Tiffany Girl

A Novel

Deeanne Gist

HOWARD BOOKS
An Imprint of Simon & Schuster, Inc.
New York Nashville London Toronto Sydney New Delhi

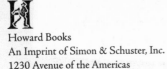

Howard Books
An Imprint of Simon & Schuster, Inc.
1230 Avenue of the Americas
New York, NY 10020

First Howard Books trade paperback edition May 2015

HOWARD and colophon are trademarks of Simon & Schuster, Inc.

For information about special discounts for bulk purchases, please contact Simon & Schuster Special Sales at 1-866-506-1949 or business@simonandschuster.com.

The Simon & Schuster Speakers Bureau can bring authors to your live event. For more information or to book an event contact the Simon & Schuster Speakers Bureau at 1-866-248-3049 or visit our website at www.simonspeakers.com.

Interior design by Davina Mock-Maniscalco
Full-page Tiffany art provided by Vidriera / Shutterstock.com

Manufactured in the United States of America

10 9 8 7 6 5 4 3 2

Library of Congress Cataloging-in-Publication Data
Gist, Deeanne.
  Tiffany girl : a novel / Deeanne Gist.
    pages ; cm
    1. Women artists—Fiction. 2. World's Columbian Exposition (1893 : Chicago, Ill.) —Fiction. 3. Chicago (Ill.) —Social life and customs—19th century—Fiction. I. Title.
  PS3607.I55T54 2015
  813'.6—dc23   2014037862

ISBN 978-1-4767-3853-6 (hardcover)
ISBN 978-1-4516-9244-0 (pbk)
ISBN 978-1-4516-9247-1 (ebook)

This will be the first time in my career that
my dad will not have read my book.
I love you and miss you so much, Dad.

In Memory of
Harold LaVerne Graham

Both before and after I lost my dad, my beloved PIT Crew (Personal
Intercessory Team) committed to stand in the gap for me every
single day while I was writing this book. Their commitment,
reassurance, comfort, and unfailing diligence helped me make my
page counts one day at a time until the manuscript was complete.

So it is with a full heart and much emotion that I thank:

Catherine Brake
Daree Stracke
Norma Jean Ursey

When gentle suggestions for the manuscript came in from my
wonderful and talented editor, my PIT Crew stepped
in again and were joined by my Community Group
(whom my husband and I meet with every
Tuesday night for fun and fellowship).

York and Robyn Whipple
Mark and Lisa Chadwell
David and Karen Danielson
Jodie Faltynski
April Garcia
Ryan Walters

Thank you for the support, the encouragement, and the shoulders you
offered during this incredibly difficult time. I will never, ever forget it.

Bless all of you a hundredfold to how you have blessed me.

ACKNOWLEDGMENTS

I knew I wanted to write about the Tiffany Girls ever since my mom told me of their existence four years ago. When I found out there was a traveling museum exhibit featuring them, I flew my sister and assistant, Gayle Evers, to Florida to see it because I was on deadline with one of my other books.

A few months after that, she flew to the Northeast to scan thousands of pages of handwritten letters by Clara Driscoll, the manager of Tiffany's Women's Department in the 1890s. It took Gayle an entire week, working from morning to night. She then spent an untold number of months preparing them for me. Those letters were the cornerstone of my research, and I could not have done the book without them. It was an enormous job, and I am so very grateful to her for all she did. She has now retired and is taking a well-deserved rest and enjoying a brand-new grandbaby—her fourth. Thank you so much, Sis. You're the best!

My critique partner—gifted author Meg Moseley—went above and beyond this time around. She has been my critique partner for ten years and is the only person on the planet who sees my work "raw." I send it to her each week—and she sends me hers. We critique each other's material, send it back, then do it all over again the following week. Sometimes, however, life gets in the way. This year was one of those years, and I found myself writing the lion's share of the book very close to my deadline.

As a result, I sent Meg my chapters daily instead of weekly. She turned them around in twenty-four hours most every time. She did it again when my revisions came in. I have no words to express what her sacrifice meant to me, both professionally and emotionally. Thank you, my friend. If there's ever anything you need, I'm your gal.

My editor, Beth Adams, offered suggestions, deletions, and additions to the manuscript that brought it up to a whole new level. She was also extremely patient and understanding during one of the most difficult seasons of my life. Thank you, Beth. Thank you, thank you, thank you.

My new agent, Lacy Lynch with Dupree/Miller, has swooped in with mounds of energy, ideas, and a go-get-'em attitude. Thanks for all you've done, Lacy. I stand amazed.

I can't wait for you, my readers, to see the photos and illustrations we've included in this book. Since our heroine, Flossie Jayne, is an aspiring artist, I thought it would be fun to sprinkle in a few pieces of art she'd done. So I contacted the talented Monica Bruenjes—who did the wonderful stop-animation for my video adventure RompThrough1893.com. Problem is, Flossie hasn't yet perfected her craft, so I wasn't sure what Monica's reaction would be, but she was very gracious and tried to make her work look "less than professional." (I still think the results are delightful. Just can't hide that talent under a bushel, even when she tries to.) In any event, I so appreciate her agreeing to be "Flossie" and on such a tight timetable. When I wasn't able to secure licenses for an existing image of the Tiffany Chapel, Monica also agreed to do a rendering for us. It is simply gorgeous, and I'm so thrilled to be able to include it. Thank you, Monica!

There were many other folks along the way who offered wonderful contributions and information about our subject matter. Lindsy Parrot, the director/curator at the Neustadt Collection of Tiffany Glass in New York; Vincenzo Rutigliano at the Schwarzman Building of the New York Public Library; authors Kellie Coates Gilbert, Kristan Higgins, Jenna Kernan, Jenny Gardiner, Miriam Berman, and Richard Alvarez; Riccardo Gomes of the East New York Project; Lauren Sodano at the Strong National Museum of Play; Arlie Sulka of Lillian Nassau LLC; Elisha Gist; and Michael Gurrola. A huge thanks to all of you!

Deeanne Gist ♡

NOTE TO READER

I wanted to warn you that privacy as defined by a turn-of-the-century Victorian looks a great deal different than how we, today, define it. So don't be alarmed if fellow lodgers at a boardinghouse move freely in and out of one another's rooms without permission and with no regard as to whether the occupant of the room is even present. This was the case in private boardinghouses which catered to genteel urbanites, as well as those of more modest means. This trend is supported in many resources I studied, including first-person accounts.

I also wanted to let you know that what was politically correct in the Victorian era is hardly so today. While writing this novel, I worked extremely hard to depict what society believed at that time and have presented things from an 1893 viewpoint as best I could. (So please don't kill the messenger!) As for the exposés our protagonist writes for his newspaper, rather than making them up, I decided to record, in many cases almost word for word, quick little snippets from articles that were written during the time. (And which are, of course, in the public domain.) I did this mostly because they were such eye-opening glimpses into our past.

Last, other than our heroine, Flossie Jayne, and her nemesis, Nan Upton, all the Tiffany Girls depicted are based on real ones, including their manager, Clara Driscoll. I have no idea what their temperaments were like or what they looked like, so I made all those parts up—including any words spoken by them, of course.

For more insider information, refer to my Author's Note after the last page. But you might want to read the book first, because there are many spoilers in the Author's Note.

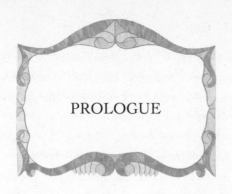

PROLOGUE

Reeve remembered everything about that morning. He remembered the scratchy wool of his short pants. His stiff collar and bow tie making it hard to swallow. The branches of the willow tree whipping against the window. The women sitting in the parlor, the air around them saturated with their homemade herbal fragrances.

But mostly he remembered his mother. So still. Lying on a table—and in the middle of the morning when everyone knew it was the time she snapped beans from the garden. Her eyes were closed, her lips turned down, her skin a funny color.

Father shifted Reeve farther up his hip. Leaning over, Reeve reached for her. Her chin was as hard as the rocks Father skipped across the creek, and as cold, too. He jerked his hand back and looked at his father in question.

Father didn't make a sound, but tears streamed down his cheeks.

"Poor child," someone sobbed.

Turning away, Reeve buried his face into Father's neck, the smell of his shaving soap sharp, his neck moist from sweat, or maybe tears.

Within three months Father's dry goods store had failed.

Within six, he'd taken Reeve to the doorstep of his grandparents' house. Grandparents he'd never even known he had. Grandfather motioned him inside with a jerk of his head, then latched the door, cutting off the sight of Father.

Reeve stood in the entry hall, its walls bare, its air stale. Grandfather's flinty eyes took in his mismatched stockings, his threadbare jacket, his stained hat. Reeve didn't need to touch him to know he was hard as the rocks by the creek and just as cold.

"Flossie used to love this room, with its northern light
and view of Stuyvesant Park. Its mauve floral walls and
Baghdad rug had hosted many a happy occasion."

CHAPTER

1

New York City, 1892
Twenty-two Years Later

"Your father has decided to withdraw you from the School of Applied Design."

Flossie Jayne looked up from the muslin in her hands, her fingers pausing, her needle protruding from the cream-colored fabric. "What do you mean?"

Mother secured a porcelain button to a short basque waist of a Louis Seize brocade in rich shades of burgundy and claret. The buttons had miniatures painted onto them. Miniatures Flossie had put there with her own brush.

"I mean," Mother said, "when your current winter session at the design school is over, you will not be going back."

Flossie lowered the bodice lining to her lap. The whalebone sandwiched between the two pieces of muslin slipped. "But, why? The painting classes won't be complete until next summer."

"Your father is aware of that." She snipped the end of the thread, then picked up another button.

"Has something happened?"

Mother said nothing. Her hair was no longer as black as Flossie's, but had softened with silver strands and was pulled up into a twist.

"Mother, I . . . I live for those lessons. Painting is the only thing that gets me through this endless sewing."

Even though Mother was working, she had dressed with extreme care. Her emerald gown was not as fancy as the ensembles she sewed for the upper echelons of New York society, but it was certainly nicer than that of most barber's wives. When customers came by the house, they'd see what a fine figure she cut and would often order something similar but significantly more expensive. Thus, she and Flossie both dressed exquisitely and in the very latest fashions no matter what their plans were.

"The sewing we do is not endless," Mother said. "Endless sewing is what those poor unfortunates in factories and sweatshops do. You and I work in our warm, cozy sitting room and handle all manner of silk, velvet, mink, lace, and jewels."

"We sew from first light until last light, until our eyes hurt and our heads ache. We stop only to do the cooking and cleaning." The thought of sewing without interruption was bad enough, but to give up her passion, the one thing that not only offered her a reprieve but infused her with renewed energy, was not to be borne.

"You stop every afternoon for your lessons," Mother said.

"Which is my whole point."

Mother *tsked*. "You should be happy we have the work. With so many men losing their fortunes, many seamstresses are finding themselves with fewer and fewer customers."

"You will never lose your customers." Flossie once again worked her needle along the edge of the whalebone, boxing it in with neat stitches. "Not when every gown you make is nothing short of a work of art."

Mother allowed herself a small smile. "Your pieces are not far behind."

"Even if that were true, the difference is you love to sew. I hate it. No, I loathe it. The only thing that keeps me in this chair is knowing that if I want to attend the School of Applied Design, Papa said I'd need to bring in the income myself. But if he's not going to let me go, then what's the point?"

The fire in the grate popped, its heat warding off December's chill. Flossie used to love this room, with its northern light and view of Stuyvesant Park. Its mauve floral walls and Baghdad rug had hosted many a happy occasion. The sense of warmth and well-being it once induced, however, had long since dissipated, leaving dread and drudgery in its wake, for this was where she and Mother did their work week after week, day after day.

She pushed the floor with her toe, setting her rocker in motion. "He went to the races again, didn't he?"

Mother tied off the last button. "You really did do a lovely job painting these miniatures. Mrs. Wetmore is going to be very pleased with them."

"How much did he lose this time?" Flossie rued the day her father had been invited to the races by one of his customers. What should have been a day of leisure ended up becoming a consuming passion. He'd even started to close the barbershop on Saturdays in order to go to the racetrack.

"It's not for you to question how your father spends his money."

"What about how he spends *our* money?"

"Hush." Mother glanced at the door as if someone might hear, but they didn't have a maid anymore, nor a cook. "You and I don't have any money. It's all his."

"Why is that? We're the ones doing the work. We're the ones designing the clothes. We're the ones taking care of your clients. Why don't we get any of the money? Why do we have to hand it all over to him?"

"Because we do."

"What if we don't?"

"That is quite enough."

"I mean it, Mother. What if we simply told him no? Told him he couldn't have it?"

Standing, Mother shook out the bodice, then held it up by its shoulders, the light glinting on its gold-braided trim. "These buttons will become more popular than they already are once the senator's wife wears this. Perhaps tomorrow you should paint some more."

"Let's go on strike."

Glancing at her sharply, Mother draped the bodice over the back of her chair. "What on earth are you talking about?"

"Let's tell Papa we refuse to do any more work until he gives each of us a percentage of our earnings."

Narrowing her eyes, Mother snatched up tiny scraps of fabric littering the worn oriental rug that had been in her family for generations. "You've been reading too many newspapers. If you're not careful, your father will disallow it."

"You ought to read them, too. The *New York World* gave a very detailed account of the feather curlers when they went on strike. It brought the entire feather industry to a standstill. By the end of it, night work was abolished and the women had won. Well, they'd won the first skirmish, anyway." She scooted forward in her chair. "Don't you see? If we both told Papa we wouldn't work another day until he agreed to give us each a percentage of our work, he'd have no recourse but to give in to our demands."

"No."

"Then let's just keep a portion and not tell him. They pay you, so he'd never know."

Mother studied Flossie, her brown eyes catching the fire's light. "Look around you, daughter. The rocker you are lounging in, the cup of tea at your elbow, the very walls that protect you from the cold . . . these are all a product of your father's hard work. Surely you remember we haven't always lived so well. It has taken him years to provide such nice things for us. If he wants to give himself a little treat, then I will not begrudge him and neither will you."

"I remember we lived much more modestly until you started to take in sewing. Until you discovered you had a talent—no, a gift—for creating gowns of the highest caliber. I remember Papa being so delighted that he hired a maid and then a cook so you could devote more of your time to your sewing." She folded the muslin lining. "Everything was wonderful at first, but it was never the same after we moved here and away from all our friends. Papa opened his new shop with fancy chairs and even fancier equipment. He joined those clubs. He stayed out late. He went to the races. He fired the help."

Mother stood stiff, her lips drawn.

"I've heard you crying, Mother." She looked down, picking a loose thread from the muslin. "I'm not a young girl anymore. I'm one-and-twenty. Old enough to see that something is very, very wrong."

"We're just going through a bad spell right now. Everyone is." Her voice wavered.

Setting her sewing aside, Flossie stood. "But we shouldn't be. Your business is booming and so was his, but he hardly ever opens his doors anymore. He simply takes the money we make and spends it."

"He enrolled you in the School of Applied Design."

"Only because you made him. And the reason I didn't feel guilty about it was because I earned every penny of the tuition." She bit her lip. "But as sure as the sun rises, I know that as long as we keep handing everything over to him, he'll never change his ways. Why would he?"

"Your father's a wonderful man."

"He is. And I love him—very, very much. But what he's doing to you—to us—is wrong and I'll—I'll not be party to it. If you want to work yourself to death and give it all to him, you are certainly free to do so, but not me. If I do the work, then I'm going to keep a portion of the wages."

Mother closed the distance between them and lowered her voice. "You will not."

"It's time, Mother," she said, matching her quiet tone. "Well past time."

Mother slapped her.

Gasping, Flossie fell back, covering her stinging cheek. Tears sprung to her eyes. Never in her entire life had either of her parents raised a hand to her.

"We are women." Mother's hands trembled. "You can read all you want about unfeminine women who want to be treated like men, but no matter how hard we try, nothing will change the facts. We aren't men. Not now, not ever. And if those women aren't careful, they just might get what they are asking for, and then where will we be? Do you wish to load your own steamer trunks onto a wagon? To shovel snow from the sidewalk? To drive six horses? To fight in wars? To wear trousers? Well, I don't, and I will have no such talk in this house. Have I made myself clear?"

Still cradling her cheek, Flossie ignored the tears spilling onto her fingers. "Crystal clear."

Turning, she fled from the room and up the stairs. Flinging herself onto her bed, she buried her face into her pillow and sobbed. Not just for herself, but for her mother and all the other women who didn't see that men—even the ones who loved them—were very careful to keep the fair sex in a state of subjection and complete subservience.

CHAPTER

2

Flossie squinted her eyes, blurring the woman at the front of the room to nothing but shadows, highlights, and midtones. The model was young and sat extremely still in a stout oak armchair, her ankles crossed, her hands folded atop her lap. Her simple green gown and white lacy collar offered a wonderful contrast to her rich, dark hair.

Swishing her brush in turpentine, Flossie glanced at the other art students, some of them men, most of them women. They'd covered their clothing with paint-smudged smocks and worked quietly while the instructor, a master whose paintings were sold in galleries all over New York, circulated throughout the room and offered quiet suggestions.

She dabbed her brush on a rag, then picked up some sapphire blue from her palette and mixed it with crimson. She still couldn't believe Papa wasn't going to allow her to return after the new year. She'd secretly hoped he'd change his mind come Christmas, but that morning had come and gone with strained politeness as she'd unwrapped the paints and canvas he'd given her. She loved the gifts, of course, but nothing had been the same since Mother had struck her. In that one moment her entire childhood had fallen from her like a snake casting off its skin. Mother had made up with her almost immediately, for she'd been horrified with herself and followed Flossie to her room after only a few moments. They'd held each other, both of them apologizing, both of them stricken. It had made them closer than ever before, but in a completely different way—a more grown up, woman-to-woman way.

Still, she'd decided it was time to make a break. With quick brushstrokes, she swiped dark lines of shadow along the upper edge of the arm she'd sketched, then dabbed at the hairline and gave a squiggle beneath the jaw. It was one thing to determine she wanted to be on her own. It was quite another to go about finding a job, especially when she couldn't seek the advice of her parents. She wondered how much the model on the platform made.

A murmur rippled throughout the room. She glanced toward the door where their instructor, Mr. Cox, hustled to greet a couple who'd entered.

"Tiffany," he said. "Great Scott, what a surprise. I didn't know you were coming."

Tiffany? Surely not *the* Tiffany of the jewelry empire? But no, this man looked to be in his forties. He wasn't nearly old enough to be the real one. And the woman with him didn't dress in the manner Tiffany's wife would. Although her organdy waist and black silk skirt were nice enough, they were nothing like what Flossie's mother would make.

"Forgive our intrusion." Tiffany's headful of brown hair expanded as it was released from his derby hat.

"Nonsense. You're welcome any time." Mr. Cox wiped a beefy hand on his apron, then held it out, his wiry black mustache crinkling when he smiled.

Tiffany clasped the offered hand. "Allow me to introduce you to Mrs. Driscoll. She's head of my Women's Department." He turned to her. "This is Mr. Kenyon Cox. We painted together at the National Academy of Design."

Women's Department? Department of what? And Mr. Cox had painted with a member of the Tiffany family? For though this man was too young to be the jeweler and though he lisped with every *s* he pronounced, the cut of his coat and the fine cloth it was made from left no doubt that he was somehow related.

"A pleasure." Mrs. Driscoll gave a slight bow, the greenish-black rooster-tail feathers in her hat trembling. The woman was no wilting flower, but she was a single-stemmed bloom to Mr. Cox's solid oak trunk. It had always amazed Flossie that a man of such proportions could paint with the delicacy of Michelangelo.

"To what do we owe this honor?" Mr. Cox asked.

Tiffany draped their coats across the back of an old wooden chair. "We'd like to have a look at your students' work, if you wouldn't mind."

His eyes widened a bit. "Certainly. Are you interested in anything in particular?"

Mrs. Driscoll moved to one end of the room while Tiffany and Cox began to make a slow circuit around the other. They glanced at the men's work, but stopped and studied the women's.

"I am," Tiffany said. "I'm sure you heard the lead glaziers and glass cutters went on strike?"

Mr. Cox pulled a face. "I saw that in the papers and thought of you immediately. I'm assuming it has brought everything to a halt?"

"Indeed it has, but that's not the worst of it. The Chicago World's Fair starts just five months from now and I am in the middle of preparing an exhibit for it—a chapel using every type of glass known to man."

Mr. Cox gave him a sharp look. "There's going to be a display of American stained glass?"

"Not officially, but when the fair executives realized they'd overlooked provisions for an ecclesiastical art display, they told my father about it. He agreed to portion off a section of his exhibit space so it could be devoted to such. Naturally, Father approached me for the execution of it."

Flossie dipped her brush in the turpentine. So he was the heir apparent, Louis Comfort Tiffany. His windows graced her church, and she'd spent more than one Sunday admiring their vibrant colors and luminosity.

"I hadn't heard that." Mr. Cox clapped Tiffany on the back. "That's marvelous. Congratulations."

A lovely smile flashed across his face, then dimmed. "It will all be for naught if I don't get myself some glaziers and glass cutters—and quick."

Across the room, Mrs. Driscoll chatted with Aggie Wilhemson, one of Flossie's favorites here at school. Aggie stood six feet tall, her blond Swedish heritage evident not just in her bearing, but in the lilt of her voice.

"Are you going to give into the workers' demands, then?" Mr. Cox asked, recapturing Flossie's attention.

Mr. Tiffany shook his head. "Even if I did, I wouldn't be able to convince all the other glass manufacturers to do so. No, these things take time and I don't have any time. That's why I'm here."

"I can't imagine how I can help, but I'm willing to do what I can."

Slipping his hands in his pockets, Mr. Tiffany tilted his head to the side and studied Elizabeth Comyns's painting. She'd illustrated some books, and though Flossie had never seen them, three of her designs for china painting had been published in this year's *The Art Amateur*.

"I was thinking of hiring some women to do the work," Mr. Tiffany said.

Flossie froze.

Mr. Cox's eyebrows shot to his hairline. "Women? To do *glass cutting?*"

"To do it all."

"Do you think they can?"

"Mrs. Driscoll seems to think so, and I put a great deal of stock in her opinions."

Mr. Cox's gaze drifted to Mrs. Driscoll, who now conversed with Louise King. The quiet, unassuming girl was Mr. Cox's star pupil, not just because of her extraordinary talent, but because of a growing attraction between the two.

"Wouldn't hiring them get you into trouble with the unions?" he asked.

"I don't see how." Tiffany shot him a conspiratorial look. "Women aren't allowed to be members of unions."

Throwing back his head, Mr. Cox gave a bark of laughter, then swept his arm in a half circle that encompassed the room. "Look all you want, then. There isn't a student in the room that I wouldn't recommend."

CHAPTER

3

From the time Flossie was twelve, she'd watched over the children of Mother's clients during fittings and design sessions. She'd diapered Eleanor Roosevelt, burped Harold Vanderbilt, and bottle-fed Henry Du Pont. To her, Mr. Tiffany was nothing more than an ordinary man who happened to have a lot of money. And though the Tiffany women had never sought out Mother for their clothing needs, she knew this man ate, worked, and slept just like the rest of them.

Therefore, she could only attribute the drying of her mouth and the queasiness in her stomach to his interest in hiring female artists for his studio. If she could get a job with Tiffany Glass and Decorating Company, she'd not only be able to move away from home and be her own woman, but she'd learn a great deal about art, color, texture, and design.

Mrs. Driscoll paused beside her, glanced at her underpainting, then moved on to the next student. Frowning, Flossie took a step back and studied her work. It looked pretty good to her. Why hadn't Mrs. Driscoll visited with her the way she had Aggie and Elizabeth? Perhaps she wasn't the decision maker. No, of course she wasn't. She was a woman. Mr. Tiffany had said he valued her opinion, but everyone knew men didn't really—not deep down.

By the time Mr. Tiffany made it to Flossie's station, he'd suffered through girls blushing, stammering, giggling too loudly, gawking, and refusing to make eye contact. She felt horrible for him. How tiring it must be to only be seen as an object of wealth and talent instead of a flesh-and-blood man. So great was her pity for him that her queasiness completely vanished.

Stepping up beside her, he watched her for a moment. "You have a good eye for shadows and highlights."

"Thank you." She mixed some white paint with a touch of umber, then thinned it with turpentine. "The underpainting is one of my favorite layers."

He lifted his brows. "It is? Why is that?"

Shrugging, she squinted at the model, then made a slash of muted white on her figure's shoulder. "I guess because I get to use the bigger brushes and I can be loose and sloppy. It's . . . I don't know . . . freeing, I guess. What's your favorite part of painting?"

He gave her a startled look. "The underpainting."

She paused. "It is? Why?"

He looked to the side in thought before turning back to her. "Because I hate to stay in the lines."

A smile began to form. "You make your living in stained glass. If that's not painting inside the lines, I don't know what is."

He answered her smile. "That's different, Miss . . . ?"

"Jayne. Florence Jayne." Propping a hand on her waist, she lifted a brow. "And just how is it different?"

"It's all in the coloring of the glass. That's where I am free."

She turned back to her work. "So, picking colors and painting them onto glass gives you a sense of freedom?"

He whipped himself straight. "I do not use painted glass. Its results are dull and artificial. No, I *infuse* my glass with color and swirl it up while it's still hot." He made a whirling motion with his arm. "The men pour a heavy ladle of molten glass onto a giant iron table, then, in rapid succession, ladle on additional colors. They drag a rake-like tool through it with big, haphazard movements." He pantomimed the motion, using his entire body to comb the imaginary liquid fire. "The color begins to swirl throughout the glass. Sometimes it streaks, sometimes it pools, sometimes it twists, sometimes it spirals." His eyes brightened, his face shone. "But no two pieces ever come out the same."

The words were lost in his animation and love for the process. He spoke passionately of using paddles along the edges of cooling glass to make it buckle so that it looked like folds in drapery, or jostling tables to make the glass ripple, and sometimes blowing a thin glass bubble, then shattering it and strewing it over the hot glass.

Oh, to be a man and have the privilege of working a furnace burning at two thousand degrees, to have the freedom of movement their trousers allowed them, the power their muscles afforded them.

They stood facing each other, his breaths deep, her painting forgotten, her brush loose in her hand.

"I opened my own glassworks and furnaces this year in Corona, Queens," he said, his voice soft, his lisp pronounced.

"Did you?"

"Yes." He gave her a lovely smile, a smile that would make any woman catch her breath, even if he was twice her age. "We're no longer restricted, as we were when we used other glassworks." He shook his head, his curly hair loosened and tumbled from his earlier theatrics. "We try all kinds of experiments in Corona to see what accidental effects we might have, and I must tell you, Miss Jayne, we have produced every imaginable color in every shade, tone, and hue known to man."

"But what if you want to reproduce a particular color and style?"

"We can't. That's the whole beauty of it." A twinkle appeared in his eye. "My superintendent told me just yesterday that there are only two things more uncertain than the manufacture of colored glass—the mood of a woman and the heels of a mule."

She laughed.

Mrs. Driscoll joined them.

"I've found a friend, Mrs. Driscoll. This is Miss Florence Jayne." He turned to Flossie. "This is the head of my Women's Department."

"How do you do?" Flossie asked.

"Nice to make your acquaintance." The woman turned to Mr. Tiffany. "I've decided upon five girls who I think will do quite nicely and who have agreed to join us."

"Excellent," he said. "What if we make it six?" He turned to Flossie. "Would you like to come and work for Mrs. Driscoll in our Women's Department, Miss Jayne? I must warn you, it would require staying within the lines."

Her pulse jumped. Her hand flew to her chest. "Oh. Oh, my. Why, yes. I would love to. I . . . I . . ."

Nodding his head, he looked around the room. "Mrs. Driscoll will give you all the details, but if you ladies will excuse me, I'm going to speak with Mr. Cox for a moment."

"Yes, of course. Thank you."

But he'd already walked away, his footfalls sounding briskly on the wooden floor.

She set her brush down on the palette, then turned to Mrs. Driscoll. "Did—did that just happen?"

The woman's face softened. "I believe it did."

She was older than Flossie and a good deal younger than Mother. Perhaps thirty? Thirty-two? No more than thirty-five, certainly. She'd fashioned her brown hair into a sensible twist, her brown eyes missing nothing. "We'll be entirely focused on completing the windows for Mr. Tiffany's World's Fair exhibit. There will be little time for training—more of a baptism by fire, I'm afraid."

"I understand. How long do you think it will take to do the windows?"

"Every bit of time between now and May first, when the fair starts. You'll be expected to put in a full day's work Monday through Saturday and will be compensated with five dollars a week. Will that suit?"

Five dollars a week. All of it hers. "Yes, that will suit very nicely. When do I start?"

"January second. Our studio is at the southeast corner of Fourth Avenue and Twenty-Fifth Street. The Women's Department is on the third floor."

"I'll find it."

Mrs. Driscoll gave her a nod. "See that you do."

After Mr. Tiffany and Mrs. Driscoll left, Flossie's hands shook so much, she could no longer paint—not even the sloppy parts. She'd need to find someplace to live that was closer to Tiffany's studio. Not just because her parents' house was too far away to be practical, but because her father would keep her wages if she stayed home. And she needed those wages, needed them so she could save up tuition for art school.

She wondered how to find a room, how much they cost, and what her parents would say. Shying away from that last thought, she glanced at the other girls whom Mrs. Driscoll had singled out. Maybe one of them would be interested in sharing a room with her. Either way, she would now be what the papers called a New Woman, and what her father called an abomination.

" 'We decided on some sleeves entirely of velvet for the *plissé crépon.*' "

CHAPTER

4

M other had a customer in the back. Flossie wasn't sure who it was, but she used the time to whip up some marmalade pudding. Orange marmalade was the thing Papa loved most and which he insisted be kept upon their table at all times. Chopping up some suet, she tried to decide how best to break her news to them.

Should she tell Mother, then let Mother tell Papa? Tempting as it was, it seemed rather cowardly. The question then became, should she tell them separately or together? She gathered up the suet and dropped it into a bowl, gave Mother's vegetable soup a stir, put a different pot on to boil, then spent the next several minutes collecting ingredients. By the time Mother's customer left, Flossie was whipping up the breadcrumbs, flour, sugar, soda, and marmalade.

"That was Mrs. Cutting," Mother said, coming into the kitchen. Taking an apron from a peg, she slipped it over her neck, then tied it around her waist. "She's ready for the black *plissé crépon*, the flowered brocade, and the peau de soie gowns to be remade."

Flossie added a touch of buttermilk to her mixture. Mrs. Cutting was known for never being seen in the same gown twice, so Mother designed them to be remade, added to, and subtracted from.

Grabbing an agate bowl, Mother began to grease it. "We decided on some sleeves entirely of velvet for the *plissé crépon*, a round waist of black baby lamb for the brocade, and a spangled satin collar with pointed tabs for the peau de soie."

"That's nice."

Mother glanced at her, then paused and put down her rag. "It was your last day at school. I'm sorry. I should have realized. Are you all right?"

Flossie whipped the ingredients more feverishly. "Yes. Is that bowl ready?"

Mother brought the greased bowl and steadied it while Flossie scraped the pudding into it. A sweet, citrusy aroma wafted up and around them.

"Thank you for preparing this." Mother's voice was low, gentle. "Your father hasn't been himself ever since he realized you'd have to quit. This gesture, well, it will mean a great deal to him."

Avoiding her gaze, Flossie set the pudding, bowl and all, in the pot of boiling water, then placed a lid on the pot so it could steam. Mother stood at her side. Flossie stared at the pot.

"I'm so sorry," Mother whispered, placing a hand on Flossie's arm.

Swallowing, Flossie looked down. "Mr. Tiffany—the younger Mr. Tiffany who does the stained glass? Well, he stopped by our class today."

Mother said nothing. Just kept a soothing hand on Flossie's arm.

"He was looking to hire women who could make stained-glass windows for his World's Fair exhibit." The heat from the stove warmed her. The scent of orange began to permeate the room. "He . . ." She took a deep breath. "He asked me to be one of them."

Mother went completely still. "What did you say?"

Flossie fiddled with the apron strings wrapped about her waist. "I said yes."

Releasing her, Mother took a step back and rested her fingertips against her mouth. "How much is he going to pay you?"

"Five dollars a week."

"Oh, Flossie. You make much more sewing for me."

Flossie looked out the window above the kitchen worktable. The view was no more than a wall of soot-covered bricks from the building next door. "I make nothing working for you."

"But you won't make anything working for him, either. You'll be giving it all to your father either way, so what difference does it make?"

Flossie moved her gaze from the window to her mother, her mother whose brown eyes were so much like her own. "I won't be giving it to Papa because I won't be living here. I'm moving out."

Mother sucked in a breath. "You're speaking nonsense now. You can't move out. You're an unmarried, beautiful young woman. What will people think?"

"I suppose they'll think I'm a New Woman."

"You cannot," Mother hissed. "Your father will, oh my, he will—"

The front door opened, muffled sounds from the street outside briefly reached them before being shut off as the door closed.

Mother paled. "Good heavens. Oh, my. Goodness me." She whipped off her apron, patted her hair, and rushed toward the hall. At the last moment she turned back to Flossie. "We'll talk about this later. Do *not* mention anything to your father."

Blowing out a quick breath of air, Flossie collected plates from the kitchen cabinet and took them to the dining room. A few minutes later Papa joined her, Mother just behind him.

"There she is," he said, his voice bright. "My little sunshine."

With charm and grace, he relieved her of the final plate, took both her hands in his, and placed a kiss on her cheek. "How are you, moppet?"

Unlike Mother, he wouldn't have forgotten it was her last day at the School of Applied Design. He knew she'd be understandably upset. And as he always did when she was unhappy, he took it upon himself to lift her spirits.

He was quite accomplished at it, actually. He'd had twenty-one years of practice putting on a jovial mood to coax her out of her pout. She couldn't think of a time when his engaging smile and sparkling brown eyes had failed to do so.

She studied him anew. He'd benefited from Mother's handiness with a needle. His well-cut jacket and gray striped trousers marked him as a New York man—perhaps not one of rank, but certainly one who did well for himself. Never did he have a piece of black hair out of place or a white collar anything less than perfectly stiff. Only in the last couple of years had gray begun to touch his temples.

Her favorite part of his careful grooming, though, the one she always associated with him, was the subtle aroma of coconut that wafted about him. It was his secret ingredient for enriching the lather of the shaving soap he used in his shop and in his own toilet.

Slipping an arm around her waist, he danced her about the table and sang, his beautiful tenor filling the dining room.

"Of all the days that's in the week
I dearly love but one day—
And that's the day that comes betwixt
A Saturday and Monday."

Unable to resist, she added the alto harmony to his favorite song.

"For then I'm drest all in my best
To walk abroad with Flossie;

She is the darling of my heart,
Her hair so fine and glossy."

The real words didn't use her name, of course, but those of a girl named Sally who lived up in an alley. Still, Papa had changed the verses so often that when Flossie heard anyone else sing it properly, it always jolted her.

He spun her through three more verses until he had her laughing and out of breath.

"Now, there's a good girl," he said, bringing them to a stop. He lifted his nose and sniffed the air. "Am I smelling what I think I'm smelling?"

She nodded. "You are."

"Did you make it?"

"I did. It's not quite ready, though. It's only just now been put on the stove."

Studying her, his face slowly sobered. "You're a very good daughter to have done that, especially today."

She looked down and took a step back. "Papa, I—"

"Come, you two," Mother said, surging forward. "It's a good thing I had soup on the stove, for Mrs. Cutting didn't leave until just before you got home, darling. So sit down and, Flossie, you come with me."

Papa grabbed Flossie's hand, stopping her. "Not tonight, Mother. Tonight Flossie will sit at the table with me. No bringing in food and no scrubbing of dishes for my moppet. I have need of her at the table with me."

Flossie gently disengaged herself. "Don't be silly, Papa. Mother needs some help. I'll only be a minute."

He put on a pout, but took his chair as she knew he would.

In the kitchen, Mother grabbed some applesauce that had been chilling on the windowsill. "Slice up some bread and, for heaven's sake, don't say anything about Mr. Tiffany's offer."

Instead of answering, Flossie concentrated on her task, and within a few minutes all was on the table. Papa said grace, then kept them entertained with anecdotes about the men who'd visited his shop. When any lulls in the conversation occurred, Mother quickly filled in the silences.

If Papa noticed Flossie's reticence, he must have attributed it to melancholy over leaving the design school. Finally, she and Mother took the plates from the table and returned with his orange marmalade pudding.

Despite Mother's insistence on discretion, Flossie screwed up her courage. "Mr. Louis Comfort Tiffany came to the studio today."

Mother gave her a sharp look.

"Did he?" Papa asked. "Don't tell me he was a guest instructor?"

"No, he just came by to examine the students' work."

"Did he see yours?"

"He did."

Leaning back in his chair, Papa wiped a hand on the napkin tucked into his neck, a look of pride touching his face. "And what did he think?"

"He said I had a good eye for shadows and highlights."

Papa's eyebrows crinkled a bit. "That's it?"

"That's what we were working on today, the underpainting."

"Ah." His expression smoothed. "Did he see your *Woman at the Seashore* painting?"

She shook her head. "No, I brought that painting home day before yesterday. I've been bringing a little bit home each day so I wouldn't have so much to carry at the very end."

He placed his hand against the table, palm up. She slipped hers into it.

"I'm sorry you had to quit, moppet. It won't be forever. And it isn't as if you earn any diploma or anything. They don't even have a set curriculum."

"I know, but every day I miss, I fall behind."

"You're already so accomplished."

"I want to be more than accomplished. I want to have my paintings hanging in a museum."

Squeezing her hand, he gave her a placating smile. "All the great artists are men, my dear. That's just the way things are. The sooner you accept that, the better. Yet another reason to take a break from the design school. I don't know if they're the ones putting these ideas into your head or if it is some half-formed aspiration thrilling upon your nerves that is to blame, but you must stop for a minute and consider how very comfortable your life is."

She removed her hand from his.

He scraped the inside of his pudding cup, the glass clinking with each stroke of his spoon. "You certainly have more diversion than I do, as you look after our household, go to afternoon teas, and consider the complicated problems in women's fashion." He took his final bite of pudding. "No, only someone content with life could have as excellent an appetite as you and could sleep eight hours every night. You will get married before you know it and will find the rearing of your children infinitely more rewarding than having some piece of canvas hanging on a wall of a stuffy old museum."

Her shoulders tensed. The skin about her mouth tightened. Rearranging the spoon beside her pudding cup, she lined it up perfectly straight. "Because of a strike, Mr. Tiffany has lost his glaziers and glassworkers."

Mother nudged her under the table.

She refused to make eye contact with her. "He needs someone to help him finish making stained-glass windows for his exhibit at the World's Columbian Exposition."

"*Flossie*," her mother hissed.

"He offered me and five other girls the men's jobs."

"I'm sure you told him no." Papa wiped his mouth with the napkin hanging from his collar. "Wonderful dessert, my dear. Simply wonderful."

"I accepted the position. I start January second."

He gave her a look of loving tolerance. "You will write him a very nice note then, thanking him, but telling him you are needed at home."

"I'm moving out."

Removing his napkin, he pushed back his chair. "Do not test me anymore, Flossie. You will not move out of this house until you are good and wed. And you will not take a job, ever."

"I am taking this job, Papa. You can go to the races on it. I will leave as soon as I can secure a room in a boardinghouse."

He'd narrowed his eyes at the word "races," but it was the word "boardinghouse" that sent him completely over the edge.

"A boardinghouse?" He gripped the table and leaned forward. "A *boardinghouse?*" His voice shook. "Have you lost your senses? You would be in grave moral danger. Why, men of highly questionable character swarm those places. You'd be ruined. No decent man would ever have you."

She sat on her hands, willing herself not to panic. "The world is changing, Papa. Lots of respectable women live in boardinghouses these days. The papers are filled with women who have become doctors and lawyers and all kinds of things."

He slammed a hand onto the table. She jumped. Mother squeaked.

"No daughter of mine will be written about in the paper," he roared. "Not unless she's getting married or she's dead."

She squeezed her hands into fists. "No one's going to write about me in the paper."

"They most assuredly are not," he continued, his voice blistering her ears. "Because no daughter of mine will hold a job, nor will she live in a *boardinghouse.*" He spewed the last word out as if it were Hades itself.

She set her jaw. Out of respect for him, she'd not argue any further, but there was nothing he could do to stop her—and it wasn't the first time she'd ever dug in her heels. She could tell he recognized the determination on her face.

He waved his hand in a gesture of exasperation. "Do something, Edythe."

Mother clasped her hands. "Flossie, dear, think. If you do this, you will become a . . ." She glanced at Papa. ". . . a *New Woman*." She whispered the last two words as if they were unfit for delicate ears. "You will be choosing the life of an old maid. Why would you do that? Don't you want a man to love? Some children to enrich your life?"

She did want that, there was no denying it. For years, all she'd ever dreamed of was growing up and becoming a wife and mother, but that was before women had any choices. Now they were earning degrees. They were asking for the vote. They were even securing jobs in professions never before accessible to them. But in order to keep those jobs, they had to remain unmarried.

A moment of clarity and calm washed over her. Her shoulders relaxed. If she were going to be an old maid the rest of her life, then she certainly wasn't going to stay in her father's house, where her salary would not be her own. Besides, who ever heard of a New Woman living with her parents?

No, if she was going to be a New Woman in the truest sense, she'd have to leave. There was no other way. "I'd love to have children, Mother, but I can't seem to work up any enthusiasm for a husband who will withhold money from me when I'm the one earning it and who will keep me on a leash because he thinks he knows better than I what's best for me."

Mother sucked in her breath.

Papa's face exploded with color. "He *will* know what's best for you! Clearly."

Looking down, Flossie picked a crumb from her skirt and dropped it into her empty pudding cup.

Papa squeezed the bridge of his nose. "Fine, fine," he barked.

"You can have the job at Tiffany's, but by all that is holy, you will stay here at home."

She lifted her chin and looked at a point just above her mother's head. "I'm sorry, Papa. I cannot."

Taking in a wheezing breath, he drove his fingers into his hair and fisted his hands, the gesture ruining the perfection of his appearance. Genuine concern for his health swept through her. Surely her actions wouldn't cause his heart to fail?

No, no. She had to get ahold of herself.

After a tense moment, he lowered his arms, weariness settling over him. His hair stuck up in tufts. "Your mother and I have spent a lifetime caring for you, training you, teaching you, encouraging you, loving you—even spoiling you, at times. We have put everything—everything—into preparing you for life as a wife and mother. You are all we have, Flossie. Why, after all we've done, would you do this to us?"

Her eyes filled, her throat swelled. "Are you afraid I'll fail, Papa? Are you afraid I'll make you ashamed of me?"

He gave her a look of acute sadness. "No, moppet, I'm afraid you'll succeed. As a matter of fact, I know you'll succeed. You're so beautiful, and talented, and smart—too smart for a woman, actually. So much so, I'm afraid once Tiffany realizes what he has, he will pull you from the glasswork and make you a designer of his windows. Then you'd never come back home."

Love for him burst within her. She didn't dare thank him for his unfailing belief in her, but it warmed her clear down to her toes. "And would my being a designer for Tiffany shame you?"

Pursing his lips, he examined his immaculate fingernails. "No, I'd be quite proud of you, actually. Imagine us going to church and telling the people next to us that our daughter designed the windows." He gave a wistful smile. "So long as you were designing them, it would be okay. Just like painting is suitable for a lady of your upbringing. But, sweet girl, how could we ever explain that you'd given up the very purpose God created you for? And all for a job? Especially one where you solder lead and cut glass? That's man's work, not woman's." The pain and injury in his eyes made her resolve waver. "It's possible we could hide what you were doing—if you lived at home, that is. Then once you became a designer, if you still insisted on living somewhere else, we could look into it."

She swallowed. "I can't stay here, Papa. I have to move out."

"Why?"

"Flossie." Her mother looked close to tears. "Please."

Papa tilted his head. "What is it?"

Some inner sense kept her from stating the driving reason— that she wanted to keep her earnings for herself. She'd hinted at it before and he'd not picked up on it. Besides, no matter what she thought, she simply couldn't bring herself to confront him about that or his gambling. But there was another reason, one she'd thought of on the way home from school, one that had been building up a great deal of steam and excitement within her.

"If I lived in a boardinghouse," she said, "I'd have siblings for the first time in my entire life, and I've always, always wanted them."

Mother clasped her hand over her mouth, the tears that had threatened earlier spilling over her cheeks.

Too late, Flossie realized how her mother must have interpreted that. "No, Mother, I didn't mean—"

Shoving her chair back, Mother tossed her napkin on the table and fled from the room.

Flossie rose halfway out of her chair, but her father stopped her with a hand on her arm. "No, moppet, I'll go to her in a moment. Sit, and let's finish this."

She sank back down. "I didn't mean it as a criticism."

"Of course you didn't, but your mother, she feels she failed me. I've told her a thousand times that you are enough, more than enough. You are more than any father could ever hope for, but it never occurred to her, I don't think, that she'd failed you."

"But she didn't fail me."

"Then why this sudden need to have siblings?"

Setting an elbow on the table, she rested a palm against her forehead. It wasn't a sudden need. It had been a lifelong need, or wish, anyway. "This is such a mess."

"We'll get it sorted out, but you must stop this nonsense about a boardinghouse."

"Oh, Papa. Don't you see? I want to spread my wings. I want to see what it's like to be on my own, to be part of a big family. If I move into a boardinghouse, I'll be able to do all of those things."

"If you move into a boardinghouse, what you'll have is a soiled cloth on the dining table, a mattress stuffed with pigs' hair, and filthy bed clothing which holds an unspeakable odor, not to mention unemptied slop jars and dirty washing basins."

She wondered if he realized who washed his bed clothing, who emptied his slop jar, and who cleaned his washing basin.

"What is Tiffany paying you?" he asked.

"Five dollars a week."

"Then you won't be able to afford a boardinghouse unless you share a room with someone, which means the second bed would be occupied with a person not of your choosing, but of the landlady's choosing. What if she is of an unpleasant nature?"

"What if she isn't? What if she's—" *like a sister*, she finished to herself.

He studied her. "You're going to do it, aren't you? No matter what I say, no matter how much it will injure your mother and me, and no matter all that we've done for you."

"I'm sorry," she replied. "I can't really explain it to you, but my mind is made up. I would very much like your assistance in choosing the boardinghouse, but if you won't help me, then I'll have to do it myself. But I will do it, Papa."

She didn't know how she'd do it, though. The other girls at the School of Applied Design already lived in houses without any vacancies or were going to stay at home, but the more Flossie thought about a boardinghouse, the more excited she became about it. She'd have no one to answer to. No one. Not her father. Not her mother. Not even a husband. She wouldn't just be a New Woman, she'd be a whole new person.

"The new boarder swept by Reeve Wilder's open door in a whirl
of extravagant haberdashery and fur-lined clothing."

CHAPTER

5

The new boarder swept by Reeve Wilder's open door in a whirl of extravagant haberdashery and fur-lined clothing. Behind her was their landlord, Mr. Klausmeyer, a giant trunk strapped to his back, his gait slow and plodding. Snow had saturated the lower portion of his dingy brown trousers and clung to his hobnailed boots. Reeve wondered if the man had finally gotten around to shoveling their front landing.

He hoped the carting of trunks wouldn't tax Klausmeyer so much that he abandoned the task. The boardinghouse betty was a former lodger who'd settled his back rent by marrying the landlady, making him her third husband and making it the third time the house was given a new name. It was rare, indeed, for Klausmeyer to even make an appearance. He was much more likely to lounge about in the back without ever lifting a finger to help.

"Hello! Are you Miss Love?" The new boarder's voice held a lyrical component, flushed with innocence and enthusiasm. Reeve had expected her to continue to the stairwell, for all first-floor rooms were occupied. Instead, she'd stopped at Miss Love's room. The room right next to his.

"I am, indeed, Miss Love. You must be Miss Jayne, the Tiffany Girl."

The entire house was much atwitter about this Tiffany Girl who was coming to board with them. He'd kept his thoughts to himself, though. He wasn't sure Tiffany's women could manage the kind of work they'd been hired to do, but far worse was the fact that they'd undermined the hundred-plus men who were striking for reasonable hours and better wages.

"Yes, I'm Miss Jayne, but if we're to be roommates, I insist you call me Flossie."

Roommates? he thought. Miss Love was taking on a roommate?

"Then you must call me Annie Belle."

"Annabel Love?"

"Annie Belle Love. I was named after my grandmothers, Annie and Belle."

"Oh, isn't that lovely? My name is short for Florence, but no one ever calls me that, thank goodness." She paused. "Oh, dear. I hope you don't have any loved ones named Florence. I meant no offense, of course. Where should Mr. Klausmeyer set my things?"

A solid *thunk* indicated the placement of her trunk before any response was given.

"Oh, thank you, sir. Thank you so very much."

Klausmeyer hauled in three more trunks—how many clothes could one woman have, for crying out loud? And how would that tiny room have space for them?

He didn't have long to wait for his answer, for unpacking commenced, and as soon as one trunk emptied, Klausmeyer carried it back out. Just when Reeve expected things to settle, the man commenced to lug in a bookshelf, a rocking chair, a lamp, an artist's easel, a small table, several paintings, a brass headboard, and three rugs.

Death and the deuce, there was no chance of Klausmeyer completing his shoveling now. He'd done more work in the last two hours than he had in the last two years. Worst of all, Miss Love's door remained open through it all.

"What beautiful clothes." The awe in Miss Love's voice bordered on covetousness. "I've never seen such fine garments up close."

"My mother's a seamstress for the wealthy set. She tries out her ideas on my wardrobe."

"Oh, it must be wonderful to have so many gowns."

"You and I appear to be close to the same size. Is there one in particular you like? Why don't you try some on, then wear your favorite to dinner tonight? What do you say about that?"

"Oh, no. I couldn't. I simply couldn't." Miss Love's voice, however, said she'd be more than willing.

"I insist." Their door clicked shut.

He glanced at the clock sitting on the corner of his desk. He'd mentioned the Tiffany Girl to his editor at the *New York World*. It had spurred a long discussion between them that culminated in an assignment where Reeve was to write a series of exposés on this breed of New Women who were trying to infiltrate what had been—and what should certainly remain—man's rightful and exclusive dominions.

His first piece was to be sent out in two hours. Yet he'd only managed three paragraphs since Miss Jayne's arrival. He closed his door, too, even though it would disrupt the flow of air between the hall and his cracked window. Still, the women's voices and exclamations came through the thin walls as easily as if they stood in his very room.

"Have you met Mr. Tiffany?" Miss Love's voice flowed like old rye whiskey, easily discernible from Miss Jayne's, whose was of a more bubbly, champagne variety.

"He wasn't at all what I'd pictured him to be," Miss Jayne said. "There's nary a gray hair on his head, yet I just found out his forty-fifth birthday approaches. And such a lovely man. I can't comprehend how all those lead-glass workers walked out on him at such a critical time."

Miss Love's response was muffled beneath layers of clothing being whisked on and off. Perhaps he should interview one of the glassworkers. There were less than a hundred and fifty men in the entire city who knew how to do the work Tiffany required. With the exhibits for the World's Columbian Exposition due to Chicago in a few short months, it was the perfect time to stage a strike.

He dipped his pen in an inkwell.

Women of today have a perceptible restlessness for something which baffles this writer and others of the stronger sex. When asked, the New Woman can give no particular reason for her malcontent, though, in a rather mystical way, she expresses a desire to attain what she calls her "true place" in the social and economic world. Yet what could be a truer, more perfect place than the position which she currently holds?

"Oh, dear. No, no," Miss Jayne said. "This color is all wrong. Here, let's try this one."

More rustling of clothing.

"Mrs. Klausmeyer tells me you teach school," Miss Jayne continued.

"Yes, I teach the primary grades."

"Do you ever whip any of the children?"

Reeve paused.

"Goodness, yes," Miss Love answered, her voice not the least bit repentant. "I've whipped lots of them. In my class right now I have a boy who last year put his master right out the window. So at the first sign of trouble, I had Georgie take off his coat, then I gave him a good whipping with a strong switch. He's almost as large as me, but he's behaved good as gold ever since."

Tightening his jaw, Reeve wondered if she'd be quite so quick to use the rod if she'd ever been subjected to such ignominious torture in front of all her peers. Trying to tune them out, he reread what he'd written, then again wet his pen with ink.

> *Everyone knows men were created to do the world's hard work,*
> *to blaze a path for civilization, to strive, to battle, and to conquer.*
> *Everyone ought to know woman was created to make it possible*
> *for man to do this work. To ease his struggle with her sympathy, to*
> *keep him from faltering by her belief in him, to supply him with*
> *a love so great it inspires him to achieve. This, then, is a woman's*
> *part in life.*

"Oh, Annie Belle, you look absolutely beautiful. This is the gown. You must wear this one. Now, what would you say to letting me style your hair? It's such a beautiful shade—a mix of ochre and burnt sienna. I could fluff it up into the Gibson girl style everyone is wearing. I'm very good at it."

He listened to them chatter while he finished his piece. An hour later, all that was left was the last sentence, but everything he tried fell flat. Finally, it came to him. First, he jotted down two stanzas from a popular essay.

> *Why has not Man a microscopic eye?*
> *For this plain reason—Man is not a Fly.*
> *Why is not Man served up with sauce in dish?*
> *For this plain reason—Man is not a Fish.*

Smiling to himself, he added a couplet of his own making.

> *Why has not Woman all jobs overran?*
> *For this plain reason—Woman is not Man.*

He blotted the ink and reopened his door, having learned in the course of the afternoon that Miss Jayne had been attending the New York School of Applied Design when Tiffany acquired her—oil paint being her favorite medium. She was the apple of her parents' eyes. And she could talk the ears off an elephant.

He rubbed his eyes. For better or for worse, it seemed the serene life he'd known here in his room at Klausmeyer's Boardinghouse had come to an unexpected and unwelcome end.

TIFFANY GLASS AND DECORATING COMPANY[4]

"Tucking her head against the wind, she headed from the streetcar toward Tiffany's grand four-story building on the corner."

CHAPTER

6

J anuary's wind caught the corners of Flossie's midlength coat and flung it back to reveal a bluish-purple skirt with subtle stripes of mignon. She'd never had a first-day-of-work before and wanted to make a good impression. Picking a gown should have been a simple task. Heaven knew she had a gown for every occasion, or so she'd thought. Yet there was nothing in *Harper's Bazaar* or *The Ladies' Home Journal* that discussed the appropriate attire for a Tiffany Girl.

At first she'd thought to wear a simple skirt and shirtwaist, much like what she wore to the School of Applied Design. But everyone at the boardinghouse had made such a fuss about her working for Mr. Tiffany that she'd begun to wonder if perhaps she shouldn't dress up a bit. She'd tried on four different outfits before finally settling on her grosgrain. She hoped to heaven she wasn't overdressed.

Tucking her head against the wind, she headed from the streetcar toward Tiffany's grand four-story building on the corner. She was almost at the entrance before she realized something was amiss with the tight cluster of men congregated at the juncture of Fourth and Twenty-Fifth. Some tall, some short. Some stocky, some thin. Some old, some young. All of them displeased.

Slowing, she made eye contact with one of them. Red hair peeped out from beneath his hat, its color echoed in his closely cropped beard and mustache. His boxy overcoat was worn and scuffed with dirt.

He raked her with his gaze. "What do ya think yer doin', lady?"

Her steps faltered.

"We got families, ya know." This from another man gripping a rolled-up newspaper. "We got kids and wives and babies. Ya ever think o' that?"

Low murmurs and grumbles bubbled up in all directions like a pot of soup starting to boil. Grasping the collar of her coat, she squeezed it against her.

"What's the matter with you? Takin' our jobs like that?" A man not too much older than she looked at those around him, gaining confidence from their nods of support. "You oughta be ashamed o' yerself, that's what I say."

She continued to make her way to the door, not sure whether to look them in the eye or ignore them completely. Out of nowhere, a snowball pummeled her in the face, knocking her off balance. Gasping, she wiped it off and looked to see who'd thrown it. A little boy of six, maybe seven, leered at her and scooped up another chunk of snow. She picked up her pace.

A wiry man pushed his way to the front. "If'n you were a decent gal, you'd turn around right now and get yourself back to hearth and home where ya belong."

"You know what we call folks like you?" This from an older man waving his cane at her. "*Scabs*. That's what we call 'em. And if you think them skirts'll protect you from how we deal with scabs, then yer mistaken. We got ways." He narrowed his eyes. "We got ways."

She shivered, then hurried up the steps and into the building. It was one thing to read about strikers in the paper, quite another to come face-to-face with them. By the time she climbed the third flight of stairs, she was shaking so much she couldn't even undo her buttons. Closing her eyes, she leaned against the wall and took a deep breath. When she opened them, she noticed a wad of spittle clinging to the skirt of her coat.

She pressed a hand against her mouth, then fumbled in her pocket for a handkerchief. Crinkling her nose, she swabbed her coat, then folded the handkerchief gingerly around its ugly cargo and returned it to her pocket. A door down the hall opened. Flossie straightened. Botheration. The woman who'd stepped out wore a black serge skirt and simple white-striped shirtwaist. Flossie had overdressed.

"Hello," the woman said. "You must be one of the new girls." She had an owl-like appearance—large head, hooked nose, squatty neck, and buggy eyes. The color of those eyes were a deep, lovely blue. Flossie wondered if she could reproduce it with her oils. Perhaps sapphire with a touch of umber? She'd have to try it and see.

"Yes, hello. I'm Flossie Jayne. There were some . . ." She pointed a thumb behind her shoulder, indicating the front of the building.

"I heard. I'm sorry. Most of them work for other glass manufacturers, though Mrs. Driscoll recognized a couple of them from our glassworks. Either way, Mr. Tiffany is already devising a plan for everyone to get to work through another entrance."

Flossie's shoulders relaxed. "Thank you. That would be wonderful."

"Of course." The woman tilted her head. "Are you all right?"

"A little shaken, to tell you the truth. Nothing like that's ever happened to me."

"It's a nasty business, that's for certain. We're glad you're here, though. There were only six of us before, not counting Clara."

"Clara?"

"Clara Driscoll. She would have been with Mr. Tiffany when he visited the School of Applied Design." Tightening her lips, she looked toward a window at the end of the hall. "It was supposed to be me."

"I'm sorry?"

The woman gave a little shake of her head. "Nothing. I'm Nan Upton. I select the glass. At least, right now I do, but I know how to do all of the jobs, including the designing, so if you need any help with anything, you just let me know."

Flossie smiled. "I wish I'd known that this morning when I was trying to decide what to wear. I'm afraid I've overdressed."

Nan flicked her gaze over Flossie's coat and skirt. "Don't worry. I'll see if I can find a smock for you."

The strain of the morning began to ease. "Thank you. It's wonderful to think I might have made a friend before I've even stepped into the shop."

Nan's smile faltered, as if she were forcing herself to maintain it. "Think of me more as someone who can guide you if you are in need of direction. It's been like that between me and the other girls since long before Clara came back."

"Came back?"

"Yes, she was part of the Women's Department several years ago, then left when she married. Quite recently, she became widowed and asked Mr. Tiffany if she could return. Right out of the blue. Right after Agnes had told Mr. Tiffany she couldn't stand to be manager for another minute. Sometimes I wonder if it wasn't Agnes who put her up to it."

Flossie blinked. "I see." Though she didn't, of course. Who was Agnes? And how could someone be encouraged to become a widow? Rather than ask, she simply waited to see if Nan had anything further to say.

Instead, Nan waved her toward the door. "Well, the shop is right through there. Go on in. I'm going to go wait in the lobby for the rest of the girls. The men outside aren't exactly the welcome we had planned."

CHAPTER

7

From the back of the crowd, Reeve tugged down the rim of his hat and watched Miss Jayne scurry into the building. One of his contacts had told him there were to be protestors outside Tiffany's this morning, so he'd come to see if he could find someone to interview. Never had it occurred to him the men would harass a lady. New Woman or not, scab or not, she was of the fair sex and therefore commanded a certain amount of respect.

Certainly, she had no business trying to usurp a man's job. She should, indeed, return to hearth and home as one fellow had suggested, for if women abandoned their homes, who would take care of the children? Reeve knew firsthand what it was like to grow up without a mother.

It wasn't her fault she'd died, of course. He knew that now, but it hadn't made him feel any less deserted at the time. If his mother had chosen a mere job over staying home with him, the repercussions would have cut deep and been everlasting. He'd heard some women argue no children would be left at home because only unmarried women could hold positions, but it was a slippery slope they walked. Today they might have to be unmarried, but tomorrow, who knew what might happen?

All that aside, he couldn't stand here and watch while women were abused, so he'd best find himself someone to interview or take his leave. A fellow with frowsy brown whiskers and a paper collar stood back from the others, his brows knit, his weight shifting from one foot to the other. Reeve couldn't tell if it was due to the cold or discomfort over the men's conduct.

"You a glazier?" Reeve asked.

"A glassworker. What 'bout you?"

"A reporter from the *New York World.*" He held out his hand. "Reeve Wilder."

The man gave him a wary look, but returned the shake. "You gonna report what the fellows here are doin' to these gals?"

He glanced at the group. Two more women approached, their expressions anxious. Hooking elbows, they began to walk the gauntlet as men hurled their barbs and insults.

"That's not why I'd come," Reeve said. "I'd come to see if I could get your side of the story."

"What is it you want to know?"

"Can I buy you a cup of coffee? Sit down with you someplace warm?"

The man shook his head. "I don't much like what's goin' on here, but I'm not leaving. Not till the rest of 'em do."

"Then let's at least stand over by that lamppost there where it's not so loud."

After a slight hesitation, the man followed him a few yards down the street.

"Tiffany sure took everybody by surprise hiring these women, didn't he?" Reeve asked.

"I'll say. Never crossed our minds." He scratched his beard. "We figured this strike would be over in a hurry, with the fair coming up and all. Now, we don't know what to think."

"Do you suppose the women have the strength to cut the glass? To manipulate the metal?"

"If they're anything like the strong-armed ironers down in the garment district, then I'd say they probably do. They might not have the muscle to cut as many pieces per day as we can, but I definitely think they could do it. That's why we're so worried."

Reeve swiped a hand across his mouth. "Surely they won't be able to solder the joints."

The man gave a snort. "No, they wouldn't be able to do that, but the boys who solder are still working. It's the glassworkers and glaziers who are striking, not them."

"What do you think about Tiffany? Is he a good man to work for?" Reeve didn't know if this man worked for Tiffany Glass and Decorating Company or one of the other manufacturers, but he'd learned to phrase his questions in such a way that people answered without him ever having to ask.

"Mr. Tiffany seems to be a good man, but he may as well be President Cleveland. Too far out o' reach for the likes of me."

Reeve withdrew a notepad from inside his jacket. "If he weren't out of reach, what would you say to him?"

"You mean, besides us wantin' to work fifty hours a week instead of sixty? And wantin' twenty dollars for cutters, and eighteen for glaziers?"

Reeve nodded. "The union's already told him that."

"Maybe I'd like to see how good o' work he'd do on bread and ale to stifle his hunger. How he'd feel watching his woman and little ones grow skinnier by the day. He might know all there is about what colors would look just right in a picture window, but I know—and the boys here know—nobody can do good work on an empty stomach."

"What's your name?" Reeve asked, scribbling on his pad.

"No names."

"All right, then. Tell me—"

A woman's voice captured his attention. "You throw that, and you'll be sorry."

She was taller than most of the men there, easily six feet. Her shoulders were broad, her posture erect, her expression fierce. The crowd was stunned to a momentary silence. The boy with the snowball hesitated. It was enough for her to get through the door unmolested.

It had barely closed behind her when the snowball sailed toward it, splatting against the wooden barrier, sticking for a brief second, then sliding to the ground.

The men roared in anger, making promises of retribution if she dared to challenge them again. Reeve had seen protestors throw tomatoes, rocks, and fists. He'd seen things escalate to the use of knives and guns. The fact that they'd only thrown snowballs was an indication of just how deferent they were being. He feared they wouldn't be so accommodating tomorrow. And if they resorted to rougher measures, he wasn't sure what the public's reaction would be.

One thing was certain, even if Miss Jayne was a magpie and a New Woman, he didn't want to see her hurt. Perhaps he should speak to her tonight, implore her to quit this nonsense and return to her home.

"Flossie glanced at a woman behind Mrs. Driscoll who crouched
in front of a giant stained-glass window, her skirts pooled about
her as she held up different pieces of colored glass."

CHAPTER
8

Flossie's insides bobbed like a cork. In a few moments she'd be assigned to the role she'd have at Tiffany Glass and Decorating Company. She hoped to be awarded the job of painting faces on leaded glass windows, for portraits were her specialty—particularly women's hair swirling in the breeze. She could do the Virgin Mary with flowing hair, or the woman at the well, or Esther.

She frowned, trying to recall if she'd ever seen swirling hair in a stained-glass window, then pulled her mind back to the present. Nan had mentioned six women being in their department, but she only counted five, all busy working.

A wall of windows flooded the room with light. Beside one window, a huge white painter's canvas as big as a palace-sized tapestry hung against a wooden frame. An intricate geometric pattern had been sketched across its surface. A young woman added watercolor to the sketch, her arm propped against a maul-stick to keep it from tiring. It was clear the rendering was for a yet-to-be-made stained-glass window of enormous proportions.

The six girls Mr. Tiffany had chosen from the School of Applied Design sat on one side of a table. It was made of nothing more than giant boards set upon sawhorses, its surface so large she felt sure two front doors could have lain side by side atop it.

At the head of the table, Mrs. Driscoll studied Flossie and her schoolmates as if they were insects beneath a magnifying glass. Everyone except for Flossie wore serge skirts, simple shirt-waists, and no hats. Folding her hands in her lap, she tried not to squirm.

Mrs. Driscoll cleared her throat. "As you know, the Chicago World's Fair opens in five months, and Mr. Tiffany is planning to debut a first-of-its-kind exhibit—an enormous one-thousand-square-foot chapel whose interior is made up of nothing but reflective glass mosaic surfaces."

Flossie glanced at a woman behind Mrs. Driscoll who crouched in front of a giant stained-glass window, her skirts pooled about her as she held up different pieces of colored glass. The entire window was one-and-a-half times as tall as Flossie, yet it stood propped against the bank of windows along the wall. It was a wonder it didn't go crashing right through them.

"Without lead-glass workers," Mrs. Driscoll continued, recapturing Flossie's attention, "Mr. Tiffany's project will not be completed on time and his dream will not be realized. And that is where you come in." Her expression softened. "He believes our gender is well-suited to this work. Our fingers are more nimble than men's, our eyes are more sensitive to nuances of color, and we possess a God-given disposition for decoration."

Flossie kept her expression neutral. She'd never in her life heard a man admit such a thing. Were those truly Mr. Tiffany's words or Mrs. Driscoll's interpretation of them?

"The carved plaster arches of the chapel, the mosaic columns, the electrified chandelier, the white glass altar, and the dome-shaped baptismal font have all been completed by the men."

Flossie lifted her brows. What on earth was left to do?

"But there are several windows that have yet to be completed. And those, my dears, are what you will take on. You will do them as well, if not better, than the men and with a delivery date that will ensure the Women's Glass Cutting Department is not a temporary department, but a department that will outlive the fair and many years beyond it."

Flossie sat up a little straighter, knowing she was ready for the challenge and relishing the thought of turning those men outside onto their ears—once they'd returned to work, anyway.

A WOMAN SELLING FLOWERS[6]

"Hands behind his back, he bent over and examined a sketch of
a woman selling flowers to a well-dressed gentleman."

CHAPTER

9

A diminutive man paused at Reeve's door, his hair flatly brushed, his face clean-shaven. "Excuse me, would you happen to know where Miss Jayne's room is?"

"I'm afraid she's not in."

"Yes, I'm aware of that."

Reeve hesitated. As a rule, gentleman callers waited in the parlor, even well-dressed ones twice her age.

The man pointed toward the foyer with his thumb. "I knocked and waited just inside the door, but no one ever came."

Reeve sighed. "No, I don't suppose they did. Was there something I could help you with?"

"I just wanted to see her room, is all, then I'll be on my way. If you could tell me where it is, I'd be obliged."

Placing his pen in its holder, Reeve chose his words carefully. "Did you have business with the lady?"

"I'm her father."

"Are you?" Reeve stood and held out a hand. "Reeve Wilder."

"Bert Jayne." They shook. "I just wanted to make sure my girl was settled in all right."

"She seems to be. Today was her first day of work."

Looking down, Mr. Jayne ran a thumb over the rim of his hat.

"I never thought to hear words of that sort about any woman, but most especially not about my daughter."

"I'm sorry." And he was. He couldn't imagine being the father of a working girl, even if she did work for a prestigious employer like Tiffany. Perhaps it was best not to mention the strikers who'd harassed his daughter.

"I'm sorry, too." Jayne sighed. "Still, I wanted to see for myself that she was okay. If I'd waited until she was home, then it would look like I was condoning what she was doing—and I'm not. Not by a long shot. All the same, I'd like to see her room."

Pushing in his chair, Reeve stepped into the hallway. "Her room's right here next to mine."

Jayne frowned. "So close? Isn't there a woman's floor?"

"Much to my sorrow, there is not. I'd give anything to have the women on their own floor, but Mrs. Klausmeyer lets out rooms on a first come, first served basis with no regard to gender."

"Well, that's certainly distressing news." Jayne rubbed his forehead. "I do feel for you, though. Flossie's definitely a jabber box, but I confess to missing the chatter. Home has become so quiet all of a sudden."

Reeve could just imagine. Opening the door to her room, he stepped inside, then held it open for her father. A hodgepodge of rugs lay in a maze-like pattern on the floor, some circular, some rectangular. Every wall had furniture up against it with pictures, sketches, paintings, and china plates hanging above. One bed was shoved against the back wall like his, but unlike his it had a white quilt with intersecting rings made up of colorful fabrics. At its head, a matching pillow cover.

He'd never been in Miss Love's room before. He wondered how much of this was hers and how much of it was Miss Jayne's. He looked behind the door at the other bed. Her bed. It was up against the wall he shared with them—her voice always easier to hear than Miss Love's. No simple quilt for Miss Jayne, though. Her bed was covered with a fluffy white spread and a white lace pillow bordered with white lace ruffles. Above its brass headboard, a large painting of a woman at the seashore captured his full attention.

He moved closer, looking for the signature. And there it was. *F. Jayne.*

"It's the best one she's ever done," her father said, standing just behind Reeve's shoulder. "Far and away my favorite."

Reeve tilted his head. It was actually quite good. The woman leaned against a railing, her red hair flowing in the breeze and changing color depending on where the sun hit it. The water was blue and sparkling, the sand white and begging to be walked upon. He could almost hear the waves, taste the salt, and feel the grit of the sand on his skin.

Standing there, beside the painting and the white linens on the bed, he felt as if he'd stepped into a summer day, full of light and sunshine and happiness. Sort of like her.

He took a quick step back and bumped into her father. "Excuse me."

As much as Reeve wanted to return to his room, he didn't feel right leaving. The man said he was Miss Jayne's father, and he could see a little bit of resemblance around the mouth. Still, until he knew for certain, he'd stay put.

Mr. Jayne walked about the room, looking at the walls as if he were in a museum. Hands behind his back, he bent over and examined a sketch of a woman selling flowers to a well-dressed gentleman. A dress form holding a fashionable gown. A crowd of people boarding a steamer. A group of children playing hopscotch on the street. "Such a talent my girl has. Must have gotten it from her mother. I can't draw to save my life."

Reeve glanced at the sketches and paintings he referred to. Some weren't bad, but he wasn't sure he'd call Miss Jayne a talent. She was competent, as the seashore painting proved, but she was hardly the next Rembrandt.

Mr. Jayne stopped in front of a washstand. Instead of a wooden affair on spindly legs, the women had a full cabinet with an assortment of glass vials, china bowls, and porcelain vessels surrounding a fancy washbowl and ewer with floral designs and gold-leaf edges.

Mr. Jayne lifted a few of the lids and peeked at the various creams and liquids. "I'm a barber, you know."

No, he didn't know, but he didn't say so.

"Taught her a thing or two about creams and such, and she caught on awfully fast. She's a smart girl, my Flossie. She'd have made a great barber if she'd been a man." He held a jar of liquid to his nose. "Smells just like her, don't you think?" He held it out to Reeve.

Out of politeness, Reeve took a sniff. It smelled of roses. "I couldn't really say, sir. I only see her at dinnertime, and the table we sit at is awfully large."

Mr. Jayne screwed the lid back on and returned it to the washstand. "Well, of course you couldn't say, but I could, and I can assure you, it smells just like her." He took one last look about the room, then withdrew a card from his pocket. "Well, don't tell her I was here. I want her to come home. If she knew I'd been here, she might take it as a sign of approval."

Reeve accepted the card. So it was her father after all. "Mum's the word, sir."

Mr. Jayne clapped him on the shoulder. "That's a good man. If we want to keep this women's movement from gaining momentum, we'd best stick together. Good day, Wilder."

"Good day."

The man left as quickly and as quietly as he'd come. A shame his daughter wasn't more like him.

"She hadn't been chosen to paint faces on the leaded glass
windows, nor to paint watercolors onto the large hanging
canvas, which she now knew they called a cartoon."

CHAPTER
10

With aching feet, Flossie squeezed onto the crowded street-car that would take her home. Home to Klausmeyer's Boardinghouse. Exhausted as she was, she couldn't suppress the thrill of completing her first day of work. She hadn't been chosen to paint faces on the leaded glass windows, nor to paint watercolors onto the large hanging canvas, which she now knew they called a cartoon. Instead, she'd been sent to the storeroom to restock colored glass.

Nan Upton, the Tiffany Girl she'd met out in the hall, had stood beside a cartoon going through trunks full of colored glass. She'd pick up a small sheet, hold it to the window, mutter something under her breath, then do the same thing with a different one. When she'd sorted through all the trunks and not found the color she was looking for, she'd started on barrels of colored glass. By the time she'd laid aside a selection weighing no more than a few pounds, well over a ton of glass had been strewn from one end of the storeroom to the other.

It had been Flossie's job to put the pieces back, but rather than return them to any old trunk, she'd decided to sort them by color. All the greens in one trunk, the reds in another, and blues in yet another. No wonder Mr. Tiffany had lit up when he'd described the characteristics of his opalescent glass to her. Never had she seen anything like it in her entire life.

Touching it, holding it up to the light, seeing how different textures created different results enthralled her, and slowed down her work considerably. When Mrs. Driscoll had come to find out what was taking her so long, she'd given Flossie a bit of a scolding.

"For heaven's sake, look at all this glass. What on earth have you been doing?"

"Sorting it by color," she'd answered. "It might take a bit of time up front, but I think it will save time in the end."

"Nonsense. No one could ever sort Tiffany glass. It's too variegated. How would you ever be able to decide? No, no. Just get it up off the floor and tables and into the trunks, then come along. There's much to be done."

With a great deal of disappointment, she'd done as she was told. It was hard to pout, though, when she'd been able to work with such a plethora of colors and designs.

The streetcar conductor gave a savage ring of the bell and tore around a corner, throwing Flossie into the men crammed up next to her in the overcrowded quarters. She hung on to a leather strap above her head. No one offered her a seat, no one offered her any space.

It was the same for all women on streetcars this time of day, whether they were students or working girls. This was the time reserved for men who rushed home to their wives who served up meals, fetched slippers, and birthed children. At least the glass strikers hadn't been outside of Tiffany's at the conclusion of the day, so she and the others had gone unmolested to the streetcar stop.

Still, the men on the five o'clock cars didn't like them being there, and even though she knew better, it felt as if they'd all had some secret meeting and agreed to teach women students and laborers a lesson: if you want to enter into a man's world, then don't expect to be treated differently.

But the women *were* treated differently. They were touched inappropriately under the guise of being helped on and off the car. They were groped by "bustle pinchers" taking advantage of crowded conditions, and they had things whispered to them the men would never dare to utter under normal circumstances.

She tightened her hold on the creaking strap. No matter how stiff she made herself, she couldn't keep the men from brushing against her in an intimate fashion. All pretended it wasn't happening, but all were very aware it was.

In an effort to distract herself, she tried to imagine what it would be like if she were to be the one selecting glass instead of restocking it. She'd realized at once it was the most critical step of the entire window-making process.

She definitely would have chosen a different piece for the Virgin Mary's hair. The flow, density, and texture of the piece Nan had chosen was lovely—all of Mr. Tiffany's glass was lovely—but Flossie had run across some others that were even better. She'd considered showing them to Nan, then recalled Nan had seen them and set them aside, which was why Flossie was having to restock them in the first place.

"West Fifty-Seventh!" the driver shouted, pulling the horses to a stop.

Excusing herself, Flossie pressed her way to the front and had almost made it to the door when her coat caught on something and her backside received a strong pinch. Squealing, she whirled around, grasping her coat and swatting the area behind her.

She made eye contact with each of the men in her vicinity and they with her. She let her irritation and disgust be seen. They offered amused indifference in response.

Clasping her coat closed, she refused help dismounting, then hurried down the street. The brisk wind combined with the cold air made her nose hurt and her ears sting. Cabs, drays, and wagons slung snow up behind them. Drivers shouted at their horses.

She pressed her lips together. Bustle pinchers. She'd had to deal with them when she was returning home from the School of Applied Design, and she'd have to contend with them now as well. The only way to avoid them was to walk home, but that wasn't a viable option, either. The winter days were short, and women traveling alone after dark did so at their own peril.

Maybe she'd save a little money each month and buy a bicycle come spring.

PLACE CARD[8]

"After giving her a sympathetic squeeze on the shoulder, he went in search of his place card. It had chickadees painted on it, of all things. He hated chickadees."

CHAPTER
11

Tilting her head to the side, Flossie studied the long, scarred table stretching across the expanse of Klausmeyer's dining room. The mingled aromas of stew and soda bread drifted in from the kitchen. In twenty minutes the dinner bell would ring and the house's boarders would descend. Boarders who simply sat down, ate, and then returned to their respective rooms.

And why shouldn't they, when the table offered no cloth or centerpieces to soften its rough wooden surface? When the seats of its mismatched chairs were sunken from overuse and their uneven legs kept everyone off balance? When the fireplace's mantle held no decorations or candelabras? When the blank, stained walls had nothing to soothe the spirit or inspire the imagination? And worst of all, when the boarders didn't offer up anything resembling conversation?

Well, that was going to change. She desperately missed her parents and was more homesick than she was willing to admit. Still, she'd spent her whole life as an only child and now she'd inherited a new family, a very big family. She wasn't about to sit idly by while they acted as if they weren't all sharing the same house.

First thing on the agenda was to switch up the seating

arrangement. The same people sat in the same spot night after night, never bothering to engage those around them.

Not tonight. Tonight everyone was going to introduce themselves.

She fingered the place cards in her hand. She'd spent every night of the past week painting songbirds on them, then penning each person's name. That had been the easy part. The hard part was deciding who to put where.

AT THE SOUND OF the dinner bell, Reeve glanced up at his clock, startled to see it was already seven. Though his exposé had run in the back section of the paper, it had evidently been read by plenty of women—all of whom had strong opinions.

He placed his pen into its holder, then capped the inkwell. Women may not have the right to vote, but it didn't keep them from being heard. They'd gone to the *World*'s office with his article in hand and demanded a rebuttal. The office had invited them to submit one, but Reeve would be surprised if they ran it. He hoped they would, though. The controversy would draw attention to his pieces, and if there was ever a topic that needed attention, the women's movement was it.

He'd never said anything to their new boarder about the picketers or about her returning home. It would have been wasted breath on his part, and he had no desire to engage in a discussion with her—especially not an unpleasant one.

Standing, he grabbed his jacket from his chair, shrugged it on, and stepped across the hall to Mrs. Dinwiddie's room. "I believe I heard the dinner bell, Madame. Shall we head that way?"

Setting her knitting aside, the elderly widow lumbered to her feet, her white hair reminding him of spun glass. As usual, she'd twisted it up in an old-fashioned style that had probably been popular in her youth. He couldn't imagine the time it must take her to wrap those rolls of hair around her head like stacked sausages.

"Would you like me to get your cane for you?" he asked.

She waved her hand in a negative gesture. Her gray gown didn't favor the large puffy sleeves most women wore, but instead had sensible, straightforward ones. "No, no. I'll just hold on to you."

He gave a slight bow. "Then I shall be the most fortunate of men."

"Oh, hush. No need to waste your sparking on me. You'd best save that for the young ladies who'll appreciate it." The pleasure in her tone, however, belied her words.

He gently cupped her elbow. "I only have eyes for you, as you well know."

"Fiddlesticks." Pink scalp peeked through a swath of matted-down white hair on the right side of her head. "Have you noticed our new boarder? Now there's a piece of calico for you."

He smiled to himself, not only at the antiquated saying, but that it was coming from such an unlikely source. "We've a new boarder?"

Adjusting the round glasses propped against her nose, she *harrumph*ed. "You've noticed. You're just not wanting to admit it."

"What I've noticed is the lovely scent you're wearing this evening. Is it new?"

Her eyes lit. "Why, it is. Just arrived from Montgomery Ward. They call it Meadow Blossom."

He lifted her wrist to his nose. "Just like its name."

She *tsk*ed, but when they entered the dining room, her smile was broad, her step a bit lighter.

At the threshold, the new boarder greeted them as if she were the hostess in a receiving line and they her invited guests. "Good evening, Mrs. Dinwiddie. I believe your place card is right here closest to the door. Yours, Mr. Wilder, is there, at the other end."

He gave her a sideways glance. How did she know his name? He'd never so much as said word-one to her, although he knew all about her due to the thin walls.

"Place cards?" Mrs. Dinwiddie asked.

Other residents of the house circled the table, exclaiming over various place cards. Even their landlady, a drawn, reedy woman, set down a bowl of potatoes, then showed an uncharacteristic bit of animation as she looked over Miss Love's shoulder and examined these additions to her table.

"That's right," Miss Jayne said. "I thought it would be fun to sit by someone new tonight."

He suppressed a growl. What was this?

"You didn't put me by Mr. Oyster, did you?" Frowning, Mrs. Dinwiddie leaned close to Miss Jayne, but didn't bother to lower her voice. "He's going the way to destruction, I'm afraid. You mark my words."

The mercantile clerk looked up at the mention of his name. Anyone addressed as Oyster ought to be bald, pale, and clammy. Instead, he had a full head of hair in a constant state of disarray, a warm complexion, and a smile always at the ready when a woman was nearby. He caught Miss Jayne's eye, waggled his eyebrows, then winked.

Reeve would have to keep an eye on the man. When the ladies were absent, Oyster talked of nothing but his past conquests—especially if the girl had been a New Woman on her own. Miss Jayne might be a magpie and a complete disruption to the peaceful solitude Reeve prized, but Mrs. Dinwiddie had been right. Miss Jayne was also a stunner—and ripe for being duped by a bounder like Oyster.

Reeve stalled Mrs. Dinwiddie with a slight increase of pressure when she started to move away. "I'm afraid Mrs. Dinwiddie and I always sit together."

Miss Jayne smiled. "Yes, I noticed. That's why I put you at the other end of the table from her."

"But I don't want to be at the other end of the table from her."

Mrs. Dinwiddie patted his hand. "Now, now, Mr. Wilder, it's all right. It's just for one night. Besides, it's not as if I don't see you every afternoon for a spot of tea."

He frowned. That wasn't the point. Their teas were a way to keep him from working straight through the day without stopping and a way for her to break up the monotony of her afternoons. It had nothing to do with dinner.

Still, rather than create a scene, he escorted her to her seat and held out her chair. Miss Jayne had not only put her across from Oyster, but had placed her next to Mr. Nettels, a condescending music master who disparaged everyone else to make himself look better. The poor woman was going to have a miserable dinner.

After giving her a sympathetic squeeze on the shoulder, he went in search of his place card. It had chickadees painted on it, of all things. He hated chickadees. They made the most obnoxious noise and once they got going, never ceased chattering.

Settling into his chair, he spread his napkin on his lap and glanced at the new table arrangement. She'd placed everyone boy-girl, boy-girl and stuck him beside her roommate, with the house's newlyweds assigned to sit across from him. He'd be subjected to their ridiculous billing and cooing the entire meal.

Mr. Holliday, a man of forty who'd recently taken a girl of sixteen to wife, seated his wife and gave her arm a gentle pat. Miss Jayne sat in the middle, where she could preside over the table. She'd piled her mountain of black hair atop her head in the haphazard way Charles Gibson had made famous with his numerous pen-and-ink drawings. Her brown eyes and ready smile might hypnotize everyone else at the table, but not him.

"While we pass the bread," she said, "I thought it might be nice if we played a little game."

He eyed her. She could not possibly be serious.

"Beneath everyone's plate is a question written on a slip of paper."

Mr. Oyster reached for his plate.

"Wait, wait!" She touched his arm. "No peeking. Not until you know the rules."

To her left, Mr. Holliday held the bread basket up to her in a wordless question. She gave a genteel nod. "Yes, please."

He placed a roll on her plate, then sent the basket past her to Mr. Oyster.

"During the course of dinner," she continued, "we will take turns reading the questions beneath our plates. But the question you read is not for you, it's for the person across from you. That way, you can't cheat and formulate an answer while no one is looking."

Several in the group chuckled. Reeve shifted his position on the unfamiliar lumps of an unfamiliar chair. Looking at her husband, the young Mrs. Holliday clapped her hands together. The man gave her an affectionate smile and chucked her under the chin.

"Mr. Wilder?" Miss Jayne drew his attention. "Why don't you start us off, then we'll go all the way around the table."

All eyes turned to him. Heat rushed up his neck. "I mean no disrespect, Miss Jayne, but—"

From the corner of his eye, Mrs. Holliday's expression crumpled. He realized with a start it was her question he'd be reading, for she sat directly opposite him.

Sighing, he wiped a hand on his napkin, then withdrew the piece of paper from beneath his plate. Its borders were painted with tiny figures. Two were in a toboggan. Two were having a snowball fight. One was making a snow angel. And in the bottom corner, a couple skated across a frozen pond.

The paintings were simple, but charming. Almost childlike.

"Mr. Wilder?" Miss Jayne prompted.

He cleared his throat. "Yes. Right. So . . ." He looked at Mrs. Holliday. "What is your favorite winter activity?"

Her mouth made a tiny O. Her wide blue eyes sought her husband's. "Oh, my. There's so many to choose from. I'm simply not sure. Let me see . . . I guess I'd pick ice-skating?"

Miss Jayne's expression lit. "Truly? That's my favorite, too." She looked around the table. "Does anyone else like to skate?"

Not knowing what to do with the paper, Reeve tucked it inside his jacket, only listening with one ear as the others answered in the affirmative. Though he'd grown up in New Jersey and had had a pond directly behind his house, he'd never actually skated—not because he hadn't wanted to, but because he hadn't been allowed to. He'd stood at the window of his second-story bedroom and watched the rest of the town skate. His classmates. Other families. Young lovers. Old-timers. But never him.

To his left, Miss Love removed her piece of paper. Painted onto its borders were tiny figures reading books. A man in a chair smoking a pipe. A young girl in a window seat. A boy stretched out on a carpet. A woman reading to a group of children collected about her feet.

"What is the last book you read in its entirety?" she asked Mr. Holliday.

Reeve studied the man, wondering what a girl of sixteen would see in him. He was comely enough, Reeve supposed, and well built, but he was old enough to be the girl's father and already a touch of gray had begun to show in his thick dark hair and mustache.

Stroking his chin, he smiled at Miss Love. "*The Last of the Mohicans*, by James Cooper."

"Oh, I've never read that," Miss Jayne said. "It's about some girls being captured by Indians, is it not?"

And so it went, all the way around the table, all the way through dinner. It didn't take Reeve long to realize Miss Jayne had made a careful study of everyone in the house. Her questions were too specific to be accidental.

Mrs. Holliday had probably made snow angels and ridden in toboggans as recently as last year. He wondered if ice-skating really was her favorite winter activity or if it was simply the one she considered most suitable for a married woman. Though her husband was a photographer, he often had a book tucked beneath his arm and was thrilled to give a synopsis of *Mohicans* while Mrs. Klausmeyer brought in stew from the kitchen.

Miss Jayne had stuck to a safe topic with Mr. Oyster and asked what food he'd give up if he were forced to choose one. Mrs. Dinwiddie said the key to a happy marriage was making sure the person you chose loved you more than he loved himself.

The music master's favorite holiday was Christmas. Miss Love's favorite smell was that of honeysuckle, and Miss Jayne confessed her favorite thing to do as a child was to go on walks with her father—even in the rain.

Turning away, he wiped his mouth with his napkin. What a charmed life she'd led. A mother who garbed her in clothes worthy of a princess and a father who treated her as if she were one. Walks in the rain? He'd never walked anywhere in the rain for the sheer pleasure of it. Never even crossed his mind.

"Mr. Wilder?" Mrs. Holliday's bright eyes looked at him with expectation, a notecard in her hand.

He flushed. "I'm sorry. I wasn't listening. Is it my turn?"

"It is."

"Could you repeat the question, please?"

She looked to her husband, as if to ascertain whether Reeve was serious or merely toying with her, but the man nodded his encouragement and she read her paper again.

"If you were to change one thing about society, what would it be and why?"

He swung his gaze to Miss Jayne's. Her expression was one of polite interest. Nothing to indicate she'd studied him so thoroughly that within two weeks of moving in she'd sensed the passion he held for the preservation of home and community.

Certainly, the walls between their rooms were thin, but he had no one in his room to confide in. Any visiting he did occurred in Mrs. Dinwiddie's room, not his. So, she hadn't overheard him say anything. Neither he, nor anyone else that he knew of, gathered in the parlor in the evenings. She rode the streetcar to work in the mornings, while he stayed in his room to write. So how did she know to ask him such a question? Unless she'd read his articles. Still, was he that transparent? That easy to see through?

"Mr. Wilder?" Mrs. Holliday's tone held a touch of uncertainty.

"I'm sorry." He again wiped his mouth with his napkin. "That's a rather big question. One I couldn't possibly answer succinctly. What if I told you what my favorite season was instead?"

Miss Jayne gave him a tolerant smile. "Nonsense. Anyone who writes the kind of articles you do would, I feel sure, be able to briefly sum up what he feels our society could do to better itself."

He stared at her. She *had* read them. He shifted in his chair again. "My favorite season is winter."

She lifted a brow. "Scared to answer the question?"

"Certainly not." He was tired of this game. Tired of all the chatter. Tired of sitting in a different seat when everyone knew his chair was the more comfortable one Mr. Nettels now occupied. "I'm simply finished with my meal and have a deadline to meet. So, I'm afraid—"

Again, young Mrs. Holliday's face began to crumple. Death and the deuce. If he didn't answer the blasted question, she'd take it personally.

Heaving a sigh, he pulled his napkin from his lap and set it on the table. "If I were to change one thing in society, I'd put a stop to the crusade of today's New Woman who wishes to break with conventions of the past and trample all tradition underfoot."

He slid back his chair. "The reason her pursuit of economic independence is so serious is because the place she currently occupies in society is vitally important. Any change to it would result in enormous consequences to every individual and even to the entire human race."

Standing, he grasped the top rail of his chair. It wobbled in his hands. "As much as she wishes it, she cannot simply rush off with a conceited notion that all the teachings of human history can be easily reversed, and society cannot suddenly be turned into a social and economic paradise by the application of some simple formula she's concocted."

Miss Jayne's lips parted.

He should stop. This wasn't exactly appropriate dinner conversation. And it wasn't as if he could actually change society. Still, the entire situation fired his fear and his anger and he found himself unable to stem the flow of words. "It is man, not woman, who throughout the centuries has battled with the forces of nature and subdued them to his will. It is he who swept away the jungle and the forest, who made the desert blossom like a rose, who reared great cities and created states and founded empires. It is he who flecked the ocean with his fleets, who girdled the earth with the cincture of civilization, who united humanity into one great brotherhood, and who established law and evolved the sciences."

Pushing in his chair, he straightened his spine. "If woman has it in herself to do the work of man, which he has fearlessly performed for unnumbered centuries, then why didn't Eve choose to live her life apart from Adam from the very beginning? Why didn't she treat him on equal terms? Become his rival?" He flattened his lips. "I'll tell you why. Because giving woman economic independence would breed mistrust and jealousy between her and man. It would corrode the very foundations every society in the world is built upon. Our future as a human race depends upon her keeping her life joined to his in a spirit of trust and reverence and affection. Now, if you'll excuse me, I have work to do."

Spinning, he stalked from the room, leaving total silence in his wake.

Fourteen-Hour Wives
of Eight-Hour Men, need
GOLD DUST
Washing Powder

To enable them to get through work as early as their husbands.

GOLD DUST saves time, strength, patience and money.

Made only by
N. K. Fairbank & Co.,
CHICAGO,

St. Louis,
New York,
Philadelphia,
Boston,
Montreal.

" 'I've no desire to condemn women to imprisonment in greasy kitchens, forever debarring them from intellectual growth. It's their best interests I have at heart. Theirs and their children's.' "

CHAPTER
12

Flossie held herself perfectly still at the open doorway of Mr. Wilder's room. The patter of rain outside and the hall's worn carpet runner had covered her approach. His back was slightly turned, for he was sitting on the end of his bed, his body angled toward the window. The precipitation had stirred the ever-present slime in the city's streets, tainting the room with its subtle odor.

She took advantage of the unguarded moment to study him. Jacketless, his white shirt stretched across a broad back. Criss-crossing black suspenders trapped parts of his shirt and caused it to wrinkle, then drew the eye down to brown trousers hugging a trim waist. Muscular thighs strained the fabric encasing them.

The moisture in the air made her hair wilt, but made his short blond curls more wavy. At his feet, a gray, pathetic-looking cat purred as he stroked its matted, wet fur. She'd often wondered why he kept his window cracked, even on the coldest of days. Well, now she knew. He whispered to it, then chuckled as it rolled onto its back seeking a tummy rub.

A dull green blanket had been thrown over his pillow in a man's way of making the bed. No curtains hung on his window, no ornaments graced his bedside table. She'd never seen such a sparse, barren room, totally devoid of personal mementos and pictures.

Only his desk gave a peek into the man he was, but even that held a minimal amount, and what was there was kept in an orderly manner. His papers were neatly stacked, his oil lamp flickered, his pen protruded from its stand, his inkwell was tightly capped. So much for having work to do. Clearly, that had been an excuse to escape from their dinner party.

After his departure, the boarders had been more taken by the number of words he'd spoken than the actual topic of his discourse. According to them, he'd said more in those few minutes than in the entire year he'd lived there. For her, however, it was the subject matter and the passionate delivery that impressed her. She'd read his articles, had known the women's movement concerned him. What she hadn't realized was the degree to which it did.

Her father would certainly like him. They'd find much in common if they were to ever meet. But with the way her father felt about her being here, the chances of that were slim. Still, it had been illuminating to hear Mr. Wilder voice what Papa had not—or perhaps could not. She'd sort of stumbled into being a New Woman because of circumstances. She wasn't a member of any women's association. She hadn't attended any women's rallies or lectures. She merely wanted to be paid for her labor so she could go to art school. She had a hard time seeing how that was going to lead to the deterioration of the entire human race.

Even so, despite his speech, her game had been a wonderful success. Everyone stayed at the table, visiting, until Mrs. Klausmeyer finally kicked them out. They agreed to adjourn to the parlor, but Flossie wanted everyone in the family to join them. So, she'd excused herself for a moment to come and fetch Mr. Wilder.

Lifting her hand, she tapped on his door.

He looked over his shoulder, then slowly straightened his spine.

"Don't get up," she said. "I just came to check on you."

He glanced at his jacket, which had been draped on the back of his desk chair, and started to rise.

"Don't get up," she said again, then pointed to the cat. "I see you have a friend."

He sank back down. "It's raining."

"Actually, I think it's snowing now."

He glanced at the window. "No, I mean, the cat always comes when it's raining . . . or snowing."

"Does he?"

"She. It's a she. And, yes, but Mrs. Klausmeyer wouldn't like it."

"I won't tell."

He studied her, his eyes hidden, for the lantern light on the desk didn't reach quite that far.

"I don't let her on the bed," he said. "I make her a little pallet on the floor. She doesn't bother anybody. Never cries. Just purrs."

Crossing her arms, Flossie propped herself against the doorframe. "What's her name?"

"I don't know." Teasing the cat, he touched its nose, paws, and ears in quick succession while it swiped at him.

Why hadn't he named it? she wondered. Instead of asking, she simply offered him an invitation. "Everyone's in the parlor. We're going to play The Board Game of Old Maid. I found it on one of Mrs. Klausmeyer's shelves."

Instead of responding, he rubbed his knuckles against the cat's ear. Closing its eyes, the cat leaned in to the rub and purred.

Flossie tilted her head. "We'd like you to join us."

"I'm afraid I can't. I need to do some work."

She looked again at the clean desk and capped inkwell. "But everyone's there."

"Perhaps next time." He still hadn't looked up, but kept all his attention on the cat.

"Is it because I'm a New Woman?"

Pausing, he rested his elbows on his knees. "Not at all. I'm sorry about that. I don't know what came over me."

"Don't be sorry. I asked you a question and you answered."

He studied her again. "Why did you ask it? Why was it so different from everyone else's?"

"I don't know." That wasn't completely true. "Well, okay. Perhaps it had a little something to do with your articles in the *World*."

"Did it?" He leaned back. "Well, I have a question for you now. What kind of paintings did you surround my slip of paper with— the one Mrs. Holliday read to me, I mean?"

Looking toward the upper corner of his ceiling, she bit her lower lip. "Well, let's see. One painting was of a man dragging a woman by a chain around her neck. Another was of a woman being turned away from a university by a pack of men in black robes. Another of a woman in sordid labor over a soap vat. And the last a father pocketing all the money his daughter earned."

"Perhaps he needed it to help feed his family."

"Perhaps he didn't."

He blew out a puff of air. "We men aren't tyrants, you know."

"No?"

"I've no desire to condemn women to imprisonment in greasy kitchens, forever debarring them from intellectual growth. It's their best interests I have at heart. Theirs and their children's."

Rather than challenge him further, she decided instead to extend an olive branch. "Then there's no reason not to join us in the parlor."

A beat of silence. "I'm sorry."

She supposed she could blackmail him. Tell him she'd report him for harboring a stray, but, of course, she'd never do that. Still, she'd have to think of something, but for now she'd let him off the hook.

Pushing herself off the frame, she took a step back. "Next time, then. Good night, Mr. Wilder."

"Miss Jayne."

The cat took a quick swipe, catching him across the hand.

He jerked it back. "Oh, ho, ho. Easy now."

The sound of his one-sided conversation followed her back down the hall.

Mr. Tiffany poked his head inside the storeroom. "Well, there she is."

Flossie rose to her feet. "Mr. Tiffany! It's so good to see you. I've been dying to tell you how much I love your glass. It is the most beautiful thing I've ever seen and such a privilege to work with."

With an arm against his waist, he gave a bow. "Thank you very much." He straightened. "I've been wanting to come by, but hadn't been able to pull myself away from the factory in Corona."

She couldn't imagine that he'd been dressed like that at the factory or he'd have looked as out of place as she'd been on her first day of work. Still, she took a moment to appreciate the quality of his mixed cheviot coat, his brown worsted trousers with a thin dark stripe, and his russet shoes that had gained such popularity men were wearing them with everything but their evening dress.

"Miss Upton," he said, acknowledging Nan.

"Good afternoon, Mr. Tiffany." Nan picked up a sheet of glass, her owl-like eyes bluer than normal in the bright sunlight.

He returned his attention to Flossie. "I wish you could have seen the glass we made yesterday. It was the purest of yellows with just enough red added to turn parts of it the exact orange of the sun the moment before it disappears behind the horizon."

Flossie rested a hand against her chest. "Oh, I wish I could have seen it, too. It sounds like it would be the perfect thing to use for flames. Too bad we aren't making any windows about the fiery furnace Shadrach, Meshach, and Abednego were thrown into."

He laughed. "Perhaps I can talk someone into commissioning one, but what I'd really like to use it for is daffodils."

"Daffodils?"

With a sheepish expression, he shrugged. "Don't tell anyone, but I'm growing a bit weary of always making windows for churches. All they ever want are traditional religious figural pieces. It doesn't leave a lot of room for creativity. For quite some time, I've been wanting to try some nature-inspired still lifes or even a panorama of a pastoral scene."

"Like your paintings," she said.

"Like my paintings." He smiled at her, then glanced at Nan as she held up a section of aquamarine glass to the window.

"Ah, look at that one, Miss Jayne."

"Wouldn't it make the perfect scales for a mermaid?"

"A mermaid." Shaking his head, he chuckled. "It would indeed. Now, is this the glass you've selected so far?"

"Miss Upton has. I just do the restocking, but wait until you see what she's selected."

With a lift of her chin, Nan proceeded to show him each piece, then pointed to its corresponding color on the cartoon.

With hands in his pockets, Mr. Tiffany listened and watched. When she was finished, he looked at Flossie. "What do you think?"

Biting her lip, she glanced at Nan. The girl's eyes turned steely, her posture stiff.

"For the most part I loved what she picked," Flossie said, keeping her tone neutral.

"You'd make no changes, then?" he asked.

She shifted her weight. "Well, perhaps, but only a couple."

"Which ones?"

Without looking Nan's way, Flossie walked to a pile of glass the girl had deemed unworthy, flipped through it, then removed a piece the deep color of a ginger plant. She held it up to the light. "I'd have used this for the section of fabric that runs along the Virgin Mary's lap—right here." She pointed to the corresponding part on the cartoon. "I think that piece needs to be fairly dark in order to add a bit more shadow and dimension."

He nodded. "Since you are doing the preliminary selecting and the final decision will occur later, you need to give your selector as many choices as you can without including the entire storeroom. That's the first thing to keep in mind. So from now on, Miss Upton, I recommend you choose a few more options for your selector. Second, you were right, Miss Jayne, to note the piece Miss Upton chose for the Virgin's lap wasn't quite right, but I'm afraid yours isn't, either."

"No?" she asked.

"No, the color is good, but you need a piece of heavily wrinkled glass. That will give the illusion of the fabric being gathered in her lap, and will also give the dimension you were missing before. Let me see if I can find one."

For the next thirty minutes Mr. Tiffany critiqued Nan's selections, giving both the girls a chance to find different pieces before selecting even better ones himself. A couple of times Flossie felt like her selections were just as good as his, but she savored every moment of the time he spent with them. His vast wealth had not overly impressed her, but his vast talent had.

By the time he left, she had learned more about color, texture, and design than she had in a month of classes at the design school. "Oh, Nan, isn't he wonderful?"

"I could hardly understand him with that lisp." With little

regard to their fragility, she stacked the pieces they'd decided upon onto a tray.

"Goodness, I hardly even notice his lisp anymore."

"You two are certainly very friendly."

Flossie began to return the unused pieces to their trunks and barrels. "We became acquainted the day he and Mrs. Driscoll came to the School of Applied Design."

Picking up the tray of glass, Nan gave her a hard look. "Well, don't think that just because he gave you a little attention today means he's grooming you to be a selector. That position requires a great deal of experience and talent—neither of which you have. I suggest you don't get ahead of yourself."

Nan flounced out the door before Flossie had the opportunity to formulate a response. It was just as well. By the time a response did come to mind, it wasn't exactly one that would promote camaraderie, and she had no wish to make an enemy of Nan—or any of the Tiffany Girls. Now, more than ever, women needed to stick together.

"Clearly, she was not going to give him the kind of questions she gave everyone else, such as: when did you last climb a tree?"

CHAPTER

14

What is your earliest childhood memory?"
Seeing my mother in a coffin. But he couldn't say that.

Tonight it was Miss Love asking his question from across the table. A question Miss Jayne had planted there. Clearly, she was not going to give him the kind of questions she gave everyone else, such as: when did you last climb a tree? If you were given a boat, what would you name it? If you could be a piece of furniture, what would you be?

No, his questions were never simple. They appeared innocent enough on the surface, but in reality probed rather deeply. And she knew it. Was doing it on purpose. Would he receive easier questions if he joined them in the parlor each night? Or if he ceased to write articles about the New Women? He wished he could take dinner in his room, but Mrs. Klausmeyer would only allow that if he were sick, and there was no telling what Miss Jayne would do if she thought him ill.

He cut a bite of sprat, then jabbed it with his fork. "My earliest memory is of sitting in church with my father."

Everyone turned to Miss Jayne. Clearly, his answer was insufficient. The green gown she wore, with its lace and bows and big puffy sleeves, befitted a duchess rather than a working girl. He'd noticed she no longer wore fancy dresses to Tiffany's studio, though. Saved them instead for dinner and parlor games.

She took a sip of cider. "What was it about that particular day in church that made it so memorable?"

I'd been told earlier in the week that my mother lived in heaven.

He took a deep breath. "I'd asked my father where heaven was."

Everyone looked at one another with smiles and amusement.

Miss Jayne tilted her head, her black hair swept up in artful disarray. "And what did he say?"

"He didn't say anything. We were in church. He simply pointed upward."

Her focus narrowed, concentrating the full force of her brown eyes onto him. His stomach clenched. She was very perceptive, a little too perceptive.

"You didn't believe him, did you?" she asked.

"I believed him."

"But . . . ?"

He sighed. "But for a long time afterward, I thought heaven and the church attic were synonymous."

Good-natured chuckles rippled about the table.

Miss Jayne didn't so much as smile. "How did you discover they weren't synonymous?"

"I climbed up into the church attic and my mother wasn't there."

The clinks of silverware ceased. Mugs stalled midair. All fidgeting froze.

"I'm so sorry," she said softly, and she meant it. He could see her genuine sorrow.

Emotion rose to the back of his throat. Emotion he'd long since buried, right beside his mother. At least, he thought he had. Not trusting himself to speak, he simply nodded and returned his attention to his plate. It was a long time, however, before he could swallow the rest of his dinner.

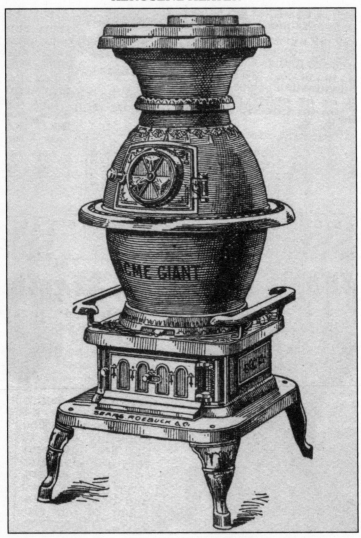

"Kneeling in front of Mrs. Dinwiddie's kerosene heater, Reeve tilted
the upper portion back on its hinge and lifted out the tank."

Kneeling in front of Mrs. Dinwiddie's kerosene heater, Reeve tilted the upper portion back on its hinge and lifted out the tank. "This shouldn't take too long, then I'll have it fired up again and we'll get you warm in no time."

"I'm fine," she said. "Take your time."

He couldn't quite suppress a smile. She sat in her overstuffed chair with a blanket about her shoulders, a lap robe over her legs, a winter scarf about her neck, and a pair of gloves protecting her hands. He couldn't believe she'd chopped the fingertips off of a perfectly good pair of gloves just so she could keep her hands warm yet have her fingers free to sew.

Removing a pocketknife from his trousers, he scraped off some char along the edge of the flame spreader. His fingers were stiff with the cold, making even the simplest task take longer. "So what are you making now?" he asked.

"I'm hemming a tablecloth. Be careful not to get any of that on my rug, dear."

"Mrs. Klausmeyer gave me an old sheet to double up and put over your rug. I'll be careful, though." He glanced about her room. Her accent tables already had cloths, and the other pieces of furniture were covered with doilies. "Where are you going to put your new tablecloth?"

"It's for the dining room."

"The dining room?" The gallery on top of the tank refused to budge. Raising up onto his knees, he grasped it and forced it in a counterclockwise direction until it finally came loose.

"Yes," Mrs. Dinwiddie replied. "Miss Jayne asked if I'd mind making one up. She thinks it will make our meals much more homey and pleasant. I quite agree with her."

He frowned. He couldn't imagine their landlady parting with coin for something as frivolous as fabric for a tablecloth. "Where did the material come from?"

"Oh, it's some old stuff I had stored under my bed. We found some other fabric I had that would make lovely drapes for the parlor."

"We?"

"Miss Jayne and I."

"So you're making drapes as well?"

"No, Mrs. Holliday agreed to do those up for us."

"With your fabric?"

"Mmm-hm." She wove her needle along the edge of the white cloth.

He wiped his hands on a rag. "What if you want to use that fabric for something else?"

"I won't."

"Not yet, perhaps, but you might later."

Glancing over the rim of her glasses, she gave him an affectionate smile, her hands still working. "No need to get fierce, young Wilder. I'm thrilled to put the stuff to good use."

He still didn't like it. Miss Jayne was taking over the entire place. Name cards at supper. Questions under their plates. Parlor games in the evenings. And now she'd commandeered the use of Mrs. Dinwiddie's personal belongings. What if that fabric had been in her family for years? What if she'd had secret plans for it that she hadn't yet had an opportunity to initiate? She'd never say so to Miss Jayne or anyone else.

"Do you have any petroleum jelly?" With great effort, he kept his voice civil. It wasn't Mrs. Dinwiddie he was irritated with, but that blasted New Woman who'd evidently decided that if she couldn't take over the world, she'd take over Klausmeyer's Boardinghouse instead. He tightened his jaw. Over his dead body.

"There on the dresser." She pointed with her head to a large marble-top dresser crowded with frames, candles, jars, and hat stands. "On the far left."

He stood before the dresser, overwhelmed and uncomfortable about reading the labels of such personal things, much less rifling through them.

"Oh my, it's freezing in here." Miss Jayne walked in with a wooden easel and set it up by the door. Her hair was in its usual artfully-arranged-to-appear-unarranged pouf. She'd changed out of her Sunday clothes and now wore a plain brown skirt and striped shirtwaist.

"Come in, my dear. Come in." Mrs. Dinwiddie paused in her work. "Mr. Wilder is changing out the wick in my heater. It won't be long now."

"Hello, Mr. Wilder." Miss Jayne gave him a bright smile as if she had every right to be here when everyone knew Sunday afternoons were the times he did for Mrs. Dinwiddie what their landlady's husband neglected to do himself.

Reeve didn't feel at ease with very many people. He much preferred to be alone. Yet Mrs. Dinwiddie was not like everyone else. She was a kindly old lady who'd lost her husband and son within a year of each other and had no one left in the world. He knew only too well what that was like.

But more than that, she always put others before herself. He'd never in his life seen such a selfless person. It wasn't fake, either.

He'd watched her for a long time before he'd finally responded to her overtures of friendship.

The same characteristic that was her greatest strength, however, was also her greatest weakness. She'd give anyone anything without a thought to her own wants, needs, or comfort. Which brought him back to the tablecloth and draperies. There was no way to know what that fabric had been earmarked for, but one thing was certain, Mrs. Dinwiddie wouldn't have used up precious space in this tiny little room to store it away if it meant nothing to her.

"Show him where the petroleum jelly is, Miss Jayne." Mrs. Dinwiddie pointed a finger toward the left side of the dresser. "It's there by the licorice powder."

He quickly scanned the jars, bottles, and containers littering the left side of the chest. He could find it. He didn't need any help from the likes of her.

Miss Jayne stepped up beside him, paused for no more than a second, reached over him, then whisked up a little tub clearly marked with the Vaseline label. "Here you are."

He snatched it from her. "What's the easel for?"

Her face lit. "I've decided to paint a portrait of every member of our family here at 438, starting with Mrs. Dinwiddie."

"A portrait? Right now? Today?"

She laughed. "Heavens, no. It will take much more than one sitting. Today I'm doing the sketch. Then every Sunday, about this time, I'll come back and do the next step."

"Every Sunday?"

"Yes."

"At this exact time?"

"More or less."

"Why?" he asked.

"Because it's the only afternoon I have off, and because if I come at the same time each week, the lighting will not have changed too drastically."

He spun around and pierced Mrs. Dinwiddie with his gaze. This was their time. *His* time. Not his and Miss Jayne's times.

But Mrs. Dinwiddie wasn't looking at him, she was looking to the side and tapping her lips with a fingerless glove. "Oh, my. Will I have to wear the same outfit every single Sunday?"

"It would be helpful if you would," Miss Jayne replied.

"You absolutely do not," Reeve all but growled. "You wear whatever you want. Miss Jayne will make do."

"Well, yes," Miss Jayne said. "I can certainly make do, I'm just saying—"

"She knows what you're saying," he snapped.

Mrs. Dinwiddie looked at him, lifted her brows, and followed his progress as he stalked back to the heater, plopped onto the floor, and crisscrossed his legs. He knew he was being churlish. And so did she. Still, was nothing sacred anymore?

Yanking off the lid of the Vaseline, he dug into it with his rag and wiped it onto the threads of the gallery so it wouldn't stick next time he needed to unscrew it.

Miss Jayne made a few more trips, carrying in a stretched canvas and propping it onto the easel, bringing a sketchpad and leaning it atop the canvas, then scattering a few supplies onto Mrs. Dinwiddie's bedside table. Reeve intentionally didn't offer to assist her. Instead, he brushed off the cobwebs, dust, and dirt from the gallery.

Finally, Miss Jayne pulled a smock over her clothing and began buttoning it closed.

Mrs. Dinwiddie set her sewing aside. "I guess I should remove all these blankets so you can see."

Reeve slammed the gallery onto the floor, causing it to rattle. "You will *not*." The pulse in his jaw hammering, he impaled Miss Jayne with his stare. "Would you have her catch a chill just so you can get a sketch?"

Miss Jayne flushed.

"Mr. Wilder," Mrs. Dinwiddie hissed. Never, ever had she used that tone with him. "That is quite enough."

He flexed his fists. "I'll not have you becoming ill. She can jolly well wait until I'm done and the room has warmed or she can come back tomorrow."

"She will be working tomorrow."

"Then she can go straight to the de—"

"*Mr. Wilder.*" Another warning, this one fiercer than the last.

He cranked the stem with sharp turns until the gears came to the end of the wick carrier.

"He's right," Miss Jayne interjected into the yawning silence. "Quite right. I wasn't thinking. I'll wait."

Finally. Some inkling of sense. Praise the saints that be. Maybe now she'd leave.

"Come and sit beside me, then, while we wait." Mrs. Dinwiddie's voice held great affection and not a little reassurance, as if Miss Jayne were the one who'd been wronged. Grabbing the wick with two fingers, he lifted it up and pulled it out of the carrier.

"No, no," she said. "That's all right. I'll just do some warm-up sketches." Her charcoal began to scrape along the pages of her sketchpad.

Mrs. Dinwiddie did not pick her sewing back up. A sure sign of her displeasure. With him. And it was all Miss Jayne's fault. He and Mrs. Dinwiddie had been having a perfectly fine visit until she'd entered into their conversation, then actually shown up in the flesh.

Lining the cotton tails of the new wick onto either side of the wick tube, he held them in place with one hand, brought his pocketknife to his teeth, opened it, then used it to tuck the tails down inside the tank. As he worked the wick down, the hairs on the back of his neck began to rise. Somehow, someway, he knew he was being stared at. Not by Mrs. Dinwiddie, but by *her*.

He slanted a glance at her. She was drawing on her sketch

pad. She flicked her gaze to him and froze. He immediately returned his attention to what he was doing, refusing to look at her again. It took a little persuasion, but he finally slid the wick down until the adjuster made contact with the wick carrier.

He wiped his brow with his shoulder. The gears were meshed. By the time he leveled the burning surface, reassembled the tank, filled it with fuel, and installed it back into the heater, the extended silence in the room had caused the tension to rise to even greater heights.

"We'll need to give it fifteen minutes to soak up the kerosene before I can light it," he said, collecting the discarded wick and drop cloth.

"That will be fine." Mrs. Dinwiddie's voice was civil, but not warm. Nothing like it normally was.

He looked at her.

Her lips were pressed together, her eyes full of censure.

His chest tightened. Scooping up his mess, he scrambled to his feet, swept past Miss Jayne, and headed out back to dispose of it. It wasn't until he returned to light the heater that he saw Miss Jayne's sketch.

He pulled up short. A muscular man with broad shoulders and curling, untamed hair held a gallery in one hand, while he crammed a wick into it with the other, elbow out. The lines were quick, rough, and careless, yet he knew immediately what it was. Who it was.

She sat in the chair beside Mrs. Dinwiddie, both of them looking at him. They'd ceased speaking when he'd appeared. Had they been talking about him?

"Excuse me," he mumbled, then lit the wick, closed the heater, returned the Vaseline to the dresser, and left, feeling angry, confused, and hurt. A hurt not unlike the one he'd felt many times before when he'd been shut inside his room at his grandparents' house and stood in front of the bolted-down window, looking out at the world from behind a barrier as impenetrable as a solid brick wall.

"Pressing down with her stylus, she outlined each individual color on
a giant cartoon Grace de Luze had painted with watercolor."

CHAPTER

16

M r. Tiffany had been sequestered in Agnes Northrup's office for almost forty-five minutes. Flossie glanced again at the woman's door, wishing she could simply sit at the man's feet and listen. Already she'd been able to apply what she'd learned from him to her painting techniques. If she could just shadow him, she'd be able to learn so much more. Especially since it was going to take her forever to save up enough money for tuition to the School of Applied Design, much longer than she'd originally thought.

She wondered what he and Miss Northrup were discussing. Was he critiquing her work? Miss Northrup had been with Mr. Tiffany since 1888 and was the manager before Mrs. Driscoll. Nan said the woman had hated it and complained it interfered with her designing. So Nan was to have taken her place. Then Mrs. Driscoll, who had worked for Mr. Tiffany before, swooped in and swiped the managerial position. Miss Northrup had become a full-time designer and been given her own personal office. Nan was given nothing—no promotion, no special working space, no title. She was simply a Tiffany Girl, just like the rest of them.

This morning Mrs. Driscoll had moved Flossie and Nan from the storeroom to the workshop with the rest of the girls. As much as Flossie loved putting the glass away, it was a rather lonely affair. Out here, she not only enjoyed the camaraderie of the other girls, but she was able to see all the other tasks they performed.

Pressing down with her stylus, she outlined each individual color on a giant cartoon Grace de Luze—a designer who'd been with Tiffany for three years—had painted with watercolor. Finding a spot of rich blue, Flossie ran the point of her stylus around the edge of that single color. She was careful to exert a good deal of pressure on the stylus, for underneath the cartoon were two sheets of carbon transfer paper atop two sheets of heavy manila paper.

When she was finished, Mrs. Driscoll would pull back the cartoon. Underneath, on the manila sheets, would be a perfect outline of where each fragment of colored glass would eventually be placed. Before the two sheets of manila were separated, however, one of the other girls would number each individual section Flossie had delineated. Nan told her they would use those numbers over and over when putting the window together.

Stepping out of Miss Northrup's office, Mr. Tiffany clapped his hands together. "How are my windows coming along, ladies?"

Flossie wondered if he changed into his fine clothes every time he wanted to visit the Women's Department, for she'd never seen him looking anything less than the gentleman.

"What do we have here?" he asked, stepping up to watch two girls cut templates with three-bladed scissors.

They were cutting around carbon lines on manila paper that someone else had already traced and numbered. Their special scissors cut an eighth-of-an-inch border around each piece to compensate for the lead that would be soldered there. The glass cutter would eventually use the numbered pieces of paper as her templates.

"Wait a minute. What's this?" He frowned. "Mrs. Driscoll, this looks like the western section of our *Adoration* window."

Weaving between the tables, Mrs. Driscoll approached him at a sedate pace. "That's exactly what it is. They're cutting out the wreath the woman is holding."

He pulled out his pocket watch and popped it open. "But, we've twelve windows to make before May. How can we still be cutting out templates for the first one?"

"The men's tasks are new and unfamiliar. Our speed will improve with time."

"But we don't have time."

"Nor can we afford careless errors because we are hurrying when we should be paying attention to detail."

His lisp became pronounced. "Well, then, let's give the ladies a little incentive, shall we?"

Mrs. Driscoll folded her hands in front of her. "What did you have in mind?"

"The two girls who do the best work, who complete their tasks quickly and without errors, and who never miss a day of work will be sent to the fair. By me."

Flossie touched her fingers to her lips.

Mrs. Driscoll gave a small smile of approval. "That would be extremely generous of you, but even more than that, they would like to maintain their positions as Tiffany Girls even after the chapel is complete—even after the men return. My suggestion would be to award them permanent positions if they complete the windows in a timely manner."

"All of them?" He widened his eyes.

"All of them."

"Impossible." He pursed his lips. "But I could probably keep two of them."

"Two of them get to stay on and two go to the fair, then?"

A slow smile grew on his face. "I'd forgotten what a negotiator you are, Mrs. Driscoll. All right, then, two will remain in the Women's Department permanently and two will go to the fair."

The girls squealed with delight, clapping their hands and talking all at once. Flossie, however, had a stirring of unease. Certainly, she was thankful to Mrs. Driscoll for being their champion, but, at school, these girls had been her classmates. Now they would be her competition.

Flicking her fingernail and thumbnail against each other, she glanced about the studio. She wasn't overly worried about Louise. Their instructor at school was in love with her and it wouldn't surprise Flossie if a marriage proposal would soon be forthcoming. Theresa, a typewriter girl, had painted nude figures in Paris and done quite a good job of it. Though Flossie was the first to appreciate good art, the very idea of having a nude woman stand at the front of the room made her cheeks warm. Lulu had studied in Boston at the School of the Museum of Fine Arts. Elizabeth's designs had been published in this year's *The Art Amateur*.

Aggie, however, was more like Flossie. Neither of them had any distinguishing recommendations in the art world, but they were both hard workers, they both loved to learn, and they both loved to paint. At the beginning of the school year, they'd made a pact. One day their paintings would hang in the Metropolitan Museum of Art right next to all those men's.

Now, perhaps, they could make another pact. One day they would attend the World's Columbian Exposition and they would become permanent additions to the Women's Department of Tiffany Glass and Decorating Company.

She caught Aggie's eye from across the room. The giant Swede gave her a conspiratorial wink and their pact was made.

CHAPTER

17

Reeve hovered at the door to Mrs. Dinwiddie's room, unsure of whether or not he'd be welcome for tea.

"Sit," she said, pouring the brew into his cup.

He hated tea. Would have much preferred coffee, but he'd never, ever said so. He lowered himself into the upholstered chair next to hers, its fabric a fancy swirl of maroons, greens, and gold.

"You behaved very poorly yesterday."

Stretching out his legs, he crossed his ankles and studied the tips of his shoes. "I'm sorry."

"Are you really?"

"No."

She remained silent so long, he finally braved a look.

The slightest hint of amused tolerance softened the lines of her mouth. "What in the world possessed you? I've never seen you act like that. Good heavens, Mr. Wilder, it was as if you were two and ten."

"Miss Jayne started it."

She laughed, actually laughed. "Are you listening to yourself?"

He scowled. "You've seen her. She's disrupted the entire house. Has everybody scrambling to do her bidding. Did you know she has Mr. Holliday repairing the legs of the dining room chairs so they no longer wobble? That Mr. Nettels is using his music connections to have the upright in the parlor tuned? That Miss Love borrowed Miss Jayne's paints to add color to some sort of fading flowers on the parlor's wallpaper? And that Miss Jayne herself installed two of her own oil paintings in the dining room?"

Mrs. Dinwiddie put two lumps of sugar into her cup, none in his. "She's been a breath of fresh air."

"She's been a stench in our nostrils."

Mrs. Dinwiddie handed him his cup. "It's as if spring has come early and filled the entire house."

"It's as if the Antichrist has come and hypnotized the entire bunch of you."

The old woman's eyes crinkled, then filled with an emotion so close to love that he turned away and took a big gulp of tea, burning his throat.

"For shame." She stirred her tea, then tapped the spoon on the cup's rim, making a delicate *tink-tink-tink*. "What would the others of your sex say if they heard you assign such a heralded position to a woman?"

He *harrumph*ed. "It certainly would fit in with their ideology."

"Whose? The men's or the women's?"

"Don't start with me." He set his cup on the table. "She's not only causing trouble in the house, she's causing trouble between you and me. We've never had a cross word between us. Not once. Not until she showed up."

"She was a guest in my room, Mr. Wilder."

"What was I?"

"You, sir, were and are one of my most beloved friends and, as such, your actions are representative of me—particularly in that instance. I will not tolerate such abuse to those who are my guests. I will not."

Never, ever had he been referred to as beloved. Still, it was the scolding he heard. The disappointment. The ultimatum. Propping his elbows on his knees, he pressed the pads of his hands against his forehead. "You're right. I know that in my mind, and I'm sorry, but she just . . ." He jumped to his feet and began to pace. "She just . . ."

"Just what?"

"Irritates the very devil out of me." He stopped. "Right or wrong, polite or not, she's driving me to distraction and she is *always* talking. She's worse than a magpie, if that's even possible."

Mrs. Dinwiddie took a sip of tea. "Interesting."

"Interesting?" He buried a fist against his waist, flicking his jacket back. "What's that supposed to mean?"

Setting down her cup, she leaned back, then folded her hands in her lap. "I'm afraid you wouldn't want to hear what I happen to think the problem is, so I shall keep my thoughts to myself."

"When have I ever not wanted to hear what you had to say?"

"You won't this time. Trust me."

He studied her for a moment. "All right. I trust you. Besides, it's so refreshing to find a female who's willing to keep her mouth shut, I dare not spoil the moment."

She chuckled under her breath. "Go on out of here, Mr. Wilder. I believe you have some work to do."

He nodded. "I do, actually, and I am sorry about yesterday."

She lifted her hand. He took it into his.

She gave it a squeeze. "I know."

"How long do you think this portrait of yours is going to take?"

"I have no idea, but I get the impression it is a drawn-out process."

"I mean no disrespect, but I may wait until everything is back to normal before I resume my Sunday duties."

She frowned. "But I have a list of things for you to do."

"You can give me your list tomorrow and I'll get it done, just not on Sunday afternoons."

She sighed. "Very well."

"You try and get some rest before supper." Releasing her hand, he returned to his room, if not refreshed, then at least no longer with a sick knot in his stomach.

CHAPTER

18

B ut we need you, Miss King," Mrs. Driscoll said. "Can't you postpone your vows until after the chapel is finished?"

Flossie glanced up from the cartoon she traced. She could have told Mrs. Driscoll any efforts to dissuade Louise from marrying Mr. Cox would fall on deaf ears. Flossie had been watching those two from September to Christmas. Ordinarily the instructors at school rotated. Mr. Cox, however, had volunteered to take on most every class Louise attended and had then taken an inordinate amount of interest in her work.

"I know you need the help," Louise said, her red hair clashing with her purple hat. "And I'm truly sorry, but I simply can't stay."

"But why? There's absolutely no reason to rush." Mrs. Driscoll hesitated. "I mean, unless . . . ?"

Louise's face flooded with color. "Oh no, no. It's nothing like that. It's just that Mr. Cox has been commissioned to paint a dome for the Manufacturer's Building at the World's Fair and he's asked me to help him. Well, I, of course, want very much to help him, but I can't run clear across the country with him unless, well, unless . . ."

"Unless you're married," Mrs. Driscoll finished, her shoulders wilting a bit.

"Yes, exactly."

"A dome." Mrs. Driscoll shook her head. "What a very lovely way to spend your honeymoon."

Louise's smile bloomed. "We thought so, too."

"Well, can't the girls and I at least throw you a little party before you go?"

"Oh, Mrs. Driscoll, what a lovely thing that would have been, but I'm afraid there isn't a moment to spare. We've a whole dome to paint and only a few months to do it in, so Mr. Cox is waiting for me on the front step right this very minute."

Flossie didn't even pretend to keep working, but stood filled with delight not just for Louise's betrothal, but for her opportunity to paint a dome for the fair. The *fair*. She glanced toward the front of the building wishing she could run out and congratulate Mr. Cox. The strikers had long since quit loitering about the entrance, but Mr. Tiffany wouldn't like it at all if she went out. He still insisted everyone access the building through a circuitous route that involved the building next door.

"Very well, dear, you'd best not keep him waiting, then."

She did keep him waiting, however, at least until she'd gone about the room giving each of the girls a farewell. When she reached Flossie, the two clasped each other's hands.

"Congratulations." Flossie smiled at Louise. "A dome. Painted by a woman! And for the whole world to see."

"It will only be partly done by a woman. Kenyon will, of course, be leading the way."

"Even still, I'm so excited for you."

Louise glanced to the left and right, then leaned in and lowered her voice. "Then you must do everything you can to be the one chosen by Mr. Tiffany. Then you'll be able to see it. But remember, Flossie, do *exactly* as you are advised by Mrs. Driscoll and the other designers. They are quite knowledgeable, and if you listen to them very carefully, I think you'll have just as good a chance as all the other girls."

Wrapping her arms around Louise, Flossie closed her eyes. "I promise. I'll do everything I can."

"Good girl. Now I have to run." She blew a kiss to everyone, laughing, smiling, her excitement contagious.

Waving back, Flossie couldn't think of anything more romantic than running off to do a collaborative work of art with a painting master who loved you.

With a sigh, she spun around and crashed into Nan. Sheltering the tray of glass she carried, Nan twisted sideways, launching Flossie backward. Nan managed to stay on her feet and keep her tray level, but Flossie lost her balance.

Wheeling her arms, she stumbled backward, backward, until her feet lost all traction.

The girls screamed.

Flossie careened into a hard surface and slid to the floor, covering her head with her hands.

The girls screamed again, then total silence.

Flossie didn't have to look to know what she'd done. She'd landed against a giant sheet of plate glass propped up next to the windows. Thousands of fragments of colored glass, which made up their *Story of the Cross* window, had been adhered to the plate glass with tiny bits of beeswax. With her backside, she'd brought down an entire section of their work.

Mrs. Driscoll rushed to her. "Are you hurt? Did the glass cut you?"

Flossie sat stunned for a moment. "I don't know. I don't think so."

Mrs. Driscoll and Aggie helped her to her feet.

Flossie looked over her shoulder, then sucked in her breath. "Our window!"

The Story of the Cross was to eventually include five scenes giving tribute to Christ's birth, ministry, resurrection, and reign. Flossie had wiped away an entire decorative section in the lower quadrant.

She covered her mouth. "Oh, nooooo!"

Mrs. Driscoll plucked off pieces of colored glass, which were now stuck to the back of Flossie's skirt. "At least you didn't bring down the plate of glass. It could've killed you. Are you hurt?"

"No, I'm fine. My petticoats must have protected me, but look." She turned to Mrs. Driscoll, her legs beginning to shake. "All that work. All that work. I'm so sorry. I don't know what happened, I just turned around and—"

"It was bound to happen sooner or later, as crowded as it is in here." Mrs. Driscoll handed Flossie one of the pieces of glass. "If they hadn't slid down with you, they probably would have broken. Come on, let's get these back where they belong."

Accepting the glass, Flossie looked from it to Mrs. Driscoll to the window. Never, ever had she fastened the finished colored pieces on to the glass easel. Every part of the glassmaking process excited her, but this was where the magic happened. This was where the composition came to life.

"I'll start at the top," Mrs. Driscoll said, rolling a piece of wax between her fingers, then sticking it onto the back of an ochre-colored fragment. "You start on the border."

Flossie looked at the cartoon. A string of maroon lined the bottom edge of this section. Kneeling to the ground, she collected the maroon pieces she'd knocked to the floor. A moment later, Aggie knelt beside her with some trays. The two of them sorted the fallen glass by color until all had been separated.

"Good luck," Aggie whispered before returning to her table.

When Flossie had been outlining individual colors on a cartoon, she hadn't really thought about the sheer magnitude of glass that would eventually have to be cut and incorporated into each window. It was one thing to watch someone else do this job, quite another to be faced with it yourself. When quitting time came, Flossie and Mrs. Driscoll still had hundreds of pieces left.

"I'm afraid I've come down with a migraine," Mrs. Driscoll said, rubbing her forehead. "We'll have to finish this tomorrow."

"I'm so sorry." Flossie pressed a piece of olive-colored glass to the giant sheet of clear glass they called an easel. "You go on home. I'll just finish up this row."

Mrs. Driscoll hesitated. "Don't stay too late, mind you. It wouldn't do for you to be out after dark."

"I'll be careful."

Heaving a sigh, Mrs. Driscoll lumbered to her feet. "All right, then. Good night, Miss Jayne."

The other girls left shortly after Mrs. Driscoll until it was just Flossie and Aggie.

"You want some help?"

Flossie glanced up. Aggie's blond hair and blue eyes contrasted sharply with Flossie's black hair and brown eyes. The girl was all length and joints, while Flossie was padded with curves.

"You don't have to stay," Flossie said.

"I don't mind." Settling down cross-legged beside her, Aggie picked up a piece of glass and held it to the light. "It's like a puzzle, isn't it?"

"Except there are no interlocking pieces, only the cartoon, the numbered manila guide, and the lines of demarcation painted onto the glass easel."

"This is only going so slowly because you don't have the templates anymore."

Flossie glanced at the parts of the window that had yet to be done. At the top, all the pieces of numbered manila paper that had been cut into templates had been stuck to the glass with wax. Each piece of paper was separated by an eighth of an inch. Ordinarily, the selector would remove only one template and pass a piece of colored glass over the clear space until she found one that matched the color on the cartoon.

She'd then hand the selected piece and the template to the cutter. The glass cutter would cut around the template, put a piece of wax on the back of her fragment, and affix it in that same spot on the massive sheet glass. Since her template had a number, she could easily locate its exact position on the easel by finding its corresponding number on the giant manila guide. Day after day, week after week, the pair did this until every piece of paper had been removed and replaced by colored glass.

When Flossie knocked off the pieces, there weren't any numbered templates left behind to use as cross-references. Only the fallen glass.

"You're going to stay until it's done, aren't you?" Aggie asked.

"I am, but you don't have to."

"How will you know which color goes where when you've no sun to hold it up to?"

"I'll have to make do with a lantern, I suppose."

"No, *we'll* have to make do with a lantern."

The girls exchanged a smile. Neither paid attention to the snow that had started that afternoon and picked up momentum once darkness fell.

CHAPTER

19

Reeve stepped into the vestibule, stomped the snow off his feet, and blew onto his hands. It had been coming down all day and all night. Yet still no sign of Miss Jayne.

She'd not made it home for dinner—leaving the entire household in a state of confusion. It was as if they couldn't figure out where to sit without place cards. He'd simply returned to his normal chair and everyone else eventually followed suit.

But there were no painted slips of paper beneath the plates, and no Miss Jayne to facilitate conversation. Mr. Oyster made a few feeble attempts at engaging those present, but without Miss Jayne, the discussion fizzled.

After dinner, everyone adjourned to the parlor. He'd normally have returned to his room, but he was too familiar with the streets of New York. Too familiar with the desperation of union strikers. Too familiar with the dangers that could befall an unescorted lady after dark.

With a mumbled excuse, he'd wrapped a scarf around his neck, pulled on his coat, placed a derby atop his head, and gone outside—three times—to see if he could find her. She may have been a New Woman, she may have thrown a wrench into his and everybody else's routines, but he didn't really think she was as equipped for independence as she thought she was. And now she was out there alone and perhaps in trouble.

He'd hoped Mrs. Dinwiddie would say something to him, encourage him to go look for her. That way he'd at least have justification for all this effort. But the woman hadn't said a thing, had instead adjourned to the parlor along with everyone else and exclaimed over the curtains Mrs. Holliday had sewn.

He kept thinking about Miss Jayne's father, how he'd come to check on her, to make sure the boardinghouse was on the up-and-up. What would Reeve say to the man if something happened to his daughter? How would he explain that he'd blithely gone to bed knowing full well she was out there somewhere?

He couldn't. He wouldn't. He'd never had anyone check up on him like that, and the way her father looked when he talked about her, the way he'd gloated over her art simply because it had been done by her hand, had affected him deeply. So, he'd braved the storm in an effort to find her, for her father's sake.

The first time out, he'd walked up and down their block. The second, he'd checked a few paths in Central Park. The third, he'd hiked a good mile down Madison.

This last time, he was tempted to walk all the way to Fourth Avenue where Tiffany's studio was, but it was simply too far. The streetcars were no longer running, so wherever she was, she was going to have to hail a driver. He wondered if she carried enough money for that.

Shrugging off his coat, he hooked it and his hat on the hall tree, then pulled off his scarf. The other boarders had long since retired. The fire in the parlor had deteriorated to softly glowing ashes.

Maybe she'd returned while he'd been out. He strode down the hall, the carpet runner softening his footfalls. At his own door, he saw that the cat had slipped inside and curled up in a corner by his bed. At Miss Jayne's door, he hesitated. He couldn't simply open it. He placed his ear against the door. Nothing.

Straightening, he rubbed his jaw, then gave a quiet knock. "Miss Jayne? Miss Jayne? Are you home?"

"She's still not back." It was Miss Love's voice, cracking with sleep. "Do you think she's all right?"

"I'm sure she's fine," he lied. "I was just"—he grappled for an excuse—"just thinking I might have heard something. You go on back to sleep. She probably went home with one of the other Tiffany Girls."

But he knew she wouldn't do that, not without telling anyone. She treated every boarder as if they were a member of her family.

Family. He shook his head. She was so naive. They were no more her family than the milkman or the lamppost lighter, but in her mind, they were her adopted siblings, cousins, and grandparents. She'd never have left them to worry about her— not that anyone was actually worrying. They'd all gone to bed without a moment's pause.

Returning to the parlor, he knelt in front of the fire, threw on new logs, and stoked the embers until they began to spread. Bit by bit, his fingers thawed and feeling returned to his toes. He knew the protestors had long since quit picketing, but he couldn't seem to shake a feeling of unease. Should he call the police? He rubbed his face with both hands. He simply didn't know. Maybe he should wake up Mrs. Dinwiddie and see what she thought.

In a *whoosh* of wind, the front door banged open. Miss Jayne trudged inside, her coat whipping about her skirts, snow swirling in behind her. Jumping to his feet, he crossed the room and forced the door closed. In the sudden quiet, wind whistled against the windows while the mantel clock reminded him of the time.

"You're home awfully late." He kept his tone measured and neutral.

Snow clung to her slumped shoulders, her coat sleeves, her wet skirts, and the scarf wrapped tightly over her head. "Y-you're up awfully late, too."

He allowed himself a small smile. At least she still had a bit of pluck left. "Where have you been?"

"Work."

He double-checked the clock in the parlor. "At three in the morning?"

She tried to untie her scarf, but her frozen, curled, gloved fingers were too clumsy. Brushing her hands aside, he untied it and lifted it from her head. The snow-filled scarf bowed like a hammock. He shook it out into the umbrella stand, then draped it onto the hall tree.

When he turned back around, she hadn't so much as moved. Her Gibson hair pouf had an amoeba-like quality to it. Some black locks bunched up at an angle, others drooped to the side. He saw no sign of ill treatment, but the only skin he could see was her face.

"Have you been harmed?" he asked.

"No, but I-I'm c-c-c-cold." Her body began to shake.

Of a sudden, instead of looking for bruises, he registered her ice-coated gloves, red nose, and bluish lips. Guiding her to the parlor, he positioned her near the fire, but not directly in front of it, then proceeded to thumb open the buttons of her double-breasted coat. It was of an excellent quality, of course, and had kept her torso dry, thank goodness. Tossing it to the side, he cupped her upper arms and rubbed them back and forth with quick strokes.

She closed her eyes. "*Ummmmm.* F-f-f-eels g-g-good."

"We'll have you warm in no time."

But the lower reaches of her skirts were saturated and her gloved hands were still stiff.

He turned her palm toward him and unbuttoned the pearl clasp at her wrist. Thick ice caked the leather. He broke off what he could, then peeled the glove backward. Ice cracked as each new patch of skin was uncovered.

She winced. "Ou-ouch."

He finally managed to remove it, then enclosed her tiny hand between his, knowing better than to rub it or force it flat. Eventually she unfurled her fingers. He slipped her hand underneath his jacket and trapped it beneath his armpit. Its cold temperature seeped through his shirt.

Her body began to teeter.

He steadied her. "Easy there, little magpie."

She lifted her lids. Even her eyelashes held crystals of ice and snow. Holding her gaze, he continued to imprison her hand. He'd never really had a good look at her eyes before. They were the color of Mr. Nettels's violin. Polished spruce with deep brown accents.

Her lids closed, then opened. Closed, then opened.

"Stay with me," he said.

A small smile formed on her pale-blue lips and something deep within his chest stirred. He moved his attention to her right hand and repeated the glove-removal process. As he sandwiched it in his, he noticed calluses and wondered if they were from the work she did at Tiffany's. Finally, he tucked this hand beneath his other armpit. Her shakes slowed to shivers and color began to return to her lips.

Grasping her waist, he eased her to a chair, surprised to discover his hands could almost completely encircle her. "You need to get out of those wet boots."

Her fawn-colored skirt pooled about her, a good ten inches of it soaked all the way through. There'd be no removing that, of course. At least, not in front of him. But since her torso had been protected, he'd feel comfortable sending her to her room once he'd ensured her feet were not in danger.

Crouching down in front of her, he held out his palm. "Your boot, please, Miss Jayne."

She looked at her skirts, her arms limp. "Too tired."

"Are your feet cold?"

"My toes hurt."

He brushed her hem aside, stopping short at the sight of pink-satin ribbon trimming her petticoat. He tracked its serpentine course, a plethora of wet, soiled, gray lacy ruffles spilling from beneath it. He glanced up at her, but her eyes were closed, her chin resting against her neck. She took a trembling breath.

His dropped his gaze to her chest, her waist, then the pool of skirts hiding her hips. "Just extend your foot, at least, so the warmth in the room has a chance of reaching it."

She didn't move.

Swallowing, he flicked the ruffles aside, but they only revealed more ruffles. How many petticoats was she wearing? He sat back on his heels, resting his hands against his thighs, his pulse acting as if he'd just run the entire perimeter of Central Park.

"How did you get home?" he asked.

"Walked." Her head remained down, her eyes closed.

"From Fourth Avenue?"

No answer.

"In the middle of the night?"

No answer.

"Alone?"

No answer.

His jaw began to tick. "Why didn't you hail a driver?"

Still, no answer. But if she'd walked all that way, her boots would be encased in ice. As exhausted as she was, he didn't trust her to do more than tumble into bed, boots and all. And if her toes were in danger of frostbite, what he did—or didn't do—could mean the difference in losing toes or keeping them.

Groping beneath her petticoats, he pretended he was searching for something under his bed, but when he latched onto a tiny booted ankle, he had no illusions as to what it was he had ahold of. He pulled it from its shelter.

A film of ice covered a long row of minuscule black leather buttons. Buttons he'd never be able to undo with his fingers.

"Sit tight," he said. "I'll be right back."

Jogging to his room, he tried to keep his footfalls soft lest he wake the other boarders. He opened his desk drawer, fumbled around for a box at the very back, opened it, extracted a button-hook from his mother's things, then grabbed two towels off his washstand.

Miss Jayne had vacated the chair while he was gone and curled up on the floor, her hands acting as a cushion for her head.

Tossing the towels in front of the fire, he went on another hunt for her foot, uncovered it, and worked on the ice and buttons until he could finally wiggle off the boot. He gave himself only a moment to register the pink-and-white-striped stockings before trying to tug them down, but they wouldn't budge. He wasn't about to reach up under there and remove her garter. Despite her fond belief that the Klausmeyers' boarders were one big happy family, he and she were decidedly not brother and sister.

He rose onto all fours and jostled her shoulder. "Wake up, Miss Jayne. Your stocking is soaked and you need to remove it."

She shrugged him off.

He shook her again. "Wake up. Only long enough to remove your stocking. I'll take care of the rest."

With a grumpy huff, she reached down.

Spinning around, he waited, then heard a whimper and looked back over his shoulder. With a grimace, she was grasping her bare foot, her petticoats spilling about her.

"It hurts?" he asked.

Biting her lip, she nodded.

Shooing her hands away, he pressed her arch against his thigh and covered as much of her foot as he could with his hands. "It's good that it hurts. And the skin is red instead of white, soft instead of hard, which is also good."

"The fire." She gave it a longing glance. "Can we get closer to the fire?"

He shook his head. "That will make it worse. We need to warm you by slow degrees. I have some towels on the hearth, though. When I've warmed your foot as much as I can with my hands, then we'll wrap it with a towel."

He repositioned his hands.

"Don't look." Another grimace of pain flickered across her face. "I have ugly toes."

"Too late, I'm afraid. I've already seen the middle one is a bit curved and is much longer than all the others." He shook his head. "Hope I don't have nightmares."

Her lips twitched, then a slow smile began to smooth out her features. A smile that accentuated her cheeks and drew attention to the Cupid's bow of her lips. "Maybe it'll get frostbite and fall off."

"Now there's a thought. Shall I leave it stranded so it continues to freeze?"

"Yes, if you don't mind."

He found a reluctant smile tug at his own lips, though he didn't give into it. Still, he was careful to keep the offending appendage protected within his warmth. "I aim to please."

"Do you?" She cocked her head, more fully awake now. "Then why won't you join us in the parlor after dinner?"

He returned his attention to her foot. It wasn't just her toes that were unorthodox. She had huge feet for a woman her size. Even so, they were nicely formed, had a high arch, and were surprisingly soft for a working girl.

"What kept you at work so late?" he asked.

"A portion of a stained-glass window had to be redone, so I stayed late."

Lifting her foot from his thigh, he cupped it in one hand and covered her toes with the other. "Redone? What happened? Did something break?"

"No, thank goodness." Her voice dropped, along with her gaze.

Reaching for one of the towels, he wrapped her foot inside it, then held out his hand. "Next."

She pushed herself to a sitting position. "I can do it."

He handed her the buttonhook. "I'd have thought Tiffany would run a cleaner operation than that. Doesn't sound very efficient or cost-effective if his windows have to be redone."

Whatever ice had covered this boot had now melted, but she couldn't get the buttons to work. Confiscating the buttonhook, he took over.

"It wasn't Mr. Tiffany's fault," she said. "It was mine. I bumped into one of the windows we were making, knocked off a bunch of pieces, and had to stick them all back on."

"And that took until three in the morning?"

"It was a bit like Humpty Dumpty." Withdrawing her foot from his grasp, she placed one hand on the heel of her boot and the other at the toe, then worked off the shoe. "At least Aggie stayed to help me or I'd still be there."

"Aggie?"

"Miss Wilhemson. A friend of mine and one of the Tiffany Girls I work with." She lifted her index finger and twirled it in a spinning motion.

He turned his back and waited while she removed her stocking. Its pink-and-white-striped mate lay crumpled on the floor next to a pink garter with a giant decorative bow. He slammed his eyes shut and forced his mind to the topic at hand. He couldn't believe she'd knocked over one of Tiffany's windows. She was lucky she still had a job. At least, he assumed she still had one.

When all had settled behind him, he looked over his shoulder. She sat grasping her foot and squeezing her toes, her features scrunched up.

"Don't do that."

"It itches and burns and feels like a thousand tiny needles are poking my skin."

"That's good. That means you'll keep all your toes whether you want them or not." He knelt before her, then pressed her foot against his trouser leg. "Did he fire you?"

"No, thank goodness."

"But you had to stay and work until it was finished?"

"I wasn't required to stay. I did that on my own." She propped her hands behind her on the floor and leaned back, some of the tension falling from her expression.

"Why?" he asked.

"Why? You mean, why did I stay?"

"I mean, why did you stay so long that you risked bodily injury walking home alone at night, not to mention frostbite?"

"I wasn't in any danger of being accosted. Who in their right mind would be out in this mess?"

"Quite so," he mumbled, picking up her foot and warming it within his hands. "Nevertheless, you shouldn't do it again. You don't have to prove yourself simply because you're a woman."

She straightened, her relaxed posture disappearing. "I wasn't trying to prove anything."

"No? You work until three in the morning and walk home alone in a snowstorm and you weren't trying to prove anything?" He lifted a brow. "Either you're extremely foolish or you're lying."

She jerked her foot from his grasp.

He reached for the second towel, opened it, and waited.

"I can do that," she snapped.

"Not as easily as I can."

"I said, I can do it."

"Trying to prove something?"

She whipped the towel from his grasp and swaddled her foot in a haphazard fashion.

"What were you doing up so late, anyway?"

Good question, he thought. Ice and snow struck the windows with a rapid *klink-klink-klink.*

She lifted her gaze. "You weren't actually waiting for me, were you?"

"Certainly not." He stood.

Her eyes widened. "You were. You . . . you were worried about me, weren't you?"

"Of course not. I simply had a lot on my mind, couldn't sleep, and heard you come in."

There it was again. Cheeks that lifted and bow-shaped lips that stretched into a rather becoming smile. She looked him over from top to bottom. "I see. Nice nightclothes."

Heat rushed into his face. "I changed before I left my room."

Her brows lifted. "Into jacket, tie, suspenders, socks, and shoes? All in the time it took for me to cross the threshold?"

Leaning down, he snatched up her stockings, garter, and gloves, wadded them up, and handed them to her. "You'd best get out of those wet clothes before you catch pneumonia."

Her eyes lit, but for once she didn't say anything.

Helping her up, he grabbed her boots, then assisted her to her door as she struggled to walk with towel-wrapped feet. "Good night, Miss Jayne."

"Good night, Mr. Wilder." She took the boots, then stopped him with a hand to his arm. "And thank you. I mean it. I truly do appreciate you assisting me and . . . well, being awake when I arrived home."

With a curt nod, he returned to his room, closed the door, and rested his head against it. He could hear her moving around. The cat stirred, then came and wove between his legs. Reaching down, he lifted it to his chest and rubbed behind its ears until all had settled in the room next to his.

It was almost dawn, however, before he managed to fall asleep.

WORLD'S COLUMBIAN EXPOSITION, BIRD'S-EYE VIEW[13]

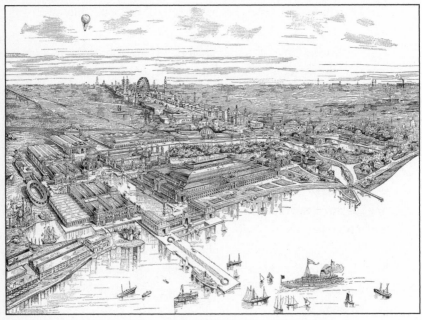

"'Mr. Tiffany is going to send two of his girls, but we don't
yet know if Miss Jayne will be one of them.'"

CHAPTER

20

I f you could snap your fingers and appear somewhere else, where would you be?" Mrs. Dinwiddie put her card next to her soup bowl and looked at Mr. Wilder in expectation.

Flossie bit back her satisfaction. She'd get him out of his room—figuratively, if nothing else.

"My room," he said.

Flossie narrowed her eyes.

"Nonsense." Mrs. Dinwiddie, bless her soul, waved her soup spoon in an *I don't think so* gesture. "You're a writer, Mr. Wilder. Use your imagination."

"I'm a newspaper reporter. I don't make things up."

Mr. Nettels snorted.

Mr. Wilder gave him a piercing glare.

"Nevertheless," Mrs. Dinwiddie continued, "try to enter into the spirit of the game. If you could go anywhere in the world, where would you go?"

He looked to the corner of the room as if weighing his options before returning his attention to Mrs. Dinwiddie. "I suppose I'd go to the Chicago World's Fair—once it opens, of course."

The elderly woman's face lit, creases rippling out on either side of her smile. "What a marvelous choice. I'd love to go as well. Mr. Tiffany is going to send two of his girls, but we don't yet know if Miss Jayne will be one of them, do we, Miss Jayne?"

"No, it will be a while before he makes a decision."

"How will he decide?" Mr. Wilder asked.

"It's based on performance." She tucked a piece of hair back up into her coif. Only Mr. Wilder knew of her blunder at work—other than the Tiffany Girls, of course. But over the past month she'd worked doubly hard and arrived even earlier in the mornings. Last week she'd been moved from tracing cartoons to working with Nan. Nan would select the glass, then Flossie would cut it the exact shape of the paper template. It was harder than it looked and her arms and fingers had been sore all week.

Smoothing the napkin on her lap, she directed the conversation away from her in order to include the others. "Since you weren't in the parlor with us last night, you might not be aware that it will be Mrs. Holliday's birthday on Sunday."

Mr. Wilder turned his attention to the young woman beside him. "Congratulations, Mrs. Holliday."

"Thank you." She looked up at him, her excitement palpable. "You'll come to my party, won't you?"

Mr. Holliday patted his wife's hand. "Of course he'll come."

Mr. Wilder balked. "Party?"

"Why, yes." Mr. Oyster removed a piece of food from his teeth with his tongue. "Miss Jayne has arranged for us to all go ice-skating at Central Park this Sunday."

The full weight of Mr. Wilder's gaze turned to her. "I'm afraid I'm—"

"Even Mrs. Dinwiddie is coming," she interjected, cutting off his refusal. She knew he longed to engage with them, to be a part of their family, yet he simply refused. It didn't make a bit of sense.

" 'Course I'm coming." The elderly woman dabbed her mouth with her napkin. "Wouldn't miss it, and neither will Mr. Wilder. Will you?" Her blue gaze drilled into his.

Mrs. Dinwiddie might have been in her seventies, but she'd been married to a retired colonel and had raised a son of her own. Flossie marveled at the skill with which she handled the men in the house.

Instead of answering, Mr. Wilder made a noncommittal sound, then took another spoonful of his soup.

CHAPTER

21

Reeve studied the half-finished portrait of Mrs. Dinwiddie. It didn't look like much, other than a pair of eyes with different shades of red war paint blocking out parts of her face.

"Does it tire you to pose for these painting sessions?" he asked.

Mrs. Dinwiddie poured his cup of tea, the scent of camphor oil clinging to her. "Not at all. Miss Jayne keeps me quite amused."

He *harrumphed*.

"Maybe she'll do your portrait next."

He gave her a look of warning, but the woman simply handed him his cup. He settled into the chair beside hers and they discussed the trial of Lizzie Borden, the failure of the Philadelphia & Reading Railroad, and his most recent article on the New Woman.

"You cannot deny," Mrs. Dinwiddie said, looking at him over her glasses, "there is a mercenary element in our present form of marriage."

"Not you, too." He frowned at her.

"Admit it. A wife, more often than not, performs the lowest grade of unskilled labor."

He sighed. "I will admit that there are a great many women

who bend over the washtub, but it's not as if their husbands' lives are any less sordid or monotonous. He's out wrapping up codfish or selling five-cent cigars and engaged in a laborious occupation not a bit more idealistic than her own."

They spent another quarter hour in an invigorating debate. He conceded a bit of ground, but took even more. Already he was brimming with ideas for his next article.

"So, are you going to the ice-skating party?" she asked, picking up her knitting. Whatever she was making was of a dark navy blue.

"I'm afraid I'm going to pass," he said.

"Why?"

"I don't have any skates and I'd rather not spend the money to rent them."

"You can borrow Herschel's."

"You still have your son's skates?"

"Indeed, I do."

He shifted in his chair. "That's very generous, thank you, but I'm still not going."

"Why not?"

He rubbed his hands on his trousers. "I don't know how to skate."

"Pshaw. There's nothing to it. You strap the skates on to your shoes and off you go."

It had looked easy when he'd watched others from his window, but it couldn't be as simple as it appeared or he wouldn't have seen so many people fall.

"You can't mean that you're going skating?" he asked.

"Heavens, no. I'm way too old. I'd crack my noggin open for certain. No, I plan to rent a chair sled."

He stiffened. Once again, Mrs. Dinwiddie would be spending her own coin because Miss Jayne desired it to be so. "Aren't those rather costly?"

"Not terribly so." The *click-click-click* of her knitting needles sounded loud in the quiet of her room.

He tapped his thumb against his leg. At what point should he interfere? What if she didn't have a head for numbers? What if she overspent by accident and couldn't pay her rent? He'd never asked about her finances before because there'd never been any need to. "Mrs. Dinwiddie, do you think that's wise, spending your resources on such frivolous things?"

Her knitting needles paused. "Is that a philosophical question or a practical question?"

"A practical question."

She lowered her knitting and stared at him for several beats.

His face warmed. "It's really none of my business. Please forgive me."

She shook her head. "No, I appreciate your concern. That's not why I didn't answer." She looked to the side, took a breath, then turned back to him. "Since we are such good friends and since I trust you to keep a confidence, I shall entrust you with a little secret. I'm rather well off. If I'd wanted to, I could have lived in the lovely brownstone Robert and I shared for fifty-four years. But I decided instead that I wanted to live in a boardinghouse so that I'd be around people, so I'd have someone to eat dinner with, someone to linger in the parlor with after my meals."

He blinked. He'd had no idea.

"I'd tried some of the fancy boardinghouses," she continued. "But I tired of the airs the boarders put on. So, I simply looked for someplace clean, in a good part of town, and with salt-of-the-earth people." Reaching across the table, she patted his arm. "I certainly found one in you."

He sat up a little straighter. "I'm sorry. I had no idea. I meant no offense."

"Of course you didn't. That's why you'll go to Mrs. Holliday's ice-skating party."

"Wait, what?"

"She's very young, Mr. Wilder. You'd cause her great offense if you did not attend. She would think it had something to do with her, that perhaps she wasn't engaging enough, or pretty enough, or a good enough wife to Mr. Holliday." She picked her knitting back up. "No, you must go to the party, even if only for a little bit. You'll find Herschel's skates in a box on top of my wardrobe over there."

After several seconds of hesitation, he mumbled his acquiescence, pushed himself up, and retrieved the skates.

ICE SKATING IN CENTRAL PARK [14]

"Stretching out his legs, Reeve crossed his ankles and leaned back
on the bench, content to watch the others do all the skating."

CHAPTER

22

Stretching out his legs, Reeve crossed his ankles and leaned back on the bench, content to watch the others do all the skating. A cloudless sky allowed the sun's unrestricted rays to provide a bit of warmth against winter's bite.

Hundreds of skaters soared across Central Park's pond in what he imagined would be the next best thing to flying. A man in a dark-blue frock coat, hands behind his back, sailed past, gliding first on one leg, then the other. A young boy whizzed by him, filching a red cap from another little shaver. With a shout of protest, the hatless fellow gave chase, paying no more attention to his skates than he would to his feet if he were running.

Reeve shook his head in wonderment. It was different watching the skaters from a bench as opposed to a window. He could hear the cutting of the blades, feel the sting of crisp air, smell the woodsmoke from the warming fires, and almost taste the roasting chestnuts.

Mrs. Dinwiddie waved to him from her sleigh chair, barely recognizable beneath her pelts, cloak, and scarf, the latter wrapped about her mouth and nose. Mr. Nettels skated behind her, holding on to the chair's handles and propelling her forward.

"Come join us, Mr. Wilder," Miss Love shouted, gliding beside them, the breeze snatching away her laugh.

He waved back, then scanned the other skaters, looking for the rest of their party. He spotted Mrs. Holliday in a dark jacket and skirt gripping her husband's arm. She wobbled along with a slow shuffle, fighting to navigate the frozen pond marred with uneven marks from other skaters.

Without even searching, though, he knew where Miss Jayne was, what she was doing, and whom she was skating with. She was hard to miss. A plush maroon gown accentuated her curves, and its trimming of white fur brought attention to her neck and wrists. A matching hat was anchored with a white snowy scarf tied beneath her chin. Oyster skated in time beside her, their right and left hands joined in promenade style.

They pushed off with their left feet then held them slightly lifted behind them as they slid in perfect harmony on their right blades. Oyster angled his head toward her, saying something to make her smile.

Reeve tapped his toes together in rapid succession and slipped his gloved hand into his coat pocket, warming it on a hot potato Mrs. Klausmeyer had provided him. He forced himself to look away.

A group of kids played snap-the-whip, the boy at the end of the line barely hanging on as he was flung this way and that. A father a few yards from Reeve held a young boy between his legs, catching him as his feet slipped out from beneath him. Reeve briefly wondered if his father would have done the same for him had Mother survived.

Beyond them, Oyster slipped an arm about Miss Jayne's waist and spun her in front of him, recapturing Reeve's full attention. Oyster led her in a brisk waltz across the pond. Or perhaps it was a mazurka. He couldn't tell. But one minute she was skating backward, the next he was. The moment after that they were side by side again.

Around and around they went, her skirts whipping in the

wind, his trouser legs flapping as he stretched in a graceful ballet. He spun her out, he pulled her in. He twirled her about, he clasped her waist. And, finally, he whirled them in a tight circle like a twister, faster and faster until they blurred in Reeve's vision.

Eventually, Oyster brought her to a slow stop, pulled her close, and dipped his head, whispering into her ear. Reeve pulled his feet in. Straightened his spine.

Laughing, she placed her hands on Oyster's chest and used it to push away from him, skating backward, then she turned and headed straight toward Reeve. She made no move to slow down, no indication that she was going to do anything other than plow right into the snowbank.

Jumping to his feet, he stepped to the edge of the pond and stretched out a hand.

She did the same. "Come join us, Mr. Wilder."

"Careful," he replied.

She slowed with graceful ease, clasped his hand, and allowed him to assist her onto the snow.

Oyster made an abrupt stop at the edge of the pond, spraying Reeve with ice granules. "You're missing out on all the fun, Wilder. Aren't you going to put on your skates?"

Reeve glanced at the pair of skates Mrs. Dinwiddie had loaned him. "Perhaps."

With rapid breaths, Miss Jayne placed a gloved hand against her chest. "Well, I, for one, am going to take a rest. Mr. Oyster took me out for quite a spin."

"So I saw."

She smiled. "You did?"

Oyster made an elaborate bow. "You were the perfect partner, Miss Jayne. The best I've ever had."

Reeve scowled. Why did everyone do that? Tell her she was the best at everything? He'd concede her skating was impressive. Still, the best partner? *Ever?*

Puffs of white vapor came from her mouth. "Might I share your bench with you, Mr. Wilder?"

"Of course." He walked her to the bench and helped her settle while Mr. Oyster skated off, most likely in pursuit of another young innocent.

Removing the now lukewarm potato from his pocket, he handed it to her. "How are your fingers?"

She cupped the potato with gloved hands. "Definitely a bit tingly. This feels wonderful. Thank you."

"You're welcome. And your toes?".

"Still okay. What about yours?"

"Mine?" He lowered himself beside her. "Fine. Just fine."

She fell back against the bench and scanned the other skaters. "It's been quite some time since I've skated like that."

It was on the tip of his tongue to tell her she was very good at it, but he kept the thought to himself. The last thing she needed was one more person singing her praises.

They sat in silence, her studying the skaters. Him studying her. Her oval face. Her slim nose. High cheekbones. Cupid's-bow lips. Classic jaw. And—he squinted—a very, very slight dimple in her chin. So slight, he'd never noticed it until now.

"I love to skate," she sighed, her cheeks lifting with a small smile. "It's so . . . I don't know . . . freeing. Don't you think?"

When he didn't answer, she turned to him. "You don't agree?"

He shrugged.

She tilted her head. "Where did you say you were from?"

"New Jersey."

"Then, clearly, you've skated."

Again, he said nothing.

Her eyes widened. "You've never skated?"

He glanced at a concessionaire. "Can I get you some hot cocoa?"

"How could you have grown up in New Jersey and never had cause to skate?"

"I just didn't."

"Why?"

He pulled a hand down his face. "I wasn't allowed."

She straightened. "Weren't allowed? You mean, your parents forbade it?"

"Grandparents, actually. I was raised by my grandparents."

He could see her struggle with herself, then give in to her curiosity. "You lost both your parents?"

"In a manner of speaking."

Another hesitation. Another concession to curiosity. "Is it painful to talk about?"

"Not particularly, no."

An additional poof of air formed a quick cloud in front of her mouth. "Why do you do that?"

He lifted a brow. "Do what?"

"Have conversations that consist of nothing more than three-word sentences."

"My sentences have more than three words."

"No, they don't."

"Yes, they do."

"All right, then, what happened to your parents?"

"They died."

She lifted her hands in an *I give up* gesture. "See?"

"That was two words."

"You know what I mean."

And he did. He knew exactly what she meant, but he never talked about his past. Not because he had some great objection to it, but because it rarely came up.

He stood. "I'm going to get a cup of hot cocoa. Would you like one?"

"Yes, thank you."

He used the time standing in line to try and ascertain why he was so reluctant to tell her about his parents. Or about anything, for that matter. And he could only come up with one viable reason. She frightened the very devil out of him, this New Woman.

CHAPTER

23

Here you are." Reeve handed Miss Jayne a steaming cup of cocoa, hoping she hadn't become too chilled while he was gone.

She exchanged the now cold potato for the cup, wrapping her hands around its tin sides. "Ahhhh. So warm."

"Are you getting chilled?"

"A little. This will help, though. Thank you." She blew on the liquid.

He settled next to her. "You'd better drink up. It won't stay hot for long out here."

She studied him. "So your grandparents raised you?"

Death and the deuce, but she was persistent. Still, he wouldn't put it past her to place the question beneath someone's plate at suppertime if he didn't go ahead and tell her what she wanted to know.

Taking a swallow of cocoa, he allowed the heat to flow down his throat. "They did. My mother died when I was four. I was never told of what. My father died of pneumonia when I was eighteen."

"I'm so sorry." Her face softened, her tone gentled. "You must have been very lonely."

He said nothing.

"Your father never remarried?"

"Not until much later. And by then, well, I was sixteen and his wife was eighteen."

An older couple holding hands glided by. It was something he didn't see very often. Usually the man would take the woman's elbow, or clasp hands in a promenade fashion. But holding hands. That was different. It spoke not just of love, but of companionship, familiarity, friendship, and ease. An ease unique to only those two.

"Why didn't they let you skate?" she asked. "Your grandparents, I mean."

He shrugged, following the couple with his gaze. "Same reason they wouldn't let me go barefoot to school, even though everyone else did. Same reason they made me eat lunch at home instead of carrying it to school like the other kids. Same reason they forbade me from visiting the lending library—although they did eventually relent on that one."

"Did you ever sneak out to skate?"

"I thought about it plenty of times, but the penalty had I been caught wasn't worth it to me. So, instead, I watched them."

"Watched them? But how did you do that if you didn't sneak out?"

A cloud passed over the sun. He tightened the winter scarf slung about his neck. "The pond was right behind the house. I could see them from my bedroom window."

She sucked in her breath, her stricken face making him regret his words.

"Don't look like that," he said. "I enjoyed it."

She bit her lower lip. "But not as much as you'd have enjoyed actually doing it."

"Perhaps." Squinting, he noted Mrs. Holliday had found her sea legs and was moving across the ice with a bit more ease.

"Well, what do you say we do something about that? How would you like to go skating, Mr. Wilder?"

He cut his eyes to hers. "Right now?"

"Right now."

"With you?"

"With me."

Taking a breath, he held it for a second before letting it out with a gush. "No, I'm sorry. It's . . . it's not you, I just . . . I just have no desire to go skating."

"I think you do. I think you're dying to get out there."

"Well, you'd be wrong, then."

A teasing glint entered her eye. "I'm hardly ever wrong."

"You might be surprised."

"I'm hardly ever surprised."

"I'm not going skating."

"I believe you are." Downing the rest of her cocoa like a shot of whiskey, she set down the cup, dusted off her hands, and stood. "Come on, now. Up we go."

"No."

She picked up his borrowed skates. "Strap these onto your shoes. And don't worry, I'll be right beside you the whole time."

The sun came back out, making his eyes squint from the bright reflection of the vast pond and snow-covered grounds.

"I appreciate the invitation, but I prefer to watch."

"All my eye and Betty Martin." She wiggled the skates at him.

He snatched them from her. "God gave you two ears and one mouth for a reason, Miss Jayne."

Laughing, she twirled her finger, encompassing his feet. "Put them on."

"I really—"

"Thou doth protest too much, methinks." She propped a hand on her hip.

His jaw began to tick.

She leaned over and placed her face level with his. A hint of rosewater drifted about her. "I am not leaving this pond until you have at least made an attempt. Shall I put them on for you?" She began to kneel.

He grabbed her elbow. "Absolutely not. I can do it."

She straightened with a self-satisfied smile.

Slamming the metal skate onto the bottom of his shoe, he strapped on the buckles, yanked them tight, and stood. "Well, don't just stand there. Let's get this over with."

"You're going to love it." She cupped *his* arm as they stepped onto the ice.

He jerked it away. His feet immediately went out from under him, landing him on his backside in the snowdrift, its softness cushioning his fall.

She bit her bottom lip, her eyes playful. "So, now you have that over with. Everyone falls. It's part of it." She held out both hands. "Come on. Let's try again."

He stared at her, trying to decide if he'd give in to her or not.

She tilted her head. "I know and you know that you've always wanted to be out here. So you may as well let yourself enjoy it. Please?"

Deep down, he knew she was right, but he'd wanted to do it on his terms and on his time line. He wasn't fighting it because he didn't want to skate. He was fighting it because he'd been forced into it. And now she just expected him to snap his fingers and enjoy it simply because she wished it to be so.

Well, he'd go through the motions, but he wouldn't enjoy it until he was good and ready.

After a slight hesitation, he took her hands and stood.

"Good. Now, I'm going to start going backward. All you have to do is keep your ankles locked and your blades underneath you."

He gave a curt nod. For several yards he cut through the bumpy, rutted ice, determined to keep his balance.

"You're doing splendidly. I'm going to bring us to a stop." She'd taken them to the middle of the pond, where some stood and conversed while others tried trick moves.

"When I let go of you," she said, "I want you to try to march— once you have your balance, of course."

March? He looked around. No one else was marching. "I'm not going to march."

She closed her eyes. "March, Mr. Wilder. Hup-to."

He didn't budge.

"The sooner you march, the sooner we can go back."

He marched. She encouraged him, praised him, and steadied him when he began to fall. From there, she took both his hands again and skated backward as she taught him to push off with one leg while gliding on another.

Before he knew it, they were making slow loops together around the edge of the pond. It wasn't anything like the brisk movements of all the others, but he was skating. He hadn't yet decided whether he was going to enjoy it or not.

"I've been reading your articles," she said, the breeze fluttering her collar.

"And you disagree with them." He stiffened his ankles to keep them from bowing on the rough ice.

"Parts of them. I suppose it is natural enough to assume that since women have stayed home all this time and the world has gone on, that if women suddenly ceased to stay home, the world would cease to go on." She shrugged. "It just doesn't seem like much of an argument to me."

"A warhorse and a fawn cannot be fitted for pursuits that are identical, Miss Jayne."

They slowed down, then veered around a father holding the hand of his young son.

"I will give you that men and women differ," she continued. "But it's not a question of masculinity or femininity, it's a question of humanity. Women are human, just like men. Therefore, we have just as much right to hold jobs as you do."

"You talk about rights, yet when you took that job at Tiffany's, you undermined more than a hundred men who were fighting for *their* rights. The rights to higher wages and shorter hours. Not only that, but they have families to feed. You've no one but yourself."

"If women had the right to be members of the union, then perhaps we could have put up a united front, for I have no objection to those men getting fewer hours and higher pay. As a matter of fact, I'd love for them to receive everything they're demanding. My filling in for them has nothing to do with that. It has to do with helping Mr. Tiffany achieve his dream, his goal."

"Tiffany?" He scoffed.

"Everyone has dreams and goals. The strikers do, I do, and Mr. Tiffany does. It's as if Mr. Tiffany is, I don't know, one of the debutantes my mother sews ball gowns for."

"Debutantes?" Wiggling his toes, he tried to generate more feeling into them without losing his balance.

"Yes. The debutante and her mother put months, sometimes years, into planning the young lady's presentation into society. If someone was to tell the girl she couldn't go to the ball after all that planning and expense simply because, at the last second, her dressmaker refused to make her gown, well, that would be inexcusable. The girl would be crushed. She only has one chance, one opportunity for her coming-out. I can tell you one thing, if I were the girl's mother, I'd knock on every seamstress's door for miles and miles until finding whomever I needed to get the job done."

He rolled his eyes. Leave it to a woman to argue labor laws by using dresses and debutantes as an example. "And Mr. Tiffany is no different from a debutante?"

"Exactly." She smiled at him. "Only his presentation into society—into the entire world—is to be in the form of a mosaic chapel at the World's Columbian Exposition. He plans to make a name for himself there. The men tried to snatch that away from him, his once-in-a-lifetime dream that he'd invested an enormous amount of time, energy, and money on."

"He didn't spend it on the workers," Reeve mumbled.

She either didn't hear him or pretended not to. "So I was happy to help Mr. Tiffany in any way whatsoever. If that meant walking through a line of picketers, being called ugly names, being abused by little boys and spit on by grown men, so be it."

He sobered. "I didn't agree with the way they treated you."

"Neither did I." Her voice was soft.

The cold had long since breached Reeve's wool socks and his ears had turned all but numb. He slowed to a stop. "Mr. Tiffany has more money than he could possibly spend in a lifetime. He could have afforded to treat his workers better. If he had, he'd never have jeopardized his 'debut,' as you call it."

"Have you ever met Mr. Tiffany? Visited with him?"

"I don't need to. His actions speak loud enough."

"As do the actions of the men who spit on me."

He adjusted his hat. "Yes, well, thank you for the skating lesson, but I'm going to head back now."

"Because I defended Mr. Tiffany?"

"Because I'm cold."

"Oh. Well, just one last thing, then, before you quit."

He sighed. "What's that?"

Looking around, she turned in a small circle, so comfortable on her skates she didn't even seem to think about what she was doing.

"There," she said, pointing. "Do you see the warming hut?"

He followed the direction of her gaze to a small, white, four-sided structure. "Yes."

"I want you to skate to it as fast as you can."

"Why?"

She shrugged. "So you can feel what it's like to let loose and just go."

"I don't need to feel what it's like to let loose."

She lifted a brow.

"I don't."

"Maybe you do, maybe you don't, but on the off chance that you are too stubborn to ever get on the ice again, I want you to know what it feels like to skate. I mean, really skate."

He pinched the bridge of his nose. "Miss Jayne, I appreciate what you're trying to do, but I'm just going to go back to my bench, take off my skates, and walk home."

She touched his arm. "Please? You picked everything up so quickly. You're a natural. I know you'll be able to do it. Just do the same bend-push, bend-push, only a little faster."

"Aren't you forgetting something?"

"What?"

"I don't know how to stop."

She swooped her hand down in a *don't worry* gesture. "Just skate into the snowbank. That'll stop you."

He had no interest in experiencing whatever it was she felt he needed to experience. He also had no interest in creating a scene with her in the middle of the pond if she didn't get her way.

Mumbling to himself, he pushed off, making a direct line for the warming house. *Bend-push. Bend-push.* His blades scraped against the ice like a knife against a sharpening stone. Snowflakes melted on his face but stuck to his lashes. Laughter and conversations from those around him ebbed and flowed.

He picked up more speed, surprised to find it a bit easier to balance at this faster rate. Concentrated laughter and squeals came from his right. It was all the warning he had, and then they were there. A line of youths hanging on to one another by their waists, going full tilt and weaving about skaters in a game of snap-the-whip. Only, they didn't weave around him. They cut right into his path.

"Watch out!" he cried. He had no idea how to stop. Options careened through his mind in the mere seconds he had to react.

If he fell and slid into them, his blades might slice someone's ankles. If he dove, his fingers and face would be cut to smithereens. If he charged through them, he'd scatter them like a rack of billiard balls.

In the end, he bent his knees and attempted a ninety-degree turn, ice spraying, but he couldn't manage it. Shocked faces turned to him right before impact.

He scooped up the boy he plowed into, then fought to regain his equilibrium and protect the child in his arms. Other youths fell like bowling pins, one spinning across the ice and directly into his path, tummy down, limbs outstretched.

Cursing, Reeve jerked to the left. It was too much. His legs whipped out from underneath him, cutting across the youth's gloved finger and slamming Reeve onto his tailbone. The boy in his arms rolled off of him and jumped to his feet.

The youth Reeve had run over screamed. It was high-pitched and excruciating, traveling up and down the scale in agonizing sharps and flats.

Oh, God. Oh, God.

Ignoring his own pain, Reeve rolled onto all fours and scrambled to the boy, who looked to be about fourteen. Curling up his legs, the boy cradled his hand, screaming and rocking his body.

"Let me see." Reeve pried the boy's arm free and lifted it so it would be above his heart. Blood seeped through the glove.

"No! No!" The boy pulled back, tears pouring down his face.

Reeve held firm. Other skaters descended, surrounding them and talking at once.

Placing a hand against the boy's head, Reeve tucked it against his chest "I'm sorry. I'm sorry." He squeezed his eyes shut. "We need to get your glove off, son."

"No," he whimpered.

A commotion in the crowd drew Reeve's attention.

"Let me through," said a voice. "I'm a doctor. Let me through."

The throng around them broke, allowing a middle-aged, portly man access. Kneeling beside them, he gave the boy a reassuring smile. "How you feeling, young man?"

"My finger."

The doctor nodded. "I'm going to remove your glove."

"No!"

Reeve held him fast.

"I'm not going to pull it off," the doc said. "I'm going to cut it with my pocket knife."

The boy stiffened.

"*Shhhhh.*" Reeve rested his cheek against the boy's head. "It'll be all right now. I want you to close your eyes, though, okay?"

The boy slammed his eyes shut. Reeve and the doc exchanged glances.

"You the boy's father?"

"No, I'm . . . I . . ." Emotion stacked up against his throat. "I'm the one responsible."

The doc began slicing the fabric of the glove with his knife. "It was an accident. That's why it's called that, because it's unintentional."

It might have been unintentional, but it was also preventable. He should have stayed on that bench. He had no business getting on the ice. None whatsoever.

The boy jerked, screaming again as the doc removed the part of the glove stuck to his injured finger. Reeve tightened his hold. The finger was still attached, thank the Lord, but it was cut to the bone.

"What's your name?" Reeve asked.

"Paschal Smith," he whimpered.

The doc wrapped the finger, exerting pressure. Paschal screamed again. Reeve pressed his mouth against Paschal's wooly cap and prayed. *Don't let him lose his finger. Don't let him lose his finger.*

"Paschal!" A burly man with leathery skin pushed his way through. "Paschal, what happened?"

"Papa." His voice had weakened. "I don't feel so good."

"We need to get him to the warming hut," the doc said. "I'll stitch him up in there."

Reeve would be of no help on skates, so he relinquished Paschal to his father. Several men surged forward to assist. They pulled the boy to his feet and headed toward the warming hut.

Reeve ripped the straps from his skates and freed himself, his hands trembling. The pain in his tailbone made itself felt for the first time. With care, he placed his feet beneath him and stood, grimacing. When he looked up, Miss Jayne stood a few feet away, hugging herself.

"Are you all right?" she asked, the distress in her voice audible.

He made fists so she wouldn't see his hands shaking. "Stay away from me. I don't want to talk to you. I don't even want to see you."

Her face paled. "I'm sorry. I'm so—"

He cut her off with a slice of his hand. "Not one word. Not one."

A tiny sound came from the back of her throat, but he hardened his heart. He was plenty angry with himself, but he was absolutely furious with her. Turning his back on her, he headed toward the warming house, the ice almost as difficult to traverse in his shoes as it was on his skates.

CHAPTER

24

Flossie paced in front of the parlor's fireplace, berating herself for the umpteenth time. What had she been thinking to send Mr. Wilder off like that without teaching him how to stop? There was no excuse. None. And now a boy might lose his finger because of it.

She'd wanted to go to the warming house, but after Mr. Wilder's directive, she didn't quite have the nerve. She knew he didn't mean what he'd said, that he was just reacting. Still, she felt it best not to push him until he'd had time to calm down.

The rest of the family at 438 had retired to their rooms for some quiet time before supper, but Flossie could not sit still. So she'd changed, then built up a fire in the parlor while she waited for him.

She glanced at the mantel clock. Usually she found the *tick-tock* of clocks a comforting and soothing sound. Today, however, it offered no such solace. Only reassurance from Mr. Wilder would give her relief. Reassurance that the boy was going to be all right and that Mr. Wilder didn't loathe the sight of her—though she knew he didn't. Still, she felt it would be good for him to say so. That way, he'd know it, too.

It was another hour and a half before the door finally opened.

She whirled around. Mr. Wilder stepped inside, his shoulders slumped, his face grave. Her throat closed. *Oh, no. Oh, no. Please tell me the boy will be all right.*

He hung his hat on the hall tree, his dark-blond curls more pronounced than usual. Peeling off his gloves, he stuffed them into his coat and closed his eyes in what looked to be exhaustion. Without opening them, he unbuttoned his coat, but instead of removing it, he simply stood with head down, arms at his sides.

Her heart squeezed for him. She took a step forward. He lifted his head. Their eyes connected, hers pleading for understanding, his hardening.

"The boy's finger?" she asked, barely able to voice the words.

His lips tightened. "Still intact, but if infection sets in . . ."

She swallowed. "I owe you an apology. It was my fault—*is* my fault."

"And that's supposed to make everything okay? Just like that?"

"Well, it . . ." She looked around in confusion. It wouldn't heal the boy's finger, of course, but she'd hoped an apology would smooth things over between him and her.

His eyes thunderous, he whipped off his coat and crammed it onto a hook, followed by his scarf. "Did I not make myself perfectly clear on the ice, Miss Jayne?"

She clutched her hands. "You did, but you didn't mean it. You know you didn't."

Narrowing his eyes, he jutted out his jaw. "Oh, I meant it, Miss Jayne. I meant it. And I expect you to honor it. And so there is no confusion, I'm not interested in speaking to you. Not now. Not at dinner. Not even in the hallway. I'll let you know if and when that changes."

She shook her head. "Please, I said I was sorry and I am, truly, I am. I'd give anything to—"

Spinning, he stormed down the hall, never allowing her to finish.

Reeve slammed his door, anger whooshing through him all over again. He could not believe she had the nerve to tell him what he meant and what he didn't mean. Or maybe he could believe it, for it was typical of a New Woman. Typical of her.

He'd planned to fall straight into bed and escape for an hour or two in sleep, but there was no chance of that now, not with the rage she'd roused up. Once again, Miss Jayne had interfered with his plans.

Loosening his tie, he whipped it free, wadded it up, and threw it against the wall. It slithered to the bed. He kicked off his shoes. Next came his jacket, his shirt, his trousers, all of them damp. Plopping down into his desk chair, he ripped off his soaked stockings and held his toes, trying to warm them.

His heater had run out of fuel since he'd not returned in time to fill it, so his room was freezing. He couldn't go into the parlor to warm up, not with her in there. Shivering, he crawled under the covers and curled up. Not to sleep, but to try and get warm.

You're dying to get out there, she'd said. *Don't worry, I'll be right beside you the whole time,* she'd said. *Thou doth protest too much,* she'd said.

His anger rose even further. He'd told her no politely. Then firmly. Then outright. Still, she'd insisted. *I am not leaving this pond until you have at least made an attempt.*

He flipped onto his back. Not only was she a New Woman, she was exactly the kind of boarder who gave boardinghouses bad names. The kind journalists and novelists loved to satirize. He flung an arm over his eyes. Maybe he should write a novel. He could populate it with a condescending singing master, a disreputable bachelor, a mismatched married couple, and a nosy New Woman whose main goal in life was to wear trousers. It'd be the easiest money he'd ever make. Probably even run in the front section and earn him a huge wage.

Possibilities ran through his mind. He'd name her Merrily. No, Marylee. Wait, Marylee Merrily. That was it. She'd be bossy, nosy, and impossibly sure of herself. She'd drive her fellow boarders to the brink of insanity. She'd bring calamity down onto the entire household, then be summarily tossed out onto her very delectable backside.

His chest rose and fell. His mind continued to churn. Finally, he tossed aside the covers, pulled on dry trousers and shirtsleeves, fueled his heater, then sat at his desk with a fresh piece of paper.

"Mrs. Gusman tapped the spoon against the side
of the pot, then turned back around."

CHAPTER

25

Reeve's childhood home was for sale. He stared at the Brooklyn address printed in all capital letters. 85 GEORGIA AVENUE. He'd lived in many places throughout his life. He'd spent his youth at his grandparents' house in Princeton Junction, a year at his stepmother's house in Seattle, a couple of years in a college dormitory, and the rest of his days in a smattering of boardinghouses. But of all the places he'd lived, he'd only had one home, and now it was for sale.

He tried to recall everything he could about it. His most vivid memories were of the front parlor where his mother had been laid out. They'd pushed back all the furniture and brought in the kitchen table for her coffin. When the funeral was over and the table returned to its proper place, Reeve had refused to eat at it. Instead of making him, his father had taken their plates out to the front porch steps.

Reeve reread the advertisement. It didn't have a price listed. He was a saver, though. Once he'd finally paid off college, the only thing he ever bought was books, and only then on rare occasions.

The cat jumped up onto the windowsill, then down into the room. Leaning toward the floor, Reeve wiggled his fingers.

"Hello there, little lady. Where have you been? I saved some fish for you."

Tail up, ears perked, she pranced to him. He slipped a hand inside his jacket pocket and removed a few bits of fish meat wrapped in three handkerchiefs. She ate her offering right from his hand, then curled up at his feet and began grooming her whiskers.

"I bet you'd like a home, too, wouldn't you, girl?"

After one more glance at the ad, he pushed it to the side and began to work on his article, but his gaze drifted back to the newspaper. 85 GEORGIA AVENUE. Even from here the words jumped out.

He turned the newspaper over. He put it under his chair. He stuffed it in the desk's drawer. But his mind would not leave it be.

He couldn't afford a house. At least, he didn't think he could. But what if the sellers were in a desperate situation? What if they were selling it cheap? What if somebody else got to it before he did?

Expelling a breath, he tore out the ad, pushed in his chair, and gave the cat a pat. "Don't wait up for me, girl. I'll probably be late."

Reeve approached the cottage-like house, paint peeling from its sidings. He remembered it as being a lot bigger. A row of shrubs plucked bare by winter's hand flanked its facade. Beneath a covered door stoop, a worn white rocker had icicles dripping from its arms.

He stared at the steps he'd sat on with his father and tried to picture eating their meager meals. Had his father even known how to cook? He must have, for they'd eaten something. Reeve had no recollection of whether it was any good or not. Either way, it had been summer then. Now it would be too cold to eat outside.

The front door opened. A woman with a faded but clean blue gown stood at the threshold, a baby on her hip and a boy old enough to start school clinging to her skirt.

"Can I help you?" she asked. He wondered how long she'd lived there. Was it her childhood home, too? Had she grown up within its walls, then married and birthed her own babies right there in his parents' room?

He held up the newspaper clipping. "I'm Reeve Wilder and I was hoping to speak to your husband about the house."

The baby grabbed a chunk of his mother's blond hair and yanked. Without even acknowledging the pain, she clasped his hand and unfurled his fingers. "He's not here."

"I see. Do you know when he'll be back?"

She glanced up the street, black rings shadowing her eyes. "Won't matter. He won't be in much shape to talk when he does get home."

Reeve took a moment to absorb the implications. Maybe the house was cursed. Maybe no one had ever found happiness there. Maybe he was better off without it. He gave himself a mental shake. He didn't believe in curses, and the happiest moments of his entire life had been spent inside that house.

"Clive's asking eight-hundred ninety-nine for the house," the woman said.

A wave of disappointment crashed through him, then was quickly followed by uncertainty. Was she expecting him to discuss the terms with her? He'd never done business with a woman before.

"We're selling it cheap because we're wanting to go south. We got family there." She made a motion that encompassed the porch. "We keep a good place."

He studiously avoided looking at the peeling paint, the uneven boards on the left side of the landing, and the water stains on the eaves. It could've had gaping holes in its sides and he'd still have wanted it. "How long have you lived here, Mrs. . . . ?"

"Gusman. Since '88. Clive bought it from an old-timer who'd lost his wife, and his wits, as well."

Somebody else's wife had died in that house? He sighed. After all these years, he supposed it was inevitable, but he didn't like hearing about it.

"You want to see the rest of it?" she asked.

"You don't mind?"

"Nope." Turning, she disappeared inside, leaving him to follow or not.

He climbed the steps. *Hello, Dad.*

At the door, he removed his hat, stomped the snow from his boots, took a deep breath, and stepped across the threshold. It took a moment for his eyes to adjust. It was tiny. A rag rug sat in front of the fireplace, anchored by a rocking chair, a kitchen chair, and a miniature-sized chair, almost as if Silver Hair's three bears had been living there.

He looked to the spot where his mother had been laid out. There was no furniture there, just a wall with dark rectangular patches on it, making him wonder if they'd recently held framed images that had been sold to make ends meet.

"Kitchen's through here." She walked into a connecting room, the little boy eyeing Reeve. His delay in following his mother caused her skirt to stretch.

"You like it here?" Reeve asked, his voice low.

Mrs. Gusman tugged on her skirt. "Come on, Archie."

The boy scurried after her without answering.

Reeve made it no farther than the doorway when he came to an abrupt halt. Light poured through a storm door and side window whose frame held fluttering red-checked curtains. Cabbage simmered on the stove, its aroma filling the little ten-by-ten room. A hip bath sat propped against one wall. A lump of bread dough rested atop a well-used cabinet dusted with flour. It held one bin, a cutlery drawer, and a removable chopping board.

He tried to picture his mother in here, but had only fleeting glimpses that vanished before he could fully grasp them. Still, he was standing where she'd stood. Walked where she'd walked. He again tried to feel her, get a sense of her, but it had been too long.

Mrs. Gusman slipped the baby into a chair. Someone had modified it with rails to keep the tot from slipping out. "Climb on up in your chair, too, Archie, and I'll give you some dough."

A yearning slammed into Reeve. Had his mother ever done that for him?

Archie took the bit of dough his mother tore off for him and began to roll it into a snake. Reeve watched in fascination.

"Would you like some coffee, Mr. Wilder?"

"What? Oh, no." He rotated his hat in his hands. "I, you, um, you wouldn't know where your husband is, would you?"

"I imagine he's at Krummenacker's Saloon down at Pennsylvania and Jamaica." Her voice held no bitterness, only resignation. She plucked an apron off a peg, then threaded the sash behind her waist to tie it on. "You thinkin' you might be interested?"

"I'm interested."

"You got the money?"

He hesitated again, unused to discussing such things with a woman, but under the circumstances, she might be the only one capable of it. It was hard to fathom. "I don't have eight-hundred ninety-nine dollars, if that's what you mean. And with all the banks broke and no one lending money, I don't think I could come up with it, either, but I might be able to take on the payments for you."

Her shoulders wilted. "We'd need more than the payments. Like I said, we're heading to Tennessee. Clive's going to start fresh out there. We can't go empty-handed."

He rubbed the back of his neck. "How much do you need?"

"Bottom dollar would be two hundred, plus picking up these last two years of payments."

It was an amazing deal, and bespoke their desperation if they were willing to let it go so cheaply. Still, a heaviness pressed against his chest. "I'm afraid I don't have that much."

Turning toward the stove, she stirred the cabbage. "How much have you got?"

"Forty-eight."

The baby gurgled, waving his hands and making spit bubbles.

Mrs. Gusman tapped the spoon against the side of the pot, then turned back around. "I'm sorry, Mr. Wilder. If we had to, we could come down to one seventy-five, but not to forty-eight."

He glanced into his parents' room on the right. The room he was born in. The room he'd slept in. The footboard of a sturdy wooden bed with a patchwork quilt was just visible. He could have the only home he'd ever known for one seventy-five and two years of payments.

It might as well have been a hundred thousand for all the good it did him. He looked down. A bit of snow had fallen off his boot and made a muddy smudge on the wooden floor. It wasn't the first time he'd ever tracked mud into this house, but he was sorely afraid it would be the last. He released a long breath. "Well, thank you for your time. I'm sorry to have troubled you."

"No trouble."

With a nod, he let himself out the front door, the lump in his throat so big he couldn't swallow, much less breathe.

"Worrying her lip, she glanced about the room. Aggie wrapped foil around cut pieces of glass, using beeswax as adhesive. Mary, the daughter of a portrait painter, worked on a new cartoon. Ella, who drank enough tea for the entire British Empire, selected glass for a window while Elizabeth worked as her partner cutting it."

CHAPTER
26

W e are behind, girls." Mrs. Driscoll rose from the table, then began to pace. "With Louise married, Lulu home sick, and Theresa's hand stiffening up again, we are losing a lot of ground."

Flossie glanced about the studio. They might have only completed five windows, but they'd made inroads on five more and it was just a matter of time. Still, there were a dozen to do in all and every single one involved thousands of steps, thousands of pieces of glass, and thousands of hours.

"Must I remind you how much is at stake here?" Mrs. Driscoll stopped and grabbed the back of her chair. "What we are doing is of great significance. Millions of people from all over the globe will be attending the fair. Imagine what it will do for our sex if we accomplish our goal. Then imagine the damage if we don't."

Flossie hadn't thought of that. She'd been so focused on her own goals she hadn't really thought of the bigger picture. Still, she was growing weary of everything always being about gender. Did every move they make always have to be viewed through a lens that focused on how females were compared to males?

Mr. Wilder's articles had been particularly fierce this week in his denunciation of the New Woman. She supposed that was inevitable, all things considered, but it saddened her just the same.

"I know you are working hard." Gripping the chair more firmly, Mrs. Driscoll leaned in toward them. "But you *must* work faster. The fair starts in one month. It is clear we will not be ready, but we mustn't be any later than we absolutely have to be."

Mona Van Ness, their errand girl, hurried into the workroom, her long black braid bouncing. She handed Mrs. Driscoll a note, then chatted quietly with Grace near the front.

Sighing, Mrs. Driscoll handed the note back. "Thank you, Mona. Mr. Mitchell told me to send you to the showroom next time I saw you."

"I'll go find him right now, then." The girl waved to the rest of them, them hustled back out.

"It appears I need to go out to the factory in Corona." Mrs. Driscoll shook her head. "I'll probably be gone the entire day, so when I return tomorrow, I will be reviewing what each of you did and how quickly you did it. I challenge you to surprise me."

Returning to their stations, each Tiffany Girl picked up her weapon, as it were, and answered the call to battle. Flossie wasn't sure how to cut the glass more quickly yet still adhere to the shape of the paper template. Her arm and hand muscles had gained strength over the weeks, but some of the pieces were tiny and the cuts intricate. Still, she put her head down and bent her mind to the task.

Nan also sped up her work. Normally, she'd pass anywhere from a half to a full dozen colored sheets of glass in front of the easel before deciding on one. Today she simply chose the first sheet she tried. Flossie had long since learned that the selection wasn't just about color, it was also about texture and transparency. Mrs. Driscoll even had the selectors stack their glass pieces behind each other sometimes in order to achieve the perfect color, or to project a third dimension, or to alter the transparency.

This fast and reckless method of Nan's caused a great deal of glass to stack up on Flossie's table in a very short amount of time.

The higher the piles, the more pressure Flossie felt, and the more anxious she grew. She managed to bite her tongue until Nan started pulling glass for Christ's throne. It sat in the innermost spot of the entire window and it needed to be spectacular—the perfect color, the perfect texture, and the perfect amount of transparency.

Turning, Flossie sorted through a selection of rippled glass Nan had passed over and chose an iridescent goldenrod dotted with metallic-looking speckles. "What about this one?"

Nan huffed. "Hardly. You just worry about cutting the pieces I've chosen and be sure to line them up so the grain flows in the same direction."

Flossie bit back her retort. What would Mrs. Driscoll say when she returned? Flossie didn't fancy the idea of having to recut all these pieces simply because Nan couldn't be bothered to slow down.

Grimacing, Nan placed a hand against her stomach. "I hope I'm not getting whatever it is that drove Lulu to leave yesterday."

Flossie hoped so, too. The last thing she needed was to get sick. "Your stomach ails you?"

"It does."

"Maybe you'd better rest. I've plenty of cutting to do."

Rubbing her stomach, Nan glanced around at the others. "No, I'll be all right."

But throughout the next two hours, she continued to worsen, as did her selections. By noon, she wasn't even holding the sheets up to the window. She simply grabbed colors, slapped a template onto them, and set them on Flossie's table.

"Nan, it's clear you feel wretched. Go home. I've plenty to do."

After a great deal of waffling, Nan finally acquiesced. With her coat slung over her arm, she tapped a stack of glass she'd just put on Flossie's table. "It's imperative that you use these pieces for the nativity. Do you understand?"

"You needn't worry. Everything will be fine."

The moment she left, Flossie's mood lifted. She'd not realized how oppressive Nan had become, but the sun shone brighter, the work went faster, and the other girls' banter became infectious.

She finished cutting the pieces for Christ's throne, then studied the cartoon. The sheets Nan had chosen for a nativity scene disrupted the flow, had the wrong texture, or didn't produce the luminosity of a true Tiffany piece.

Worrying her lip, she glanced about the room. Aggie wrapped foil around cut pieces of glass, using beeswax as adhesive. Mary, the daughter of a portrait painter, worked on a new cartoon. Ella, who drank enough tea for the entire British Empire, selected glass for a window of Christ blessing evangelists while Elizabeth worked as her partner cutting it.

Flossie looked again at the cartoon depicting the nativity scene. She could do a better job selecting than Nan had. She knew she could. If Mrs. Driscoll had been there, she'd have asked permission first. But she wasn't.

Flossie wasn't worried, though. Mrs. Driscoll had asked to be surprised. Well, once she saw the glass Flossie selected, she'd not only be surprised, she'd be pleased. Turning to the trays of discarded sheets, Flossie pulled new glass. Her fingers flew to the different selections, much like a typesetter who was so in tune with the type he hardly had to look to find the exact letter he needed.

Once she'd made her final decisions, she cut the pieces and pasted them to the glass easel. Never had she worked so fast and with so much joy.

When she finished the section, she stared at her work, a sluice of euphoria sweeping through her. This was what it meant to be an artist. This was what she wanted to do. This was where her talents lay.

Once again, she imagined Mrs. Driscoll's reaction, then hugged herself. She could hardly wait.

CHAPTER
27

What is the meaning of this?" Mrs. Driscoll made a sweeping gesture with her arm to indicate the section of window Flossie had redesigned.

The maroons and golds of the wise men's robes offered a rich contrast to Mary's brown outer tunic. The sky in the background hinted of morning colors. Yet Mrs. Driscoll's tone indicated displeasure. Perhaps she was referring to the section where a bearded Jesus preached to the apostles. Flossie hadn't much cared for the color selections in it, but she'd only had time to change the nativity scene.

"Which part exactly?"

"These!" Mrs. Driscoll pointed to the nativity scene—the exact part Flossie had changed.

She fingered a button on her shirtwaist. "You mean, the places I selected colors for?"

The other Tiffany Girls had yet to arrive. Flossie, however, made sure she was always the first one in and the last one to leave. Her parents had told her over and over to be the very best at everything she did. Arriving early was part of that, and so was picking out the very best colors for the windows. At least, so she'd thought.

"What on earth possessed you to select colors? You cut the glass, and at a more leisurely pace than ideal as it is."

Leisurely pace? She might not be as fast as Elizabeth, but she wasn't slow, either. She shifted her weight to the other foot. "Nan wasn't herself yesterday and I was simply trying to keep us from having to redo anything." She looked to the door to make sure no one was coming, then lowered her voice. "You should have seen the selections Nan made for this section. They weren't very good at all. I tried to offer my suggestions, but she refused to listen."

Mrs. Driscoll stared at her with an incredulous look. "Miss Upton didn't select the colors for this section. Didn't you notice she failed to hold them to the light, but instead simply took them from the tray, pulled the template, and handed them to you?"

Flossie stiffened. "That's why I was so distressed. I thought she was trying to hurry things up and was sacrificing the quality of the window." She looked at the nativity scene. "Was there something you didn't like about the glass I chose?"

"Yes, I liked the glass that had been previously chosen."

"I mean no disrespect, Mrs. Driscoll, but did you look at the glass that had been chosen for that part of the cartoon? I don't know who did the selecting, but whoever she was, she picked ridged glass for the Virgin Mary's gown, rippled glass for the wise men's gifts, and fibrillated textures for baby Jesus."

For a long moment Mrs. Driscoll said nothing. Her light-brown eyes merely studied Flossie as if she were an oddity in a curiosity shop. "I'm sure this will come as a shock to you, Miss Jayne, but Mr. Tiffany himself selected the glass for this section of the window."

Flossie's mouth slackened. She took a step back.

Looking to the side, Mrs. Driscoll let out a huff of air, then turned back to Flossie. "Mr. Tiffany also *invented* ridged glass for the specific reason that when it is made by his formula, it looks like clothing draped into folds. As for fibrillated glass, he uses it in places which call for a rather soft glow—much like a baby would have. He developed rippled glass because it creates a sort of fiery glitter, which would be quite suitable for the treasures the wise men bestowed upon Jesus."

Flossie's breathing grew deep. Her head became light.

Placing her hands on the table, Mrs. Driscoll leaned toward her. "Just this once, I'm going to pretend you never said the things you said, nor did the things you did. But if you *ever* do another task you were not personally assigned by me to do, I will dismiss you. Do we have an understanding?"

"Yes, Mrs. Driscoll."

"Good. Now, I suggest you get back over to your station and start looking for the templates you discarded yesterday. You have done us a great disservice. I will have to find the pieces Mr. Tiffany chose—if I even can. If I can't, then he will have to do them over, and he will not be pleased about it."

Flossie's heart began to hammer. "I'm—"

"In addition to that, you are going to get even more behind on your cutting because you'll have to put the templates back on the easel once you find them, you'll have to remove all the glass pieces you have up there, and you'll have yesterday's and today's cutting to do instead of just today's. We won't even mention the cost of the glass you've ruined, but from here on out, if you make any mistakes or break any pieces, the cost of the glass will be taken out of your pay."

"Yes, Mrs. Driscoll. I'll be careful. And I'll hurry. You'll see."

After curtseying, she rushed back to her station, tears stinging her eyes, the cut marks in her rough wooden table blurring. Shoving her glasscutters to the side, she rifled through the trash bin for templates. She couldn't see a thing, but she made sure no sounds escaped as her shoulders shook.

What if she wasn't chosen to go to the fair because of this? She had to be. She simply had to be. It was just one mistake. She'd work doubly hard—harder than any of the other Tiffany Girls, so hard that she'd be irreplaceable.

Finally, with a trembling breath, she wiped her eyes, laid out what numbered templates she had, then began to switch them out for the pieces she'd cut.

"Everyone looked at the Trostles, the new elderly couple who'd just moved in."

CHAPTER

28

"Does anyone know where today's *New York World* is?" Nettels asked. "It's not in the parlor."

Everyone looked at the Trostles, the new elderly couple who'd just moved in, assuming it was them who'd removed it from its proper place.

"Oh, dear." Mrs. Holliday worried her lip. "I'm afraid I'm the culprit. I was reading *The Merry Maid of Mumford Street.*"

Reeve choked on his coffee.

Oyster slapped him on the back. "Oh, I saw that this morning. A delightful story, indeed."

Capturing his breath, Reeve looked up. How in the blazes did they know about the satire he'd written?

"We should have someone do a reading of it tonight," Mrs. Trostle suggested. The woman exuded a level of wealth none of the other boarders could match. Reeve briefly wondered if Miss Jayne's mother might have sewn for her, but if that were the case, what was the woman doing in Klausmeyer's Boardinghouse?

"But Miss Jayne isn't here," Mrs. Holliday countered.

"Miss Jayne?" Mr. Trostle shouted, overcompensating for the fact that he couldn't hear too well. He was every bit as old as his wife, but hadn't aged as gracefully. His forehead was stacked with wrinkles like a pug, and his gray goatee bobbed at the end of a protruding lower jaw that was missing a few teeth. "Is she the Tiffany Girl?"

The start of the fair had come and gone, but the Tiffany Girls still hadn't finished the windows and had been kept at work for long hours, so the Trostles had yet to meet Miss Jayne. Reeve had heard her leave early every morning and come home late in the evenings. He never waited up, nor did he go looking for her, but, much to his frustration, neither could he fall asleep until he heard her return.

Smoothing his tie down his chest, Nettles straightened in his chair. "I suppose I could read it in Miss Jayne's absence."

Reeve only listened with one ear to the rest of the conversation. His day had been taken up with some follow-up interviews with glass strikers. Surely the story Mrs. Holliday mentioned wasn't his. Yet, he'd not noticed it in his drawer lately. Had he somehow accidentally stuffed it in an envelope with one of his other assignments?

Even if he had, his editor would have realized it wasn't anything worth publishing. After all, Reeve didn't write fiction. He was a journalist. He wrote serious pieces. Important pieces. Pieces about real people in real situations with real consequences. The farcical pseudonym of I. D. Claire alone should have clued Mr. Ulrich in to knowing it wasn't a legitimate submission.

As soon as he could excuse himself, he did. He needed to have a look at today's paper.

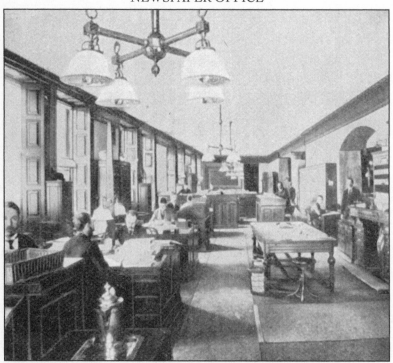

"Wooden desks lined a bank of windows on one side of the
room, standing desks and shelves lined the other."

CHAPTER
29

Wooden desks lined a bank of windows on one side of the room, standing desks and shelves lined the other. Reporters, proofreaders, and clerks looked up as Reeve walked past them toward the editor's office. Pipe tobacco smoke mingled with cigar, creating a hazy fog and a woodsy odor.

"Hey, Wilder." Bob Tarver unhooked his glasses and loosened his tie.

"Tarver."

Reeve glanced at the paper on his desk. "What're you working on?"

"News just came in that the opening of the Ferris wheel has been delayed for another month."

"They're that far behind? I thought it was supposed to be ready by now."

"It was." Tarver scratched his head, making a couple of strands of hair stick out—what there was of it anyway. His hairline had receded so far back that his part was only a couple of inches long. "It's not Mr. Ferris's fault, though. It's those Chicago bureaucrats. Took them so long to agree that the wheel was the best way to upstage the Eiffel Tower that Ferris wasn't able to start on the thing until the fair was almost upon him."

Lifting the cloth of his trouser leg, Reeve propped a hip on the edge of Tarver's desk. The Eiffel Tower had been built as the entrance arch to the Paris Exposition in '89, but Chicago had been determined to outdo the thousand-foot monument. "They should have had the fair in New York. We'd have had everything finished on time."

"That we would have."

Reeve glanced toward the back wall. "Is Ulrich in?"

Tarver used his thumb to point behind him. "He's been typing away on his Smith Premier all morning."

Rising, Reeve clapped him on the shoulder, then walked to the back, exchanging greetings with several of the men while noting three of the desks had been cleaned out. He reached his editor's office and tapped against the open door.

Ulrich waved him in. His cowlick was in rare form today, combed up into one giant red curl, creating the perfect foil for his equally bright goatee. "I'm glad you're here, I need to talk to you. Have a seat while I finish this up."

An oversized window behind him cut a swath of light across the desk, highlighting a stack of papers on his right, a dictionary half a foot thick, three competitors' newspapers, and several notes tacked to the wall.

Reeve settled into a spindle-back chair and propped his ankle on his knee. Ulrich had removed both coat and waistcoat, leaving him in shirtsleeves, suspenders, and tie. A spot of ink marred the left breast of his wrinkled shirt.

Finally, he whipped the piece of paper he'd been working on out of the typewriter's roller and pointed to a basket of mail on a table in the corner. "You see those letters over there?"

Nodding, Reeve rested a hand on his ankle.

"Those are from subscribers who read your boardinghouse satire."

"I was going to ask you about that." Reeve eyed the stack of mail. "I could have told you we'd get complaints. I didn't even mean to send it in. I just wrote it as a joke. It must have gotten mixed up with my other stuff."

"Since when do you make jokes?"

"Since this once, I guess. I wish you'd sent word before printing it."

Leaning back in his chair, Ulrich tucked the ends of his tie inside his shirt between the third and fourth buttons. "I'm in the newspaper business, Wilder. When my boys send me stories, I assume they're for printing."

"Didn't you see the pseudonym?"

"I saw it." He smiled. "Wasn't much like you, but then, neither was the story."

"I wrote the thing over two months ago. When did you receive it?"

"Last week."

Reeve rubbed a hand down his face. "I see. Well, I'm sorry. I should have burned it the minute I finished it. I shouldn't have even written it. Are the higher-ups mad?"

"No, they're not mad."

"Well, that's a relief."

Ulrich dropped the legs of his chair onto the wooden floor with a *thump*, then removed a pipe and a pouch of tobacco from his top drawer. "The higher-ups want you to serialize it."

He stilled. "They what?"

"They want you to serialize it."

He frowned. "Why?"

Opening the pouch, Ulrich took a pinch of tobacco, dropped it into the pipe bowl, and tapped it with his finger. "Because the readers are going crazy over it. The letters have been pouring in ever since it ran."

Reeve looked again at the mail basket. "Those aren't complaints?"

"Nary a one." Striking a match on the side of his desk, Ulrich waited for it to flare, then held it to his pipe, puffing until the tobacco lit. With each draw, more and more smoke seeped from his mouth. A pungent odor filled the room, not unlike the smell of burning leaves. "With subscriptions down, the higher-ups are looking for ways to draw in new readers, and they're willing to pay for it. So they told me to have you serialize this Marylee character."

Reeve rubbed his temples. "But . . . the story is stupid, and I don't even write fiction, don't know the first thing about it."

"Well, I could try and find somebody else." Ulrich fired up his tobacco again for a deeper light, then waved away the smoke. "Didn't occur to me you wouldn't want an increase in pay."

Reeve tapped a thumb against his leg. "How much of an increase?"

"Two-fifty. If the serialization does well and subscriptions go up, so will the fee. If they don't, you'll have to wrap up the story prematurely."

Reeve studied a calendar on the wall. Ulrich hadn't flipped the page for two months. "How high could the fee go?"

"Up to five dollars."

He lifted his brows. "Per installment?"

"Per installment."

At five dollars per segment, he could double his forty-eight dollars of savings in two months. Even the two-fifty a week would be quite a boon. He jiggled his foot. "What would the storyline be?"

"Whatever you want, so long as it takes place in a boarding-house and the New Woman—Marylee, I think—remains the focal character. That's what most of the letters mention." Ulrich shrugged. "I'd suggest throwing in a few more eccentrics. You know, meddlesome landladies, coquettish daughters, slovenly servants, ill-mannered housemates, horrific food—don't you live in a boardinghouse? Just fictionalize the people who live there."

Reeve thought of the boarders at Klausmeyer's. After the question-and-answer game they'd been playing, he knew them much better than he used to. It wouldn't be hard to turn them into caricatures of themselves, except for Mrs. Dinwiddie. He'd never do something like that to her. It's just that the rest of them weren't particularly interesting.

Well, there was Miss Jayne. She was interesting. Compelling, even. And definitely complex. Still, to cast her in a leading role of an entire serialization? He wouldn't know the first thing about it. The extra money would help him garner money for that down payment, though. A down payment he very much wanted.

He scratched his jaw. If writing this serialization would accelerate his chances of getting the Brooklyn place back, then maybe he ought to do it. It wasn't as if anyone would know he was the one writing it.

Taking a deep breath, he uncrossed his legs and pushed himself to his feet. "I still want to write my regular articles. And the satire can only be published under the pseudonym."

"Agreed."

"All right, then. I'll have something for you by the end of the week."

Clamping the pipe at the corner of his mouth, Ulrich held out his hand. "That's the spirit, Wilder. That's the spirit."

Reeve clasped his hand, but couldn't help wonder if he'd just made a deal with the devil.

CARTOON FOR DISPLAY AT WORLD'S FAIR [19]

"Mr. Tiffany looked at the designers, who were all bunched together at the
other end of their line. 'I have agreed to send them a cartoon by Miss McDowell
and some sketches by Miss Northrup, Miss de Luze, and Miss Emmet.'"

CHAPTER

30

Flossie, Aggie, Nan, and all the other Tiffany Girls gathered around to admire the sections of *The Story of the Cross*. It was the final window they'd completed for the chapel—the largest and most important work the Women's Department had ever done— and it took up almost every window in their workroom. A sense of accomplishment rushed through Flossie.

Some ten-thousand pieces of colored glass had been selected, cut, foiled, and arranged to make up the circular window. Seeing the entire composition, knowing it was mannish work yet had been completed by women, made her want to throw open the shutters and shout out to the world.

Look what we did! Look what we—twelve women—did all by ourselves!

Of course, the pieces still needed to be soldered, then ultimately installed, and no woman would be allowed to tread into that territory. Still, they'd done work that before had been done solely by men. Men who'd gone on strike and would be very surprised to see what the Women's Department had accomplished in their absence.

She wished her family at 438 could see it. Even Mr. Wilder. Especially Mr. Wilder. She'd done as he'd requested and left him

alone. Not that it was hard, what with the hours she'd been working. But she hoped time and the advent of spring had helped
soften his feelings toward her.

Drawing in a breath, she pulled herself back to the present
and studied the window's nativity scene—the one she'd first
thought was poorly designed. She shook her head. The selections
were perfect. *Perfect.* The nuances of each piece making up Mary's
robe flowed from one segment to the next, emulating shadows
and highlights, folds and bunches. The pieces she'd wanted to
use would have worked, but not like these. Not like the ones
Mr. Tiffany had chosen.

She studied the other sections. Sections where Mrs. Driscoll
had been the one to decide which glass went into which spot, as
had Nan and Ella as well. Pride swelled within her. She'd bet every
penny she had that no one would have dreamed women had the
skill and ability to create such a spectacular work of art.

A door opened and a male voice intruded upon the quiet that
had fallen over the girls.

"Mrs. Driscoll?" Mr. Tiffany shouted.

"We're in here," Mrs. Driscoll replied, giving their creation one
last lingering glance before turning her attention to him.

Flossie wished she could sit Mrs. Driscoll down in a chair
and do her hair for her. She'd taken to parting it down the
middle and slicking it back into a bun that looked like some sort
of outgrowth from her head. It would look a hundred times
better in the Gibson-girl style.

Mr. Tiffany stepped through the door, then paused. "Would
you look at that? You did it, ladies. You did it, and not a moment
too soon."

The girls had grown accustomed to him and his visits over
these last five months and had lost their nervousness, but not their
wonderment and respect. With hands behind his back, he walked
down the line of windows inspecting their work like a general

inspecting his troops. By the time he reached the end of the row, not a one of the girls was breathing.

He turned to Mrs. Driscoll. "Perfect. Absolutely perfect."

Mrs. Driscoll smiled. The girls clapped and cheered. Flossie wished she were a man and could throw a hat in the air and whoop. Instead, she hugged Aggie on her left and Nan on her right.

"I suppose you'll be wanting to know which of you girls I've chosen to go to the fair."

They quieted immediately. Propping a hip onto one of the tables, he half-sat and half-stood. "Well, before I tell you that, I have a surprise to share with you. Have you heard about the Woman's Building at the Fair? It's a building designed by women, built by women, and stocked with exhibits made exclusively by women. I have been approached by the Board of Lady Managers. They have asked for a sampling of your work to be displayed in their building."

Flossie sucked in her breath. Most of her work would already be incorporated into the windows, but she could certainly cut a few pieces of glass for the display. Or they might want to show one of the manila sheets she'd made with her stylus and carbon paper. Oh, wouldn't her parents be thrilled? It would make up for so much. She saw them every Sunday at church, and a week didn't go by without them imploring her to return home, especially when they found out the Tiffany Girls had been returning to work on Sunday afternoons in order to finish the windows.

Mr. Tiffany looked at the designers, who were all bunched together at the other end of their line. "I have agreed to send them a cartoon by Miss McDowell and some sketches by Miss Northrup, Miss de Luze, and Miss Emmet."

Flossie leaned forward and glanced at the girls he'd mentioned. They had been with him long before she and her classmates had arrived. They blushed and smiled and looked at one another.

He folded his hands in his lap. "I, of course, would not dream of leaving out my new girls. I am so proud of you and will be sending three samples of your work. One of magnolias, one of grapes, and one of chrysanthemums."

Flossie's heart sank. She'd not worked on any of those and neither had Nan. Still, he hadn't announced who would be attending the fair. As wonderful as it would have been to have her work displayed, she'd much rather go to the actual fair. She'd worked more hours than any of the others, she'd not missed one single day of work, she'd arrived early and stayed late, and she'd only had two mishaps—crashing into the glass easel, which wasn't her fault at all, and reselecting Mr. Tiffany's pieces, which she'd set to rights immediately.

"Would you like to tell them, Mrs. Driscoll?"

The woman's cheeks pinked, then she faced the girls. "I honestly didn't know how we would decide, but the choice ended up being simplified when the Board of Lady Managers asked Mr. Tiffany if one of our selectors and her glasscutter could do a demonstration in the Woman's Building for fairgoers."

Flossie's pulse soared, her breath held.

"Mr. Tiffany and I each wrote down the names of the team we wanted to send and both came up with the same names."

Aggie slipped her hand into Flossie's. There was no question now that Aggie would not be going. Her job had been to bend foil around the edges of the cut glass for soldering, but Flossie was one of two cutters, so it was between her and Nan and the other team, Ella and Elizabeth.

"Our choice is Nan—"

Flossie sucked in her breath, her heart filling with joy, her eyes stinging with tears.

"—and Elizabeth."

She froze. Nan covered her mouth. The girls squealed. They surrounded Nan and Elizabeth, hugging, applauding, and all talking at once. Flossie turned to Nan and smiled, her congratulatory words drowned out by the others.

It was as if she wasn't in her body, but was floating above the room watching herself, seeing herself share in the excitement and say all the right things. She hugged the designers and asked which sketches they were going to send. She expressed to Mrs. Driscoll her pleasure over what their windows would mean for the women's movement. And she chatted with Mr. Tiffany, telling him she couldn't wait to hear everyone's reactions when they saw his chapel. Yet during it all she wanted nothing more than to run and run and run until she'd outrun the pain and disappointment.

CHAPTER

31

All lights were out at Klausmeyer's. Closing the door behind her, Flossie groped along the hallway.

A moment later Mr. Wilder stepped out of his room, an oil lamp in his hand. He was in his shirtsleeves and stocking feet. His suspenders hung down by his sides, and his hair was mussed. "Oh, it's you."

"Who were you expecting?"

"Nobody at this hour. That's why I was coming out to check. What are you doing getting in so late?"

"I stopped by my parents' house before coming home. I'm sorry I didn't tell anyone. It was somewhat last minute." After leaving work, she'd gone straight to her father's arms, seeking refuge, and though he and Mother hovered, they also pleaded with her to "stop this ridiculousness" and come home. In the end, she wished she hadn't gone to them at all.

He narrowed his eyes. "What's the matter?"

Her lips parted. How could he tell something was the matter? Not trusting herself to speak, she shook her head and started to pass him.

"Something's the matter," he said, partially blocking her way. "What is it? Is it the strikers?"

Pressing her knuckles to her mouth, she shook her head again.

"Did someone hurt you?"

"Not like you mean."

"Then, what?"

Her eyes filled. "Mr. Tiffany picked someone else to go to the fair." She barely managed to get the words past her throat.

He lifted the lantern. "Are you crying?"

Swiping a tear, she looked away. "I'm disappointed, is all. I thought . . ."

She didn't want to tell him what she thought. The faint hissing of the lamp filled the silence. His cat came into the hall. Latching on to an opportunity to divert his attention, she tried to steady her voice. "Is that a different cat from the one I saw before?"

He lowered the lamp. "It's the same one. I bathed her, is all."

"Did you?" She squatted down and ran a hand along its back. "She looks a hundred times better. And so soft."

He shifted his weight.

"Have you named her yet?" she asked.

"I call her Cat."

Scratching its chin, she leaned down and brought her nose close to it. "That isn't much of a name," she whispered in a baby voice. "Is it?"

Cat purred, then lifted her nose and touched it to Flossie's. The gesture was so sweet, so unexpected, it completely undid her. With her emotions so close to the surface, she was unable to suppress them. Sinking the rest of the way to the floor, she covered her face.

Mr. Wilder set the lamp down, then knelt on one knee beside her. "Should I, should I get Miss Love?"

She shook her head, keeping the sound of her sobs in, but her shoulders still shook.

He opened and closed his fists. "Don't cry, now, just a few more steps and you'll be in your room."

"You don't have to stay," she said into her hands. "I'm sorry to have disturbed you. I know I'm a bother to you, so, please, I'll be all right. I'm just going to sit here for a few minutes."

He rubbed his hands on his trousers. "Come on now, little magpie. I can't leave you in the middle of the hall like this."

A sob escaped.

Blowing out a breath, he sat down beside her and pulled her up against his side, holding her and letting her cry into his shirt.

"I'm sorry," she whimpered. "I didn't think I had any tears left."

"*Shhhhh.*" He leaned his cheek against her hair. "It's all right."

"I w-wanted to go so bad."

"I would have, too."

"I worked so hard. Going in early. Staying late. Never complaining."

"*Shhhhh.*"

She cried some more until finally the tears began to subside. Cat crawled up into Mr. Wilder's lap, then crossed over to hers. Flossie petted her, drawing comfort from the action and from being held in Mr. Wilder's arms. He felt so different from her father. So hard and firm, yet not the least bit uncomfortable. Much as she wanted to stay there, she straightened.

"Better?" he asked, his voice quiet.

She gave a shrug, her eyes filling again.

He studied her face, his eyes surveying her much like a painter who was trying to capture every nuance of his subject's features. The lantern's light flickered in his pupils. He hooked a tendril of hair behind her ear, then lowered his hand to the floor.

Warmth flooded her. She burrowed her fingers into Cat's coat.

"You'd best go on to bed," he said. "The morning's not far in coming."

"Yes."

Neither moved. Her heart shifted. Her stomach tensed.

Drawing in a breath, he pulled his feet beneath him and rose, then held out a hand for her. She picked up Cat, nuzzled her neck, then looked up at Mr. Wilder. "Can I sleep with her tonight?"

His Adam's apple bobbed. "All right."

With her hands full, she was unable to take the one he offered. Leaning down, he placed his hands at her waist and lifted her clear to her feet. Flossie held Cat tight. The animal dug her claws into Flossie's bodice, but made no attempt to spring free. Mr. Wilder's hands lingered for the slightest of moments, then he stepped back.

"Good night, Cat." He rubbed a knuckle between Cat's ears.

Flossie's chest rose and fell. The warmth inside her grew. Moving to her door, she gave him a quick glance, then let herself into her room, but the picture he made in his shirtsleeves, stocking feet, and swinging suspenders would stay with her for many a month to come.

CHAPTER

32

I don't really care for the Marylee character," Miss Jayne said, cutting into her codfish cake. "She's so, I don't know, shallow. And a bit irritating, don't you agree?"

Reeve's fork stalled halfway to his mouth before he realized it and carried it the rest of the way.

"Oh, but wait until you read today's installment." Leaning in, Mrs. Trostle looked up and down the table. "I think the bibliomaniac is starting to fall in love with her."

Reeve choked. Oyster pounded him on the back. "You okay?"

Reeve held up a hand, then hit his chest a couple of times. "Just swallowed wrong, but I'm curious, Mrs. Trostle. What makes you think that about the bibliomaniac?"

Miss Jayne's eyes widened. "You read Mr. I. D. Claire's column?"

"That is a ridiculous name," he said.

She smiled. "I like it, I do declare."

With a *humph*, he returned his attention to Mrs. Trostle. The woman was again dressed to the knocker in a gown whose upper sleeves were as full and round as a person's head. Perhaps she, too, had a seamstress in her family, but then, that wouldn't explain the jewelry.

Looping a long strand of pearls round and round her finger, Mrs. Trostle pursed her lips. "All the signs are there. The bibliomaniac's perfectly composed and well-spoken in every situation until Marylee enters the room, then he becomes tongue-tied and self-conscious and only too anxious to make his exit."

Reeve blinked. "He does?"

She gave him a patronizing look. "Well, I can understand why you didn't see that, being a man and all, but we women have a sixth sense about these things."

He scratched his jaw. "Interesting. I missed that completely."

"Heavens." She swatted the air with her hand. "It's as obvious as the nose on your face."

Unless you were the author, he thought, then shook his head. The bibliomaniac was the normal character. Sure, Reeve had given him a few idiosyncrasies, like reading the dictionary from cover to cover, but for the most part that character was reason in a world of confusion. Order in a world of chaos. Practicality in a world of unfeasibility. For the bibliomaniac to have feelings for the flighty Marylee confounded not only him, but the entire plot.

By the time he drew himself back into the conversation, the topic had shifted to Miss Jayne's paintings.

"You really have a remarkable talent, Miss Jayne." Mrs. Trostle turned to her husband. "Don't you think so, Chester?"

"Eh?"

"*Don't you think Miss Jayne has remarkable talent?*" she said, her voice raised.

"Yes, yes." Propping a monocle on his right eye, he looked at Miss Jayne. "Remarkable talent, indeed. The others have been telling us about you being a Tiffany Girl and the tremendous work you have done for Mr. Tiffany. You must tell us the things that they could not. Did you study art in Paris?"

She flushed. "Oh, no. I simply attended art school during the summers of my youth and then enrolled in the New York School of Applied Design."

"The School of Applied Design." He nodded. "Is that where you did the seashore portrait that hangs above your bed?"

"No, I did that last summer."

"Well, it's an excellent piece. You have a definite affinity for painting women with auburn hair. Best I've seen, in fact."

She smoothed the napkin on her lap. "Thank you. Red hair is my favorite."

"Did you see her portrait of Mrs. Dinwiddie?" Miss Love asked.

"Indeed I did." Mrs. Trostle tapped her mouth with her finger. "I wonder if Monsieur Bourgeois would be interested in seeing it."

Her husband leaned close to catch her words. "Bourgeois? Jean-Pierre Bourgeois? An excellent idea. I'll ask him when I see him next week."

Holliday wiped his mouth with his napkin. "Who's Jean-Pierre Bourgeois?"

"A gallery owner." Mrs. Trostle placed her flatware across her plate at a precise angle, as if she'd just completed a meal at the queen's table.

Mrs. Holliday imitated the woman, placing her flatware in the same position even though she'd not finished eating.

Miss Jayne craned her neck to better see the Trostles. "You know an art gallery owner?"

"My, my, yes." Mrs. Trostle took a sip of tea. "We've known Monsieur Bourgeois from when we were living in Paris years ago. He's opening a new gallery on West Twenty-Third, and instead of catering exclusively to European art, he also wants to promote interest in American art."

Miss Jayne exchanged a glance with Miss Love. "And you think he might be interested in my paintings?"

"I do, but for some reason I seem to remember he was looking for landscapes." Mrs. Trostle shrugged. "It's of no matter. Chester will speak to him and if he is interested in portraits or ladies with glorious auburn hair, then we shall arrange for you to meet him."

Miss Jayne's entire face lit. "Oh, thank you, Mrs. Trostle. *And thank you, Mr. Trostle*," she said, projecting her voice.

The man relaxed the muscles around his eye and tucked the monocle into his vest pocket. "No promises, my dear. Monsieur Bourgeois is very particular, but as my wife mentioned, he is always willing to look at new talent. So, we shall see."

The conversation turned to the arrival of the princess of Spain at the Chicago World's Fair, but Reeve could see Miss Jayne's mind was a million miles away. He hoped her disappointment wouldn't be too great if her painting was refused. Maybe he could work something similar into his Marylee story. The bibliomaniac situation, however, was a concern. He'd definitely need to do something about that.

DELMONICO'S RESTAURANT[20]

"The maître d'hôtel opened a door leading to an outdoor dining area, the summer breeze stirring her gray-and-rose-striped taffeta gown."

CHAPTER
33

Flossie stood uncertainly inside the doorway of Delmonico's in Madison Square, the aroma of sweet bread a favorable portent of the meal to come. The Trostles had not only spoken to their friend, Monsieur Bourgeois, but they'd shown him her paintings last week while she was at work. He'd been impressed and had asked if she'd join him for lunch.

She scanned the dining room in search of a Frenchman by himself. The mirrors lining the walls of the restaurant multiplied its size. Crisp white cloths covered the tables. The fresh flowers gracing their centers could not compete, however, with the stunning summer toilettes of the women surrounding them. A robust fountain in the center added the soothing sound of water to the low murmur of voices. Never had she been in a restaurant so fine. Certainly, her father was a member of a few clubs, but nothing like this.

A clean-shaven maître d'hôtel in an impeccable black suit stepped forward.

She clutched her parasol. "I'm to meet Monsieur Jean-Pierre Bourgeois."

"Right this way."

She glanced up at the frescoed ceiling, briefly thinking how much prettier a Tiffany glass mosaic would be. The maître d'hôtel opened a door leading to an outdoor dining area, the summer breeze stirring her gray-and-rose-striped taffeta gown.

A diminutive man with olive skin and warm brown eyes sat alone. At their approach, he stood. "Mademoiselle Jayne?"

"How do you do."

He took her gloved hand and kissed her knuckles, then held the chair for her as he addressed the maître d'hôtel. "Punch à la Romaine for the lady," he said, his French accent thick.

She'd never been without the buffering presence of another person when partaking of a meal with a man, but he looked to be her father's age, so what could be the harm? Besides, she was a New Woman now. If she were going to make her way in the world, she'd best learn to stand on her own two feet.

"I was expecting someone older," he said. "Your paintings suggest an expertise not often seen in such youth."

"Thank you." She flushed with pleasure.

Over calf's head soup, chicken cutlets, and stewed beef à la Jardinière, she told him of her work at the School of Applied Design and at Tiffany's. He told her of his exhibitions in Paris and London, his affiliation with the Society of French Artists, and the relationships he'd established with American painters living abroad—including Remington, Chase, and Sargent.

"I've been much impressed with the art coming out of this country." He gestured with his hand, a gold ring on his pinkie finger catching a ray of sunshine. "I was stunned, therefore, to discover the galleries here only show European work. I couldn't resist the opportunity to introduce your patrons to something that's been right under their noses this whole time."

"You'll only be showing American work, then?"

The clamor of iron-shod wheels on Fifth Avenue's Belgian blocks partially drowned out his answer. ". . . include European art, of course, but my main focus will be on American painters, which brings me to your work. I was quite taken with the painting of the woman at the seashore. Tell me about it."

Lifting one shoulder, she spooned up a raspberry in a delicate long-stemmed crystal dessert bowl. "I love to paint women's hair, especially in the breeze. Red hair's my favorite. It's so beautiful in the sunshine, isn't it?"

He gave her a small smile. "*Oui*, Mademoiselle, it most certainly is. Where were you when you painted it?"

"In Gloucester, just north of Boston. Our instructor took us down to the beach." Swallowing the raspberry, she shook her head. "It was so windy, my canvas blew over two or three times, but I wish you could have seen the sky that day. It was the clearest blue I've ever seen in my life."

"I did see it."

"You've been to Gloucester?"

"In your painting I have."

Her cheeks warmed. "Thank you."

"*Je vous en prie.* That's why I asked Monsieur Trostle if I could meet you. If you will allow me, I'd like to include it in my exhibit with the intention of selling it."

She knew this was what they were to discuss, but she'd thought she'd have to convince him somehow. Heavens, had he taken her to this lavish restaurant to convince *her*?

She glanced over the decorative rail separating Delmonico's patrons from the pedestrians. Across the street, a nursemaid pushed a perambulator along the park's winding pathway and past the monument of Admiral Farragut. A stately carriage with two liveried footmen passed by, momentarily blocking the view, then pulled up to the curb.

Smoothing the ribbon about her waist, she swallowed. "Nothing would please me more, sir. How much do you think you would be able to sell it for?"

"I will ask four hundred, and will take no less than three hundred."

Her jaw slackened. "Dollars? Four hundred *dollars?*"

"*Oui.*" He caught the waiter's eye. "*Un petit café, s'il vous plaît.*" He studied her. "Have you ever had your work shown in a gallery before?"

She tried to concentrate on the question, but was still reeling from his estimated selling price. Three hundred dollars would be an entire year's worth of wages. Four hundred dollars was unthinkable. Especially for *one* painting. "I, um, no, I'm afraid I've never had my work in a gallery before."

"It is nothing for you to worry over. I will take care of everything."

Her heart soared. If she did well in this showing, surely it would lead to more. This was the break she'd been waiting for. Every single artist in the Metropolitan Museum had started out in a showing just like this. What Monsieur Bourgeois didn't realize was she'd have paid him for the opportunity, not the other way around. Beneath her skirt, she covered one toe of her boot with the other. "So, all I do is bring you the painting?"

"Well, you'll need to direct me to the man who takes care of your business affairs."

Touching her napkin to her lips, she scooted up in her chair. "I'm a New Woman, so I take care of my own affairs."

Propping an elbow on his armrest, he tapped his mouth with his knuckle. "You have no father? No future husband?"

"I have a father, but I live on my own. I'm a working girl. All business is to be discussed with me."

The waiter served their coffee, then removed their empty dessert bowls.

"You'll forgive me," he said. "But it seems most indelicate."

"I won't take offense, I assure you. Now, what is it you wanted to discuss?"

Pulling his brows together, he took a sip of coffee, then gave a tiny shrug. "Well, I'm not sure if you are aware or not, but there is much involved in putting on an exhibit, so I require a fee up front."

She blinked. She hadn't thought about his fee, but, of course, he would have one. "I see. How much is your fee?"

"One hundred fifty dollars."

She sucked in her breath.

"But you would keep the full price of the sale," he said. "Be it three or four hundred."

She shifted in her seat. One-hundred and fifty dollars? Panic made her stomach tighten. "I'm sorry, but I don't have that kind of money. Would it be possible to remit payment after the sale is made?"

"I'm afraid it doesn't work that way. There are many up-front costs involved." Leaning forward, he rested his arms on the table. "A man would understand this. Are you sure you wouldn't like me to speak with your father?"

"No, no." The sun had moved across the sky and now cast its rays directly onto her. Tiny beads of moisture formed along her spine. "It's just, I, well, I simply don't have a sum of that magnitude at my fingertips." She ran a finger around the rim of her china cup. She wanted this so badly. Imagine, earning a year's worth of income in one easy sale.

He tapped the table with his thumb. "I don't usually interfere with my artists' financial concerns, but perhaps you would not mind a suggestion?"

"Not at all." She pulled a handkerchief from her cuff and dabbed it along her hairline.

"Is there someone you can go to? An uncle? A grandfather? You would be able to reimburse them as soon as the painting sold—and I know it will sell, otherwise I wouldn't offer to feature it." He finished his coffee. "What if we did this, what if I lowered my fee to one hundred dollars? You are such a lovely girl who I think will one day become a very important artist. So, I will lower it for you, but you mustn't tell anyone else."

She bit her lip. Maybe her father would give it to her. According to her mother, he'd done rather well at the races, for once. Perhaps she could convince him it would be like investing in a horse, only it was his daughter and his chances would be much better.

Nodding, she stuffed her handkerchief away and sat up straight. "Let me see what I can do."

"Excellent. I would hate for us both to lose this opportunity and for the public to lose the joy you could bring them." He smiled. "I have a feeling this is going to be the beginning of a long and rewarding relationship, Mademoiselle."

"I'd like that, sir. I'd like it very much."

CHAPTER

34

"Mrs. Vanderbilt came by this week." Mother threaded tiny beads onto her needle, slid them down, then sewed them onto the bodice of a ball gown she was making.

Tucking her feet up under her skirt, Flossie rocked herself in the chair. "Did she stay long enough for tea?"

"Indeed she did. As a matter of fact, her cousin is getting married. Mrs. Vanderbilt has asked me to sew the dresses for the wedding."

Flossie took a quick breath. "Oh, Mother, congratulations. What a testament to the quality of your work."

Mother threaded another set of beads. "I've not decided yet whether I'm going to do it. It would be a great deal of work."

Seated on the couch reading the *Times*, Papa turned down a corner of his paper. "And a great deal of money."

"I fear it would be the death of me." Mother sighed. "My headaches have started up again."

"I'm sorry to hear that," Flossie said. "Perhaps you shouldn't do it, then."

"That's what I keep telling your father, but I admit it would be lovely to have the extra income. We could buy that parlor grand piano I've been wanting so badly."

Folding his paper, Papa crossed his legs. "I'd like to hear a little bit more, Flossie, about this art gallery your mother was telling me of."

Flossie rocked her chair. "Well, the owner of the gallery, Monsieur Bourgeois, took me to Delmonico's yesterday."

"Delmonico's?" Papa frowned. "Who went with you?"

She lowered her legs and sat up in her chair. "I went by myself."

"Oh, Flossie." Her mother looked up from her sewing. "You mustn't do things like that, dear. It's too forward."

Ordinarily she'd have argued with her, but tonight she decided it would behoove her to be on her best behavior. "Yes, Mother."

"How old is this Bourgeois fellow?" Papa asked.

"He's an older man—about your age, I think. He's secured a space over on West Twenty-Third that he plans to use as his gallery."

Mother lowered the fabric in her hands. "What did he say about your paintings?"

"He liked my seashore one very much. And guess what? He thinks he can get four hundred dollars for it."

Papa's brows shot up. "Four hundred dollars?"

"Yes, and if he can't get that, he said he wouldn't take any less than three hundred. Can you imagine? He's going to be featuring European artists, of course, but he wants to make a name for himself as the gallery with premier American artists."

"Like who?" Papa asked.

"Remington, Chase, and Sargent are the ones I know of for certain. I'm not sure who else."

"That's quite the company you'll be keeping."

She gave a small smile. "Yes, it's rather hard to believe. I'm very excited."

He tapped his finger on the back of the couch. "Is he only taking that one painting?"

"I wouldn't be able to afford more than one."

"Afford?" He frowned. "What do you mean, afford?"

Reinforcing a pleat at her waist, she glanced at Mother, then back at him. "Well, artists are subject to set-up costs."

"What kind of set-up costs?"

She took a deep breath. "A hundred dollars paid in advance."

He jerked himself upright. "A hundred dollars?"

"It was one-hundred-fifty at first, but I bargained him down to one hundred."

"That's thirty-five percent. Highway robbery."

Mother set her sewing on the table beside her. "But even if she sells it for three hundred, Bert, that would still leave her two hundred. Think of it. Two hundred dollars—for *one* painting."

He scowled at Flossie. "Why isn't he taking his cut out of the sale? Why is he making you pay it up front?"

She clasped a locket at her neck and ran it back and forth across the chain. "He says it's very expensive to put on an exhibit, but he's confident my painting will sell, and when it does, the three hundred dollars will only be the beginning."

He leaned forward, resting his elbows on his knees. "And just where are you going to get a hundred dollars?"

She said nothing, simply looked at him.

He began to shake his head. "Oh, no. Not this time, little girl. It's one thing to send you to the School of Applied Design, but this, this is totally different. I'm sorry, honey, but I can't give you that much."

"I wasn't asking you to give it to me. I'll pay you back."

"And if the painting doesn't sell?"

"For heaven's sake, Bert." Mother shook out her skirt. "The painting will sell. It's outstanding. Your favorite, in fact."

He rubbed his eyes. "It's a lovely painting, and I don't wish to upset you, but realistically I'm simply not sure someone will pay three hundred dollars for it."

Flossie swallowed, her heart in her throat. "I know it's a lot,

Papa, but people come into Mr. Tiffany's showroom all the time and pay twice that amount for nothing more than a vase."

He peeked up at her. "His name is Louis Comfort Tiffany. That's why he can demand those prices. Your name is Florence Rebecca Jayne. It's not the same."

"Mr. Tiffany's name didn't always mean what it does now." She looked him directly in the eye, knowing better than to show any weakness. "As a matter of fact, Mr. Tiffany—his father, the jeweler on Fifth Avenue, I mean—originally borrowed a *thousand* dollars from his father, a mere miller, when he was first starting out. He used it to open a small stationery and gift shop, and look at him now." She clasped her hands. "I'm only asking for a hundred, Papa. And I'll pay you back, just as soon as it sells."

Much as she wanted to mention the races, she couldn't quite work up the nerve.

"I want you to consider it, Bert." Mother wet her lips. "If Flossie's painting sells—and I'm sure it will—then she won't have to work for Tiffany anymore and she'd be able to come home."

Clasping her hands, Flossie said nothing. She wasn't coming back home. She loved living in the boardinghouse and she loved her job at Tiffany's. Now wasn't the time for that quarrel, though.

With a pained expression, her father pushed himself up off the couch. "I'm sorry, moppet. It's too much. And we really don't know anything about this Bourgeois fellow."

"But the Trostles know him and they—"

He looked at Mother. "I'm going to retire now."

"Bert, I—"

Leaning over, he gave Flossie a peck on the cheek. "Come have dinner with us soon. I miss having you at the table."

She watched him walk from the room, tears stacking up against her throat. "I didn't expect him to say no."

Scooting to the edge of her chair, Mother lowered her voice. "It's of no matter. I'll lend you the money."

Flossie whipped her head around. "You?"

"Yes. Your father doesn't know this, but when he started going to the races on a regular basis, I began taking in jobs that I didn't tell him about, and I hid the money away."

"What?" Flossie's eyes darted to the door. "But how?"

Mother waved her hand in the air. "Keep your voice down. I only worked on them while he was gone. He never knew the difference, and neither did you. That's why I had so much extra work for you, because I kept getting behind on the jobs he did know about."

She stared at her mother with incredulity. "But what about, what about when you . . ." *Slapped me*, she wanted to say, but didn't.

Mother understood what Flossie meant, though, for the lines of her forehead creased. "I still feel awful about that, and quite ashamed. I think the reason I reacted so vehemently when you suggested I secrete money away was because I was already doing that very thing." Her eyes filled. "I'm so sorry."

The fire in the grate popped, its warmth toasting the room.

Flossie lowered her voice to a whisper. "Don't cry, Mama, and don't be sorry. Even if he didn't gamble your money on races, it's still perfectly acceptable to keep some back."

"Whatever the case, I want you to have it."

"You have a *hundred dollars*?"

Mother ran her hand up the back of her hair. "Well, no, not a hundred, but I do have seventy-five. Do you think Monsieur Bourgeois would take seventy-five?"

"Even if he would, I'll not take it." She shook her head. "Absolutely not."

"But I want you to have it. It's doing nothing but sitting there."

"And if Papa loses big?"

"After this last win, he said he's going to stop."

"And how many times has he made that promise?"

Mother stood. "No more arguing. Either you give it to the

Frenchman or I'll give it to the Trostles myself and ask them to pass it on to Monsieur Bourgeois. Besides, I can take the Vanderbilt wedding job and make a good portion of it up."

"You cannot possibly do an entire wedding without Papa knowing about it, and besides, you said the wedding was too much work. You said you were getting headaches."

"I'll be fine."

Flossie rose. "No, Mother. What if the painting doesn't sell?"

"It will."

"What if it doesn't?"

"Then at least I'll know I did everything I could to help." She hesitated. "Botheration, I can't get it for you now, not with your father home, but I'll bring it to you tomorrow."

"I really don't like this, Mother. Let's just forget the whole thing."

"Since you'll be at work, I'll go to Klausmeyer's and put it inside your brown leather boots. Now, you'd best get going. It's late enough as it is."

Looping her hand through Flossie's elbow, Mother all but pushed her out the door.

CHAPTER

35

Ever since Miss Jayne has been here, she's been putting questions under plates, organizing games in the parlor, and painting portraits of the boarders. Now that the chapel is complete and she's home in the evenings, she's doing it all again. This time she's painting Mrs. Holliday's portrait. I'd forgotten how much of a disruption she is. I won't be able to include that aspect of Miss Jayne's personality in my column. No one would believe it.

Still struggling to write his satire each week, Reeve had put together quite a collection of notes about Miss Jayne.

Try as I might, I can't seem to separate Marylee and Miss Jayne in my mind. At first, I'd only planned to use Miss Jayne as inspiration. Now, however, I find I study her constantly and she never disappoints. Every night she does something that gives me an idea for the story.

Miss Love peeked into Reeve's room.

"Am I disturbing you?" She glanced at the papers on his desk.

Having heard the numerous conversations between her and Miss Jayne, he knew her much better than he'd ever known any woman—other than Mrs. Dinwiddie—and the same went for Miss Jayne. But neither one knew it.

"Not at all." He returned his pen to its holder, then covered his notes with a blank piece of paper.

She looked about his room, her gaze touching on Cat, who licked her paws and smoothed her whiskers. "Mrs. Klausmeyer knows about your stray."

"Yes. She's upped my rent."

"Oh, my. You might not be able to help us, then."

He leaned against the back of his chair. "Help you with what?"

"A collection. Mrs. Trostle started one up since Miss Jayne's a bit short of the deposit Monsieur Bourgeois is asking of her."

Straightening his leg, he pulled a handful of coins from his pocket. "A bit short? According to Mrs. Trostle, she's an entire month's wages short. Passing a hat amongst us won't raise the twenty-five dollars she needs."

"All the same, every little bit helps."

He counted out fifty cents, and handed it to her.

Her eyes lit with surprise. "That's very generous of you."

"It's a foolhardy thing she's doing." He returned the remaining coins to his pocket.

Miss Love stiffened.

He held up his hand. "Just my opinion, but in my experience, an agent earns his percentage after the piece is sold, not before."

"And what experience do you have with agents?"

Threading his fingers together, he rested them against his stomach. "None."

She gave him a knowing look. "That's what I thought."

He tilted his head. "You don't like me very much, do you, Miss Love?"

She tugged down her cuffs. "I don't like your articles about the New Woman."

"But you're a schoolteacher, not a New Woman."

"My roommate's a New Woman and, therefore, I take it personally when you say all those things about her."

Of late, he found he didn't really think of Miss Jayne as a New Woman. Even though she called herself one, she didn't entirely fit the mold, at least not the mold presented on the lecture platforms and in print. She didn't have a chip on her shoulder. She didn't malign men or call them tyrants. She didn't argue that his gender's only desire was to make women cower, cringe, and be helplessly dependent, always ministering to man's wants, whims, and fancies. Not once had he heard her even hint that men were selfish, violent brutes greedy for power, or that they wished only to have the companionship of an inferior rather than one who was his equal. No, she wasn't a New Woman, she was simply a naive girl trying to make her way in a man's world. His arguments were not with her.

"I'm not talking about her specifically," he said. "Just the New Woman in general."

"But there are no generalities. When you write those articles, you are talking about Miss Jayne and many of my other friends." With a glance to the side, she took a step back. "In any event, I'm sorry to have bothered you. Thank you for your contribution."

She flounced down the hall toward her room. He sighed, knowing he'd just wasted fifty cents, for Miss Jayne would never be able to afford Bourgeois' fee.

CHAPTER

36

Out of all the Tiffany Girls, Lulu Sturtevant was the quietest. She didn't style her hair. She didn't wear any jewelry. She didn't visit or interact. She simply numbered manila carbon copies and cut them out. Sometimes Flossie even forgot the girl was there.

She wasn't forgetting today, for Mrs. Driscoll had asked her to help cut glass. Lulu took the same seriousness to glass cutting as she had taken to her previous assignments, and by the end of the day she was cutting two pieces for every one of Flossie's.

Now that the chapel was finished and had finally opened at the fair, the Women's Department had been working on windows commissioned by churches. Their current window was based on a thirteenth-century painting by Pietro Perugino. Mr. Tiffany had returned from Chicago to briefly check on things here and had taken particular interest in this project, for he planned to make Joseph of Arimathea look like his own father.

"I'll be sugared," he said, his lisp pronounced. "Look how much you ladies accomplished today."

"It was because of Miss Sturtevant," Nan said. "Look how much she cut—and in just one day." With a wave of her hand, Nan indicated the robe of the pious woman, the white shroud Christ lay on, and the burgundy folds of Joseph's cloak. "And did you see this?" She pointed to a piece of reddish-purple glass that held a dramatic swirl of black pigment. "Look how she cut the piece so the swirl of the glass looks like the swirl of Joseph's hem."

Mr. Tiffany bent over, inspecting the piece. "Excellent work. Just excellent."

Color high, Lulu somehow managed to look him in the eye. He was so generous with his praise of her, but he didn't so much as greet Flossie. It was the first time since she'd been there that they hadn't exchanged pleasantries.

He might not have realized his slight, but Nan did, and she gave Flossie a triumphant glare when he left. Turning away, Flossie continued to cut her pieces. She'd also worked on Joseph's cloak and had positioned her templates so the peculiarities of the glass caused the garment to appear as if it bunched and twisted.

She'd said nothing, however. It was Lulu's first day to cut glass and the girl never received any notice whatsoever. Flossie wouldn't begrudge her the attention. A moment later, however, she couldn't help but feel a pang of resentment when Lulu reached over and began to start on Flossie's stack since there was no more glass in her own.

CHAPTER

37

Flossie stepped into the art gallery, light streaming through its front window. The newly applied BOURGEOIS' ART GALLERY made an arch across the window, the letters backward from this angle. The scent of beeswax, linseed oil, and vinegar testified that the paneled walls had recently been polished. There was no furniture, only a barren floor and gleaming walls. Framed artwork wrapped in brown paper lay propped against its perimeter. Scrawled across the papers were names such as Audubon, Granger, Jayne, and Cloudman.

Her heart skipped a beat. Jayne. Right there between two great American artists. She still couldn't believe Monsieur Bourgeois had agreed to accept her painting when she'd been short the deposit by twenty-two dollars and change.

"Mademoiselle."

Turning, she smiled. The petite Frenchman pulled a jacket over his shirtsleeves, though he had no tie or waistcoat beneath it. Even still, his black hair was in perfect order, a fine complement to his dark skin and eyes.

"I caught you in the middle of working." She clutched her reticule with both hands. "Did I misunderstand what time I was to call?"

"Not at all. The fault is mine. I'm afraid the time got away from me." He looked around. "I'd offer you a seat, but I regret to say I have none. The furniture was due to arrive this morning, but it has yet to make an appearance."

She loved his accent, could listen to it all day long and never grow weary of it.

"It's all right." Opening her reticule, she removed a pouch heavy with coin. "I just came by to give you your fee. It's all there if you'd like to count it. All seventy-seven dollars and thirty cents."

Frowning, he slipped it into his coat pocket. "I know you are a—how do you say it? A New Woman? But I'd expected a man to deliver this on your behalf."

She lifted her chin. "And as I told you before, I take care of my own affairs."

He studied her, his brown eyes unreadable. "I see. Well, New Woman or not, I'd never be so crass as to count coins in front of you."

"Would you count them in front of a man?"

He took her elbow. "That is not for you to worry over."

Stiffening, she carefully withdrew. "I'm afraid I must insist."

"I trust you."

"And if you find I've counted incorrectly?"

He rubbed his jaw. "Have you counted incorrectly?"

"I have not."

"Then that is good enough for me." He took her elbow again. "Now, let me walk you around and tell you how I have envisioned everything."

For the next twenty minutes they circled the room. He told her which types of paintings would hang in what sections. Where he planned to place the seating. Who he thought would attend. And then he showed her a sketch of the invitations he was having embossed. He even unwrapped Audubon's painting to let her have a peek. "It's a barred owl."

A brown owl in a threatening pose with wings arched back screeched at a squirrel who'd invaded his tree limb.

"Exquisite," she said. "Look at the bark, and the fuzziness of the squirrel's tail. His attention to detail is simply incredible."

"Quite so." He wrapped it back up.

"Are there any other woman artists being displayed?" she asked.

"There are not. You are my only female, but that shall be our little secret. I think it best not to put any barriers in front of the buyers. Let them fall in love with the painting the way I did. When they are all vying to purchase it, only then will I reveal your true identity."

She wrapped the ribbons of her reticule's handle about her finger. "I'm very eager to see it up and on the wall with the others. When can I come back?"

He waved his index finger in a negative motion. "*Non, non.* I don't allow the artists to come by in advance. It is a rule. Otherwise, they tell me they want me to move their painting to here and someone else's to there." He took her hand in his. "You must trust me, *ma chère.* I will make sure your work is displayed to perfection. We will see you on opening night, but not a moment before. Promise me you will do as I request?"

She nodded. "I understand. And I promise."

"That's a good girl." At the door, he kissed her hand. "I shall see you two weeks from Saturday for the opening. Be sure to wear something beautiful."

"I will. And thank you, Monsieur Bourgeois. For everything." With a tiny wave, she stepped back onto the sidewalk, excited and scared to death all at the same time.

DINING CAR[21]

"'I'll be eating in its fancy dining car and sleeping in an actual berth.'"

CHAPTER

38

The front door slammed and the sound of rapid footfalls hurried toward him. Reeve looked up from his work in time to see Miss Jayne fly by in a blur of navy and white. What was she doing home in the middle of the day? He was on his feet and in the hallway before he even realized he'd moved.

"Has something happened?" he asked, still gripping his pen.

With a hand on her doorknob, she turned to him, eyes bright, color high, smile radiant. The wallop it packed nearly sent him to his knees.

"Guess what?" She hugged herself and gave a little bounce.

"Your painting sold?" He couldn't fathom it, for not only was the gallery not open yet, the picture wasn't of the caliber one would expect to see in an art gallery. Still, he was no art expert, so perhaps he was wrong.

"I'm going to the fair!" A laugh like the jingling of chimes filled the hallway.

"The fair? How? When?"

"Tomorrow!" Throwing her hands wide, she spun in a circle, advancing toward him, her skirt belling out. At the last moment, she stopped a mere foot away and listed to the right.

He reached out and steadied her.

"Elizabeth is very ill and can't go." She covered her mouth, looking like she'd just been caught in the midst of a deadly sin, yet wasn't completely sorry for it. "That sounds horrible. I shouldn't be so thrilled she's sick. And I'm not, truly I'm not, but I can't help being just a little excited because they asked me to go in her stead."

"What's all that ruckus out there?" Mrs. Dinwiddie's voice held the scratchiness of one who'd dozed off in her chair.

"Oh, Mrs. Dinwiddie, guess what?" Miss Jayne raced into the woman's room, took the knitting from her hands, pulled her to her feet, and gave her a giant bear hug. "I'm going to the fair! I'm going to the fair!"

Mrs. Dinwiddie patted Miss Jayne, seemingly more out of reflex than anything else. "What? What's this?"

He returned his pen to his room, then propped a shoulder against Mrs. Dinwiddie's doorframe. Miss Jayne raised the old woman's arm and twirled beneath it as if they were in the middle of a ballroom. Finally, she let go and proceeded to jump. She clapped her hands, she bounced like a bunny, she laughed with unrestraint.

Mrs. Dinwiddie chuckled and, in spite of himself, he found a grin tugging at his mouth.

"I can't believe it." Clasping her hands, Miss Jayne pressed them beneath her chin. "Mr. Tiffany is already there, but he's having a carriage sent for me in the morning which will take me to Grand Central Station where I'll meet up with Nan. From there, I'm to take a Pullman car to Chicago. Can you imagine? A *Pullman*. I'll be eating in its fancy dining car and sleeping in an actual *berth*. I can't even fathom it."

She danced to him, grabbed his hands, pulled him into the room, and spun them in a circle as if they were children. "I have to go pack. What in the world will I wear? I can't wait to tell my parents." She stopped, their hands still clasped, her eyes filling.

"Oh, Reeve, they're going to be so pleased and proud. I'm going to do a demonstration of glass cutting at the Woman's Building. I'll get to see our chapel. I'll get to see my friend's mural in the Manufacturer's Building. Oh, my goodness. How am I going to have time to do all the things I need to do before I leave? I must get busy." She rushed out of the room, then a moment later was grabbing the doorframe and swinging herself back in. "Could you do me the biggest favor, Mr. Wilder? I know you're busy, but it would mean so much. Could you get word to my mother? I'm going to need her help or I'll never be ready in time. Would you mind?"

He found himself shaking his head. "Of course not. I'll be glad to."

"Oh, thank you!" Arms wide, she launched herself at him.

Eyes widening, he stumbled back, but there was no stopping her momentum. She wrapped her arms around his neck, kissed him on the cheek, then raced off to her room before he had a chance to respond.

Every nerve in his body went on alert. The blood in his veins moved so forcefully he could almost feel it. The place on his cheek where her lips had touched tingled.

With a pleased look, Mrs. Dinwiddie shooed him with her hands. "Don't you dare send a message, you go fetch her mother and bring her back post haste or that girl might explode into a thousand different pieces."

His cognitive functions began to operate again. "I don't have time to—"

"Yes, you do. If it means you have to work a little late tonight, so be it. Now, go. And for heaven's sake, don't dawdle."

He was out the door and on the sidewalk before he realized he had no idea where the Jaynes even lived. Turning back around, he reentered the house.

Mrs. Dinwiddie met him halfway down the hall with a piece

of paper in her hand. "Here you are. Their address is on here. Now, hurry."

It wasn't until he'd flagged a cab and had a chance to catch his breath that he realized Miss Jayne had used his Christian name. Even more than the kiss, that shook him to his very core.

"On every side, every horizon, were colossal white palaces, gilded
domes, lofty pillars, decorative statues, and curved bridges."

CHAPTER

39

The train trip Flossie enjoyed so thoroughly brought great distress to Nan, whose stomach could not adjust to the constant motion of the car. When they finally arrived in Chicago and made it to their hotel, darkness had once again fallen. Nan fell into bed. Flossie pulled back the curtains of their window.

Their room overlooked the mile-long Midway Plaisance and the giant Ferris wheel at its center, which had opened the day before. In awe, she watched it turn, its edges gleaming with hundreds of electric lights so bright they hurt her eyes. The wheel was huge, enormous, the grandest thing she'd ever seen. She'd read about it, of course, but seeing it for herself was entirely different.

Lampposts, Japanese lanterns, and spotlights were everywhere, turning night into day. People crowded the Midway's broad walkway from end to end and side to side. Costumed foreigners mingled with sober-clad businessmen and tourists dressed in their best.

Farther down, spectacular white-domed buildings loomed against the dark sky. She couldn't help but think of Columbus, whose discovery of America was being celebrated at this World's Columbian Exposition. Four hundred years ago, he'd expected to find a city of fabulous wealth with sky-kissing temples and gold-tipped spires. He'd been disappointed then, but he wouldn't be disappointed now. For this was more beautiful and more imperial than any city he could have ever imagined. It was indeed the city of his dreams—and of hers.

Flossie touched her fingertips to the cool window, her heart stretching toward the joys that would come with the morning sun.

She rose extra early and slipped out of their room, careful not to wake poor Nan. She crossed to the Madison Street entrance, showed her exhibitor's pass to a tall, handsome Columbian Guard in blue regalia, and then she was in.

She wanted to see the chapel alone and in all its glory before the gates opened to the public. Street cleaners swept away the last bit of debris from the night before, their bristles making a rhythmic *swish-swish-swish* and stirring up clouds of dirt. The midway's queer villages slept behind striped awnings and arched entrances. A thick-set man with a white flowing cloak and enormous straw hat with tassels took a pull on a cigarette and watched her as she passed beneath a viaduct and into the official White City.

Nothing could have prepared her. On every side, every horizon, were colossal white palaces, gilded domes, lofty pillars, decorative statues, and curved bridges. Cutting between these majestic structures was a sapphire-blue waterway—a liquid street—that reflected back to her in twofold the beauty of the marble-like facades.

She had no trouble spotting the Manufacturer's Building. Being the largest building ever erected, it had been touted as the Eighth Wonder of the World. The guidebooks even said the Eiffel Tower could lie flat inside it without ever touching the enveloping structure and still have thousands of feet to spare.

Her circuitous route took her past a set of descending marble steps leading to the water's edge. A half-dozen gondolas bobbed in the lagoon awaiting their first passengers. Gondoliers fresh from Venice lounged about in brigand's leggings and colorful sashes, their broad-brimmed hats shading brown faces and black eyes, their quiet conversations in musical Italian.

Crossing a bridge, she glanced into what looked like a wooded fairy island with winding paths, fragrant bowers, and shadowy glades. A brood of ducks glided out into the water, cutting an arrow-shaped swath across its surface.

The closer she came to the Manufacturer's Building the more it dwarfed her. Climbing its steps to the grand portal, she passed beneath a triumphal arch, then paused at the imposing entrance. She looked behind her, almost expecting to find the celestial city had vanished like an illusion, but the magic spell of its ravishing vista remained unbroken.

"Shallow stairs at the front invited her to approach, their risers covered in mosaics, their designs simple at the bottom but gaining complexity with every step up she took. To her left, a white mosaic lectern stood like an angel, silent and impressive. To her right, an ornate baptismal font rested in an alcove backed with one of their windows."

CHAPTER

40

Under any other circumstance, Flossie would have been captivated by a miniature city inside a building—complete with streets rather than aisles. Instead, she looked up, up, up to the dizzying height of a pendentive dome, and there it was. The mural that Louise and Mr. Cox had painted.

With one hand holding her hat and the other touching her throat, she noted that instead of painting the upper part of the vault, they'd placed female figures in each of the triangular segments dropping down from the four corners of the dome. In one shield-shaped space, a robust woman testing a sword suggested steelworking. For ceramic painting, a graceful girl in blue-and-white drapery decorated a vase. A tall, shapely woman in golden-green robes wielded a carpenter's square to represent building. And in the final pendentive, a maiden of fair complexion held a distaff to symbolize weaving.

Flossie couldn't imagine how on earth Louise was able to paint something all the way up there. It made Flossie's stomach fill with butterflies just thinking about it. Still, their work was breathtaking. All of the literature she'd read only mentioned Mr. Cox's name, but Flossie felt sure Louise would have signed her name alongside his.

Try as she might, though, she was too far away to distinguish anything as tiny as a signature.

When her neck couldn't stand the strain any longer, she lowered her chin and scanned the building until she spotted the clock tower, then headed toward it and the American section of the building. The Tiffany exhibits were not hard to find, for Mr. Tiffany, his father, and Gorham Manufacturing had footed the bill for the entrance to the American pavilion. As such, their names were prominently displayed, their exhibits the first inside the gate.

Grasping the gilt handle of the chapel's door, she opened it and stepped inside, then caught her breath. God's presence filled the place. Didn't matter that it was an exhibit. Didn't matter that no services were held. Didn't matter that there was no pastor or priest. Holiness encompassed every corner, every crevice, and seeped into her very soul.

A peace settled over her, chasing away all the upheaval of coming and going. The sound of her boots on the marble floor echoed as she walked down the aisle between highly polished pews. Shallow stairs at the front invited her to approach, their risers covered in mosaics, their designs simple at the bottom but gaining complexity with every step up she took. To her left, a white mosaic lectern stood like an angel, silent and impressive. To her right, an ornate baptismal font rested in an alcove backed with one of their windows.

Joy rushed through her as she absorbed the full impact of the window—a halo of light and color. The stained glass didn't overwhelm the font, but instead complemented it.

Shaped like a bejeweled globe, the font was the perfect tribute to the Garden of Eden, where innocence once lost had been recaptured and sealed forever by the miracle of baptism.

Another step and she stood before the altar. Pairs of columns made a semicircle around it and her. Multicolored swirls of mosaic climbed up them as if the waves of the stairs had crashed into breakers upon reaching the holy of holies. They supported rounded arches in the shape of concentric rainbows.

Worked into one were Latin words she didn't understand and couldn't pronounce. She'd asked Mr. Tiffany about these words, though, and learned they translated into, *Holy, holy, holy, Lord God Almighty, who was, who is, and who always will be.*

Nearer and nearer the columns drew her, each one more extravagant than the last, all leading to the masterpiece framing the altar. A chef-d'oeuvre of mosaic art, the reredos held an iridescent crown of the King, worshiped by spreading peacocks, the Byzantine symbol for eternal life.

She knew she should pray, should say something profound to her Savior, but no words came. Only awe. And then, thanksgiving.

With a deep breath, she turned around and looked up, taken by the heavy, green glass chandelier hanging overhead. From any angle, it could be viewed as a cross. A halo of white lights encircled its lowest level, bestowing grace and peace to all who passed beneath it.

But as beautiful as it was—all of it—none could compare in her mind to the radiant stained-glass windows that she and the other girls had made. Stepping down the stairs, she returned to the nave, flanked on either side by the windows. Her breathing grew labored. Her eyes pooled. Seeing them in pieces on the easels was nothing like seeing them completed and installed.

The circular *Story of the Cross* shone with resplendence. That one window had required hours and hours of toil. She pictured sweet, quiet Lulu cutting out the paper templates. Her dear friend, Aggie, who never objected to wrapping each piece of glass with foil, hour by hour, day by day. Tens of thousands of pieces she'd wrapped, yet not a word of complaint passed her lips.

She recalled Theresa, with her cherub face and sunny disposition, tracing a cartoon with her stylus for so long that her hands began to stiffen and her fingers began to permanently ache. Darling Louise, before Mr. Cox whisked her away, had placed Theresa's carbon copy beneath a sheet of glass and painted the doubly grooved lead lines onto it. And, of course, Nan had pulled the colored glass, then given the pieces to Flossie for cutting.

Each of the girls had a part. No part more important than the other. And each of the parts had been arranged exactly as the designer wanted them.

Standing in the center of the nave, she turned in a complete circle, savoring glorious window after glorious window. Because of twelve girls, millions of people would experience the fruit of their labor, the blessing of Tiffany's creations. Their signatures might not be on the bottom, but each one of them had signed them with their very soul.

BYZANTINE GATE TO RUSSIAN SECTION [24]

"Russian women had produced its intricate design by burning
out the oak and overlaying it with gold leaf."

CHAPTER

41

The wide front door of the Woman's Building clicked shut behind Flossie. A Columbian Guard in a smart blue uniform glanced at her, then tugged the rim of his cap. "Ma'am," he said, his Southern drawl charming her at once. "Welcome to the Woman's Building." Like all the guards, he was much taller than average, his brown eyes missing nothing. "If there's anything you need, you just give me a holler."

"Thank you, and actually, maybe you'll be able to point me in the right direction. I'm a Tiffany Girl and here to do a demonstration. Before I do, though, I'd wanted to take a quick peek at our display."

"Yes, ma'am. Your demonstration will be upstairs at the far end in the Assembly Room. Some fellows came earlier and set everything up for you. As for the Tiffany Girls' stained-glass exhibit, it's right around the corner. Follow me and I'll show you."

When they reached the exhibit, she sucked in her breath. "Oh, my. Would you look at that? I didn't realize Mr. Tiffany was going to include that in the display." She turned to the guard, her spirits buoyant. "I made that."

She pointed to a paper pattern she'd outlined with a stylus. It was one of the first cartoons she'd traced way back in January.

"You painted that?" he asked, referring to the cartoon hanging beside it.

"No, no. Miss McDowell painted the cartoon. I made a carbon copy of it onto manila paper."

"Is that right?"

She nodded.

"Well, I have to make my rounds," he said. "But if I can, I'll poke my head in for a look-see at your presentation upstairs."

"Wonderful. I'll watch for you, Mr. . . . ?"

"Scott. Hunter Scott."

She smiled. "I'm Florence Jayne. It's nice to meet you."

"Likewise, ma'am." He again tugged on the rim of his cap, then headed back to the main atrium, stepping aside to allow a young couple into the room.

It was all Flossie could do not to jump up and down and tell them she'd made the paper pattern. Instead, she held her tongue and listened to their reactions.

"Look at this, Cullen. I didn't know women even made stained-glass windows."

"I'm sure they don't do any of the heavy work," he replied. "Just the painting and that sort of thing."

"There's supposed to be a presentation of it upstairs in about fifteen minutes. Perhaps we can go to it?"

"If you'd like."

Flossie opened her mouth to set the man straight, but they'd already turned around and sauntered through an elaborate Byzantine gate. Russian women had produced its intricate design by burning out the oak and overlaying it with gold leaf. She shook her head. So much to see and no time to see it.

Hurrying from the room, she made her way upstairs, fully expecting to find Nan. Instead she found Mr. Tiffany examining sections of glass on a table. A line of plate glass easels in various stages of completeness leaned against a wall of windows, faced by rows of chairs.

"Hello, sir," she said.

He turned. "Miss Jayne, it's always a pleasure."

"Thank you. I just came from your exhibit downstairs and it's quite impressive."

"It's you ladies who are impressive." He looked behind her. "Where's Miss Upton?"

Flossie looked over her shoulder and onto the gallery. "I'm not sure."

"Well, you'll have to carry the presentation, then. I plan to sit in the audience."

A trio of women entered and took some seats at the front.

Flossie crossed to Mr. Tiffany and lowered her voice. "They would much prefer to hear from you, I'm sure."

He gave an adamant shake of his head. "I never speak in front of crowds. Besides, this is about what ladies do, so I'll leave it to you."

She flushed, realizing, of course, that he'd be naturally shy about his lisp. She kept forgetting he had one. They spent the next few minutes deciding on a course of action. By the time they'd finished, quite a crowd had accumulated.

Stepping to the side, Mr. Tiffany remained standing near the wall.

Flossie cleared her throat. "Thank you so much for coming today. My name is Florence Jayne and I'm a Tiffany Girl."

Starting at one end of the plate glass sheets, she spoke about the making of Tiffany glass in the factory, then explained each step of the window-making process, from the cartoon to the cutting of glass.

"You can see here on the cartoon, Miss McDowell has painted leaves on a tree in multiple shades of green." She picked up a piece of light-green rippled glass and held it up to the window. "Do you see how the wrinkles and ripples in this piece are suggestive of leaves ruffled by the wind?"

Nan rushed into the room, her footfalls loud on the wooden floor as she hurried toward the front. She'd almost reached the staging area when Mr. Tiffany placed a hand on her arm and gave her a gentle shake of his head.

"I'd thought to take a short cut," she whispered, her voice carrying. "So I crossed over into the Wooded Island, then couldn't find a bridge on the other side."

People glanced at her. Mr. Tiffany kept his attention on Flossie while gently holding Nan back. He gave Flossie an encouraging nod.

"Yes, well, as I was saying . . ." Flossie held the glass back up to the light. "The texture is perfect, but the color of the glass doesn't quite match the one on the cartoon. So at that point, the selector goes back and looks for another one."

Mr. Tiffany directed Nan to the table of glass sheets. She quickly picked up a green piece, held it up to the light, then handed it to Flossie.

"This one is a much better color," Flossie said. "But the ripples in the glass are spaced too far apart."

Nan chose another.

"Miss Upton here is one of our best selectors, as you can see from this last piece she picked, but sometimes it can take hours or even weeks before the perfect tint and texture are found."

The audience murmured. At the entryway the guard she'd spoken to earlier leaned against the archway, one foot crossed over his ankle.

"At this point, the selector—in this case, Miss Upton—hands the piece to the cutter, who in this case is me. Now, I know many of you think cutting glass is too mannish for a woman to do, but you want to know a secret?" She glanced to the right and left, then leaned toward them. "The weaker sex is not as weak as most assume." She quickly released the cuff at her right wrist, pushed up her sleeve, and flexed her arm. An impressive muscle sprang to life.

Some women tittered and fanned themselves. Others clapped in appreciation. The couple she'd seen downstairs turned very red. The Columbian Guard lifted one corner of his mouth in the beginnings of a grin.

She buttoned her cuff. "I've been cutting glass for months now and I'll admit it was difficult at first, but I've become quite proficient." She began to demonstrate, then looked up. "If you'd like to gather round so you can see better, feel free to come forward."

The audience rose and huddled around her as they watched. Nan continued to select glass and hand it to her, but it was Flossie the spectators interacted with. When the presentation was almost over, she sent everyone back to their seats with a promise of a wonderful surprise.

"Now, as you know, the genius behind all this glass is Mr. Louis Comfort Tiffany and you might not realize it, but he's standing right over there."

There were gasps as people craned to have a look at him.

"He won't be taking any questions, but perhaps I could convince him to come and make a few selections for me to cut so you can see the real master at work."

Without a word, he approached the table. Even Flossie became lost in watching him as he held up glass after glass before settling on a magnificent piece for a swath of sunset sky, all apricot and salmon pink and the palest lavender.

"We call this streaky glass," she said. "And only Mr. Tiffany would be able to combine as many as five colors into one recipe and still make them all compatible."

At the end of the demonstration, they received a standing

ovation. Mr. Tiffany gave her a wink. She glanced at Nan, then waved her to the front. Instead of joining them, Nan stood to the side, her posture stiff and her neck corded. Flossie didn't have time to consider what was wrong, for the crowd surrounded her, all talking at once.

"Reeve's editor took a puff on his pipe. 'Why don't you see
if you can find some of those Tiffany Girls.'"

CHAPTER

42

Looks like the Lead Glaziers and Glass Cutters' Union is about to come to an agreement with the manufacturers." Reeve's editor took a puff on his pipe. "Why don't you see if you can find some of those Tiffany Girls and see what they think about that."

"Tiffany Girls?" Reeve stared at his boss. "What is it exactly you'd want me to ask them?"

"Well, for starters, they finished Tiffany's chapel. You can ask them about that, and I'm sure they'll also have plenty to say about the men coming back because, after all, once they do, Tiffany won't need the women anymore, right?"

Reeve had been wondering that same thing. Miss Jayne had returned from the fair last week, but he didn't really want to ask her if she expected to lose her job. It somehow didn't seem right.

Ulrich picked up a piece of paper and fed it into his typewriter. "By the way, your boardinghouse satire has brought in a great many new women readers, so you need to ramp up the romance between Marylee and the bibliomaniac."

Reeve tightened his jaw. "Marylee and the bibliomaniac are not attracted to each other."

"'Course they are, and it's time to capitalize on it. Women love that kind of thing." Hitting the carriage return lever, he slid the roller to the far left margin.

Reeve looked at the toes of his shoes. The house on Georgia Avenue was still for sale. The first thing he did every Sunday was check the paper to see if it was listed. He had a ways to go, though, before he had two hundred dollars. "What about that raise I was to get if the boardinghouse column was successful?"

"What about it?"

"I'd say it's been successful, so how about it?"

Ulrich scratched his neck. "You'll ramp up the romance?"

Reeve closed his eyes. "If I have to."

"You have to." Ulrich moved his pipe to the corner of his mouth. "The raise will be reflected next time you collect wages, but I'll expect to see a new development in this week's submission along with something on the Tiffany Girls by next week."

Releasing a breath, Reeve answered in the affirmative and let himself out.

CHAPTER

43

Y ou're up early." Flossie peeked into Mr. Wilder's room. It was still as barren as ever, though Cat was curled up on his bed.

"I have a new assignment I'm working on." He took a blank piece of paper and used it to cover up whatever he was writing.

She stepped into the room, crossed to his bed, and ran a hand down the cat. "I brought you something from the fair."

Twisting around, he stood. "I'm sorry?"

She straightened. "I brought you something." Extending her hand, she opened her palm to reveal a little ball of brown paper tied in twine.

He stood completely still, staring at her offering. "What is it?"

"Open it."

"Right now? You want me to open it right now?"

"Right now."

Swallowing, he took the ball and undid the bow. Inside nested a tiny metal figurine of a cat curled up much the way Cat was now, with its head on its paws and its tail wrapped around itself.

He gave a slow shake of his head. "Is this Cat?"

"It is."

A flush rose up his neck and face, his gaze darting about the room. Fumbling, he pulled out his desk drawer and dropped the figurine inside, before quickly closing it.

She bit her lower lip. "It's a decoration. You're supposed to put it out."

"Oh!" He jerked open the drawer, grabbed the figurine, then slapped it onto his desk.

Reaching around him, she moved it from the center of his desk to the right hand corner next to his clock. "There. Now it won't be in your way when you work."

"Right." He backed up a step. "Thank you."

She closed the drawer for him. "You're welcome. I brought a little something back for everyone. I got your piece from a toy maker in the Manufacturer's Building. I thought of you immediately when I saw it."

"You did?"

"I did."

He shifted his weight from one foot to the other. She ran her finger down the side of his desk looking at the writings he'd covered up. "Are you working on an article?"

"Sort of." He stepped between her and the desk.

"Sort of?"

He rubbed his forehead. "Aren't you going to be late for work?"

She glanced at her watch pin. "Not yet, but I probably ought to head out, anyway. I just wanted to give that to you. Everyone else already has theirs and I didn't want you to feel left out."

His fidgeting stopped. His gaze veered to the figurine. "Thank you. No one's ever . . . I mean . . ."

Her heart squeezed. Every once in a while her father would go out of town, but he'd always returned with a little something in his bag for her. Had no one ever done that for Mr. Wilder?

He blew out a breath, then checked his pocket watch.

With a small smile, she stepped into the hall. "Well, I'd best be going."

He followed her to the doorway. "Good day, then, and, um, thank you."

"You're welcome. I'll see you this evening." She walked down the hall and out the front door feeling his stare the entire time.

"The Moorish women on the Midway Plaisance
clicked the castanets when they danced."

CHAPTER
44

Reeve flipped through the pages of notes he'd taken on Miss Jayne. Since she was the inspiration for Marylee, he'd taken to watching her every move during dinner.

We had corn on the cob with our meal. Miss Jayne ate hers like a typewriter—one row at a time. That's the incorrect way, of course. You're supposed to turn the cob like a wheel and eat it all the way around bit by bit.

He skimmed down further.

Someone else is putting questions beneath the plate across from Miss Jayne. I have no idea who. Tonight she was given the question, "If you could ask Noah one thing, what would it be?" She wanted to know how he could tell the two mosquitos were male and female. Mrs. Trostle was quite shocked by the subject matter.

He rubbed his forehead. Adam didn't need to tell the difference. God sent the animals to him.

Miss Jayne organized a World's Fair night in the parlor. Everyone was supposed to bring something that would have gone in one of

*the fair buildings. Ever since she's returned, her stories at supper
have been fascinating, so I made an exception and went to the
parlor. Only to watch, of course, not to participate.*

*Miss Jayne brought a set of wooden castanets which she'd
purchased while she was there. When it was her turn, she strapped
them to her fingers and said that the Moorish women on the
Midway Plaisance clicked the castanets when they danced and
wore nothing but a finely embroidered bolero—no blouse or corset
underneath, only skin and chemise. Their skirts then hung from
their hips instead of their waist.*

*Oyster, rogue that he is, asked her to explain the dance, then
pretended to misunderstand until, finally, he beseeched her to
demonstrate. I'd fully expected her to refuse. Instead, she stood,
lifted her arms, closed her eyes, and began to sway as if a snake
charmer had hypnotized her with his haunting tune. First her
head, then her shoulders, waist, and hips undulated—all in time
to the castanets snapping at her fingertips. By the time she finished
I could scarcely breathe.*

He squeezed his knees. It was his last entry, and none of his notes
showed him how to write a love story between Marylee and the
bibliomaniac. He had no idea how to proceed. He only knew his
notes were far too personal and specific.

If he hadn't wanted the money so badly, he'd tell his chief to find
someone else to write the column. But he did want the money, more
than anything he'd ever wanted before. And desperate times required
desperate measures. Gathering up his papers, he tucked them into
the back of his drawer, then made his way to the parlor.

"That had left Miss Jayne without a partner for The Board Game of
Old Maid, and Reeve with no choice but to pair up with her."

CHAPTER

45

Reeve flicked the spinner, sending its arrow into a whirl. Mr. Trostle had been called to Milwaukee on business, so Mrs. Trostle was packing his bags, and the Hollidays had retired early. That had left Miss Jayne without a partner for The Board Game of Old Maid, and Reeve with no choice but to pair up with her. They needed a two to advance to *They Meet*—the initial square all players had to reach with an exact spin. It slowed to a stop on the number five.

"Too bad," Nettels said.

Swatting the air, Miss Jayne gave Reeve a reassuring smile. "It's all right. Once we get through this first part, I'm sure we'll sail through the rest of the board."

He hoped so. This was the dumbest game he'd ever played. For the next three rotations, he spun everything except a two. Meanwhile, Oyster and Miss Love landed on *Pleased With Each Other* and advanced three spaces, then *Ride A Bicycle Built For Two*. Nettels and Mrs. Dinwiddie progressed to *Go On A Picnic*.

Reeve handed the spinner to Miss Jayne.

"No, no," she said. "I'm a terrible spinner."

"I insist."

After a brief hesitation, she spun.

"Two!" Miss Love exclaimed, clapping her hands. "Good for you, Flossie."

Miss Jayne kept her attention on the board, refusing to meet his eye. Reaching across, he scooted their piece to *They Meet*. Nettels landed on *Misunderstanding. Go back to They Meet*.

"Oh, no!" Miss Love gave Mr. Nettels a sympathetic look. "You're going to be as far back as Mr. Wilder."

Miss Jayne stiffened. Reeve leaned back in his chair. In the next spin, Oyster and Miss Love sailed over a penalty square and on to *Little Brother Takes a Hand*. Miss Jayne passed Reeve the spinner. He flicked the arrow. Six.

"Look at that, everyone!" Miss Jayne swept up their piece. "The highest number of spaces. One, two, three, f-four . . ." Biting her lip, she counted the last two spaces silently.

Nettels snorted again.

Uncongenial. Go Back 3 Spaces.

Without a word, Miss Jayne moved their token backward, again avoiding eye contact. Nettels and Dinwiddie landed on *Rushes Matters—Go To Proposal*, which allowed them to skip a good portion of the board, thank Caesar's ghost. With any luck, they'd win and put him out of his misery.

But in the next three rounds Nettels kept landing on *Papa Says No—Go Back To Proposal*, keeping the game very much alive. Reeve and Miss Jayne *Fall In Love At First Sight, Give Each Other Presents*, and *Go To The Opera* while Oyster struggled to keep up and Nettels eventually got past Papa, only to become stuck at the end where the couple had to have another exact spin. Finally, they all caught up to Nettels, everyone's pawns crowding onto one square.

What Shall the Answer Be? Exact Spin.

Reeve flicked the arrow. With a three, they'd land on *Yes*, and live happily ever after. A four, they'd land on *No* and Miss Jayne would become an old maid.

Round and round the spinner turned. Miss Jayne clasped her hands in her lap, her fingers pressed tightly together. The spinner slowed. *Two . . . five . . . one . . .* Slower. *Threeeeeeeee . . .*

He held his breath.

Four. The tip of the arrow crept into the green pie-shaped section marked with a four. After a slight hesitation, he reached into the center of the spiral path they'd just traversed, picked up their piece, and set it on a big red heart with *N-O* printed in its center.

He turned to Miss Jayne. "I'm sorry."

Lifting her eyes, she started to reach for him, then withdrew. "Please don't be. I very much enjoyed being your partner. It's not how the game ends, but the pleasure of taking a journey together."

He pushed his chair back, then what she said began to permeate. It wasn't the destination, but the journey. His attention swiveled to the board.

They Meet. Exact Spin.

Uncongenial. Go Back 3 Spaces.

Pleased With Each Other. Advance 3 Spaces.

Misunderstanding. Go Back To They Meet.

He raised the corners of his mouth. There it was. The entire love story. Mapped out right before him. From the troubles they have meeting to getting the proposal past Papa to the questionable ending—and all the ups and downs in between.

Turning back to her, he gave her a nod. "I believe you're right, Miss Jayne. I do believe you're right."

Her eyes brightened. Her shoulders lifted. "I'm glad, and I'm happy to be your partner anytime."

He glanced around the table. "Am I excused?"

Mrs. Dinwiddie gave an affectionate shake of her head. "You are excused."

With a nod and a good night, he retreated to his room to do his level best at constructing a romance between Marylee and the bibliomaniac.

CHAPTER

46

The last person Flossie expected to see in her bedroom doorway was Mr. Wilder. The rest of the family at 438 were frequent visitors, but Mr. Wilder had never so much as gone past his room.

She sat with her back to a yellow lamp, her feet propped in her bookshelf. Placing a marker in *Pride and Prejudice*, she set her feet down and placed the book her grandmother had given her onto the bookshelf next to the rest of her Jane Austen collection. "Hello."

Dragging a hand through his hair, he looked about her room, reminding her of Mr. Darcy when he'd gone to profess his love to Elizabeth but was unable to spit out the words. Of course, Mr. Wilder had no such feelings for her, but his discomfort was palpable nonetheless.

Cracking his knuckles, he took a deep breath. "I was wondering if you could do me a favor."

A favor? "Certainly," she said. "How can I help you?"

Slipping his hands into his pockets, he looked at the toes of his shoes. "Well, it's just that I've been assigned a piece for the newspaper about the Tiffany Girls and their reactions to the upcoming culmination of the Glass Cutters' strike. I was wondering if, perhaps, you could introduce me to some of the ladies you work with?"

"I see." She folded her hands in her lap. "This is certainly a departure from the point of view you normally present, isn't it?"

"Yes."

"Well, I could ask them to meet with you, but I'm not sure when they'd have the time. We work solid during the day and after the long hours we worked getting the chapel ready, everyone is anxious to leave come quitting time."

"So you don't think they'd stay and talk to me?"

"I could ask them, but I'm not optimistic."

His shoulders drooped.

She slowly straightened. "Wait, I have an idea."

He looked at her sideways. "What kind of idea?"

She stood. "Mr. Tiffany is holding a reception in celebration of the awards his chapel has won so far at the fair. It's this Saturday at the San Remo—a magnificent hotel on Central Park West. It would be perfect. He's invited all of us Tiffany Girls."

"A reception? You mean, like a ball?"

"Yes."

He rubbed the back of his neck. "And you're going?"

"Of course I'm going." She nodded. "I wouldn't miss it. None of us would. Well, actually, there are a couple of girls who don't have anything appropriate to wear and don't feel as if they'll fit in." She shrugged. "Truth be told, none of us will fit in, but I still want to go. I've lent out dresses to the Tiffany Girls who are similar in size to me, and the rest are remaking gowns they already have."

He shook his head. "*The World* would never be able to secure an invitation to that."

"The paper won't need to secure an invitation. Mr. Tiffany told us to give him the name of a guest we'd like to bring. The other girls are bringing family members. Out of my family here at 438, I'd thought to submit Mr. Oyster's name."

He stiffened. "Oyster?"

"Well, yes. I didn't want to go alone, naturally, nor take my father when I couldn't take Mother as well. I haven't yet submitted Mr. Oyster's name, though. Something kept holding me back."

He glanced up and down the hall, then approached her, lowering his voice. "You must be very careful not to encourage Oyster. He doesn't, um, speak respectfully about the fair sex, and his motives for the charm he exudes are not completely honorable."

She shooed his words away with a wave of her hand. "Don't be silly. I've every confidence he'd behave as a gentleman with me."

He clasped her arm. "You must heed me on this, Miss Jayne. There are things I know about him that you don't."

Frowning, she shook her head. "I won't hear any ill talk of him. He's part of our family."

He gave her a gentle shake. "He's not part of your family. None of us at 438 are part of your family."

"Yes you are, and he's been nothing but the consummate gentleman in my presence."

"Which is what makes him so dangerous."

She rolled her eyes. "Everyone is dangerous in your sight. Even I'm a danger to myself, according to you. But, we digress. Would you like to go to the reception or not? It would give you a chance to interview the girls and it would give me an escort for the evening. Either way, it makes no difference to me."

"And if I don't go, you'll submit Oyster's name?"

"I imagine I will."

"Then I'll go. What time?"

"You're squeezing my arm."

He immediately released it. "What time?"

"The ball won't start until almost midnight. All of the wealthy set will be attending dinners at the homes of their society friends and only afterward will they head to the hotel. I'd thought to leave here about eleven thirty. It's a good twenty-five minute walk."

"We'll leave at eleven forty-five and I'll have a carriage."

She blinked in surprise. "That's not necessary. It's not as if we're real members of society."

"Will we be entering through the front door?"

"Oh, yes. Certainly."

"Then I'll have a carriage." With that he spun around and returned to his room.

She remained in the middle of the floor, her arm gently throbbing from the heat of his clasp, her heart lifting at the thought of him hiring a carriage for her. Of a sudden, she didn't want to wear what she'd originally planned on wearing. Moving to her wardrobe, she opened the door and contemplated the gowns inside.

CHAPTER
47

Reeve paced the parlor slapping his gloves into his hand and drawing them through, only to repeat the process. The entire household had stayed up to see Miss Jayne in all her finery. All except for the Trostles. Mr. Trostle was still in Milwaukee and Mrs. Trostle had gone to visit her sister.

Oyster, Nettels, and Holliday played cards at a table. Mrs. Dinwiddie softly snored in a rocker, her knitting forgotten. Miss Love was in Flossie's room and Mrs. Holliday curled up on the couch rereading the previous columns of the *Merry Maid of Mumford Street*.

He was surprised no one had suspected he was I. D. Claire, but perhaps it wasn't so strange after all. Other than Marylee, none of the boarders in his column were anything like the ones at Klausmeyer's. Besides, boardinghouse satires were in every corner theater, in a plethora of magazines, and in several books.

Mrs. Dinwiddie had hinted to him of her suspicions when they were alone, but the others had only seen what they expected to see, though they had asked him if he'd known who I. D. Claire was. He'd carefully told them that only Claire's editor knew the writer's identity.

He adjusted his tie and new black jacket. He'd not only

had the *New York World* pay for his clothing and carriage, but he'd demanded a good deal more money for the article. Ulrich, salivating at the prospect of reporting on the event, met Reeve's terms so long as he wrote something about who was there and what the ladies were wearing.

Reeve checked his pocket watch. It had taken him a mere twenty minutes to dress. Miss Jayne, however, had started preparing in the early afternoon. Finally, a commotion in the hall pulled him up short.

Miss Love rushed into the parlor. "Just wait until you see her."

Mrs. Dinwiddie gave two short snorts, then woke up. "What? Where? What's happening?"

"It's Flossie." Miss Love helped the elderly woman to her feet. "She's all dressed and ready. Just look."

Miss Jayne rounded the corner. Reeve's breath left him in a whoosh. The other three men surged to their feet.

A gown of palest pink hugged her figure, the neckline dipping just enough to titillate but not reveal anything of import. Spangles dotted her bodice, catching the light like a sprinkling of fairy dust. Long white gloves rode up and over her elbows, leading his eye to a patch of creamy skin partially covered by pale-pink bows of satin draping over her shoulders.

Yards and yards of black hair swept up the back of her head like a series of ocean waves, the uppermost crashing back into itself, piled high and held at bay with a tiara of filigree silver.

He had an insane urge to bow and kiss her ring finger. "You're late."

"You're ravishing." Oyster rushed past him and took her hand to his lips. "My dear Miss Jayne, I am completely besotted. You will outshine even the Astors."

"My, oh, my." Mrs. Dinwiddie placed a hand against her heart. "What a sight you are. I had no idea you had so much hair. How long is it?"

Miss Love leaned close to the woman's ear. "It goes nearly to the floor when she lets it out completely."

He swallowed hard.

"You are indeed enchanting." Mr. Nettels cleared his throat. "I daresay you will be the belle of the ball."

Reeve sighed. There they went again. Telling her how special, how beautiful, how much better she was than everyone else. And although she was a glorious creature, they were on their way to a gathering of the richest of the rich. People whose spangles would be made of diamonds, not reflectors. Whose headpieces would be made of real silver, not nickel. Whose necks would be draped with jewels, not a piece of velvet.

Wasn't simply being Flossie Jayne enough? Did she have to be Flossie Jayne the Unflawed Beauty of the Century?

Her eyes found his, their depths deep and dangerous. "I'm sorry I'm late," she said.

"It was worth the wait." And it was, although he hadn't meant to add to the already inflated opinions of the others.

She gave him a soft smile. "Thank you."

Shouldering Oyster aside, Reeve held out his arm. "Shall we?"

She laid her gloved arm atop Reeve's. The courtliness of her gesture took him off guard, for he'd expected her to tuck a hand beneath the crook of his elbow. He swallowed again. This gentle riding of her arm upon his was in many ways more intimate.

Trapping her fingertips with his, he led her to the entry hall, adjusting his step to compensate for the train that dragged behind her and slowed her steps. At the door, he draped her shoulders with a light wrap, the nerve endings on his fingers shooting sensations up his arms each time he brushed her skin.

Pulling in a deep breath, he tugged on his gloves and placed a top hat upon his head. He needed to get ahold of himself. They had a long night ahead of them and they'd yet to even make it out the door.

CHAPTER

48

They sat in the unmoving carriage, gas lights from the street providing a modicum of light.

"I guess we should have left earlier." He sat across from her, her skirt and train covering his boots, his trousers, and the floor like a swath of snow. "I didn't think about everyone's carriages arriving at the same time."

She toyed with a silver bracelet on her gloved wrist. "It's all right. It's rather nice to have this calm before the storm."

He'd hardly describe these moments as calm. His breathing was labored. His pulse hammered. And his fingers ached to stroke the skin from the tip of her chin to the edges of her décolletage. "Since I'm to write about who's in attendance and what they are wearing, perhaps you should tell me what to look for. Who to take special note of."

She looked out the window, ducking her head a bit in order to view the sky. Her position gave him an unrestricted view of her long, smooth neck and the skin between it and the bows at her shoulders. "Not yet. If you don't mind, I'd rather just sit and absorb the moment. It's not often I get to dress up and go to the San Remo."

He'd never in his life done such a thing. And with the way she looked, if they didn't discuss something—anything—he'd very likely become as besotted with her as everyone else.

"What about the other Tiffany Girls?" he asked. "Which of them will be there?"

Sighing, she pulled back to center. "My dearest friend at work, Aggie Wilhemson, will be there."

Aggie. He knew of Aggie. Miss Jayne had spoken of her often, at least to Miss Love. What he hadn't known was her last name. "Tell me about Miss Wilhemson."

"Well, let's see. She's six feet tall. Very fair and noble looking. She's from Sweden and is engaged to a forty-year-old butcher."

He lifted his brows. "Six feet tall?"

"She really is. I know you think I'm exaggerating, but I'm not."

He vaguely remembered a tall girl the day the men were picketing. "Okay. Who else?"

She told him of the girls, giving anecdotes about each. Instead of distracting him from his disquieting thoughts, her undivided attention made it worse. He very rarely had her all to himself, but to have her alone and with nothing else to look at, he found himself fascinated with the way her dimple flashed when she spoke. The way her hands did as much talking as her mouth. The way her lower lip was just slightly fuller than her upper one.

Of a sudden he realized she wasn't talking anymore.

He shifted his gaze to the window. "We're moving."

"Yes. We've been moving for a while now." Her voice was soft, husky.

He didn't dare look at her. Instead, he nodded. "Good. That's good."

The air in the carriage thickened. He kept his focus on the street. Finally, they pulled up in front of the hotel. A footman whisked open their door and assisted Miss Jayne to the ground. Reeve pressed his head back against the wall of the carriage, took another deep breath, then joined her and escorted her inside.

"Mr. Wilder had been extremely attentive at the beginning of the
evening when Flossie pointed out the Astors, the Vanderbilts,
the Roosevelts, and, of course, the Tiffanys."

Bustle pinchers?" Mr. Wilder asked, his expression stormy. "On the streetcars?"

"Yes." Nan crinkled her brows, her wide forehead accentuated by the clips holding back her long brown hair woven with fresh flowers. "We all suffer because of them."

Suppressing a sigh, Flossie turned her attention to the dancers on the ballroom floor. Eight of the twelve Tiffany Girls had come. Mrs. Driscoll instructed them to sit in chairs in the far, far corner.

Mr. Wilder had been extremely attentive at the beginning of the evening when Flossie pointed out the Astors, the Vanderbilts, the Roosevelts, and, of course, the Tiffanys. He'd glazed over a bit at her descriptions of the gowns, but took notes all the same. He'd then spent the rest of the evening sitting with each Tiffany Girl, asking about her work, her aspirations, the ending of the strike, and how it would affect her. At the moment he was interviewing Nan.

Flossie had known he would be gathering information, she just hadn't realized how much time it would absorb. It was almost three o'clock now and she had yet to dance. She wasn't sure if it was because he couldn't dance, wouldn't dance, or was too busy to dance. Whichever it was, she'd be sorely disappointed if she ended up attending her one and only soiree only to sit on the sidelines the entire evening.

"We're constantly being jostled and crowded by the men." Nan twirled a lock of hair round her finger, her lips forming a coquettish pout.

In stark contrast to the pale pink of Flossie's gown, Nan wore one of black satin, slightly relieved by white. She'd borrowed it from Flossie, and because Nan was the taller of the two, she hadn't been able to pull the sleeves up over her shoulders without the underarms cutting into her.

So she'd left the sleeves off her shoulders, showing a pretty curve of skin, in the 1830s fashion. To hold the gown up, she'd attached two straps of jet beads. Despite herself, Flossie couldn't help but admire the picture Nan made.

"We're subject to all manner of improprieties by gangs of drunken loafers," Nan continued. "You would be shocked to hear some of the things said to me in undertone."

Mr. Wilder's jaw began to tick. His dark evening jacket rested with precision on his broad shoulders, its swallow tails cut square in back instead of in the old oblong shape. The white, double-breasted waistcoat hugged his flat stomach and trim waist.

He turned to Flossie, his expression tight. "Do you experience this as well?"

She lifted one shoulder. "More often than not."

His tone deepened. "You're pinched, groped, and forced into conversation with men you've not been introduced to?"

"I don't converse with them. They do all the talking."

His breathing grew deep. "Why don't you simply sit down?"

"No one offers up their seat."

Mrs. Driscoll tapped Nan and those beside her with her fan. "Sit straight. Mr. Tiffany is coming."

Flossie scanned the room, then spotted him. He looked well enough in his evening garb, but he didn't hold a candle to Mr. Wilder.

"What a sight you ladies make." Placing an arm across his waist, he gave them a formal bow. His abundance of wavy brown hair had been combed to the side. "Has everyone had a chance to dance, I hope?"

Flossie saw Mr. Wilder blink back his surprise at Mr. Tiffany's lisp.

"Most of us, yes." Mrs. Driscoll was not of a size to borrow Flossie's clothes, so she'd added a white chiffon collar to a simple black silk dress, then trimmed the gown with black velvet.

"Most of you?" Mr. Tiffany glanced between the girls. "Who's not danced?"

"Miss Jayne hasn't yet danced," Nan said. "Nor has Mrs. Driscoll."

Flossie felt the heat in her face match the deep red flooding Mrs. Driscoll's.

Mr. Tiffany's gaze touched on Mr. Wilder and the other escorts, then he bowed once again to Mrs. Driscoll. "Well, we can't have that. Would you do me the honor?"

Mrs. Driscoll's hands skimmed over the buttons of her gown, then patted the back of her hair. Mr. Tiffany extended his elbow. She accepted it and allowed him to guide her onto the floor. Flossie kept her attention on them, waiting in silence— along with everyone else—to see if Mr. Wilder would ask her to do the same. When it became apparent he would not, Nan's brother, who'd accompanied Nan, stood.

"Miss Jayne, might I have this dance?"

Her face flamed hotter, even her ears warmed. "Thank you, yes."

She slipped her gloved hand into his, then scooped up her

train when they reached the dance floor. He spun her around the room, a proficient dancer. She smiled and nodded, paying no real attention to what he said, for it took every bit of energy she had to appear gay and happy when, for some inexplicable reason, she wanted nothing more than to tear up and cry.

"A bicyclist whooshed by, giving his bell a *ringaling-ringaling.*"

CHAPTER
50

Flossie strode down the boardinghouse hallway, nearly colliding with Mr. Wilder as he stepped out of his bedroom.

Reaching out, he steadied her, then immediately let go. "Excuse me."

With a nod, she continued toward the entry hall. She'd graduated from disappointment to outright anger. She should have invited Mr. Oyster to Saturday's soiree. He'd have been attentive. He'd have made her laugh. He'd have danced with her all night long.

Instead, she'd tried to do the nice thing by bringing Mr. Wilder, not only because he had a writing assignment, but because she thought it would help him break out of his shell. He was going to be a hermit by the time he was thirty if he didn't change his ways. She'd thought to show him that being around her and others would be fun and enjoyable. He'd repaid her by more or less ignoring her, and never once asking her to dance.

In retrospect, she'd realized interviewing the girls shouldn't have taken all night, particularly when they all said the same thing: They loved it at Tiffany's and they were concerned about what would happen to them when the men returned.

She herself was particularly concerned, for it seemed Lulu had some kind of mystical powers for glasscutting. She was not only incredibly fast, but also accurate. If one of the cutters had to go, it wouldn't be Lulu. But Mr. Wilder hadn't asked Flossie what her concerns were, only the other Tiffany Girls.

She sighed. Perhaps her concern over her job was making her overreact. Whatever the case, she was through trying to draw Mr. Wilder out, through bending over backward to make him feel included, through trying to be his friend. If he wanted to fossilize in his room with his writing and his cat, so be it.

She reached for the front door handle only to have his arm swoop around and open it. Without thanking him, she marched out onto the stoop and down the steps. He followed two paces behind. The polite thing would be to turn around and wait for him. To engage him in conversation. To ask him where he was off to this early on a Monday morning.

Instead, she headed toward the streetcar stop, widening her stride in an effort to outstrip him. Yet whether she sped up or slowed down, he kept pace. Not beside her like any normal human being, but just enough behind her to keep from having to talk to her. Typical.

Men in work trousers and gray caps rubbed down their horses and hitched their wagons, getting ready to start their deliveries. A rooster crowed from an alley, and smoke ascended from various chimneys, evidence that some women were still cooking breakfast.

Finally, she reached the streetcar stop. Only, Mr. Wilder didn't keep going, he was evidently catching one, too. At least it wouldn't be hers. He'd probably be going to his newspaper office, which was a different car.

He stood beside her, casting her occasional sideways glances. She said nothing. Did nothing. Simply stared at the flower shop across the street, her view interrupted by conveyances coming and going from all directions. A bicyclist whooshed by, giving his bell a *ringaling-ringaling*.

One streetcar came and went. Then another. And another. Finally, her car arrived, its horses shaking their harnesses and blowing gusts of air from their nostrils. She boarded, as did he. Lips tightening, she shouldered her way into the interior and grabbed onto a leather handle at the top of the car.

He followed. And though she was surrounded by men, the one at her back was not a stranger. It was him. The man facing her gave her a hooded look and suggestive smile. She scooted back to keep from brushing him. Mr. Wilder scooted back, too, giving her room.

The man in front of her began to close the gap when something over her shoulder captured his attention. He froze, then pressed back into those behind him.

She bit her lip. She could easily guess at Mr. Wilder's expression. She'd been the recipient of many a fierce look from him, but never had he used them on her behalf. The edge of her anger dissipated a little, but she hardened her heart, listing again the woes he had caused her. She needed the anger, needed it desperately, for without it, she feared more telling emotions might surface.

The man to her side gave a soft curse of surprise. She turned and saw his wrist captured within Mr. Wilder's.

"You touch her," Mr. Wilder said under his breath, "and there will be the devil to pay."

The man reddened. "I didn't know she was with you."

"She's not."

He scowled. "Then what's it to you?"

"I'll not stand by and see a woman abused."

The man curled his lip, but kept his voice down. "If she wants respect, then she needs to stay at home where her father or husband put her. But if she wants to act like a man, then she can be treated like one."

"Are you in the habit of pawing other men?"

He flushed bright red. "Let go of me."

"I'll let go, but if you even look at her disrespectfully, I'll knock you out flat." Mr. Wilder released the man's wrist.

The men on all sides of her created a tiny circle of space. When the car stopped and more people boarded, the space remained around her.

With a bang and a jerk, the horses took off again without regard for the life or limb of the car's passengers. She hung onto the strap, feeling as if each joint in her body might be separated. After a moment, a man sitting beside her stood and gave her his seat.

"Thank you." She sat, letting out a sigh of relief.

Mr. Wilder's body rocked with the motion of the car. She studied the brown weave of his sack suit jacket, the silver chain of his pocket watch, his paisley tie, his stiff collar, his sharp jawline, angular nose, and green eyes. Eyes that watched her but offered no window into what he was thinking.

Her stop was next. He followed her to the door, protecting her back and her sides. When she stepped off, she turned to ask him what on earth this was all about, but he hadn't stepped off. Instead, he paused on the bottom step.

She searched his eyes. "What is it, Reeve?"

"I like it when—"

The streetcar jerked and began to pull away.

Lifting her skirts, she walked briskly beside it. "You like it when what?"

He hesitated only a second. "When you call me Reeve."

Then he was gone. Swept away by the streetcar, yet he stayed on the bottom step, hanging slightly out as he watched her. She stared at him as he grew smaller and smaller. She gave no notice to the roaring wagons beside her, the pedestrians crisscrossing the street and whistling for cabs, for the growing confusion inside her upstaged all else.

CHAPTER
51

The workroom felt eerily vacant. Cartoons and paper patterns had vanished. Half the glass easels were gone, including the *Entombment* window with Joseph of Arimathea.

Mrs. Driscoll strode into the room, slamming the door behind her. The girls froze.

She swept the near empty room with her gaze, then fisted her hands. "As you've probably guessed, the men are back."

No one moved.

"I've managed to hold Mr. Tiffany off as far as letting any of you go, but we need to do something to justify his need for us. We need . . ." Pressing her lips together, she searched the ceiling. "We need an idea. Something we can do that will take the company in a new direction."

Flossie ran her thumb along the handle of her glasscutting tool. How in the world could they come up with a new direction? They never started on anything without first having received an order from a church or a wealthy customer.

"Mr. Tiffany has a showroom downstairs." Mrs. Driscoll began to pace in front of the windows. "Let's give him something to put into it. Something that will sell." She stopped and planted her fists onto her waist. "I want an idea from every single one of you. The new girls can give their ideas to Nan, the rest of you can give them to me. I don't care how outlandish your idea is, just come up with one. If we don't do something, a great many of you will have to go back from whence you came."

Flossie rubbed her arms. At one time, she wouldn't have been the least bit concerned about her chances of staying. Now she wasn't so sure. Being Mr. Tiffany's second choice to go to the fair had been bad enough, but the way he constantly commented on Lulu's talent troubled Flossie more than she cared to admit.

She needed to come up with an idea, and it needed to be a really good one.

CHAPTER

52

Reeve dipped his pen in the inkwell, gave a quick flick of his wrist, then brought pen to paper.

Managing comes naturally to a woman. She's been managing homes since the beginning of time. But the quality we, of the stronger sex, assume she lacks is business ability. Yet this writer had an opportunity to sit with the head of the only shop of woman glasscutters in the world. She and the dozen young women who work under her direction made—without any assistance from men—the award-winning windows of Tiffany's chapel now being exhibited at the World's Columbian Exposition.

A shadow crossed his desk. He looked up.

Flossie stood in the doorway, her red-striped skirt, navy shirt-waist, and white cuffs reminding him it was the Fourth of July. He'd ridden the streetcar with her every morning since the soiree. He'd told her he wanted to see for himself the harassment women faced.

Of course, that had been demonstrated the first morning he'd ridden with her. He'd heard plenty of talk about the loose morals of New Women, but none of the Tiffany Girls he'd met were like that, and neither was Miss Jayne. To simply assume any woman on a morning car was loose was not only preposterous but unthinkable. So, he'd continued to accompany her. Protect her. Shelter her. He never spoke to her, never bothered her, just made sure the men left her alone. His only regret was he couldn't do the same in the evenings, for her quitting hour fluctuated depending on her workload.

"Hasn't anyone told you today's a holiday?" she asked.

He glanced at his paper. "Today may be a holiday, but my deadline is approaching."

She leaned her shoulder against the doorframe. "You'll be finished in time for tonight's roof party, won't you?"

The sunlight from his window picked out the highlights of her black hair, the brightness of her eyes.

"I don't think so."

"We're going to make ice cream and watch the sunset, then enjoy heaven's glorious expanse of stars while an occasional rocket goes up in the horizon."

"Well, I'm sure you'll have a good time, then."

Looking down, she crossed her arms beneath her breasts. He took in now what he'd avoided before. The curves filling out her bodice. The tightly cinched waist. The skirts hiding the shape of her hips, though he'd imagined their shape many a time.

"Being lonely is a choice, you know," she said.

His body went rigid. "I beg your pardon?"

She looked up, her arms still crossed, her shoulder still on the doorframe, but her eyes snapping. "You heard me. You're lonely. You know it and I know it. What I can't understand is why you refuse to do anything about it."

He pushed his chair back, its legs scraping the floor. Cat shot from the bed and crawled beneath it.

"Lonely?" he said. "You think *I'm* lonely? Well, that's certainly the pot calling the kettle black."

Her arms came uncrossed. "What on earth are you talking about?"

He rose. "You. That's what I'm talking about. You, the sun which all planets orbit around. I can't imagine anything more isolating."

She pulled away from the doorframe. "The sun?"

"Yes, the sun." He swept his arm in an arc. "You have this entire household at your beck and call. When you enter a room, you outshine all within it. So much so, that the occupants are quick to do your bidding. Whether it be answering questions beneath their plates, playing games after dinner, or watching fireworks on the roof. The sad thing is, you think of them as family, but they think of you as nothing more than a housemate who keeps them entertained."

She propped a hand on her waist. "That is the most ridiculous thing I've ever heard, and we're not talking about me. We're talking about you. How many friends do you have, Reeve?"

"I have plenty of friends." His chest rose and fell.

"Name them."

"Mrs. Dinwiddie."

"Mrs. Dinwiddie is an aging widow who is very sweet, but I'm talking about friends our age."

His brain scrambled. He pictured the fellows at work. He'd never done anything with them other than visit when he went into the office, but they'd certainly do. "I have a dozen, at least."

A brow lifted. "Is that so? And how many of them do you have a real connection with?"

He reared his head back. "Connection?"

She took a step toward him. "Connection." Another step and another until she stood no more than a foot away. "You know . . . *Right. Here.*" She punctuated her words with two pokes to his chest.

He fell back a step, his mind once again scrambling.

She followed him. "Tell me. I want to know. When is the last time you've felt connected to another person? Really connected. Engaged with not just your mind, but your heart. Your very soul."

Again, he thought of Mrs. Dinwiddie, but was afraid that would prove Miss Jayne's point, not his. Then he thought of the year he'd lived with his father in Seattle. He'd been sixteen and had his first taste of life away from his grandparents. He'd had the kind of friends then that she was talking about. They went tobogganing in shoots festooned with Chinese lights while a huge bonfire crackled nearby. They picked berries, played cricket, and raced horses. He'd attended parties where he'd stayed out to all hours dancing waltzes, reels, and polkas.

But one night he remembered above all the others. The night he'd attended a wedding ball and danced with his best friend's sister. During that dance, he'd felt a connection like none he'd ever experienced before or since.

He pulled in a breath, his nostrils flaring.

"When?" She grabbed his lapels and gave him a shake. "When is the last time you've connected with another person?"

"In the middle of a dance," he bit out, shoving her hands down and away from him. "We were in the middle of a dance."

"How long ago?" she asked.

"Years."

A peddler outside passed by the window. "Roman candles! Pinwheels! Firecrackers!"

Her gaze zigzagged back and forth between his eyes. "Don't move. I'll be right back."

He was so bamboozled, he obeyed. In two shakes, she returned, winding up a tiny music box. Plopping it down on his desk, she opened the lid.

The Blue Danube filled the silence, its tinny quality unique to music boxes. Stepping up to him, she grabbed one of his hands and held it out while resting her other hand on his shoulder. She smelled of roses. An entire garden of them. He stood unmoving, his arms heavy, his legs leaden.

"Are you going to lead or shall I?" Her tone brooked no argument.

He wasn't about to let her lead. Placing his hand on her back, he applied the slightest bit of pressure. She responded immediately.

One-two-three. One-two-three.

At first, it took every bit of concentration to simply execute the steps. Then it all came rushing back. He closed his eyes, listening to the music, memories flooding him. The murmuring of the crowd. Rhythmic footfalls on a wooden floor. Corseted women. And the rush of youth roaring through his veins.

In his mind's eye, the features of the woman in his arms had transformed from a young girl on the cusp of adulthood to a fully grown woman with black hair, fair skin, brown eyes, and curves that made his mouth water.

She brushed against his desk chair and stumbled. Jerking her close, he opened his eyes, and narrowed the scope of their circle. *One-two-three. One-two-three.*

He understood now why the dance halls popping up across the city had outraged so many, for in what other instance could a man embrace an unmarried woman? Hold her flush against him, his legs lost within the folds of her skirt?

His hand spanned the small of her back. He flexed his fingers, spreading them, lightly caressing her.

Her head fell back, her eyes slid shut. The music box began to wind down, as did their steps.

One . . . two . . . three . . . One . . . two . . . three.

Slower and slower they went until they could do no more than sway, wringing every last note out of the box. Finally, the music stopped.

She opened her eyes, her long lashes heavy.

He brought the hand he held to his shoulder, then slid his hand down the whole of her arm and the entire length of her side until he had her well and truly within his embrace.

Her lips parted.

Die and be doomed, but he wanted to kiss her. Yet a man did not kiss a woman like her without following up with very real and very lasting intentions. Still, he was reluctant to let go just yet.

He moved his hands up and down her back, his fingers brushing the curve at its base, his thumbs skimming her sides, learning, memorizing, relishing.

Her fingers tightened on his shoulders.

"*Shhhhh.*" He smoothed a tiny piece of hair from her face, then brushed her eyebrow with his thumb.

She leaned her face into his hand, her eyes closing, her lashes resting against her cheek.

The front door slammed, chattering voices following it. They jumped apart. The voices ventured off toward the kitchen, but to pull her back into his arms would be sheer folly.

Her chest rose and fell, her breath fluttered the lace on her bodice. "Will you come and watch the sunset and firecrackers with us? With me?"

His chest squeezed. "I'm sorry."

Confusion filled her eyes. Her lips turned down. "Why not?"

"I have to work."

"You don't. You know you don't."

He didn't bother denying it. All he knew was that if he went to the roof with her tonight, she'd expect him to acknowledge the warmth and proximity he'd felt in her arms. Something he'd gotten along without all these many years.

And though deep inside he might long for what she offered, he was used to things the way they were. Simple. Uncluttered.

Orderly. Starting something with her would be messy and complex. He'd be on unsure footing, slipping and sliding the entire way.

Her shoulders wilted. Her expression fell. Turning, she walked from the room, leaving her music box on his desk open, but silent.

"Flossie stepped into the parlor, her accordion-pleated
skirt of blue rippling with every step."

CHAPTER

53

One look at her mother and Flossie knew Papa had gone to the races again.

"How much?" she whispered, closing her bedroom door.

Mother laid Flossie's dress out on the bed, her eyes ringed with worry. "Come, I'm anxious to see how this looks on you, and we don't want to keep everyone in Mrs. Klausmeyer's parlor waiting."

Flossie began to unbutton her shirtwaist. "How much?"

Mother's lips trembled. "Oh, now, nothing for you to worry about."

"Tell me."

She swallowed. "He said we have to move, we can no longer afford our house."

"No." Sucking in a breath, Flossie held her shirtwaist suspended in her hand. "That much?"

"He won't tell me, but it must have been a lot."

Flossie slipped off her skirt. "What are you going to do?"

"Move, I suppose." Mother picked up the new gown she'd made and slipped it over Flossie's head.

"But what about your customers? What if you move to a part of town they won't go to?" Flossie turned her back.

Mother began to close up the dress with a buttonhook. "I'll just have to go to them, then."

"What about Mrs. Vanderbilt's cousin? How are the wedding gowns going? Do you need me to help?"

A slight pause. "I told Mrs. Vanderbilt I wasn't going to do it. I didn't know this was going to happen and didn't think we'd need the money."

"Oh, Mother." Flossie caught her mother's reflection in the mirror. "Maybe my painting will sell quickly."

"Either way, I want you to enjoy yourself tonight. It's not every day a woman debuts at an art gallery—that *you* debut at an art gallery. Promise me you'll put this from your mind for now and enjoy your evening? Please?"

Flossie took a deep breath. "On one condition. You bring me some sewing. Just leave it on my bed and I'll work on it as much as I can."

"No, you need to be sketching up ideas for Mrs. Driscoll. How can you do that and sew my things as well? You can't. Besides, you hate to sew. I'll be fine."

"I mean it, Mother. I should have done that the minute you gave me the money, but we were so busy at work, I was meeting myself coming and going. It's slowed down now, especially since the men are back. So, either you bring me some sewing or I'll come and get it myself, but I am going to help."

Mother gave her a pained look.

"It will only be until the painting sells," Flossie said. "Which might even be this very night."

"Fine, fine." She fluffed Flossie's sleeves. "Now, what do you think of the dress?"

Swallowing, Flossie put on a brave smile. "You outdid yourself. It's gorgeous."

Plastering a gay expression onto her face, Flossie stepped into the parlor, her accordion-pleated skirt of blue rippling with every step. The crisscrossed front of royal-blue silk left the neckline slightly open. Velvet bows caught large puffed sleeves at her elbows, and deep epaulettes of duchesse lace rested atop her shoulders. The entire family of 438 broke into spontaneous applause. All except for Reeve, of course.

"Here she is! Our own little star." Mrs. Dinwiddie hauled her close for a back-breaking hug, the scent of camphor filling Flossie's lungs. Over the woman's shoulder, she looked up at Reeve, his expression unreadable. Even so, she knew what he was thinking.

You, the sun which all planets orbit around.

She shut her eyes. It was no longer about her debuting at an art gallery. It was about selling her painting and paying her mother back—and then some. Still, she had promised her mother she'd enjoy the evening. It was a dream come true. There would be plenty of time to worry later. If that made her the sun, so be it.

Pulling back from the hug, she looked about the room. "Where's Mrs. Trostle?"

Reeve pinched the bridge of his nose. Heat rose up her neck. She hadn't meant to imply everyone at the house was required to attend the opening. It was simply that the Trostles were the ones who'd arranged everything to begin with, so she naturally wondered at Mrs. Trostle's absence.

The sad thing is, you think of them as family, but they think of you as nothing more than a housemate who keeps them entertained.

He was wrong about that, too. They were her family. They wouldn't all gather like this to celebrate her night if they were mere housemates. Just because he'd shut himself off didn't mean everyone else had.

Over and over their conversation had replayed itself. *How long ago*, she'd asked him, expecting him to say it had been a few weeks or maybe even a few months since he'd last connected with another person his age.

Years, he'd said, and her heart had broken. How many years? She hadn't had the courage to ask, wasn't sure she wanted to know. She only knew she wanted him to be free of that wretched wall of loneliness. One little waltz, however, wouldn't break down a barricade that had been years in the making, although it had removed a brick or two.

"Mrs. Trostle is going with her sister," Mrs. Holliday said. "She said they'd see us there."

Papa snapped his pocket watch closed, his hair as perfect as ever, his eyes clouded. "Is everyone ready to go?"

The entire family made their way to the door. Flossie laughed and visited and put on a merry face. She knew Reeve wouldn't come, knew he'd stop at the door and close it behind them. She'd prepared herself for that very eventuality.

When he put on his hat and stepped outside with the rest of them, she found the summer air suddenly thick and hard to breathe. She hadn't realized until that very moment how badly she wanted him to be there. Not only to celebrate this crowning achievement with her and the rest of the family, but so she'd have his solid presence in a world that had just shifted on its axis.

"A brewer's wagon with bright green wheels ambled by,
three dozen kegs stacked against its flareboards."

CHAPTER

54

The door of Bourgeois' Art Gallery was locked, its window covered with brown paper from the inside.

"Are you sure it was tonight?" Papa asked.

"Yes, yes. I'm sure." She fumbled with her reticule, then extracted the invitation. Everyone hovered around her, reading over her shoulder. She pointed to the date. "See there? 'Saturday evening, the eighth of July, at seven thirty.'"

Papa flicked open his pocket watch. "Well, it's seven forty-five now. Where is everyone? Is it the right address? Let me see that."

She handed it to him, looking again at the number on the door plaque. "I'm sure this is it. I was here a few weeks ago. And—and Monsieur Bourgeois was inside. He—he showed me a painting by, um, Mr. Audubon. You know, one of those beautiful etchings he does of his birds?" She walked to the window and tapped on its glass. "Hello? Hello? Anyone home?"

Mrs. Dinwiddie exchanged a glance with Reeve, her brows drawn together. He lowered his chin, studying his shoes.

Flossie touched a bit of gold paint flaking off the window. "This—this used to say Bourgeois' Art Gallery." She drew an arch with her finger across the glass. "But, it's gone. I—I don't understand."

Papa's face turned red. "I'll check with the neighbors." He walked to the next shop, but it was vacant. He knocked on three more doors, shouting for someone to answer. A brewer's wagon with bright-green wheels ambled by, three dozen kegs stacked against its flareboards.

Flossie looked at her mother. "What's happening? I don't understand."

Mother took her hand and patted it. "There, there. Your father will find out what's amiss. I'm sure it's just a misunderstanding. See there? He's talking to someone now."

They all looked down the walkway, the sun so low the buildings' shadows stretched clear across the street. Papa conversed with a man in an apron, his arms making big motions and pointing in their direction.

A cab rolled by. "Anyone need a ride?"

No one said a word.

Papa shook hands with the man, then headed back toward them. A shiver raced through Flossie.

Mother pulled her close. "What did you find out, Bert?"

"Bourgeois is gone, has been for days. And we're evidently not the first to inquire about him."

"What do you mean?" Reeve asked.

"There were others, quite a few others, who'd paid him money to show their artwork."

Flossie frowned. "I don't understand."

"He skipped town, girl." His tone impatient, he snapped his fingers. "Vanished. Took the money and ran."

The blood drained from her face. "Skipped town? Took the money? Are you sure?"

He stretched both palms toward the boarded-up gallery. "What does it look like to you? A gallery opening, or a shyster who pretended to be something he wasn't?"

She wrapped her arms about her waist, a wave of nausea slamming through her. *Oh, no. Oh, no.* Her mother's money. Her mother's seventy-five dollars and the money her family at 438 had given her.

Papa shook his head. "A hundred dollars. To think he tried to take me for a hundred dollars." He closed and opened his fists. "Thank goodness I didn't give him any money."

A tiny moan escaped from the back of her throat. "Mother."

Mother placed an arm about her. "Yes. Thank goodness for that, Bert. No harm done."

"No harm done?" Papa growled. "He got away with Flossie's painting. He had no right."

"Try not to upset yourself, dear. You know what happens when you get upset."

But he was already wheezing, his face turning a deeper shade of red, almost purple. Reeve held up a hand and whistled for one of the cabs circling the block.

Mother released Flossie and took her husband's arm. "Come, Bert. Take me home."

Papa shook his head. "Flossie. She needs us. We need to, we need to . . ."

Hiding her distress, she rushed to him. "I'm fine, Papa, just fine. And look, my whole family is here."

"Family?" He pulled back, his scowl even worse than before.

"Friends." She twirled her hand toward them. "My friends. They're all here. I'll be fine."

Reeve helped Mother and then Papa inside. Before he closed the door, Papa grabbed Reeve's arm. "You'll see . . ." He took another wheezing breath. "Flossie safely home?"

"I won't leave her side."

Papa fell back into his seat. "Good man."

"A lamp lighter on the street lifted a long pole and ignited a stem on a lamppost, the flame just discernable in the onset of evening shadows."

CHAPTER
55

Her parents' cab rounded the corner. Hugging herself, Flossie bent slightly over. Something wasn't right. Monsieur Bourgeois had taken her to Delmonico's. She'd just seen him here herself, at this very gallery. The walls and floor had been freshly polished. The furniture was to have been delivered that day. Stacks of paintings had leaned against the deeply grained panels.

But, no. She hadn't actually seen the paintings. Only wrapped canvases with names scrawled across them. Had the Audubon he'd shown her been real? She didn't know. She hadn't looked that closely. Hadn't even thought to. Wasn't sure she'd have been able to tell even if she had.

Her mother. What was she going to do about her mother? Her head became light. Her vision doubled.

She turned back to her family at 438. A group of them had already filled one cab, the rest had hailed another. No one said a word. No one made eye contact.

"I'll pay you back," she said, her voice cracking.

Mrs. Dinwiddie *tsk*ed. "Nonsense. You'll do no such thing."

Mr. Nettels exchanged a look with Mr. Holliday.

She swallowed. The newspapers were filled with banks

closing, railroads failing, and farmers going belly-up. She wasn't exactly certain how that impacted a music teacher and a photographer, but it had. Mrs. Dinwiddie told her the number of students Mr. Nettels taught had diminished by half and that Mrs. Holliday hadn't received her allowance from her husband in over a month.

Flossie rubbed her temples, her chest aching. Annie Belle gave her a furtive glance, then stepped into the cab. When all had boarded, Reeve stood at the open door waiting for her.

Emotion rushed up her chest to her throat. Her eyes filled. She shook her head. "I'll . . . I'll walk."

"It's too far."

"I'll walk." She turned around and began to walk.

The door of the cab closed. The cabbie clicked his tongue and flicked the reins. Flossie kept her eyes forward, looking neither left nor right. The two cabs rolled past. She bit her lip. Her nostrils flared. Why was this happening?

Reeve caught her elbow and pulled her to a stop.

She yanked her arm out of his grip and kept going. "You were supposed to get on the cab."

"I promised your father."

She spun around. "Is that why you're not on it? Because you promised my father?" She curled her lip. "Well, of course that's why. It couldn't be because you cared. Not with that blasted brick wall you have right in there." She shoved him in the chest.

He fell back a step.

"That's waaaaaay too solid to breach, isn't it? So, thank you, but no. I'm not interested in being escorted home by someone who only pretends to care. Or worse, who denies he cares. I want you on a cab." She lifted her arm. "Cab! Cab!"

But no one stopped. No one gave her any notice, for a woman wasn't supposed to call for a cab. Only men had that privilege. Fine, she'd walk.

A man coming their way looked her up and down, then crossed to the other side of the street. She stuck her tongue out at him.

Reeve pulled her to a stop again. "Do you want a cab? If you want one, I'll get you one, but I'm riding with you."

She pushed him away. "Don't take my arm again. And if I want a cab, I'll jolly well get one myself, if I have to lie down in the middle of the road to do it."

Sighing, he raised his arm.

"No!" She slapped it down.

He lifted his brows.

"I said I'd do it, but right now, I'm going to walk." She began to stride. Big, long strides that kicked out her accordion skirt, its folds opening and closing around her feet like the instrument it was named for.

This time Reeve stayed beside her, not behind her the way he did in the mornings on the way to the streetcar.

"Why do you do that, anyway?" she snapped.

He gave her a sideways glance. "Do what?"

"Follow me to the streetcar every morning? Continue to ride with me to work?"

"Because I don't like the idea of anyone touching you."

She stopped. "I didn't expect you to give me an honest answer."

"Neither did I."

Another honest answer. Blowing out a breath, she turned her head to the side. Garbage lay strewn throughout the road, reeking. The building beside her was boarded up. Another had a glass pane broken out of its second-floor window. Why hadn't she noticed the neighborhood was so shabby, so vacant? Would a man have noticed if he'd been the one to deliver the money? Had Monsieur Bourgeois swindled men, too, or only women? Or maybe he hadn't swindled anyone.

"Maybe this is all a mistake," she said. "Maybe some terrible tragedy has happened to Monsieur Bourgeois and he's left word with Mrs. Trostle."

Reeve said nothing.

She crossed her arms. "What?"

"I didn't say anything."

"No, but you were thinking something. What was it?"

"I was wondering about your painting."

Her painting. Sweet Mackinaw. She'd been so upset about Mother's fortune, she'd forgotten about her painting. The seashore painting was Papa's favorite, and though she was angry with him about the tremendous loss he'd suffered at the tracks, she was even more angry with herself. Hadn't she done exactly the same thing he had? Gambled with money her mother had earned? Now, not only was Mother's money gone, so was the painting.

She blinked back the tears rushing to her eyes. "Do you think I'll get it back?"

He shook his head. "You misunderstood. I didn't mean *your* painting. I meant the *act* of painting."

"What about it?"

"Why do you do it?"

She touched two fingers to her forehead. "What?"

"Why do you do it?"

"Paint?"

"Yes."

Dropping her hand, she blew out another breath and once again began to walk. Only this time, at a more dignified pace. She pushed everything else aside and thought about his question. About the sheer pleasure that enfolded her when she painted. And not just the actual putting of paint on canvas, but the planning of the piece. Picking her subject. Considering all the angles and times of day so she'd get just the right light. And then, of course, the pleasure of seeing it on her wall and recapturing a tiny bit of that euphoria every time she looked at it.

She swallowed the lump forming in her throat. "I come alive when I paint. It's the equivalent for me of birds in full song, flowers in bloom, or a dew-kissed morning. It's . . . well . . . it's almost like magic, I guess."

"That surprises me."

"It does? Why?"

"Because, if you feel so strongly about it, I'd have expected to see you do it more often."

He was right, of course. She'd been working such long hours, she'd hardly picked up a brush in months. And just after she'd begun to take it up again, Mrs. Driscoll had called for ideas. Flossie had spent many a night sketching ideas, discarding them, then sketching some more.

She'd missed her painting, though, very much. "Oil painting—which is my favorite—has to be done in layers and takes up a great deal of time, something I haven't had much of lately. Besides, the oils give Mrs. Holliday and Annie Belle headaches, which has put a halt to the portraits I was doing."

"Ah." Flipping back his jacket, he slipped his hands into his pockets. "You could take your things to the park and paint there."

"I could, but it's a great many items to haul around and I'm not very good at landscapes. Portraits are my first love."

"What about having your art in a gallery?" He handed a coin to a rag woman picking bones from a garbage box.

The woman smiled at him, her skin browned and wrinkled from the sun.

He tipped his hat. "If you could see into the future," he continued, taking Flossie's elbow to help her circumvent a puddle, "and if that future did not include your paintings ever being sold or displayed, would you still paint?"

"Absolutely."

"Then why did you pay such a grand sum of money to be in Bourgeois' gallery?"

"How do you know how much I paid?"

"Despite what your father thinks, everyone at Klausmeyer's knows Bourgeois asked for a hundred dollars and that you were a bit short. At least, that's what Mrs. Trostle told us."

She rubbed her forehead. "Right."

"So? Why did you do that if you don't really care one way or another if your work is 'discovered'?"

Removing a fan from her reticule, she opened it and tried to cool herself in the heat. "It's a long story."

"It's a long walk home, too."

She took a deep breath. "Perhaps we should get a cab, after all."

It took him a few minutes to find one. Once they'd settled inside on opposite seats, she hoped he would forget his train of thought, but he was a journalist. His inquisitiveness would not be stemmed.

"Why was getting into that gallery so important?"

"I don't know. I suppose because being shown there would have been a real feather in the cap for the women's movement."

He shook his head. "I'm not buying that. Not when at this very moment women are being well-represented in the Fine Arts Building at the fair where the whole world can see their paintings, not to mention the ones in the Woman's Building."

She looked out the window.

He released the button of his jacket. "No, you didn't pay a hundred dollars because you wanted this for the women's movement. So what was it?"

She watched the buildings blur as the cab rolled by them. "Vanity, I suppose."

"I don't believe that, either."

She gave him a sharp glance.

He held up his hand, stemming her objection. "I'm sure that plays a part, but a hundred dollars is a lot of vanity. Not even you are that vain."

She lifted a brow. "Thank you, I think."

A corner of his mouth rose. Her irritation softened a little. The cab swayed back and forth. His long legs bracketed hers, bumping her occasionally when they rounded a bend.

"I'm all they've got," she said, finally.

"Who?"

"My parents. All my life, they've made sacrifices so they could give me everything within their power to give. I used to beg them to take me to museums or to buy me art supplies or to enroll me in exclusive art schools over the summer breaks." She shook her head. "So, Papa would make house visits early in the mornings for a select few, and then again on evenings when his customers had something special planned. Mother sewed herself sick, literally. I didn't even realize it until I'd moved out and had time to look back and reflect." She pursed her lips in disgust. "But even then, when I needed money, I went running right back to them."

Their carriage slowed at a corner. A lamp lighter on the street lifted a long pole and ignited a stem on a lamppost, the flame just discernible in the onset of evening shadows.

Reeve tilted his head. "They actually gave you everything you asked for?"

She looked down, fiddling with her fan. "More or less, at least until Papa started going to the races. But even after that they managed to do what they could to accommodate me. And with every milestone, every accomplishment, they praised me and boasted about it to their friends. It was as if their success depended upon mine."

"And you believe it still does?"

She bit her lip. "Their eggs are all in one basket, and when you've only one basket, it stands to reason that it had better be a good one."

"I think you underestimate your parents. It's clear they think the world of you. I'm not sure you could do any wrong in their eyes."

"That may be true, but for all these years I've been so selfish, never thinking for a minute about what my requests were costing them. And when Papa did start withholding the funds, I became indignant." She rolled her eyes. "I actually threatened to go on strike—in our own home. How could I possibly, after all that, dare to disappoint them?"

"Didn't your leaving home disappoint them?"

"Yes, another selfish act on my part." She took a shaky breath. "Selling that painting in a gallery for four hundred dollars would have justified everything, though. All those sacrifices of Papa's. All those endless seams and hems and trims Mother stitched until the wee hours. Me moving out. And now, now . . ." She pressed a fist to her mouth.

"You could always move back in with them."

"Not anymore. They're . . . they're moving to someplace smaller."

"What about your work at Tiffany's? You're in one of the most prestigious and exclusive jobs a woman has ever held. That ought to make them proud."

"They were proud of me for going to the fair, but . . ." She swallowed, her throat thickening. "I don't design anything at Tiffany's. I cut the glass. Papa hates that and Mother thinks my job is mannish. They aren't very happy with it, but they approve of my painting, very much so. When Bourgeois' gallery came along, well, it was simply too good to be true." She swiped at a tear, for it appeared the opportunity, in reality, *was* too good to be true. "You want to know a secret?"

He said nothing, but his attention never wavered from her.

With a huff of disgust, she stuffed her fan back into her reticule. "Being a New Woman isn't exactly how I'd pictured it. Don't misunderstand, I love the independence and I love working at Tiffany's, absolutely love it, but things just aren't what I expected."

"Aside from the fact you don't have as much time to paint as you'd like, what else weren't you expecting?"

"I wasn't expecting to be homesick. I wasn't expecting to be worried about my *parents*." She rubbed her thumb against the handle of her reticule. "I wasn't expecting my job to ever be in jeopardy. I assumed that when the men came back, they would let someone else go, not me. Now, I'm not so sure. The other two woman glasscutters are, well . . ." She lifted her face, tears streaming down her cheeks. "I can't go back home. Not just because I don't want to hear my father say, 'I told you so,' but because he keeps all the money my mother earns and either gambles it away or spends it on me. Don't you see? I have to keep my job. If I go home, she'll never be free and neither will I."

She'd also never be able to pay her mother back if she went home, nor could they afford another mouth to feed, but she was too raw to think about that.

"You could marry," he said.

She shook her head, dashing her tears, only to have more come. "I'd just be exchanging one man who appropriates all my wages for another. I'll not do that."

"But what about your painting?"

"I'm going to have to give it up." She barely managed to push the words past her throat. Yet she had to face the facts. Painting was no longer an option. Not anymore. Not when she had sketches to do for Mrs. Driscoll and sewing to do for Mother.

He rubbed his hands on his trousers. "Don't cry, Flossie."

If anything, his words made more tears flow.

Gripping the edge of his seat, he scooted forward, his knees bending even more. "You once told me it's not about the destination, but about the journey. I think you're right about that, and if you give up your painting, you'll ache. Maybe not today, maybe not tomorrow—but eventually." He grabbed her fingertips, squeezing them. "So it doesn't matter if you're living at home or with a husband. It doesn't matter who your wages go to. What matters is the richness painting would bring to your life."

Her shoulders slumped. Her body sagged. It did matter, because she had seventy-seven dollars and thirty cents to pay back.

CHAPTER
56

Flossie cried herself to sleep and it nearly did him in. Never had he felt so helpless. He couldn't comfort her, it wasn't his right. He couldn't track down Bourgeois, the police would have to do that. And he couldn't pay off her debts, he didn't have the money. Even if he did, she wasn't his responsibility, and he needed every penny he'd saved for his down payment.

Feeling a need to get away, he left Klausmeyer's at dawn and went to East New York to see his home. He just wanted to look at it, to luxuriate in the thought of one day returning to it. He walked down the deserted business section closed up in observance of Sunday, the day of rest. He tried to imagine his parents on this street. Which bakery was his mother's favorite? Which butcher? And what of his father? Had the harness maker on the corner made the saddle his father had rode out west in?

He glanced inside a barbershop's window. Had his dad sat in one of those chairs? Had he? He thumped the red, white, and blue barber pole and wondered where Mr. Jayne's shop was. The man clearly loved his daughter and most likely loved his wife, yet he'd gambled away his wife's earnings on horses? It had never occurred to Reeve a wife would want to keep her wages for herself or that she'd even need to. He found himself empathizing, though, for his grandfather had kept all of Reeve's earnings when he'd been living with him.

He took a left on Georgia Avenue, then walked alongside several houses. Houses with front porches, picket fences, and even a house with a swing hanging from a limb of a giant oak tree. A croquet set leaned against a gazebo, four empty chairs inside it. He pictured a group of adults laughing, talking, playing.

Had they known his parents? Had any of the residents on this street? Surely someone from back then still lived here. Would they be able to tell him of his childhood? Had he perhaps played with their little boy?

A familiar wave of loneliness assailed him. It had been his lifetime companion, though he was an expert at hiding it. No one at the newspaper suspected it, he was sure, and no one at Klausmeyer's had, either, until Flossie had come along.

Being lonely is a choice, you know.

Just thinking about her nerve in saying that still made his hackles rise. But ever since she'd spoken the words, he'd had to confront them, take them out, turn them over, and look at them. He sighed, unsure of what exactly he was supposed to do. It wasn't as if he could ask people to waltz around the parlor with him so he could make a—what had she called it?—a connection.

Reaching the cottage, he stopped and studied it. It was too early to knock, though a bit of smoke coming from the chimney indicated someone was up and about.

He took a slow breath, basking in the sense of warmth and belonging the place evoked. He didn't know how, he didn't know why, he just knew that returning to it was the first step in conquering his loneliness. And he did want to conquer it.

CHAPTER
57

Flossie plopped down on her bed, then fell onto her back, her feet dangling off the edge. Even though she was supposed to be coming up with ideas for Mrs. Driscoll, she simply hadn't had the wherewithal to be innovative. So she'd taken her sketchpad and charcoal to Central Park for a bit of peace and quiet.

"Did you get any sketches done?" Annie Belle asked, folding a stack of handkerchiefs.

Flossie draped her arm over her eyes. "No, I mostly just sat and thought."

And she'd decided she'd first pay back her family at 438, then she'd pay her mother. She'd calculated all her expenses—room, board, streetcar fares, the occasional cab fare, fuel for her heater and lamps, incidentals—and found she only had about fifteen cents a week to spare. At that rate, it would take years to pay off the seventy-five dollars. She squeezed her eyes shut, willing the tears away. How old would she be? Thirty? Thirty-five? Well past the marrying years. She hadn't even realized how much she'd wanted to someday get married and have children until the choice had been snatched away. Funny, but there was no square on The Board Game of Old Maid that said, 'New Woman Swindled. Go Straight to the Old Maid Square.'

Yet that's exactly what had happened. So, she'd best readjust her thinking. No doubt her mother would object to being reimbursed, but Flossie would not be swayed. Not only that, she would continue to sew for her mother until the debt had been paid. She'd thought about it all morning and her mind was made up.

Annie Belle opened a drawer and put her hankies inside. "I'm glad you're back. I . . . I need to tell you something."

Moving her arm, Flossie turned her head toward her. "What?"

Annie Belle crossed her arms, chewed her lip, and darted her gaze about the room.

Flossie pushed herself up, then leaned back on her hands. "What is it?"

"It's about the Trostles."

Flossie straightened. "Has something happened to them?"

"Not exactly, but they've left."

"Left?" Flossie frowned. "What do you mean 'left?'"

Annie Belle sat beside her on the bed. "You know how Mr. Trostle was called away to Milwaukee on business and Mrs. Trostle kept visiting her sister all those nights?"

Flossie nodded.

"Well, Mr. Trostle was never in Milwaukee."

She pulled back. "What do you mean? Mrs. Trostle received a letter from him most every day."

"I know. And according to Mrs. Klausmeyer, his letters promised to settle his accounts upon his return. Only, he was right here in the city the whole time, over on the cheap side of town."

She put a hand on her hip. "Now, why would he do that? Then he'd have to pay for two places."

"That's just it. He never has paid Mrs. Klausmeyer."

Flossie's lips parted. "Never paid? Not anything? Ever?"

"Not a cent. Right before rent was due, he left for 'Milwaukee.'"

And the dinner basket Mrs. Trostle took to her 'sister's' night after night?"

"Yes."

"Not only was it filled with dinners they never paid for—which she shared with him—it was also filled with stolen items from each of our rooms."

Sucking in a breath, Flossie grabbed the edge of the bed. "No. That can't be right. She stole things? Out of our *rooms*?"

Annie Belle looked down. "All of the souvenirs from the fair you brought us are gone."

Flossie jumped to her feet. "No. Surely not."

Annie Belle rose, too. Shaking out a handkerchief, she blew her nose. "It's true. That lovely fan you brought me is gone. So are my brush and comb set, and . . . and . . ." Her eyes watered. "The thimble that belonged to my grandmother."

Flossie took Annie Belle's hand into hers. "Oh, no. This is horrible. This is terrible. I . . . are you sure? Are you sure you didn't simply misplace them?"

"I'm positive. She took Mr. Nettels's metronome, some music folios, and his tuner. Anything that would fit inside that dinner basket. Several of Mrs. Dinwiddie's doilies and china cups are missing. Mr. Oyster's gun is gone, as well as a collection of stereoscopic cards. Mr. Holliday's spectacles—"

"Spectacles? She took his *spectacles*?"

"Yes, but that's not the worst of it. She took Mrs. Holliday's silver frame *and* the photograph inside."

She gasped. "Of their *wedding*?"

"I know." Annie Belle pressed the handkerchief to her mouth. "I can't believe it."

Flossie whirled around looking about the room. "What about my things? Do you know what she took of mine?"

"Oh, Flossie. She—they—took your money. Don't you see? They were in cahoots with Monsieur Bourgeois the entire time."

Backing away, she shook her head. "No, Annie Belle, no. They couldn't have been."

"Of course they were. Why do you think she wasn't there with the rest of us when we discovered the gallery was a hoax? Why do you think she donated such a generous amount to the kitty when we passed the hat?" She pressed her lips together. "Because she knew they'd get every dime back. It was even her idea to pass the hat to begin with. Just one more way to fleece us."

"But—but they're part of our . . ." She was going to say family, but Reeve's words reverberated in her mind.

None of us at 438 are your family . . . We're simply housemates who pay rent to the same landlady . . . They think of you as nothing more than a housemate who keeps them entertained.

She looked down at her hands. "And Mr. Wilder? Did she steal from him, too?"

"We don't know. He's been gone all morning, but the cat you brought him from the fair and his writing pen are still on his desk. Probably because he has so few things that he'd have missed them last night, the minute we got home, and the police would have been summoned much earlier."

"The police have been summoned?"

"Well, of course. They've already come and gone."

She began to pace in front of their washstand. "I still can't believe it. Mrs. Trostle? And Mr. Trostle, too? It's simply . . . I can't . . . I mean, how did she get her trunk out of her room without anyone noticing?"

"She didn't. It's still there, and it's empty. She must have worn two layers of clothing and left one of them with Mr. Trostle—if that's even their name. But we do know she did the bulk of her stealing while we were at the gallery. She must have been watching the house, waiting for us to leave. Mrs. Klausmeyer saw her briefly—basket in hand—but didn't think anything of it."

"What did the police say?"

"That the Trostles have been running this swindle all over town, though they use different aliases, of course."

Flossie dropped into the chair by her bookshelf, then gasped. "My Jane Austen books." She spread her hands over the now empty section. "My grandmother gave those to me."

Annie Belle gave a tiny moan. "I bet we'll be discovering things for weeks that we haven't missed yet. The officer said to keep a tally. Then, if anything turns up, they'll know who to return it to."

Flossie shook her head, unable to fathom it. The Trostles were older than her parents, for heaven's sake. They were personable, kind, engaging, and well dressed. She'd shared meals with them, laughed with them, played parlor games with them while they knowingly, wittingly planned to rob everyone. And out of all the family members in the house, they'd singled her out for the most nefarious of their plans.

Her eyes pooled. Why? Why her? What had she ever done to them other than welcome them into her family with open arms?

None of us at 438 are your family.

She wished she could put her hands over her ears and make those words go away, but they played over and over in her mind. She thought of each boarder at Klausmeyer's. What did she really know about them? Nothing. Nothing other than what they'd told her.

She covered her face with her hands. "Could this get any worse?"

"I hope not," Annie Belle said. "I really hope not."

But at dinner the next evening, Mrs. Klausmeyer announced rent would go up twenty cents next month. The bite of codfish Flossie had just taken stuck in her throat. Since she shared a room, her portion would be ten cents. That would mean she'd only be able to pay Mother five cents per week instead of fifteen. She quickly divided seventy-five dollars by five cents. She wiped her mouth with her napkin. Thirty years. It would take her thirty years to pay everything off. She'd be in her fifties by then.

For the first time since moving in, she set down her fork and excused herself from the table without waiting to hear the answers to everyone's questions.

"'I'm making a phenakistascope, except instead of drawing thirteen images, which change little by little so that when you spin the disc it looks like they're moving, I want to use thirteen photographed images.'"

CHAPTER

58

R eeve stood at Flossie's doorway waiting for her to notice him. She had a chair by the window, a sketch pad in her hand. He'd never seen anyone with such a penchant for dressing up. Or perhaps she saved her simpler clothing for work and had nothing left to wear but the ensembles her mother had previously sewn for her.

Today she wore a gown of yellow with shiny fabric and tiny flowers dotting the bodice. A giant blue bow hung alongside her waist, matching smaller ones at her neck and cuffs. He shook his head. Who sketched wearing something like that?

On her bed, a stack of clothing was folded and tied with twine. He knew it was sewing she did for her mother. Every Sunday evening she took completed work to her parents' house, then came home with new items to work on.

Taking a deep breath, he knocked on her door.

She jumped. "Goodness, I didn't hear you coming."

"I'm sorry." He held up her music box. "I have something for you."

She lowered her sketch pad. "My music box. I thought Mrs. Trostle had taken it."

"She took some books I stored under my bed, but nothing

else." He smoothed the top of the music box with his hand. "She might have taken this if it hadn't been in my room, but I had so few things out, I think she was afraid to take it."

She nodded, the depths of her eyes showing a touch of fragility. "She took my books, too. My Jane Austen ones, anyway."

"I'm sorry."

She swallowed. "Yes. Me, too."

"At least you still have this."

"I'm very glad." She waved her pencil toward her bookshelf. "You can just set it in there for now."

Crossing one of the rugs, he set it in the empty spot, then approached her. "What are you working on?"

"A design for a tea screen."

"What's a tea screen?"

"It's a little hinged screen, shaped like a dressing screen, except it is only about so high—" She placed her hands several inches apart to indicate its height. "You put it in front of your teakettle to keep the burner from going out." Tilting her head, she considered her sketch, then drew a decorative stick-like border on it. "Mrs. Driscoll has asked us to submit product ideas for the showroom. I've proposed several, but so far she's not shown them to Mr. Tiffany."

He scratched his jaw. "Are those things along the edges supposed to be something?"

"These?" She pointed to the hen scratches she'd made.

"Yes."

"They're spiders."

He chewed the inside of his cheek. "Spiders."

"Yes."

"That's a lot of spiders."

She lifted a shoulder. "Mrs. Driscoll is designing a lamp-shade with dragonflies on it, so I assumed she had an affinity for bugs."

He couldn't imagine anyone paying to have dragonflies or spiders on their stained glass, but he refrained from saying so.

Heavy footfalls along the hallway came to a stop at her threshold. Holliday stood in the doorway, camera under one arm, tripod under the other, a bag in each hand. His thick dark hair had been recently cut, if a bit inexpertly, which made Reeve think perhaps his young wife had made the attempt at it. His mustache, however, was well-groomed and shaped.

"Oh, Mr. Holliday." Flossie handed her pencil and pad to Reeve, then crossed the room. "Is it time already? Here, let me help you with that." She took the tripod, then cleared off a small table.

Holliday placed his bags on the floor and his camera on the table. "I appreciate you modeling for me. I'm afraid my wife has grown weary of posing."

"I'm happy to help. Do you need me to change?"

"No, no, you look lovely, as usual."

She smiled.

Reeve set down the sketchpad and stepped around her. "Well, I'll be getting out of your way."

Holliday raised a finger. "As long as you're here, would you mind assisting us?"

Reeve hesitated. "I'm afraid I don't know anything about photography."

"No, no." Holliday chuckled. "I don't mean with the camera, I mean with the modeling. Miss Jayne, if you'll stand on that circular rug over there and, Wilder, if you'd please join her."

"Join her?" Reeve said.

"Yes, I'm making a phenakistascope, except instead of drawing thirteen images, which change little by little so that when you spin the disc it looks like they're moving, I want to use thirteen photographed images." He tugged on his jacket. "Never been done before, but I think I can do it. I just need a couple to do a simple waltz."

"Waltz?" he asked.

"Oh, dear." Flossie's cheeks flushed. "I didn't realize you wanted, I mean, what I'm trying to say is . . . well, I'm afraid there's no room in here to waltz."

"I didn't meant waltz all over the room." Smiling, Holliday shook his head. "Quite the opposite. You'll need to stand in the one spot and waltz in a circle."

"Can't I dance a jig by myself?" she asked.

"I tried that with my wife, but I can't see any leg movement because of the skirts you women wear. I need a man. I suppose I could have a man dance a jig. Do you know how to jig, Wilder?"

"I do not."

"Waltz?"

He hesitated. "Yes."

"Well, then, go join Miss Jayne on the carpet and let's get started before we lose the angle of the light there at the window." He adjusted the camera. "I was going to ask Oyster, but he was napping when I went by his room. Still, if you're too busy, I'll go wake him."

He was not about to let Oyster hold Miss Jayne like that. "If it won't take too long, I'll do the best I can."

Miss Jayne's hands flew to her hair, then her buttons, then settled against her stomach. He knew she was thinking of the last time they'd waltzed, as was he. He placed a hand at her waist and assumed a dance position, the pulse in his neck pounding a little faster. Die and be blamed, but it felt glorious just to touch her.

"Hold it right there!" Holliday threw a black shroud over his head, then peeked through his camera. "No, no. That's not going to work." He crossed the room, arranged the two of them so they still faced each other, but were at a right angle from the camera. "I think it would be better if you let your left arm hang, Miss Jayne, rather than having it on Wilder's shoulder. That way we can see your lovely face a little better."

She removed her hand from his shoulder and let it bump against the arm he had about her waist.

"There." Holliday nodded. "Let's try that."

Her chest rose and fell. Reeve moved his thumb against her waist. Sucking in her breath, she glanced at him, then let her gaze skitter away.

"Pull her a bit closer, Wilder, you look like you're dancing with your maiden aunt." Holliday's voice was muffled beneath the shroud.

Reeve pulled her close.

"Closer."

He pulled her against him.

"Perfect."

Amen to that.

The camera clicked. "Now, Miss Jayne, I want you to stay where you are. Wilder, turn your body toward me so she's nestled up against your right hip and start to bring that right foot back."

While Holliday flipped over the film tray and slid it back into the camera, Reeve curled his arm further around Flossie's waist as he swiveled.

"Yes! Yes. Just like that. Hold it!" The camera clicked again. "Now, Miss Jayne, turn so your right hip is butted up against his right hip." Setting that tray aside, he prepared another one, slid it into the camera, and disappeared beneath the shroud.

Reeve turned her with his hand, her back now toward the camera. With his other hand, he rubbed her thumb with his. Her eyes slid shut.

The camera clicked. "Okay, Wilder. Bring her around in front of you like you're going to swoop her down and kiss her—but don't really do that, of course." The shroud moved up and down as he chuckled.

Flossie's cheeks blossomed. Reeve pulled her body across his, but didn't dip her over his arm.

"Freeze! Right there!" The camera clicked. Holliday threw the shroud off of him. "Now, don't move. Either of you. It's critical that you maintain that position, but I need to grab a couple more trays."

She must have washed with rose water. It took every bit of concentration he had not to close his eyes, bury his face in her hair, and fill his lungs with the fragrance. He thought about Miss Love saying Flossie's hair fell nearly to the floor when she unpinned it. Just imagining it made his nerves stand on end. He wondered if it was straight or wavy. Wondered what it would be like to run his fingers through it and drape it over her shoulders. Especially if those shoulders were bare. He looked toward the back wall, reeling in his thoughts.

"Almost ready." A few more slides and scrapes, then Holliday was back under his shroud. "This time, Wilder, keep her tucked up against you like she is, but pivot so that you're facing the east wall and she's facing the west. Try and keep your right leg a bit behind you if you can."

Now they were cheek to cheek. Flossie's face, nearest the camera, shielded his. Her ear lobe peeked out from beneath her coif and was within an inch of his mouth. He resisted, resisted, then could resist no more. He took a gentle tug with his lips.

Her breath whistled through her teeth. Her hand clenched his. Her body stiffened and pressed slightly into him.

"Hold still, please," Holliday barked. "Try and hold still."

"Your hair smells like roses," Reeve whispered.

She made a tiny sound at the back of her throat.

"Okay, Wilder." Holliday's voice was once again muffled. "We're going to make the next turn. This time, you'll bring Miss Jayne around so that she is the one facing me and you're the one with your back to the camera. Keep those right hips glued together."

If this wasn't the darnedest thing he'd ever done with a woman. He needed to remember Holliday could see them, was focused on them, in fact. Just because the man was under that shroud didn't mean he couldn't see them.

Reeve turned her out, while he turned in. She grabbed a handful of her skirt and held it out to the side.

"Oh, that's nice, Miss Jayne." The camera clicked. "I like that."

Her chest rose and fell, pressing against his with each breath. His blood rushed through his veins. Swallowing, he wondered how much longer this was going to take.

"Here we go again, Wilder. Swoop her around like you're going to lay her back and kiss her."

Tightening his arm about her waist, he dragged her across him, holding her much closer this time, for his back was to the camera and Holliday couldn't see. Her eyes glossed over. She raised her hooded gaze, but it never made it past his lips. Death and the deuce.

"Hold that position." Holliday began to change the film.

Reeve skated his hand lower, slowly, slowly. Only stopping when her back began to curve.

Holliday swore under his breath. "Hang on, I'm having trouble here."

She closed her eyes, her lips there for the taking.

He didn't so much as breathe.

"Okay. Ready?" Holliday settled himself beneath his shroud. "Just a few more shots."

Holliday took them through the rest of the dance, one step at a time. When she had her face shielded by Reeve's, she blew across his ear.

A shiver ran down him.

"Hold still, Wilder! For the sake of St. Peter, I'll have to do that shot over and this film is expensive."

Reeve squeezed her waist in warning. If she did that again, there would be the devil to pay.

Finally, they were back to where they started. Holliday came out from his cocoon. "I think I have what I need. I appreciate you helping me out."

Reeve released Flossie, his hand traveling as far as possible before returning it to his side. She touched the bow at her neck.

Holliday began to collect his items. "Don't just stand there, Wilder. Give me a hand."

Both Reeve and Flossie helped him carry everything back to his room. And though they never went near each other, never so much as touched, he was aware of every nuance in her expression, every sway of her hips, every secret look she sent him.

The stairwell was silent. The hallway was silent. The rooms were silent. He didn't know where everyone else was on this sunny Sunday afternoon, but he was thankful they weren't around.

He followed her back down to the first floor, narrowing his eyes. Were her hips swaying just a touch more than usual? Or maybe he was simply too attuned to her every move. When she began to enter her room, he grabbed her hand, hauled her to his room, shoved his door closed, pulled her against him, and took her mouth with his.

Great Caesar's ghost, but her lips were soft. She flung her arms around his neck and pressed herself against him. He tried to deepen the kiss, but she didn't understand. He pulled his mouth away and began to taste and nibble and kiss every inch of skin he had access to. Her neck, her jaw, her cheeks, her nose, her eyes, her forehead, her ears, her hair. Die and be snagged, but he wanted to run his hands through it.

Instead, he found her mouth again and wrapped his arms clear around her. "Open your mouth, magpie."

"What?"

He kissed her, really kissed her.

She made mewling sounds. She raked her fingers through his hair. She twisted against him.

Bracketing his ears, she pushed his mouth away. "I thought I was going to die during the photos."

"I think I did die." He kissed her again. He knew his bed was mere steps away. The temptation was huge. Enormous. He had to get her out of here. "We have to stop."

But she didn't let him go. Finally, he could take it no more.

He broke their kiss and held her at arms' length. "You better get out of here. Now."

Her lips were full, her cheeks red where his whiskers had scratched her, her hair mussed. She pressed her hands against her stomach. "Reeve, I . . . I feel so—"

"*Out,*" he barked, then spun her toward the door.

She walked to the door, her steps unsteady.

"*Wait,*" he hissed.

She froze, her hand on the doorknob. If she opened the door looking like that and somebody saw her, they'd never believe she hadn't just been ravished. "Let me make sure the coast is clear."

Opening the door, he checked the hall. "Okay."

She stared at him with wonder. "Reeve, I . . ."

He held up a hand. "We shouldn't have done that, Flossie. *I* shouldn't have done that."

Her brows crinkled. "Why?"

"Because you're the marrying kind, not the kiss and run kind."

She bit her lower lip. "And you're, you're the kiss and run kind?"

The earnestness in her expression, the natural love she had for everyone, shone through her eyes. It nearly undid him. Cupping her cheek, he grazed her lip with his thumb. "You deserve someone a lot better than me."

"But I'm not looking for a someone. I'm a New Woman, remember?"

Lifting her chin with his finger, he gave her a soft, unhurried kiss. If anything, it was even sweeter than the one before. "You may be a New Woman, little magpie, but you're not a loose New Woman. Now, out you go."

With a gentle nudge, he returned her to the hall, then quietly clicked his door shut.

A minute later, he heard the springs on her bed bounce. "Sweet heaven above." Her sighed words were barely audible through the thin wall.

He leaned his head back against his door. He shouldn't have done that. He absolutely should not have done that.

CHAPTER
59

W hat was your last thought before going to sleep?" Mrs.
Dinwiddie asked.

Flossie barely lifted her gaze. Reeve sat frozen, but didn't look at her, though she knew he knew that she'd put his question there. Still, she couldn't help it. She'd thought about him constantly for over a week, but he acted as if nothing whatsoever had happened. As if he hadn't teased her during Mr. Holliday's photographs and stolen secret touches and whispered in her ear—not to mention those kisses.

It was the first time she'd been kissed in her whole life. And oh, my, what kisses. She had no idea. No wonder preachers were so concerned about sins of the flesh. If that was any indication of what went on between a man and a woman after marriage, she could certainly see why some couples ate supper before they said grace.

Reeve held his hand out. Mrs. Dinwiddie passed him the paper.

He reread the question, then looked straight at Flossie, his voice low. "Where are the paintings on the edges that give hints of possible answers?"

Heat rushed into her cheeks. She'd agonized about what to

paint on his paper and had thought of many possibilities, none of which were appropriate. So, she'd simply left it blank. Never did she dream he'd ask her about it.

He raised a brow.

She wrapped a loose tendril of hair round her finger. "Well, there were just so many possibilities, I didn't even know where to start."

"Not for me." His voice dropped another register. "There was only one thing on my mind last night as I was falling asleep."

Her eyes widened. Dear heavens. Surely he wouldn't actually say it. She hadn't thought of that. She'd merely wanted to jog him out of his complacency, not announce to the entire household that he'd well and truly kissed her. And nibbled her ear. And she'd—

Oh, sweet mercy. She'd blown in his ear. Her face heated.

"What was it?" Mrs. Dinwiddie asked.

He kept his eyes on Flossie. "I was thinking about waltzing."

Her lips parted.

"Waltzing?" Mrs. Dinwiddie shook her head. "Of all the things you could say, that is the absolute last one I'd have guessed."

"What about you, Miss Jayne?" he asked. "Is it the last thing you would have guessed?"

"I . . . I . . ." She fumbled with a button at her collar. "I had no idea you would say waltzing."

His eyes warmed. He pulled up a corner of his mouth. "Yes, well, I've come to the realization that waltzing can be a rather pleasurable pursuit."

She looked at her plate, goose bumps racing up her arms. She certainly had her answer. He might have treated her exactly the same as before, his barricade might appear to be shored up and in place, but at night when the candles were out, he thought about her just as she thought about him. It would do her no good, though, for nothing could come of it. She wouldn't be free from debt until she was fifty-something.

She peeked up at him. He'd turned his attention to Mr. Holliday who, after giving Reeve a speculative look, began to read a question for Annie Belle.

DRAGONFLY LAMP[34]

"Along the bottom edge eight dragonflies with wings fully spread headed
downward as if they would burst from the shade at any moment."

CHAPTER
60

The murmur of a man's voice came from the hall. In another moment, Mrs. Driscoll and Mr. Mitchell entered the studio. Flossie immediately looked sharp, for he was not only vice president and manager of Tiffany Glass and Decorating Company, he was also brother-in-law to Mr. Tiffany. Mrs. Driscoll, however, couldn't stand him.

"Is this it?" he asked Mrs. Driscoll, picking up a painted cartoon of a lampshade. His brown bushy mustache connected to thick muttonchops that blended into his hair.

Mrs. Driscoll clasped her hands behind her. She'd been working on the design since shortly after they'd returned from the fair. Along the bottom edge eight dragonflies with wings fully spread headed downward as if they would burst from the shade at any moment. Hints of blue, green, and yellow flowed throughout each wing. Flossie could only imagine how lifelike they'd look once they were made with Tiffany's iridescent glass. If Mitchell approved it, it would be one of the most breathtaking pieces she'd ever see.

"You can't mean to tell me this is what you've been working on all these weeks?" Mr. Mitchell grimaced. "Bugs? On a lamp? Why, it's the ugliest thing I've ever seen."

Mrs. Driscoll gave no reaction whatsoever to his words, but Flossie held her breath. The future of the lamp depended in no small measure on what he thought of it.

He pulled a pair of spectacles from his pocket and put them on. "You cannot possibly believe anyone would buy this."

"Actually, I do." Mrs. Driscoll tilted her head. "It will be the most interesting and original item in the showroom."

"Perhaps, but people go to museums to see original and interesting items. They go to our showroom to buy things for their homes. And with the time and materials you'd use for this, we wouldn't be able to price it for anything less than five hundred dollars."

Flossie sucked in her breath.

He shook his head. "Who in their right mind would pay five hundred dollars for an oil lamp? Especially one with bugs on it?"

"There are people who will pay most anything for what they like." Mrs. Driscoll fingered the edge of the cartoon. "You have only to put it on the market and then you'll see. It will sell."

"It's too elaborate." He rubbed his eyes beneath his glasses. "Everything you do is so ornate and expensive to make."

"Mr. Tiffany likes my designs," she reminded him, crossing her arms. "No, he loves them."

He sighed. "Can't you make me some modest designs for candlesticks, ink bottles, and inexpensive lamps? Those are the kinds of things we can't have too many of."

Flossie captured her bottom lip with her teeth. Her tea screen was modest compared to Mrs. Driscoll's designs. It would meet Mr. Mitchell's criteria.

He pushed his glasses up into place. "Just for the sake of it, why don't you make me something simplistic? If you do, I will personally guarantee it will sell."

"Simplistic?" Mr. Tiffany crossed the studio, his suit crisp, his curly hair wild, his eyes alive with interest. "Are you looking at Mrs. Driscoll's new design?" Picking up the cartoon, he lifted it toward the light, tilting it this way and that.

All work ceased. A hush fell over the room.

He pursed his lips, then turned to Mrs. Driscoll. "I love it."

She smiled and uncrossed her arms. Mr. Mitchell slid his eyes closed.

Turning his attention back to the cartoon, Mr. Tiffany leaned in closer. "The color scheme is new and quite interesting. The design . . ." He gave a sigh of satisfaction. "The design is unparalleled. You have great creative ability, Mrs. Driscoll."

A flush rose to the woman's cheeks. "Thank you."

"I would not think of having it changed." He set it back down, then turned to Mr. Mitchell. "You must see that it is made."

Mr. Mitchell gave a curt nod, his jaw tight.

The three of them wove through the room while Mrs. Driscoll caught them up on what the girls were doing. Flossie wished she could show Mr. Mitchell her design. She felt sure he'd like it, but maybe he'd already seen it. Maybe that was why Nan had made her revise it so many times. To appease Mr. Mitchell's thirst for something less ornate.

Excitement bubbled up inside her. If her design was sold in Tiffany's showroom, her job would be secure and she might even get a raise.

CHAPTER

61

Sitting across from his editor, Reeve rested his mouth against his fist in an effort to camouflage his gratification. They wanted him to be a features writer. No longer would the articles he labored over be buried in the back. They'd be front and center, and they'd earn him a pay increase.

"The Erie Railroad has failed," Ulrich said, his cowlick drooping in the summer heat. "Milwaukee Bank suspended trading. The Stock Exchange is considering closing. And now Cleveland has called an emergency session of Congress to repeal the Sherman Silver Purchase Act." He pulled a hand down his face. "We need all hands on deck, and the chief wants you at the forefront."

"I accept. Where do you want me to start?"

"The first thing is to immediately wrap up the serialization. Right now. This week." He whirled his hand in a dismissive gesture. "Marry off the girl to the bibliomaniac, get them entrenched in a home, and have her happily waiting for him as he comes home from work."

Reeve slowly lowered his hand. "She's a New Woman."

"So?"

"That's the whole point of being a New Woman. They don't

want to be reduced to housewifery. They feel it would take away everything that is special about them."

Ulrich's brows shot up. "*Reduce* them to housewifery? Good gravy, Wilder. Housewifery in a home of their own is the ultimate reward."

"Not to them, it isn't."

"Who cares about them? Besides, you've spent the entire year waging war against the New Woman. Why all this squeamishness?"

He shifted in his chair, unable to answer. He didn't know why he was so reluctant, only that he was.

Ulrich moved a stack of paper to the corner of his desk. "No, you've put the poor bibliomaniac through all the paces of courtship—which you've done an excellent job of, by the way. You've quite a knack for fiction, but that's neither here nor there. The point is, you can't take him—and the readers—through all of that, then consign Marylee to the shelf as an old maid. We'd lose the subscriptions we gained and possibly some of the ones we've had for years." He shook his head. "Absolutely not. You marry her off."

Reeve crossed his legs. "Okay, I'll marry her to the bibliomaniac, but she retains her job."

Ulrich reared back. "After she's married? Are you out of your mind? No woman is allowed to work after she's married."

"Some are."

"Well, maybe if they live in the tenements and if they're desperate, but not our women. Not the women who are reading our paper."

"I think you underestimate them. I think they'd be thrilled."

Ulrich set his arms on the desk and leaned forward. "And what about their husbands, Wilder? The husbands who pay for the subscriptions? What exactly do you think they would have to say about that?"

He hesitated. They wouldn't like it. They wouldn't like it at all.

Ulrich gave him a pointed stare. "You've no choice. The story has been headed in this direction the entire time. Marry her off, put her in the home, and tie it up with a pretty little bow. Then get to D.C. and find out what will happen if the Sherman Act is repealed and what will happen if it's not."

Reeve sat up a little straighter. "You're sending me to D.C.?"

"Not permanently, just for Cleveland's speech next week, then a few days after. But before you leave, I want the final installment of the serialization on my desk. I want it in time for Sunday's paper, and I want it just the way I've asked for it. Understood?"

With a sigh, Reeve rubbed his forehead. He didn't want to end it that way. Not now, when he'd just begun to understand that not all New Women were man-haters. Some just wanted to earn a wage they could call their own. Others wanted to follow a dream they wouldn't otherwise be able to follow. And yet others wanted a bit of independence. His Marylee was that kind of New Woman. She'd started out as a man-hater, but she'd come around and now, now she was downright likable. He couldn't just marry her off willy-nilly to the bibliomaniac. The man didn't deserve her.

He took in a slow breath. They were only characters. It was fiction. He'd spent so much time with them in his head, they were beginning to feel like real people.

"Are you going to be this much trouble as a features writer, Wilder?" Ulrich asked. "Because if you are, then maybe—"

Reeve stood. "I'll have the last installment on your desk within a day and I'll end it however you want me to end it."

He'd waited too long for this opportunity and the salary that went along with it. Besides, he could write articles about real New Women, not pretend ones. New Women who had no interest in being generals or railway presidents, but who simply wanted to exercise their minds. Perhaps he'd search some out, heads of departments—like Mrs. Driscoll. Or women who were secretaries for giant oil magnates. Women who kept business secrets as well as any man, and who worked for men who had placed tremendous faith in their business abilities and judgments.

If he had to sacrifice his Marylee character for the greater good, so be it. He might have based her in many ways on Flossie, but the character wasn't Flossie. He'd do well to remember it.

With a nod at his employer, he strode from the office thrilled with his raise and the opportunity to be a features writer. Still, he was determined to bring Marylee to heel as gently as he possibly could.

CHAPTER

62

Flossie was holding a Marylee Merrily party in the parlor. The *New York World* had made much of today's column being the final chapter in Marylee's story. Everyone in the house had pledged not to read it until the party. Mrs. Klausmeyer had even agreed to hold the newspaper in safekeeping so no one would be tempted to peek.

Finally, the time had arrived. Mrs. Klausmeyer handed Flossie the paper. Though their landlady was only in her forties, her mousy brown hair had thinned out so much, her part was almost half an inch wide. Her Puritan-like gown of black alpaca had been taken up to fit her reedy frame. As with many thin women, her face sagged a bit more at the jowls than those with more robust figures.

Flossie had fully expected her to leave, for she usually kept herself separate from the rest of them. At first, Flossie couldn't understand why she was so distant, but after the Trostles, she realized the wisdom of it. It would be hard enough to demand rent from a delinquent boarder or, heaven forbid, evict them. But if she'd gone to their parties on the roof, or on the ice, or even taken her meals with them, it would have made her duties as a landlady exponentially harder.

This time, though, the woman stopped at the parlor's doorway and leaned against its frame.

Clearing her throat, Flossie shook out the paper and began to read. "*Marylee suspected what was coming. Mr. Bookish stood before her with his hair slicked down, his best suit brushed, and a bouquet of roses in his hand. He handed her the flowers.*

"*Accepting them, she buried her nose in their soft, silky petals to give her more time, more time to calm her nerves and her fears. Though she'd anticipated a moment of nerves when this momentous occasion arrived, she hadn't foreseen the fear. Before she could explore her feelings further, Mr. Bookish knelt down on one knee and took her hand in his.*

"*'Miss Merrily, will you do me the great honor of being my wife?'*"

"Oh! Oh!" Annie Belle cried. "He's asked her. He's finally asked her. Oh, my. Oh, my. I have butterflies in my stomach."

Flossie smiled at her friend, but didn't share her own thoughts aloud. For though her stomach had also jumped when the proposal had been made, it had not been a jump of joy. Yet she couldn't exactly pinpoint why.

"Carry on," Mr. Nettels said, giving up all pretense that he, too, wasn't on the edge of his seat.

Flossie continued to read. "*Marylee opened her mouth to say yes, then stalled. What of the photography business she'd built up? She'd started as an amateur, and without the assistance or backing of any man, she'd become a professional with a long list of clientele and a significant income.*

"*'What of my photography?' she asked.*

"*With a patronizing laugh, Mr. Bookish rose to his feet. 'My darling, you can give it up. You'll be free. Once you become my wife, you'll never have to toil or labor again.'*

"*She rubbed a rose petal between her fingers. She wanted to sit down, to reflect, but she couldn't do that. One simply didn't behave in that fashion when a wonderful man like Mr. Bookish had asked the question every woman longs to hear."*

"What a silly twit," Mr. Holliday said. "Does she really believe her little hobby is anything more than a frivolity? Honestly, I'm not sure but what the bibliomaniac would be better off without her. Maybe she'll say no."

"Hush your mouth." Mrs. Dinwiddie waved her hand. "Go on, Flossie."

" 'I could close up my shop, I suppose,' Marylee said. 'But I hate the thought of giving it up completely. What if we set up a little room for me in the back of our house? That way I wouldn't have to give it up completely.'

" 'And still charge a fee for it?'

" 'Well, of course.'

"The bibliomaniac pulled down his brows. 'Now, you know better than that. No woman is allowed to work once she has married. Not only is it rather crass, but all of your time will be taken up in the management of our home, in preparing our meals.' He raised her hand to his lips. 'And one day—very soon, I hope—in the raising of our children.'

"She blushed prettily."

Clasping her hands in a prayer-like fashion, Annie Belle pressed them to her heart and sighed.

"Marylee looked down, afraid to meet his eyes. All of what he said was true. And she wanted those things. She just . . . she just wished she could have them all plus her photography."

"She's starting to really annoy me now," Mr. Oyster said. "The fellow has offered her everything he has on a silver platter. Who in their right mind wouldn't want to be free to do nothing while someone else does all the work and earns all the money?"

Flossie thought of her mother, her aunt, and her grandmother. "Marylee will not be sitting around doing nothing. She'll be scrubbing, mopping, polishing, cooking, toting, and raising the children.

I daresay her photography would be much less demanding and a great deal more enjoyable."

Total silence descended. Mr. Holliday's mouth dropped open. Mrs. Holliday's eyes widened. Annie Belle gave her an incredulous stare. Mr. Nettels curled his lip. Mrs. Klausmeyer's expression remained unchanged.

Flossie moved her attention to Reeve. It was the first time he'd joined them in the parlor since the day of their kiss. Retaining eye contact with her, he propped his elbows on his knees, then rested his mouth on his clasped hands.

Clucking her tongue, Mrs. Dinwiddie smoothed her skirt. "I think you have forgotten something, Flossie. God has commanded us to be fruitful and to multiply. Marylee is being given the opportunity to fulfill the greatest commission a female can ever aspire to. The work of her hands as she takes care of her home and her children is not toil. It is a blessing."

The *greatest* commission? Flossie wasn't sure she agreed, but she decided not to belabor the point. She returned her attention to the paper. "*The bibliomaniac cupped Marylee's face. Her cheek was as smooth and soft as the petals in her hands. 'You haven't answered me, my love. Will you be my wife?'*

"*Marylee stared into his eyes and realized all he said was right. Her camera would be a very lonely substitute for Mr. Bookish and the life he was offering.*

"*She smiled. 'Yes, Mr. Bookish. Yes, I would be most honored to be your wife.'*

"*Taking the bouquet from her hands, he set it on the table, then took her arm. 'Come, let's tell our families and celebrate with them the beginning of the rest of our lives.'*"

Flossie laid the paper in her lap, her heart in her throat.

The room erupted in applause, everyone talking and exclaiming as if they were the family members Marylee and Mr. Bookish had just announced their news to. All but Reeve. He hadn't moved. Still sat with his mouth against his clasped hands, his focus on her.

He was too far away for her to see his expression, exactly, but somehow she knew that even though he didn't subscribe to everything the New Woman stood for, he was just as disturbed by the ending as she was.

She lowered her gaze. At least Marylee had a choice. Flossie didn't have any. If someone ever asked her for her hand, she'd have to say no whether she wanted to or not. Still, she wished Marylee hadn't given in so quickly and so readily. The entire thing left a bitter taste in her mouth.

"She wasn't exactly sure when her playtime changed from courtship rituals and married life to the adventures of a woman on her own, a woman artist who was so renowned her paintings were in museums all over the world."

CHAPTER
63

Flossie excused herself early and returned to her bedroom. She'd been working and sketching and sewing so much that she found herself exhausted and in no mood for the festive atmosphere pervading the parlor. Lifting her chin, she unbuttoned the clasp of her bolero and caught sight of the phenakistascope. Mr. Holliday had given it to her just last week and she'd wedged it between the wall and her mirror for safekeeping.

Reaching up, she plucked it from its spot. It reminded her of a child's pinwheel, except the face was flat and had been divided like thirteen pieces of a pie. At the end of each section was a photograph of her and Reeve. Turning it so the photographs faced the mirror, she held tightly to the wooden handle. With her other hand, she pinched the edge of the disc, then she looked through tiny slits Mr. Holliday had cut on either side of each photo. With a flick of her wrist, she spun the disc.

Before her eyes, she and Reeve danced round and round in the mirror. So fluid was the movement, no one would suspect that Mr. Holliday had positioned them for each step. That Reeve had taken a gentle pull on her ear with his lips. That he'd not kept his hand above the small of her back where it belonged. That he'd whispered sweet sentiments into her ear.

She spun it again and again, remembering the feeling of being in his arms, the potency of his kiss, and the connections they'd made—not just when they danced, but when they talked in his room, when they rode on the streetcar, when they answered each other's questions at dinner, when they'd walked home after the debacle at the gallery, and even back when he'd warmed her feet the night she'd been caught in a storm.

She thought of Mr. I. D. Claire's characters who shared a love so strong that Marylee had given up her life's passion for the man who'd asked for her hand.

She spun the phenakistascope again. Her eyes filled. The image blurred. She was in love with Reeve Wilder.

Snapping her finger and thumb on the disc, she brought it to a halt and peeked at herself over the disc. She didn't look like a woman in love. She didn't have any glow or starry expression. She had bags under her eyes, wilted shoulders, and a mouth that showed no indication of joy.

Lowering the phenakistascope, she ran a thumb over the photographs, now still and frozen. All during her childhood she'd dreamed about the man she'd eventually love. She'd made up elaborate courtships, scooting two child-sized chairs side by side and going for buggy rides with her pretend man. Setting up rows of chairs and playing church. They'd listened to pretend sermons while she fanned herself and he gave her loving looks.

Soon they had babies. Lots of babies. Gathering her dollies around them, they went on Sunday picnics on her bed. Both she and her man played games with their children. Games that could only be played with bunches of children, not just one.

The two of them collected their tired babies and rode home, the swaying of the buggy lulling the little ones to sleep. She gave the dollies baths, dressed them in their nightclothes, and when it was time to put them to bed, he came to help, too, because he couldn't stand to be away from her or them for very long.

She spun the phenakistascope again. Such a lovely fantasy, a charming dream. Back then, there was no such thing as a New Woman. There were no options for women at all other than wife, mother, and old maid. She wasn't exactly sure when her playtime changed from courtship rituals and married life to the adventures of a woman on her own, a woman artist who was so renowned her paintings were in museums all over the world.

Suddenly, instead of sitting next to her husband in church, she was surrounded by imaginary friends from the cream of society. Vanderbilts, Rockefellers, Morgans. She knew all the names of the important ones, for she'd read the society pages to see if Mother's gowns were ever mentioned.

She received imaginary invitations to dinner at the governor's house, and even the White House. First Lady Arthur was a great admirer of Flossie's work. The president's wife commissioned her to paint enough pieces to convert one of the rooms in the White House to the Florence Rebecca Jayne Room, and Flossie was invited to stay in it whenever she wanted.

Well, now she really was a New Woman and also in love. Neither looked even remotely like her fantasies. She'd been swindled. She owed more money than she could pay back. She worked her fingers to the bone. Her job was in jeopardy. She hadn't painted in ages. And even if the man she was in love with reciprocated her feelings, she couldn't act on them or she'd lose her job.

Swallowing the emotion in her throat, she began to tuck the phenakistascope back into its place, then paused. She wanted no constant reminder of a love that would never be. She ran her thumb along the edge of the disk. She couldn't get rid of the phenakistascope, not as long as she lived in the same house as Mr. Holliday. Perhaps she should give it to Reeve. He wouldn't have any problems with it.

He liked her, of course, and watched her when he thought she wasn't looking. And he'd certainly kissed her as if he had feelings for her, but he hadn't pursued her or followed up on those kisses. So chances were, this little device would be nothing more to him than a simple novelty.

With a deep breath, she headed to his room. Annie Belle passed her.

"You turning in for the night?" Flossie asked.

Annie Belle covered a yawn. "I am. Where are you off to?"

Flossie held up the phenakistascope. "I'm going to drop this off in Mr. Wilder's room. I haven't had time to show it to him yet and don't know when I will."

Nodding, Annie Belle continued into their room.

Flossie peeked into Reeve's. It was empty, other than Cat curled up on his bed. He must still be in the parlor.

Stepping inside, she set the phenakistascope on his desk. The cat figurine she'd given him held a place of honor not too far from his inkwell. She remembered struggling with her decision about what token she should bring him from the fair. His gift had been by far the hardest to select. She wondered if even back then she'd been in some degree attracted to him. Certainly, she'd always thought him handsome, but never had she expected to fall in love with him.

Cat jumped up onto the desk, startling Flossie and knocking some neatly stacked papers onto the floor.

"*Tut, tut,*" Flossie said, running a hand down Cat's back. "You know how your master is about everything being just so. He wouldn't like to see his papers scattered all over the place, so I'll collect them for you and save you from a scolding."

Cat turned around in a figure eight, butting up against Flossie's hand. She petted the cat a couple more times, then squatted down and began to pick up the pages. She turned over each one and rotated it so it was facing the right direction. Bending over, she reached for a couple that had slipped beneath his chair, saw her name, and paused.

We had corn on the cob with our meal. Miss Jayne ate hers like a typewriter . . . Someone else is putting questions beneath the plate across from Miss Jayne. I have no idea who . . . I'd forgotten how much of a disruption she is. I won't be able to include that aspect of Miss Jayne's personality into my column. No one would believe it.

Frowning, she sat back on her heels. Include it in his column? What did that mean? She continued to skim.

Miss Jayne had a set of wooden castanets which she'd purchased at the fair . . . First her head, then her shoulders, waist, and hips undulated—all in time to the castanets snapping at her fingertips. By the time she finished I could scarcely breathe.

She touched the hollow at the base of her throat. She'd done that? He'd felt like that? Skirts billowing out about her, she turned back to the pages she'd stacked and flipped through them more slowly.

We played The Board Game of Old Maid. As idiotic as the game was, it ended up being a godsend. It mapped out the entire plot of a love story. Now I know exactly what to do with Marylee and Bookish.

Sucking in a breath, she covered her mouth.

Miss Jayne's favorite thing to paint is portraits. I shall make Marylee a photographer. Close enough.

Flossie's heart began to pick up speed.

Miss Jayne has been the center of her world her entire life. Perhaps I shall give Marylee that same quality.

Breathing became difficult. She took a deep breath in, pushed a deep breath out. Cat rubbed against her. Flossie pushed the cat out of the way, picking up yet another page.

The Trostles proclaimed Miss Jayne a "remarkable talent." And because her parents have told her the same thing her entire life, she has no reason to doubt them. I worry what might happen if Bourgeois doesn't accept her work into his gallery. How can I incorporate this into Marylee's character?

Her stomach turned sour. She closed her eyes to stem the nausea. When she opened them, Reeve was there, frozen in the doorway.

"You're I. D. Claire," she said, her voice sounding funny, even to her own ears.

He looked at the papers in her hand.

"They fell off your desk." She nodded toward Cat, who now wove between his legs. "I was setting the phenakistascope on your desk. Cat jumped up, knocked off the papers, and I, of course, gathered them." She swallowed. "Until I saw my name. Then I began to read them."

He opened his mouth, then closed it.

Looking up at the ceiling, she clenched her jaw, anger seeping into her veins. "You've been using me as fodder for your column."

Still, he said nothing.

She held up the papers and shook them as their contents replayed within her mind. "A disruption to the household? The center of my own world? A remarkable talent in my own eyes?"

"I don't think that."

"No?" Pushing herself to her feet, she slapped the papers onto his desk. "You expect me to believe you lie to yourself in your own notes?"

"I wrote those parts before I got to know you."

"Is that so?" Spreading the papers out on the desk, she rifled through them in a disjointed and slapdash manner until she found the one she was looking for. "What about this one?"

"Flossie—"

She held up her hand to stem his words, then read from the paper. "*Flossie has aspirations of being a designer. At Tiffany's. I worry that she learned nothing from the Bourgeois debacle. She is simply so accustomed to having the world at her feet that she can't seem to formulate realistic expectations. Perhaps I should put Marylee in a position where she cannot order the bad times away. Where she is forced to be realistic.*"

He raked a hand through his hair. "I didn't mean anything by that."

She pointed to the date, her hand trembling. "That's the day you saw me sketching my tea screen. The day you kissed me. You wrote that after those kisses, Reeve? How could you?"

He pinched the bridge of his nose. "You're blowing this all out of proportion."

"I don't think so." Her chest began to ache. "You've spent countless weeks turning me into a satire. Poking fun at me. Watching me read out loud about *myself* to the entire household. Facilitating discussions about the merits and the flaws of *myself*!"

He shook his head. "I didn't. She's not . . . you're not . . ." He took a deep breath. "Marylee isn't half the woman you are. She's not even real. She's a figment of my imagination."

"A figment based on *me*." She jabbed herself in the chest. "And clearly, you must think me the biggest idiot you've ever encountered."

"I don't. I don't think that at all."

"Oh, I think you do. Even I can't misinterpret those notes." In a burst of anger and hurt, she swept her hand across the desk, scattering the pages. Her fingertips caught the edge of the figurine. It flew out to the side, then tripped across the floor with a succession of clanks. She didn't even look to see if it had broken.

"Flossie, please, let me explain."

"You have an explanation?" She crossed her arms, hugging herself. "And I suppose you think I'll just swallow whatever it is you feed me? After all that? Now who's being unrealistic?"

"Just listen, please? I agreed to write the Marylee story for the money. Money to use toward a down payment on a house. Not just any house, but the house I was born in, that I lived in with my parents. If I manage to buy it, it will be the first time since my mother died that I'll have lived someplace I belong. Not my grandparents' house, not my stepmother's house, not my landlady's house. My house." He searched her eyes. "I need that, Flossie. I need someplace I belong."

"Well, bully for you." She jutted out her chin. "What I'd like to know is just what that has to do with me? How, in all the chumbutted luck, did I get dragged into the whole thing?"

"I'd never written a line of fiction in my life. I didn't know the first thing about it. It was my editor who suggested I base the characters on the boarders I lived with."

Her eyes widened. "We're all in it? Who is Mr. Bookish?"

"No, no. No one was the least bit interesting, other than you and Mrs. Dinwiddie—and I couldn't include her or everyone would've known I was I. D. Claire. But you, Flossie, you . . ." He looked at her, his eyes pleading. "You made the story come alive. Basing the character on you was a compliment."

"Compliment? You expect me to believe it was a *compliment*? When you painted me in such an uncomplimentary fashion?"

"Everyone loves Marylee."

"She's spoiled and runs everyone else's lives."

He rubbed his mouth. "She had redeeming qualities, especially toward the end."

"You made me a laughingstock, Reeve, and the actual 'observations' you took of me are even worse than the ones you fictionalized." She pressed her fingers against her temples. "To think you toned me down because you 'couldn't include' my behavior in the column for it was too outlandish. Too unbelievable. Too *infantile*."

He pulled down his brows. "Now you're just making things up. I never said that."

"You didn't have to." She fisted her hands at her sides. "It was implied. If you don't believe me, go back and read it for yourself." Whirling around, she began to pace. "I should have listened to you from the start. You said you didn't want a friend. You were fine with your life the way it was. But, no, I had to have compassion for you. I had to make it my mission to befriend you. And that's just what I did. I poured myself out like an offering—an offering of *true* friendship." She covered her face with her hands. "Then I ended up offering you even more than friendship, didn't I? Right here in this very room. And you took that offering and desecrated it in the worst possible way."

"Flossie, I'd never—"

Shaking her head, she took a step back. "Not another word. I've received the message this time. I've heard you loud and clear. You can rest assured, Mr. Wilder, you won't have to *ever* deal with the likes of me again." She headed toward the door.

He blocked her way. "What's that supposed to mean?"

"It means I'm moving."

His jaw slackened. "Moving?"

"That's right. Moving. So you won't have to worry about me intruding on you or anyone else anymore. For all I care, you can take that loneliness you love so much, wrap yourself up in it, and choke on it. Now, get out of my way."

He didn't budge. "Don't move because of me."

"I can't stay here." Her throat began to clog. "Not anymore. The Trostles were bad enough, but you, Reeve, you've made a joke of me and laid it out in print for my parents, my friends, my housemates, my workmates, and hundreds of others to see."

"I didn't, Flossie. You aren't Marylee and she's not you."

She pointed to his desk. "I've seen your notes, Reeve. And, and . . ." Her nostrils flared. "I'm not staying. I can't. I simply—"

"Yes, you are. If anyone leaves, it'll be me."

She stared at him, pushing back her tears by sheer force of will. And truth be told, why should she be the one to tuck tail and run? Especially when she couldn't afford to move. With all the money he'd made at her expense, he ought to be the one inconvenienced.

She swiped her nose with her hand. "I'm going home. I'll stay at my parents' house for a week. When I get back, if you're still here, I'll pack my things. Now, get out of my way or so help me I won't be responsible for what I do to you."

After a slight hesitation, he stepped to the side.

She stormed past him and opened the door to her room, then slammed it behind her.

Annie Belle stood by Flossie's bed, a hand against her throat.

Flossie took a trembling breath. "I'm sorry I slammed the door."

Annie Belle shook her head. "I heard every word."

"What?"

Annie Belle pointed to the wall. "I heard every word. It was as if you and Mr. Wilder were right in here with me." She looked at the wall, then back at Flossie. "All this time, all these months, he's heard every single word you and I have ever said to each other. Including these."

The blood drained from Flossie's head, then rushed back in. Grabbing a book from her bookshelf, she hurtled it at the wall. "A pox on you, Reeve Wilder, you spineless, arrogant, lily-livered son of a sea cook!"

Annie Belle slapped a hand over her mouth.

Flossie took a deep, gulping breath, then covered her face and sank to the floor.

"You needn't yell, Flossie," he said, his voice muffled, but perfectly distinguishable. "I can hear you and I'm sorry."

"Shut up," she mumbled, sobs shaking her shoulders. "Just shut up."

Annie Belle rushed to her, put her arms around her, and held her while she wept silent tears, for she wouldn't give that beggarly, horse's backend the satisfaction of hearing her cry.

CHAPTER

64

Not another sound came from Flossie's room. No murmuring, no crying, not even the springs of her bed had squeaked. He'd pulled his notes together earlier that evening so he could burn them in the parlor after everyone had retired. He'd set them on the side so as not to forget. What an idiot.

He picked up the phenakistascope. For a brief moment, one part of his brain—the part that had become expert at pushing aside all emotion—noted that Holliday had done it. He'd actually made a phenakistascope out of photographs. The other part of his brain stared at the pictures.

They were in shades of black, gray, and white instead of the vivid colors that came alive in his memory. The sunny yellow of her gown, the blue of her bows, the brown of her eyes, the seashell-pink of her skin. Nor did they capture the scent of her hair and the warmth of her hand in his. He sighed. Photographs were a poor substitute for having the living, breathing Flossie in his arms.

He walked to the mirror and held the handle so that the photos reflected back at him. He peeked through slots and spun the disc. Round and round the two of them danced. The tinny tune of *Blue Danube* kept time in his mind, and that was his undoing.

It brought him back to not just the afternoon Holliday took the pictures, but the afternoon Reeve had waltzed with her in his room. The afternoon he'd *connected* with her. The afternoon she'd terrified the life out of him because she'd touched something so deep, so buried, that he'd been completely stripped bare.

No one else had ever touched that part of him before. Not the girl he'd danced with when he was sixteen. Not the girls he'd stolen kisses from in his youth. Not even his mother, for he had no memories of her alive.

And now, he'd injured her. Injured the very woman whom, he suddenly realized, he cared for more than he knew. He'd used her, she was right about that. He'd tried to deny it at first, but no excuse would make up for what he'd done. And she'd rejected him. Rightly so.

He couldn't say he was surprised. Life had taught him that some people were lovable and some weren't. He happened to be in the latter group. He wasn't complaining, wasn't moping, just stating the facts.

The only person he'd ever made any lasting connection with was an old woman who didn't have anyone else willing to take tea with her. If she had, he'd have taken second fiddle to them, he was sure, for all connections he'd ever made were brief. Fleeting. Passing. So he never allowed himself to open up. He kept to himself. He didn't dance. It was easier to be alone than to make and lose a connection.

Raising the lid of his trunk, he refused to think about how much he'd miss Flossie and how much he'd miss Mrs. Dinwiddie. Instead, he shut down his mind and began to pack.

CHAPTER
65

Flossie returned from her week at home no more refreshed than she had been when she'd left. Her parents' new place was hot, stuffy, and small. It was on the very fringes of a respectable neighborhood, just two blocks over from abject poverty.

In addition to that, living at home wasn't the same now that she'd been out on her own. The way her parents hovered and gave her constant praise used to bring her comfort and a sense of inner peace. Now it brought Reeve's words to mind over and over.

The Trostles proclaimed Miss Jayne a "remarkable talent." And because her parents have told her the same thing her entire life, she has no reason to doubt them . . . She's has been the center of her world her entire life . . . She can't seem to formulate realistic expectations . . . She, the sun which all planets orbit around.

She'd never really noticed it before, never had a reason to question it, but now she began to question everything. Was she really as puffed up as Reeve suggested? Was she only happy when she was the center of attention? Did she have any skill at painting whatsoever, or had it merely been trumped-up accolades on her parents' part?

They hadn't lied to her. They hadn't patronized her on purpose.

She had no doubt they truly meant it, but their perspective was biased, very biased.

She paused at Reeve's doorway. If she'd thought his room barren before, it now held no life at all. The bed had been stripped of linens, his desk cleared of all contents, and the window was shuttered, barring any entrance for Cat.

Had he taken his pet with him? Where had he gone? Who would he connect with?

She shook herself. It was no concern of hers. He'd used her, just like the Trostles had—premeditated and for monetary gain. At least with the Trostles, she would eventually be able to earn back the money they'd stolen. She'd never get back the self-respect Reeve had taken.

That night at dinner everyone filled her in on all she'd missed while she was away. Reeve had left the day before she returned. He'd paid his rent in full and taken Cat with him. He hadn't offered anyone a forwarding address. All were still reeling to discover the famous I. D. Claire had been none other than their very own housemate.

Two nights after that, everyone wanted to know why she'd not placed any questions under their plates. Why she'd not organized any games in the parlor.

She had no answer. What could she say? That the entire purpose of the questions was to draw Reeve out? That the entire purpose of the parlor games was to make them a family unit? She'd failed miserably on both counts, so she simply told them she was tired. She needed to take a break from organizing the activities.

Mr. Holliday frowned. "You've been working too hard, Miss Jayne. It's not good for the fair sex to tax themselves to such an extent. You must be a good steward of your vitality. No man wants a worn out hag."

Annie Belle stiffened. "She's not a worn out hag."

"Not yet."

Mr. Oyster gave her a smile he'd given her many times before. She hadn't noticed until now how suggestive it was. "Perhaps what you need, Miss Jayne, is a bit of fresh air. A little manly attention."

You must be very careful not to encourage Oyster. His motives for the charm he exudes are not completely honorable.

Despite her disillusionment with Reeve, she heeded his words.

After dinner, Mr. Oyster pulled her aside, his hair in its usual disarray, his smile lopsided and charming. "Might I interest you in a walk? We've a full moon tonight."

The fantasies of her youth came rushing back. The man of her dreams took her on moonlit walks, but Mr. Oyster wasn't the man of her dreams.

"Thank you, but I think I'll retire. Perhaps another time."

He cupped her elbow, drawing her close. "Nonsense. We could walk to the park and find a quiet, out of the way bench. You can tell me of your troubles." His eyes dropped to half-mast. His thumb caressed her elbow. "Then I will chase them away."

A shiver of alarm ran through her. She stepped away, breaking their contact. "I'm sorry, I'm afraid I wouldn't be very good company, but thank you."

Irritation flashed in his eyes, then was erased in a blink.

She'd known, of course, that he wasn't her family, but she had thought he was her friend. Now she wasn't so sure. The realization so saddened her, she retired early but didn't fall asleep until it was almost time to get up for work.

CHAPTER

66

Flossie approached the open doorway of Mrs. Driscoll's office, her heart in her throat. Her confidence in her artistic abilities had been shaken to the core, but Mrs. Driscoll had asked Flossie to come see her and to bring her sketchpad. The request surprised her, coming as it had just as she and the other girls were heading outside to the benches for lunch. She tucked away her lunch pail, fetched her pad, and opened it to the sketches she'd made of the tea screen.

"Knock, knock," she said.

Mrs. Driscoll looked up. "Come in, Miss Jayne."

Swallowing, she handed Mrs. Driscoll her sketch. Setting down her pencil, Mrs. Driscoll sat back against her chair and studied it.

"It's a tea screen," Flossie said, unable to endure the silence.

"What are these?" Mrs. Driscoll pointed to the borders.

"Spiders."

"Ahhhh." Placing one arm across her torso, she cupped her elbow and tapped a finger against her mouth. "Where are their legs, exactly?"

Flossie moistened her lips. "Right there." She pointed to them.

Mrs. Driscoll turned her head to the side so that her ear almost touched her shoulder. "These? Right here?"

Flossie chewed the inside of her cheek. "No. These." She pointed again. "Right here."

"They're rather hard to make out, aren't they?"

"Apparently so."

Mrs. Driscoll let out a long sigh. "It's not your fault. Spiders are something only a designer with a great deal of skill and experience would attempt. Even then, I'm not sure she—or he—would be able to pull it off. You'd have been much better advised to do something with cobwebs. I love the thought of light cascading through a cobweb."

Flossie looked at her sketch, picturing a cobweb stretched out between the flowers. "Oh, my, yes. That would have been lovely."

"I do like your idea of a stained-glass tea screen, though. What kind of flowers are these? Apple blossoms?"

"Amaryllis."

"Of course. They're lovely." She picked up her pencil, then sketched a design beside Flossie's. It had cobwebs with apple blossoms peeking around its edges. It was a hundred times better than any of the designs Flossie had made, yet Mrs. Driscoll had sketched hers in less than a minute.

"Something like this," the woman said. "See?"

"I do. It's . . . I don't know what to say. It's simply so much better. Mr. Tiffany is right. You truly do have great creative ability."

And I don't, she thought, looking at her creation.

"What you have isn't bad, Miss Jayne. It's just not up to Tiffany standards."

She shifted her weight. "What about Mr. Mitchell?"

"What about him?"

"Well, he's always looking for things that are simplistic. Do you think he'd like it?"

Mrs. Driscoll gave her a sympathetic smile. "There is a difference between simple and average. Your design is, . . . well, it's . . ."

"Average," Flossie finished for her.

"There's nothing wrong with average."

"Unless you work for Louis Comfort Tiffany." Swallowing, Flossie held her tears at bay. Reeve was right. All her life she'd been told she was above average, well above average. A natural-born artist. That she was spectacular at everything she did. Looking back, she wondered how she could have been so gullible. Perhaps if she'd had siblings, she'd have learned from them that she wasn't quite the genius she thought she was—or that her parents thought she was. But she hadn't had any siblings.

Pushing back her chair, Mrs. Driscoll rose and crossed to the window. Sunlight cut a swath behind her, dust particles dancing in its path. "Actually, I wanted to talk to you about that."

"About what?"

"About working for Mr. Tiffany." Mrs. Driscoll picked at a piece of paint peeling from the windowsill. "As you know, the men are back. Now that we've finished this last order of windows for Beecher Memorial Church, it appears we won't have enough work to keep all of us busy."

Flossie caught her breath. "But surely, with the success of the chapel, it's just a matter of time before the orders start flooding in."

Turning toward her, Mrs. Driscoll leaned a hip against the windowsill. "Perhaps, but for now, I've been told to reduce our numbers."

"No." Flossie breathed, her heart working as if it were pumping molasses instead of blood.

"I'm going to have to let you go, Miss Jayne. I'm so very sorry."

She took a step forward. "Please, Mrs. Driscoll, I'll work harder, stay longer, take less money, anything. Please."

Mrs. Driscoll gave her a sad smile. "No one doubts your willingness to work hard. You come in early and stay late, you never complain, and everyone adores you."

She swallowed. "Then please let me stay, please."

"I'm sorry."

She covered her mouth. "Who else? Who else is leaving?"

"Just you, for now."

She sucked in a breath. Out of all twelve girls, she was the most expendable? "I'm the worst? Out of everyone?"

"Don't misunderstand me, dear. You may not be the best of the best, but you are certainly competent. And being competent is a very good thing."

"If I'm competent, then why can't I stay?"

"Because someone has to go."

"But why did you send me to the fair, then, if I was your weakest worker?"

"At the time, you'd been cutting glass longer than anyone else and for demonstration purposes, the speed in which you cut isn't as critical as it is in our everyday work." She gave a soft smile. "Besides, Mr. Tiffany felt you'd be quite good at speaking to a crowd, and from what I understand, he was right. He went on and on about how much everyone enjoyed you." She pulled at her ear. "Unfortunately, speaking to crowds isn't something we're likely to do again. Cutting quickly and efficiently is much more important."

"I know I'm not as fast at cutting as Lulu and Elizabeth, but couldn't you let me trace the designs, or help Aggie with the foil, or—?"

"I'm sorry, truly sorry. I'll be happy to give you a recommendation, though."

Flossie's heart slammed against her chest. Her head felt light.

She handed Flossie a pouch of coins. "This is the pay we owe you. I wish you the very best. We'll all miss you, I can assure you of that." Mrs. Driscoll returned to her chair and began to work in a ledger.

Her entire body shaking, Flossie gathered her lunch pail and walked out of Tiffany Glass and Decorating Company for good.

CHAPTER
67

I've lost my job." Flossie stood in the kitchen of the boarding-house, its whitewashed plaster coated with a thin layer of grime. Green paint peeled from the tongue-and-groove dado covering the lower half of the wall. The scent of stewed tomatoes touched the air.

Mrs. Klausmeyer stood beside the stove, a stained, dull-white apron covering her black gown from neck to knee. She swiped her forehead with the corner of her apron. "You're leaving, then?"

"I don't want to. I know you do everything by yourself and could certainly use some help, so I was hoping that perhaps you'd allow me to clean the chambers in exchange for room, board, and one dollar a week."

Steam whirled above a large pot on the stove like a tornado trying to form. Mrs. Klausmeyer picked up a long-handled spoon, her shoulders wilting. "You'll be the fourth boarder I've lost. At this rate, I won't be able to keep the house, much less pay you."

"I'll just work for room and board, then, until we fill Mr. Wilder's room."

A lump of dough sat on a flour board, waiting to be punched into submission. She could help with that, too. She'd missed cooking.

Would actually enjoy doing it again—assuming Mrs. Klausmeyer would have her.

The woman shook her head. "Even if we fill his, I can't afford a dollar a week. Not after the Trostles left me in such a bind. And what if Miss Love leaves, now that her rent will double?"

"But Annie Belle's won't double. Not if room is included as part of my pay."

"You can't stay in Miss Love's room. I'll not have servants living in the house. You'll need to move to an attic room."

Flossie blinked. She hadn't really thought of herself as a servant, just as someone helping out until she could find another job. "I need to earn something. I have debts to pay because of the Trostles."

Mrs. Klausmeyer blew a tendril of hair off her forehead. "You'll have to clean plus help in the scullery, then. And I can only pay you fifty cents."

"Seventy-five," Flossie countered.

"Sixty, plus meals and a room in the attic. That's the best I can do."

Flossie picked at her fingernail. "Can it be a dollar a week once Mr. Wilder's room is filled?"

"It can be a dollar a week once all the rooms are filled—Wilder's, the Trostles', and Miss Love's if she leaves."

Flossie glanced at the windows up by the ceiling, then wiped her hands on her skirt. "All right. It's a deal."

Nodding, Mrs. Klausmeyer gave the pot a stir. "Your meals will be taken in here, not in the dining room."

Flossie lowered her chin to her chest. "Of course."

Mrs. Klausmeyer looked around the kitchen. "Well, I guess you can start by scrubbing the vegetables, then I have a pile of pans and utensils that need scouring."

Flossie surveyed the carrots, potatoes, and onions lying on a table. She didn't see any dishes, but she assumed they were in the scullery. "I'll need to change first, and move my things."

"You can change, but you won't have time to move your things until after supper is over, the dishes are washed, dried, and put away, and the kitchen is clean."

Swallowing, Flossie pointed behind her with her thumb. "I'll go change, then, and be right back."

"You have fifteen minutes."

Keeping her expression neutral, Flossie left the kitchen. It would take her fifteen minutes just to undo all the buttons on her gown. Lifting her skirts, she scurried to her room.

26TH WARD YMCA BROOKLYN ³⁶

"Reeve took a room at the new YMCA in Brooklyn's East
New York, just a couple of blocks up from his home."

CHAPTER

68

Reeve took a room at the new YMCA in Brooklyn's East New York, just a couple of blocks up from his home. He'd wanted to be where he could keep an eye on the cottage. Only after he'd gone over to see if Mrs. Gusman needed any help had it occurred to him that Mr. Gusman might mistake his motives. So he'd turned back around without ever knocking on her door.

He tried to remember the name of the saloon Mr. Gusman frequented. She'd mentioned it on Reeve's first visit, but he couldn't recall it. Something German, but then, a lot of the saloons around here had German names. Still, if he found the right one, maybe he and Mr. Gusman could work out a deal.

He placed his inkwell and pen onto the desk in his room, then positioned Flossie's metal figurine beside it. It had survived its flight across the room without any damage. Slipping his hands into his pockets, he studied its detail. It was the first and only gift he'd ever received on a day that wasn't Christmas. And the first one he'd received since his grandparents' deaths in '86.

Cat meowed and did figure eights between his legs. Reaching down, he picked her up. It had taken some fancy talking to convince the Y that Cat should be allowed admittance, too, but for an additional fee they'd finally acquiesced. He glanced at the bed on the other side of the room and wondered what his roommate was like.

Normally, Reeve paid for a room by himself, but the Y didn't offer solitary lodging. He'd chosen the Y because it furnished young men such as himself with a club life that mimicked the larger, expensive clubs only men of affluence could join. It had a reading hall, a public hall, and a game room. It offered its members fireside talks, a chess and checker club, Bible studies, receptions, and even concerts.

What had captured Reeve's imagination the most, however, was the gymnasium with flying rings, climbing ropes, parallel bars, and a side horse. It had a second-story track running along its perimeter that was mostly used as a spectators' gallery.

He lowered himself to his cot. Somewhere between Grand Central Station and Washington, D.C., he'd admitted Flossie was right. It was time—past time—to make some friends. Nothing as intimate as what he'd had with her. Never again would he risk that, but he couldn't go back to total isolation. It simply no longer offered the peace and relief that it used to. So, when he'd left Klausmeyer's, he'd come to the Y.

For now he'd attend a few lectures, join a Bible study, lift some weights, and maybe even sign up to play baseball. At least, that's what he needed to do. That's what he should do. That's what he'd come here to do.

His neck and shoulders began to tense. It wasn't what he wanted to do. The thought of all those activities scared him to death, especially the team sports. Yet they were also the most alluring. During his entire twenty-seven years, he'd never participated in a ball game. Oh, he'd watched plenty from afar. He knew all the rules, and he'd played ball with nothing more than a wall, but pretending a wall was a person was completely different from doing the real thing.

He took a deep breath, then slowly released it. No need to do everything all at once. Just having a roommate would be a start. When he'd adjusted to that, there'd be plenty of time for lectures and baseball teams.

CHAPTER
69

We want you to come home." Mother stood in stiff disapproval while Flossie took the linens off Mr. Oyster's bed. "This is simply unacceptable. Neither your father nor I will have it."

For the first time in her life, Flossie did not have the proper attire for what she was doing. Even if Mother had had the time to make up black dresses with crisp white aprons, Flossie would have refused them. So she wore the old striped shirtwaists she'd used when she'd helped Mother in the garden.

"I'm not going home."

"Why?"

Flossie shook out the sheet and let it drift onto the bed. "You know why. I owe you money and I owe the . . . boarders money." She'd almost said the *other* boarders, but her assumption of domestic chores had changed everything. She was no longer a boarder, she was a servant. And everyone in the house, other than Annie Belle and Mrs. Dinwiddie, treated her as if she were beneath them. She was even required to address Annie Belle as Miss Love or risk losing her job.

Flossie shook her head. Those she'd once considered family, and then friends, now acted as if she were invisible. They ignored her when they passed her in the hall and when she carried in dishes of food for dinner. They spoke in sharp tones if she didn't keep their chambers exactly the way they liked. Annie Belle might help her clean behind a closed bedroom door, and would occasionally leave a book from the library in her attic room, but things were strained between them, especially when others were around.

Only Mrs. Dinwiddie treated her as before, regardless of who was or wasn't present. The woman would sit in a rocker by her window and tell Flossie about the new boarders and the old and ask her how she was and if there was anything she could do. She slipped Flossie cookies and tarts. She'd even climbed the stairs once to visit her in her tiny, hot, attic room.

Mother rounded the bed and began to tuck in the sheet on the opposite side, bringing Flossie back to the present.

"I don't want your money," Mother said. "I refuse to take it. I've told you that a thousand times. What I *want* is for you to quit this ridiculousness."

Flossie handed her mother a pillow slip while she, in turn, shook out a blanket. "I know what you said. So I'm putting aside five cents a week and when I have it all saved, I'll give it to you in one lump sum."

Mother slammed the pillow onto the bed. "I don't want it."

"Then you can give it to a charitable cause once I've paid it back."

"There is no need. I've told your father about it."

Flossie froze. "You told Papa? About the money you'd secreted away?"

"Of course I told him. He was going out of his mind trying to figure out why you wouldn't come home."

Flossie hugged the blanket to her. "What did he say?"

"He was furious. What do you think he said?"

"Did he have a wheezing attack?"

"That was the least of what he had. And do you know what else?"

Flossie shook her head.

"He was more angry with me for giving you the money than he was for me secreting it away."

Flossie looked down. "I'm sorry, Mother. I didn't mean to get you in trouble."

"Well, you can make it up to me by coming home."

Flossie laid the blanket on the bed and began to smooth it out. "I appreciate all you and Papa have done. I truly do, but you are barely making ends meet. You're better off with me here than there with you."

"Your father has said I could keep the money I earned."

Flossie straightened. "What?"

"Once he got over his anger, he thought about how I'd saved all that money over the years, and how he'd probably have gambled it away if he'd known about it. So, he told me to keep mine and not let him have it unless I knew what it was going to be used for."

Flossie touched her fingers to her throat. "He said that?"

"He didn't even want to know how much I was making—said it would be less tempting for him that way."

Flossie shook her head in wonder. "I'm stunned. I've never heard of a man doing such a thing."

"Your father is a wonderful man. He just went through a bad spell, is all, and we'd both like for you to come home."

"I'm sorry, Mother. I'm thrilled Papa has turned over this new leaf, but the money you saved was to counteract the very situation you are now in, and I squandered it away. You would never have had to move to that awful place if I hadn't run to you with my hands stretched out for more, more, more."

"Awful? You live in an attic room and you think our place is *awful?*" Mother rolled her eyes. "And we don't mind that you want more. We love giving you more. I'd have given you twice the amount if I'd had it."

She tightened her jaw. "You're missing the point. I'm paying you back. Every blessed penny. And I'll not take advantage of the roof and food you'd provide while I'm doing it."

"I don't want it!" Her mother snapped. "I want you to live at home until you are well and safely married."

Flossie tucked in the blanket. "What about all that talk about me being an artist?"

She heaved a sigh. "Oh, Flossie, your paintings are very nice. I'd thought it would be a great boon if you were to sell your painting in that gallery, but my goodness, you're a woman. It was never our intent for you to be an artist the rest of your life. We always assumed you'd only do that until you found a nice young man and married him."

Flossie slowly straightened. Reaching behind her, she steadied herself against a dresser. A long silence followed.

Finally, Flossie took a breath. "You lied to me? All these years? On purpose?"

Mother gave her an incredulous look. "I have never lied to you. What on earth are you talking about?"

Anger began to simmer just below her skin. "I'm talking about telling me I'm an incredible artist. I'm talking about telling me I would achieve great things. I'm talking about all the accolades you and Papa inundated me with throughout the years."

Mother's face crumpled. "Those weren't lies. We were encouraging you. Giving you a boost. My goodness, you all but walked on air after we told you those things. When we saw how much joy it brought you, we simply continued. That's not called lying, that's called loving."

A bittersweet sadness crept over Flossie. "Well, I actually believed you, Mother. I actually thought I was the little genius you said I was. I didn't know I was average until I got the job at Tiffany's."

Mother rushed around the bed and hugged Flossie to her.

"Hush your mouth. You are not average, and don't you ever let anyone tell you otherwise. You are the most special girl on God's green earth."

Flossie rested her head on her mother's shoulder, tears filling her eyes. She wasn't sure if she choked up because it felt so good to be held or because her mother had just lied to her again.

Mother patted her on the back. "There, there. Are you ready to come home, now?"

Breaking loose of the hug, Flossie swiped her eyes. "You'd better go, Mother, or you'll get me in trouble."

Mother cupped Flossie's arms. "I will? Do you think I might get you fired?"

Flossie pulled up a corner of her mouth. "Good-bye, Mother. I'll come home Sunday for supper, but for now I need to get back to work."

Mother's face hardened. "I'm not taking your money. Not now. Not ever."

"I understand."

"What a stubborn, ungrateful girl you've turned into." With a huff of displeasure, she turned and strode to the door. "You've not heard the last about this."

"I'm sure I haven't."

And then she was gone.

For the rest of the day, Flossie's shoulders sagged, her legs felt weighted. Her parents had known she wasn't the most talented girl they'd ever seen? All this time? Then why had they pretended otherwise? Was it too much to ask for them to be proud of the fact they had an average daughter?

She didn't know. But no matter what they did or did not do, Flossie was through pretending. She was an average painter, an average stained-glass cutter, an average chambermaid. There was absolutely nothing wrong with that. Somebody had to be average. Besides, what if all parents told their children they were the most brilliant and talented children on earth? It was statistically impossible for everyone to be the best of the best. Some of them had to be average.

She shook her head. In a way, being average was a great relief. She'd still need to do the best she could, of course, for it was when she did her best that she produced average results, at least in everything she'd tried so far.

As for oil painting, even if the results were average, it brought her tremendous joy. Reeve was right about that. Somehow, someway, she needed to find time to paint. The problem was, she didn't have a penny to spare. Once her canvases, turpentine, and paints were gone, she didn't know when she'd be able to afford new ones.

Swallowing, she knelt down on the floor of the hallway, dipped her dust rag in wax, and began to polish the baseboards.

Mr. Oyster rounded the corner and let himself into his room. A moment later he stepped back into the hall. "Come here at once," he snapped.

"Is something the matter?" she asked.

He pointed toward his room. "There certainly is. You left a pile of rubbish beneath my desk."

She frowned. "I thoroughly swept your room earlier."

"Well, you did a slapdash job."

Setting down her dust cloth, she entered his room, crossed to his desk, pulled out his chair, and peeked under it. Before she could question what trash he was talking about, he grabbed her from behind.

Without thinking, she swung around, elbow up, and caught him in the jaw. Pain ricocheted up her arm.

Howling, he grabbed his face. "You wench! How dare you strike me?" He cuffed her across the cheek, then caught her by the arms and crushed his mouth against hers, groping her.

She bit his lip, stomped her heel into his toe, and kneed his groin, then raced from the room, looking over her shoulder.

Instead of running to the attic, where she'd be alone and without protection, she fled to the scullery. She hid behind the door, her heart beating so fast it nearly leaped from her chest. But no sound came from beyond. No one had followed her.

Her legs shook. Her hands trembled. Her stomach felt nauseated. Working her mouth, she touched her jaw, then looked at her fingers. No blood, thank goodness, but she could feel it bruising already.

Her first instinct was to tell Mrs. Klausmeyer, but Flossie had heard enough stories from her mother's clients to know that it was always the servant girl's fault, no matter what the circumstances. She couldn't afford to lose another job.

She could tell Mrs. Dinwiddie. She had no doubt that woman would bring the wrath of God upon him, but then Mrs. Klausmeyer would hear and she'd be in the same pickle.

No, there was nothing to do but hold her silence. Tears sprung to her eyes, not just from the pain, but from the betrayal. How could she have been so naive all these months? How could she have ever thought of Mr. Oyster as a family member? No wonder Reeve portrayed Marylee in such a despicable way at first. The girl he based the character on was an idiot. A senseless, foolish idiot who believed anything anyone told her.

Sliding down the wall and onto the floor, she rested her head on her knees and cried.

CHAPTER
70

Marylee's story was picked up by newspapers all over the country. Chicago, San Francisco, St. Louis, Philadelphia, everywhere. Suddenly, Reeve had more than enough money for a down payment on the cottage.

He sat on the edge of his bed, rubbing the cat figurine with his fingers. Just today a new payment had come in from a newspaper clear over in Oregon, but he hadn't walked over to the Gusmans' with an offer. For as badly as he wanted that house, how could he live there with a clear conscience knowing he purchased it with dirty money? Money he'd gained by exploiting the one girl he'd ever loved?

He knew that now, knew he loved her. It didn't matter that she'd renounced him, that she didn't even like him. He still couldn't bring himself to use the money. So, it had accumulated in the Wells Fargo bank. But lately he'd been weakening.

Every day, he walked to the cottage. Every day, the temptation to just get the money and buy the blasted thing had grown. He wasn't sure he could handle having it there much longer. He needed to do something with it. Something that had nothing to do with him and everything to do with her.

Freddie Blackburn stuck his head in the door. He was one of

the few fellows with a clean-shaven face like Reeve's. Being in his thirties, he was also one of the oldest guys at the Y. That might have been why Reeve liked him so much. He'd finished sowing his wild oats and had a more serious bent to his nature.

"You busy, Wilder?" he asked. "It's as cold as yesterday's potatoes outside, so the guys thought they'd put together a game of basketball down in the gym and I want you on my team. What do you say?"

Reeve smiled. Some young faculty member over at the International YMCA Training School in Massachusetts had come up with a game that could be played indoors in a relatively small space. You only needed two peach baskets and a soccer ball. The players here at their branch had to circumvent the two wooden columns right in the middle of the court that held up the gym's roof, but other than that, it was a great game. Because it was so new, Reeve wasn't any less competent than anyone else. "Have they cut a hole in the bottom of the baskets?"

"They have. And they've secured them to the track on the second floor."

Reeve nodded. "Let me change clothes, then, and I'll be right down."

"Great."

"And, Blackburn?"

Freddie leaned back to see what Reeve wanted.

"Let's say the losing team has to play The Board Game of Old Maid."

Blackburn grimaced. "That'll certainly keep us motivated. So long as we're on the same team, though, I'll make any bet you want."

Reeve had seen the game in a toy shop's window and bought it. The only way he could justify it to the guys was to tell them it was to be used as a forfeit. They all hated it, of course, but every time they played, it somehow made Reeve feel connected to Flossie.

He shook his head. If anybody again asked him when he'd last connected to someone, they'd be quite surprised to learn it was while he played or watched The Board Game of Old Maid. Still, remembering a connection wasn't the same as being connected. It was much like looking at a photograph of a moment that would never come again.

Standing, he put the figurine on his desk and quickly changed clothes.

CHAPTER
71

M rs. Dinwiddie closed the door to her bedroom as soon as Flossie entered.

"Is something the matter?" Flossie asked. She knew the woman had been summoned unexpectedly by her attorney. Flossie had hoped it wasn't bad news. She didn't know what Mrs. Dinwiddie's husband had set up to keep his widow in good standing, but the country was in shambles and suffering with the worst depression it had ever experienced. She didn't fully understand the way stocks or the Silver Act or anything else worked, but according to Reeve's articles, they certainly had a lot of people worried.

Mrs. Dinwiddie lowered her voice. "I went to see my lawyer today."

Nodding, Flossie took the woman's hand. "What did he say?"

"That a message was to be sent to you through me."

Flossie pulled back. "What?"

"Seems an anonymous donor has paid off your debts to those of us at the boardinghouse and also to your mother."

Flossie froze. "My debts?"

Mrs. Dinwiddie nodded.

"But, how . . . ?" She narrowed her eyes. "Wait. My father.

Do you think he went back to the racetrack? Do you think he won big?"

"It wasn't your parents."

Flossie crinkled her brows. "How do you know? I thought the donor was anonymous."

"Anonymous to you, and everyone else, but not to me."

"Then who was it?"

"I had to make a solemn oath not to tell."

"They made you swear an oath?"

"They did."

With a slight shake of her head, Flossie fiddled with the edge of her apron. "But no one I know would have done that. For that matter, they wouldn't have the money to pay everything off, much less pay their lawyer and your lawyer. Unless, unless . . . surely my mother wouldn't have said something to one of her customers?"

Mrs. Dinwiddie walked to the mirror and began to remove her hatpins.

"I played with many of their children, you know."

"Whose children?" Mrs. Dinwiddie dropped a hatpin into the premade hole of a porcelain container, much like a pencil in a pencil holder.

"The Vanderbilt children, the Forbes children, the Roosevelt children, any of the children who accompanied their mothers to fittings. I was particularly close to George Vanderbilt, although I'd heard he's down in North Carolina building a great chateau. Even so, if he'd heard something about my situation, he's just the type who would do something like this." Placing a hand on her hip, she cocked her head. "Still, it was an awful lot of trouble. Why would he go through your attorney instead of his?"

Mrs. Dinwiddie removed her hat.

"Am I right? Was it him or someone like him?"

Mrs. Dinwiddie made a locking motion over her mouth.

Sighing, Flossie picked up an empty hatbox on a side table.

"Perhaps he went through your attorney so I wouldn't be able to guess his identity. I just don't know how he'd even have known about you. I'm . . . I'm very confused."

Mrs. Dinwiddie patted the back of her head. "Is my hair mussed up?"

Mind whirling, Flossie pulled out a chair. "Here, come sit and I'll fix it."

She worked in silence, coiling the woman's hair as she tried to sort everything out. "Did he say when the payments would be made?"

"They already have been. I was given mine today, and the rest of the boarders will receive the remainder of theirs today as well. Your mother's will be delivered to her home."

"Good heavens." When Flossie finished arranging Mrs. Dinwiddie's hair, she rested her hands on the woman's shoulders. "I simply can't get over it. Nor can I imagine how Mr. Vanderbilt would have found out about my troubles. But who else could it be?"

A soft snore came from Mrs. Dinwiddie.

Flossie leaned over. The woman had dozed off.

Setting the comb down, Flossie stared at Mrs. Dinwiddie's hat, then fingered some silk dogwood blooms on its rim. Had her father orchestrated the whole thing? Had her mother made it as part of a payment for some gowns?

But, no, Mrs. Dinwiddie said it wasn't her parents. So who was it, then? Picking up the hat, she positioned it in the box, then placed the lid over it. Her debts had been paid. Just like that. One minute she was shackled. The next minute, free.

Heart soaring, she walked to the window. It had started snowing. The first snow of the season. Even with her debts paid, she wouldn't quit her job. She liked living on her own too much. Still, she could look for a new job, perhaps something that would give her the weekend off so she could paint.

Paint. She'd not only have the time to paint, but she'd once again be able to afford paints—only one color at a time, though. So she'd have to be very frugal. But it was a start, and once she had enough paints, she'd create something beautiful to give to the mysterious saint who'd set her free—if she ever found out his identity.

"God bless him, whoever he is," she whispered.

"It felt magnificent to be out of her drab alpaca gowns and in a fashionable ensemble, even if the sleeves were a bit less poufy than what was now in vogue."

CHAPTER
72

The pond had finally frozen over. Flossie dug into the ice and pushed off, enjoying the feel of freedom and relishing an opportunity to wear her sky-blue skating habit from last year. Mother and Papa had moved back to their old neighborhood and were gravely disappointed when Flossie again refused to come home. When it was apparent she wouldn't change her mind, they implored her to teach—anything other than keeping the chambermaid job. But she didn't want to teach and there simply weren't many other options for women, other than factory work, which was out of the question.

Still, it felt magnificent to be out of her drab alpaca gowns and in a fashionable ensemble, even if the sleeves were a bit less poufy than what was now in vogue. A crisp wind picked up the edges of her large sailor collar, making her feel as if she had wings. Stretching her arms wide, she spun in a circle, the braid-trimmed pleat on the side of her skirt flaring.

She tilted her head back, continued to spin, then pulled her hands in, resting them on the oversized buttons marching down her corsage. Faster and faster she spun until her head felt light. Finally, she slowed, stopped, and breathed in.

A group of men organized a baseball game on the far end of

the ice. Young boys played tag and keep-away. Tots just learning to skate folded up at the waist and sat. But it was the couples who drew her attention. Some skated side by side without touching, others hooked elbows, and yet others joined right and left hands promenade style. She couldn't help but think of Reeve.

No one had heard a word from him, not even Mrs. Dinwiddie. The woman saved all his newspaper articles, though, and let Flossie read them since the paper in the parlor was for boarders only, not servants.

If he hadn't become a champion for the women's movement, exactly, he'd certainly become a voice of reason. He exposed the bustle pinchers and made an entreaty for separate cars just for women. He refuted the widespread belief that any woman who was economically independent must therefore be immoral, then backed it up with fascinating articles featuring highly respectable women in all walks of life and all manner of occupations.

Just last week he'd written about a bevy of girls who'd done decorative painting on a ceiling of a downtown theater. The women worked from nine until five on scaffolding just as men did, lying down and letting their feet hang over. To lessen the chance of catching her skirt, one woman wore her brother-in-law's trousers under her blue flannel painting costume.

Flossie shook her head. Her father would have a wheezing attack for certain if she did something like that. Still, it made her wonder what Louise had worn when she and Mr. Cox had done their murals in the Manufacturer's Building, and it made her wish she could afford to go see the ceiling Reeve had written about.

An elderly gentleman in an old-fashioned jacket tipped his hat as he skated by. She smiled, wondering if he was here alone, wondering if Reeve would one day be like him.

She sighed. Reading his columns had made getting over him much more difficult. They kept her connected to him somehow, and with each piece her respect for him grew. Never, however, were there any new stories from I. D. Claire.

Blowing on her hands, she passed a dozen young men who offered inexperienced skaters lessons for twenty-five cents an hour. Most of the students were women, though there was an occasional man. Again, she thought of Reeve, then shook herself. She needed to stop. Even though she was no longer consigned to life as an old maid, it was long past time to push him from her mind. Sometimes she managed to follow her own advice. Other times, like today, she missed him so badly she almost ached.

"Flossie? Flossie Jayne? Is that you?"

Flossie spun around, skating backward and looking for the woman who'd called out.

"Flossie! Here!"

She narrowed her eyes, trying to see who was beneath the shawl-wrapped head. "Mona?"

"Yes!" The girl skated right up to her and gave her a giant hug. "How are you? We all miss you so much."

Nostalgia swept over Flossie. Mona was the errand girl at Tiffany's. She ran messages back and forth between the men's department and the women's department. She took their mail to the post office, and she ran any errands Mrs. Driscoll needed.

Flossie didn't know her well, had barely even noticed her while she was there, but Mona had clearly remembered her. Warmth flooded Flossie. "How are you? How is everyone?"

"Wonderful, though we still miss you, of course."

She smiled. "Did anyone else lose their job? What about Aggie? Is Aggie still there?"

"Everyone is still there, including Aggie. She's wrapping foil as usual."

Turning, the girls began to skate and Mona caught her up on the happenings at Tiffany's. The chapel had won fifty-four awards at the World's Fair—more than any other single exhibit—and had been brought back to New York. "They're assembling it right next to the showroom so that anyone who missed seeing it in Chicago can see it here in New York."

"That's wonderful!"

"We're very excited, though by the time they reassemble it, I'll be gone."

"Gone?"

"Yes." A large smile crinkled her eyes. "I'm getting married."

"Married!" But she was so young. "When?"

"Next week."

"Well, I . . . I . . . congratulations."

"Thank you. Oh, there he is now." She waved, and a man across the pond waved back as he made his way toward them. "I'd best go. It was wonderful seeing you."

"You, too. Tell the girls hello for me."

"I will." She pushed off and sailed toward her fiancé.

Married. Good heavens. She watched the two of them greet each other, then head in the opposite direction.

It wasn't until later that night when it occurred to her that Mrs. Driscoll would be in need of a new errand girl, for Mr. Tiffany did not allow married women to be in his employ.

CHAPTER

73

Flossie paused at Mrs. Driscoll's doorway, a rush of well being sweeping through her. She hadn't realized how much she'd missed the place until just that moment. Scraps of glass, paper, and an assortment of tools lay scattered across the woman's desk. She held a mold of what appeared to be a small lampshade in her hand. Looking over her shoulder, a man who managed the kiln made suggestions in an Irish brogue so thick, Flossie couldn't understand a single word.

Finally, she tapped on the door. "Knock, knock?"

Mrs. Driscoll looked up, pleasure lighting her plain features. "Miss Jayne, how very nice to see you. Come in. You remember Mr. Briggs, of course?"

Flossie gave a short curtsey. "Mr. Briggs."

"Hello, lassie." Wiping his hands on the white apron he wore, he headed toward the door. "We'll talk more later, Mrs. Driscoll."

But Mrs. Driscoll had already set down the mold and given Flossie her full attention. "Come in, come in. How are you, dear?"

"Very well, thank you. I know how busy you are, so I'll come right to the point. I saw Mona this weekend in Central Park and understand you may have need of an errand girl. Have you filled the position by any chance?"

She tilted her head. "I have not. Four girls have been recommended to me. I consumed about six valuable hours in the tenements going to meet them in their homes, but was disappointed in three of them. The fourth is to call at my boardinghouse this evening. Why?"

"I'd like to submit my name for consideration."

Her eyebrows lifted. "As an errand girl? But, it wouldn't pay what your other position did. Are you sure you'd be interested?"

"I actually think I might prefer it. I loved being a glasscutter, of course. Who wouldn't love working with all that brilliant glass? But as an errand girl, I'd be able to go all over the building and see what the men are doing, too. And didn't Mona sometimes go to the factory in Corona?"

"Occasionally." Mrs. Driscoll stared, her expression speculative. "The pay would only be four dollars a week, though, instead of five."

Flossie grimaced. "I understand I can't make as much money as the other girls, but did you ever think about having the errand girl stick down the paper patterns onto the glass? It would have saved us so much time, and that's certainly a chore I could do between errands. I could also cut Aggie's foil for her. That simply takes a snip of the scissors, not at all like cutting glass. There are any number of things like that I could do to speed up the others' work."

Crossing her legs, Mrs. Driscoll leaned back in her chair.

"You wouldn't have to train me," Flossie continued. "Other than to show me where everything is in the building. I might be slow at glasscutting, but I'm very nimble on my feet. I could fly all over the place with any message or errand you could think of. And Corona." She clasped her hands beneath her chin. "Oh, how I'd love to go to Corona and have even the slightest of peeks at the men forming the glass. What do you say, Mrs. Driscoll? Can I be your errand girl?"

"Well, if you don't want her," Mr. Tiffany said from the doorway, "I'll sure take her."

Flossie whirled around, a smile bursting across her face. "Mr. Tiffany! It's so wonderful to see you. How ever are you?"

His eyes twinkling, he approached them. "I'm very fine, Miss Jayne. It's been awfully quiet around here without you."

She bit her lip. "Oh, dear. Is that a good thing or a bad thing?"

Laughing, he shook his index finger back and forth. "Now, I know a trick question when I hear one." He turned to Mrs. Driscoll. "What do you think? Shall we give Miss Jayne a chance?"

Mrs. Driscoll swung her foot. "I believe you'd pout for a week if I didn't."

"I most certainly would." He clapped his hands together. "So, do you accept, Miss Jayne?"

She shifted her weight. "Do you think I could talk you into four-fifty a week instead of four? Especially if I do some of those extra chores for the girls?"

He raised his brows, then turned to Mrs. Driscoll.

The woman lifted one shoulder. "She'd probably be the best errand girl we've ever had, certainly the most knowledgeable of the window-making process, and everyone loves her."

With a sigh, he spread his hands wide. "All right, then. Four-fifty a week."

Jumping with delight, Flossie clapped her hands. "Thank you! Thank you so much. Both of you."

He grinned.

Mrs. Driscoll shooed her out. "All right, Miss Jayne, off you go. Report back on Wednesday and I'll have Mona show you the different parts of the building and where everything is."

"I will. I'll be here first thing." She all but skipped to the door.

"And Miss Jayne?"

Flossie turned back around at Mrs. Driscoll's inquiry.

"Be sure to wear something sensible, for heaven's sake."

With a laugh, she raced past Mr. Tiffany, down the hall, and into the workroom to greet the other girls and tell them her good news.

CHAPTER
74

Reeve watched out the window of the YMCA's parlor. The minute the carriage he'd sent for arrived, he threw on his coat and hat, then bounded out the entrance. He waited for the driver to assist Mrs. Dinwiddie, then he wrapped his arms around her and picked her clear up off her feet. "Merry Christmas!"

She squealed as if she were a girl, then rapped him on the head with her cane the minute he set her down, knocking his hat askew.

"You fresh young man, what was the meaning of that?" But her eyes sparkled and multiple smile lines stacked up on either side of her mouth.

Righting his hat, he brought one of her gloved hands to his lips. "Bah humbug to you, too."

Chuckling, she shook her head. "Get my things out of the carriage and help me in out of the cold before I freeze to death."

The driver handed him a basket, for which Reeve handed him a coin. "Merry Christmas."

"Thank you, sir. You, too."

Clasping Mrs. Dinwiddie's elbow, he assisted her to the door festooned with holly berries, evergreens, and wreaths, the scent of pine sharp and invigorating. "Be careful now. This walkway gets slippery from the ice."

"I've been making my way around New York longer than you've been alive."

He opened the door. "Just the same, have a care."

Once inside, he hung up her coat, then took both her hands in his. "I just want to look at you a minute. It's so good to see you."

Pink touched her cheeks, and his heart warmed as he realized she'd taken extra care with her toilette. Her lips held a slightly unnatural hue of red, as if she'd borrowed a bit of dye from the wallpaper in the entry hall of Klausmeyer's and rubbed it on her lips. Her gown, a deep forest green, made a rich backdrop for three rows of pearls around her neck. At the top of her coiled white hair, a whimsical hat with Christmas ornaments embedded in green netting looked like something a girl of twenty might wear. But it was the scent of camphor that squeezed his chest with familiarity and great affection.

"You take my breath away, Mrs. Dinwiddie."

The pink spread over her face in uneven blotches. "My, my, my, haven't you turned into quite the charmer?"

He tucked her hand into his elbow. "Only with you, Mrs. Dinwiddie. Only with you."

Opening the parlor door, he swept his hand in an *after you* gesture.

"Oh, my. Would you look at this," she said.

"The Women's Auxiliary came a couple of weeks ago to help us decorate." He looked around, once again marveling at the transformation. An evergreen garland lay across the fireplace mantel, its pinecones still intact. A crackling fire behind the grate filled the room with warmth, a woodsy odor, and soothing sounds. A white muslin cornice had been draped across two windows and tied in place with ribbons and pampas grass, but Reeve's favorite was the Christmas tree standing sentinel in the corner. He'd helped string the popcorn, cranberry, and nut strands, while others had wrapped them about the tree.

"There used to be quite a few gingerbread men hanging on it," he said. "The women baked them for us, but the boys ate them almost as soon as the girls left."

"Well, it's lovely all the same."

He took a deep breath. "It is, isn't it?"

His grandparents had always had a tree and had allowed him to help with the decorating, but it was nothing like this. Still, on Christmas morning there would be one small wrapped gift for him hanging from one of the branches. It was a magical time. The best day of the year.

They'd both passed away in '86 and Christmas had become the worst day of the year. It represented everything he didn't have—family and friends. Or at least it had until this year, for he'd made some friends here at the Y and had once again helped with decorations. Still, all but a handful had returned home for the holidays, leaving the place silent and deserted.

On a whim, he'd sent Mrs. Dinwiddie an invitation three days ago to join him on Christmas. He hadn't really expected her to travel clear over to Brooklyn on such short notice. It was only when she'd accepted that he realized how much he'd wanted her to come. As a result, he'd taken just as much care with his grooming as she had and wore his very best suit, a new collar, and carefully polished boots.

"Have you gotten taller?" she asked.

He led her to a group of furnishings by the fire. "Not taller, I don't think, but perhaps a bit broader. They have a gymnasium here that I've grown to really enjoy."

"Well, you must tell me all. I'm dying to hear."

He settled her onto a gold-and-white settee, then took a seat on the cushion beside her. There was so much the YMCA offered that he wasn't exactly sure where to start. "I wish I could take you on a tour, but women aren't allowed anyplace other than the parlor and public hall."

"Then you must tell me all about it."

They talked for almost two hours. He of his life at the Y, the friendships he'd started to form, and his work at the paper. She caught him up on who had moved into Klausmeyer's, the decline in the quality of the meals, Flossie's departure from and return to Tiffany's, and the Christmas activities they'd enjoyed in the parlor.

Bending down onto one knee in front of the fireplace, he propped a fresh piece of wood on top of some disintegrating logs, then pushed it to the back with a poker. "Only a few carols and a musical performance by Nettels? I'd have expected Miss Jayne to have much more planned than that."

"Flossie doesn't plan activities anymore." Sighing, she looked down at her hands. "She doesn't even join us at the table, much less the parlor."

He rested an elbow on his knee. "Doesn't join you at the table?"

"She was forbidden, of course, when she was a chambermaid. But even after she quit that and went back to Tiffany's, she kept her attic room and takes all her meals there."

"All of them?"

"She'll go home occasionally, but mostly, she eats in her room."

"Why? It's bound to be miserable up there. Hot in the summer, cold in the winter, and incredibly, well, lonely for someone like her."

"When I confronted her about it, she said she was worried it would make everyone uncomfortable to suddenly have a former servant at the table." Her lips pulled down. "But if you ask me, it's because she was very hurt by the way the others treated her during those months of house service. She'd thought them friends. It was quite a shock to her to find out otherwise."

Leaning the poker against the leg of the fireplace, he returned to his seat and brushed off his knee. "I thought they were her friends, too. What exactly did they do to her when she was the maid?"

She shrugged. "Shunned her, ignored her, pretended she was invisible." She gave him a pointed look. "Those were the things I saw. I'm sure other things went on that I didn't see. She was extremely skittish around Mr. Oyster."

He slowly straightened. "Did he harm her?"

"If he did, she never said so."

"Did you ask her?"

"Many times."

"And she denied it?"

Mrs. Dinwiddie shook her head. "She never denied it, simply told me not to worry. That she was careful to only clean his room while he was at work and that she was never in the same room with him except when she was serving dinner."

His jaw tightened. "If you ever, and I mean *ever*, find out he is harassing her, you send word to me immediately. Do you understand?"

"I do."

The thought of that wastrel trying to take advantage of Flossie made his entire body quake with anger, but there was nothing he could do about it from here. Not when she'd not lodged a complaint and not when she wasn't his to hold and protect—no matter how much he wished she were. Blowing out a breath, he propped his elbows on his knees and rested his forehead against his palms. "I love her, you know."

She placed a knurled hand against his back. "I know."

"She hates me, though."

"She loves you."

He turned his head, his hands now cupping the side of his face as he studied Mrs. Dinwiddie. "Why do you say that?"

"Because I've been in love before. I know the signs."

Well, he was in love, too, and if that made him an expert, he was pretty sure Flossie didn't love him back. Besides, Mrs. Dinwiddie wasn't privy to all that had gone on between him and Flossie. He pictured her swiping his papers across the desk and flinging his metal figurine across the room. Her words still echoed in his mind.

The Trostles were bad enough, but you, Reeve, you've made a joke of me and laid it out in print for my parents, my friends, my house-mates, my workmates, and hundreds of others to see.

That didn't sound like a woman in love to him. "How's she doing at Tiffany's?"

"She loves being an errand girl."

"She does?"

Mrs. Dinwiddie nodded. "She was sent to Corona a couple of weeks ago. She's talked about nothing else since."

"Really?" He raised up. "What's in Corona?"

"They make the glass there."

He crinkled his brows. "She went to a glass factory? Where the men work?"

"She did, indeed. Seems Mr. Tiffany himself took her to the furnace where they pour out the glass and mix the colors. It made quite an impression on her."

He smiled. "I bet it did. Is she painting?"

"I don't know. I only went up to her room once." She swatted the air. "I won't ever do that again. It was way too many steps for this old body to navigate."

"And you didn't see any paints?"

"Not then. She was working for Mrs. Klausmeyer at the time and the woman worked her day and night, not to mention all the sewing she did for her mother. But now that she's back at Tiffany's, she has her evenings off. And if she's not painting up there, I can't imagine what else she'd be doing."

I come alive when I paint. It's the equivalent for me of birds in full song, flowers in bloom, and a dew-kissed morning.

He hoped she was painting. Maybe that was why she'd stayed

in the attic, because then the odor of the paints and turpentine wouldn't sicken Miss Love or anyone else.

Mrs. Dinwiddie reached over and clasped his hand. "No matter what she's doing, she never would have been able to do it if you hadn't paid those debts for her."

"It was the least I could do."

"It was very generous."

"She doesn't know, does she?"

"She has no idea."

"Good." He squeezed her hand, then released it. "I'm learning to ice skate."

"Are you?"

"I have a friend here by the name of Blackburn. Freddie Blackburn. He's teaching me."

"Well, imagine that." She covered her mouth, stifling a yawn.

"I've worn you out."

"Nonsense, I'm having a marvelous time."

"Nevertheless, I'd better get a carriage for you."

"Not just yet. Hand me my basket first. I brought you something."

He stilled. "You brought me something?"

"Well, of course. We're spending Christmas together, aren't we?"

Warmth rushed through him as he retrieved the basket she'd carried with her. Taking it from him, she pulled back a checkered cloth, then handed him a heavy box wrapped in blue tissue and tied with ribbon. Emotion clogged his throat. Two presents in one year. A miniature cat from Flossie and now this.

"Well, go ahead. Open it."

With great care, he undid the ribbon, then pulled back the paper without tearing it. The box had *Tiffany Glass and Decorating Co.* embossed on the outside. "I hope this is just the box and isn't indicative of what's inside."

She shooed him with her hands. "Just open it."

He lifted the lid and sucked in his breath. If he hadn't known better, he'd have thought it was a stained-glass dressing screen for a doll. But he did know better. It was a tea screen.

Mrs. Dinwiddie craned her neck to see inside the box. "According to Flossie, the head of the Women's Department, Mrs. Driscoll, sketched this up after being inspired by one Flossie designed."

"The one with the spiders on it?"

"Yes, Mrs. Driscoll said cobwebs would have made a much prettier design, and I would have to agree. Flossie took me all through the showroom and introduced me to everyone while I was there. They adore her, of course. She runs all over the place doing things for them."

"She helped you select this?"

"She did. She picked it up and pointed out all of its features. She loves that screen, very much."

"And she knew it was for me?"

"She knew it was for you."

He ran his fingers over pink flowers and a giant cobweb, surprised to see his hands were shaking. He swallowed. She'd touched what he was touching. Her hands had been on these very pieces. A deep longing shimmied through him.

"They're apple blossoms," Mrs. Dinwiddie said.

His throat thickened. "I-I can't accept this. You spent way too much."

"Nonsense. This trinket is no hardship for me. I would be very honored if you'd accept it."

Putting the screen back in the box, he set it on the floor, reached over, and pulled the old woman into his embrace.

"Thank you." His words were thick, his heart full.

She patted his back. "There, there."

Pressing his cheek against hers, he rocked her. "You know, if I were a little bit older—"

With a *humph*, she pulled back and looked into his eyes. "If you were a little older, I'd still be out of luck because you, young man, have your eyes set on someone else."

"I guess this means I'll have to start drinking tea again."

She chuckled. "Indeed it does."

Shaking his head, he reached inside his coat. "I have something for you, too."

She splayed a hand against her chest, her pearls rattling. "For me?"

He lifted a corner of his mouth. "We're spending Christmas together, aren't we?"

She couldn't budge the twine, so she ripped off the tissue, then once again tugged on the twine.

His smile grew. "I didn't know you were such a reckless gift opener."

"Hush and help me."

Straightening out one leg, he reached into a pocket for his knife, then slit the twine.

The long, skinny box had *Tiffany Glass and Decorating Co.* embossed on the outside. Her eyes darted to his in question.

"My Marylee story has been picked up by a great number of newspapers and magazines."

She smiled. "Why, you little devil. Did Flossie help you pick it out?"

"She wasn't in the showroom when I was there. I, of course, had no idea she even might be."

"She roams throughout the building depending on where she's needed. She was only with me because she knew I was coming." She opened the hinged lid. Inside lay a long hatpin with a favrile bead at its head. Picking it up, she held it to the fire, its translucent colors changing from green to blue to purple. "It's stunning, Reeve. Absolutely stunning. Thank you."

"You're welcome."

She tucked it back into the box. "I can call you Reeve, can't I? I don't much like addressing someone who is like a son to me by his surname."

He stared at her. "Like a son?"

Her eyes softened. "For quite some time. I was adrift when you left Klausmeyer's."

His chest rose and fell. "I'm sorry. I never meant to hurt you. It was simply that I couldn't go back there. Not after what happened with Flossie. Not after everyone found out I was I. D. Claire. I missed you, too, terribly. I didn't realize you'd feel the same."

"I assumed it was something like that. It's of no matter. We're together now. That's what's important." She tilted her head. "So, may I call you Reeve?"

"I'd be honored, Mrs. Dinwiddie."

"Maman. Do you think you could bring yourself to call me Maman? It's French for mother." She tugged on her cuff. "My grandmother was French, you know. But I realize you may not feel at all comfortable with that, and I want you to know I'd understand."

He held his breath. His first instinct was to tell her no. To retreat. To protect that little bit of him that still shied away from anything and anyone who got too close.

But he could see the longing in her eyes. Could feel the tug. Moisture touched his own eyes. "Of course. I-I don't know what to say."

"Say, 'Maman.'"

He'd been hanging onto the last shred of his dignity for several minutes now. If this didn't stop, she'd completely strip him of his manhood. Still, he would not dishonor her.

He rose to his feet, then held out a hand. His throat became so thick, the best he could do was a whisper. "Maman."

She placed her hand in his and allowed him to help her to her feet. Grasping his lapel, she pulled him down and gave him a kiss on the cheek, camphor oil once again filling his senses. "You're a good boy, Reeve Wilder."

An arrow tied to a string went straight from the peck on his cheek and the words from her mouth to the innermost spot in his heart. A direct hit. And with it, his walls crumbled. For as far back as his memories took him, he'd never had the privilege of calling anyone Mother, in any language. But he'd wanted to, oh, how he'd wanted to.

Affection for her shot up from the arrow's mark like a fountain in Central Park, showering him, covering him, deluging him with a love like none he'd ever felt before.

Pulling her against him, he buried his face in her neck and sobbed.

A Merry Christmas

F. Jayne

"The snowman had a pipe stuck in a downturned mouth
and a swig of holly trapped beneath his arm."

CHAPTER
75

After all that transpired, Reeve was not about to let Mrs. Dinwi—*Maman*—return to Klausmeyer's alone. They sat on the same side of the carriage, covered with a cloak and sharing a warmer beneath it. He'd taken hold of her hand as soon as they'd settled and not let go the entire way.

When they turned onto West Fifty-Seventh, his heart began to hammer. He knew Flossie wasn't there, that she would be home with her parents, but he couldn't seem to convince his heart of the same.

"You haven't asked me why I brought such a big basket for such a small-sized present," she said.

He gave her a sideways look. "Far be it from me to question the ways of a woman."

Releasing his hand, she took the basket from the floor and up onto her lap. "There's some molasses candy and a block of fruitcake in here for you."

"There is?" He glanced at the checkered cloth. "I'll have to hide it or the boys will eat it before I have a chance."

"Flossie made it."

He froze. "Flossie?"

"Yes. She made it in her mother's kitchen, then gave it to me for Christmas."

He let out a slow breath. "This is yours, then?"

"No, this is yours. She made two batches."

He fingered the corner of the cloth. "And she said one batch was for me?"

"Not in so many words, but when she gave it to me, she handed me the first batch and said, 'Merry Christmas.' Then, she stuttered and twirled her hair and worried her lip before finally saying she knew I was going to see you and she thought we might like a bit of refreshment for our visit, so she made a little extra." Mrs. Dinwi—no, Maman shook her head. "This is much more than a 'little extra.' It'll last you a week."

He took in deep breaths, trying to understand if it was an olive branch, or if Flossie was merely worried that he would starve Maman during their visit. Which he had, he realized with a start.

"I never offered you a bit of refreshment." He struck his forehead with the butt of his hand. "I've never entertained before, so it didn't even occur to me. You must be famished."

"I'm not famished. If I'd been famished, I'd have had you give me a piece of candy."

The carriage pulled to a stop. Reeve glanced at the familiar stoop of 438, but had no time to reminisce before Maman handed him the basket.

"You keep this," she said. "And I will expect regular communications from you."

"I'll write you every week, but please don't ask me to come here. I-I—"

She squeezed his arm. "Letters will be fine for now."

The driver opened the door.

She leaned over and kissed his cheek. "Don't get out. And Merry Christmas, my boy."

Curling a finger beneath her chin, he drew her forward and gave her a light kiss on the lips. "Merry Christmas to you, too, Maman."

She blushed.

Ignoring her instructions, he escorted her to the door, but not inside. He simply couldn't bring himself to go back inside. As soon as he returned to the carriage, he uncovered the cloth, then jerked back his hand. Sitting on top of the fruitcake and candy was a Christmas card. A hand painted Christmas card.

Lifting it, he held it to the window, cold air seeping through the glass. It was of a cat and a miniature snowman. The snowman had a pipe stuck in a downturned mouth and a swig of holly trapped beneath his arm. The cat wasn't his, but was a black cat sprinkled with snow. It had approached the grouchy snowman, and stood back a bit while its nose stretched forward—sniffing, sniffing, not quite sure if it was safe to touch.

Squinting, Reeve sought out her signature painted in the bottom corner. *F. Jayne.*

He rubbed his thumb across it, then studied the card more closely, looking at things he'd missed the first time. A stone wall next to the cat. The shadows and the play of light. The collection of snow on the walkway. The white whiskers radiating from each side of the cat's face. And the color of its eyes—not quite gold, but not exactly brown, either.

A MERRY CHRISTMAS had been written in block letters across the top. She'd become better since he'd seen her little watercolor figures around the edges of their questions at dinnertime. She must be practicing quite a bit.

He wondered if she were taking lessons. But, no, she wouldn't be able to afford them. He sighed. He hated to think of her shut up in an attic like some sleeping Briar Rose.

The carriage rounded a corner and knocked him into the side wall. Straightening, he adjusted his hat, then opened the card and read it. Then, read it again.

Dear Mr. Wilder,

I hope Cat is doing well and has settled in to her new quarters. I was very happy to hear you'd become a member of the 26th Ward YMCA there in Brooklyn. No one knew where you had gone, though we were able to read and enjoy your articles, of course.

With my Jane Austen books long since gone, I've had a terrible time finding any good fiction to read. I've tried several books and a collection of short stories, but nothing seems to hold my interest. I know of a talented writer, but he's only written one thing. I do declare, but I wish he'd write something new. If he did, I would be first in line to read it.

I hope this finds you well. Please give Cat my deepest regards.

Christmas Cheer,
FRJ

Closing the card, he sat back, wondering what the *R* stood for. Rachel? Regina? Roberta?

He fingered the card's edges. She wanted him to write something, something fiction. Not about Marylee, surely. No, no. She wouldn't have meant that. But perhaps something different?

He wasn't sure what it all meant, didn't know if he should write her back or if she didn't want to hear from him until he'd written a story. Or maybe she didn't want to hear from him at all, maybe she was just being polite or wanted something to read.

After the morning he'd had with Maman, he couldn't think about Flossie. It was simply too much.

He took a piece of molasses candy from the basket and popped it in his mouth. He lifted his brows. It was very good. He'd had no idea she was a good cook.

Looking to the side, he watched the blur of brownstones go by and redirected his thoughts to possible story ideas. Maybe he'd give it a try. It couldn't hurt, and if it was anything as popular as Marylee's story, he just might be able to buy back his childhood home, after all.

CHAPTER
76

The Gusmans sold his house. At least, Reeve assumed they had. He searched the paper three times, but the listing wasn't there. Grabbing his coat, he all but ran to Georgia Avenue.

A large wagon filled with a rocker, a bedstead, and all sorts of odds and ends was parked out front. The Gusmans were nowhere to be seen. Instead, an older man with two teeners unloaded a sofa.

Reeve stood at the edge of the property, his breath vaporizing as his lungs pulled in and pushed out air. This couldn't be happening. This was his house. He was the one who'd lived in it first. He was the one who'd been born in it. He was the one who was supposed to buy it back. He searched the sky. Heavy clouds blocked the heavens and offered no answer to his inward cries of *Why? Why?*

He should have bought it when he had the chance. But, no, he couldn't have used the money from the Marylee story. He'd have never been able to live with himself. His knees weakened, his eyes stung, his nostrils flared. Jamming his hands in his pockets, he spun around, ducked his head, and began to walk back to the Y, the snow slushing beneath his boots. His body began to shake. He'd needed that house, *needed* it.

He fisted his hands inside his pockets, reminding himself he wasn't as lonely as he used to be. He'd made some friends. He had a maman. But he didn't have a home. He didn't have a place he belonged. Not like he would've in that house.

He rubbed his mouth. What would he do? Where would he go? He'd merely been tolerating his roommate. Telling himself it was only temporary. Only until he could get his home back. His roommate had gone home for the holidays, but that was hardly the reprieve Reeve was looking for.

When he returned to the Y, he tossed his coat and hat on the bed, and made himself some coffee. As soon as he had a cup ready, he sat down at his desk and stared at a stack of empty pages. Thoughts piled up like a shuffled deck of cards waiting to be drawn, turned over, and spread out for all to see. He flexed his fingers.

I do declare, but I wish he'd write something new. If he did, I would be first in line to read it.

He glanced at her Christmas card propped on the corner of his desk, the Tiffany tea screen, and the cat figurine in front of it. Sucking in a deep breath, he dipped his pen in an inkwell, gave his emotions free rein, and began to write, the nib of his pen scratching across the paper, his mind moving faster than his fingers. First thoughts, then sentences, then paragraphs, then chapters. It felt so good to get it out and onto paper where he could move it around, mark it out, or add to it.

Little by little a story began to take shape. A story. Never had he expected to write another word of fiction, wouldn't have even thought to, if it hadn't been for Flossie. He worked well into the night, only stopping when the sun began to peek through the shutters and his fingers began to cramp. Finally, he fell into bed, not bothering to remove his clothes.

Perhaps he wasn't a journalist after all. Perhaps he'd been a novelist all along and simply hadn't realized it. It was his last thought before sleep overtook him.

CHAPTER
77

Reeve stood at Freddie Blackburn's doorway, his smile wide. Blackburn looked up from his desk. "What has you in such a merry mood?"

"My house kit from Sears, Roebuck arrived." He squared his shoulders. "I'm in the building business."

Crossing his arms, Blackburn leaned his chair back onto two legs. "I take it that means I'm in the hammering and nailing business?"

Reeve chuckled. "I could sure use the help."

"When do we start?"

"No better time than the present."

Plopping his chair down, Blackburn nodded. "Let me finish up here, then, and you go see who else you can round up."

"Thank you, friend." Reeve pushed off the doorway, then went up and down the hall recruiting any who were willing.

He'd finished his book in February and sold it in March, but only on the condition that he agree to publish it under the pseudonym of I. D. Claire. Reeve fought and fought the publisher about it, but with the reputation he'd made for himself on the Marylee piece, it was a sure thing that any book with Claire's name on it would sell. He'd finally agreed.

That was the bad news. The good news was, I. D. Claire's name meant the publisher would pay him a tidy sum. It wasn't enough to buy a four-thousand-dollar home, like the ones around the Y, but it was enough for a down payment on a seven-hundred-dollar lot on Sheffield, one street over from his childhood home, and to buy a five-hundred-dollar home kit from the Sears, Roebuck catalog.

With hammers, saws, nails, and a lot of enthusiasm, the starting lineup for the basketball team of the Twenty-Sixth Ward YMCA headed out in the crisp spring air. By the time the group of laughing young men made it to Reeve's lot, the neighborhood children had come to see what all the fuss was about.

Once word spread, the men who lived on Sheffield Avenue pushed themselves up out of their porch swings to offer strong backs. The women, in turn, kept a supply of food and drinks coming—mostly made and delivered by their daughters. Some tall, some short. Some curvy, some willowy. Some giggly, some sober. But all of them swishing their skirts until they sounded like high wind in a tall grass. That ended up working out well for Reeve, because with all those young ladies prancing about, not only did his team of workers grow, but so did their efforts.

Swiping an arm across his forehead, he soaked up the heat of the sun. He couldn't help but think of how much had changed since this time last year when he'd hidden in his tiny room at Klausmeyer's full of resentment over the pretty little magpie who'd moved in next door and wouldn't shut up. If someone had told him then how much he'd be missing her now, he'd have never believed them. Putting two nails into his mouth, he set the third against the intersection of two beams, began to hammer, and turned his mind to what he was doing.

S itting on an upside-down apple crate, Reeve poked at a log in the red brick fireplace of his brand-new home. It had taken all summer and well into the fall to build the house. The fellows at the Y had been enthusiastic helpers at first, but as the months wore on and as baseball leagues were formed, fewer and fewer stayed around to help. As their numbers diminished, the neighbors went back to their porches, the ladies back to their kitchens.

That was all right with Reeve. He'd enjoyed every part of the process, from the foundation to the fireplace to the roof shingles. When it was only one or two guys helping, he found it a lot easier to get to know them.

The whole thing had ended up costing much more than he'd expected. Storm doors and windows were twenty-six dollars extra, material for steps off the front porch and rear stoop were nine dollars, and a cook stove with a reservoir was ten dollars.

That hadn't left much for furniture. Looking around, he sighed. It hadn't left much for *any* furniture. Still, building the place with his own two hands had made it, in some ways, even more personal than his birthplace.

Cat rolled onto her back, paws in the air, and soaked up heat from the fireplace.

"You'd best not get too close. I haven't bought a screen yet and those sparks will singe the hair right off of you."

Cat flicked her gray tail, but gave no indication of moving. Shaking his head, Reeve took a gulp of coffee and glanced at the only screen he did have—Maman's tea screen on the hearth. The flame from the burner made the glass glow and its colors change.

He'd tried to drink tea, but it was just too weak. So, he'd ended up brewing coffee in his pot instead. He'd not told Maman, though. She would not have been pleased.

Setting down his cup, he picked up his lap desk, opened the hinged top, and removed his metal figurine and a piece of paper.

Dear Maman,

It is finished. The last nail has been hammered. The last screw tightened. Cat and I are sitting in the parlor and the only thing missing is you. You'll be glad you aren't here, though, for I've nothing but an old apple crate to offer as a chair, and nothing in the cupboards—because I don't have any cupboards! So it has yet to feel like a home.

Dear Maman,

I have made my first piece of furniture. It is a table and the ugliest thing you've ever seen. With the house, everything was precut, but Sears, Roebuck doesn't sell any furniture kits. They do have kitchen chairs for forty-five cents apiece, however, which is cheaper than I can get them around here. They are nothing fancy—wood seats, four spindles, bowed backs, and some ornamental stripes—but I daresay they will be better than anything I could make.

When I collect my next paycheck, I will order two of those.
Maybe then the place will feel more like a home.

Dear Maman,

The boys from the Y surprised me last night and came to the
house bearing gifts. I now have a soccer ball, a fishing reel, an
abacus, a saucepan, a spittoon—of all things—and The Board
Game of Old Maid. It's the same one I'd donated to the Y's game
room. (The guys were only too glad to be rid of it.)

Since it was too cold and dark to go outdoors, we played a
rather ruthless game in the barren parlor with my soccer ball. We
split into two teams and lined up on opposite sides of the room,
then tried to eliminate the other team's members by striking them
with the ball as hard as we could. The first team with all players
down were the losers.

I didn't play, however. I, instead, was the defender of my
windows. They are still intact, I'm pleased to say, but the fellows
could tell how nervous I was and kept flinging the ball perilously
close to them. I had to make several dives to protect them. The
wooden floor is not nearly as forgiving as grass. I'm stiff and sore
and bruised, but very happy.

We made the losers play The Board Game of Old Maid,
which always generates a great deal of laughter and moans. That,
of course, was the best gift of all, that and the conversation which
filled the house. It almost felt like a home, then. Almost.

Dear Maman,

Your blanket arrived today, and I have no words. I don't have to ask to know that you knitted it with your own two hands. It is beautiful and warm and my favorite color. Well, I didn't really have a favorite color before, but now I do. It is and will forevermore be blue.

I wear it like a cloak all around the house, especially at night when the temperatures drop even more. It is so big that I roll myself up into it like a scroll. It keeps me warm the whole night through, even when the fire has dwindled down to nothing but embers.

Dear Maman,

My library rocker arrived today, and I am sitting in it right now with your blanket over my legs. I decided to save my money a little bit longer this time and buy something of value that would last, rather than buy two cheap rockers.

It's a man's chair and plenty big enough to hold my frame comfortably, but Cat thinks it's hers. I've had to kick her off repeatedly. I couldn't afford the leather, so settled instead for a brown upholstery. It has a deep spring seat and spring back and top roll. The arms and legs are of golden oak. I have figured out that at the current rate I'm going, I will have the house completely furnished by the time I'm fifty.

"Of their own volition, his legs carried him inside her self-made gallery."

CHAPTER
79

Reeve stepped into the entry hall of Klausmeyer's, two copies of his new book tucked beneath his arm. Nothing had changed in the fifteen months he'd been gone. The parlor still stretched out on the side, the furniture sat in the same place, the piano rested against the wall, the fireplace needed to be stoked.

Instead of the familiar bringing comfort, it was unnerving, for so much about him had changed. He was living a completely different life. He wrote fiction. He lived in a house he'd built himself. He played in basketball tournaments for the Y, and he had many casual friends and two really good ones.

His feelings for Flossie hadn't changed, though. Because of them, because seeing her would be too painful, he'd not crossed the threshold of Klausmeyer's again until today. But today was different. He simply couldn't wait to show Maman his book. Hopefully, Flossie would be at work or tucked away in her attic room.

He hooked his hat and coat on the hall tree, then headed to Maman's room. His old bedroom door was closed. Further down, Flossie's former room was open. He knew she didn't live in it anymore, yet his pulse quickened.

At Maman's doorway, he paused. She'd fallen asleep in her chair. He took a minute to view her room through new eyes, the eyes of a son. He shook his head. After all his lecturing to Flossie, he'd actually been the one to end up with family at 438.

A large marble-top dresser held frames and candles. Jars and bottles. Vases and hat stands. The Tiffany pin he'd given her was part of a collection of pins sticking out of a fancy porcelain cup.

Doilies covered every surface, even the arms of the two upholstered chairs next to her heater—one of which she sat in, her head down, her knitting forgotten. It was so crowded. So . . . lived in. Especially compared to his place with its two spindle chairs, one table, one rocker, and a single pallet by the fire.

His attention drifted back to the woman he'd come to see. He smiled. Keeping his tone low and his voice soft, he spoke. "Hello, Maman."

She jerked and looked up, disoriented, then her eyes lit with pleasure. Setting her needles aside, she stood and opened her arms. "Come here, my boy, and give this old woman a hug."

Placing the books on a dresser, he walked into her embrace and stayed there. "I've missed you."

"I've missed you, too, though your letters are wonderful. You ought to be a writer."

He chuckled, kissed the top of her head, and stepped back. "The books are here. I brought you a copy."

Clapping her hands together, she pressed them against her mouth. "I can't wait. Let me see."

He picked one up and handed it to her.

She sat and simply held it. "I'm so proud of you, Reeve. So proud. Sit down and pour me some tea while I look at it. I've kept it warm for us."

He stood flatfooted for a moment. Proud of him? No one had ever said those words to him. Not ever. The rush of well-being they induced surprised and somewhat embarrassed him. He headed toward the tea service, glad to have something to do. Glad she was already looking at the book and he wasn't required to give her a response.

Her crooked hand smoothed the title page, then she ran her finger over the words *I. D. Claire*. "Whatever were you thinking?"

"I never intended to have to use it. Have regretted it a hundred times over."

She patted it. "Don't regret it, son. Not even for a minute."

He *harrumph*ed and poured tea into her cup, his hands shaking at the use of the word "son." It was how she addressed all her letters to him, and he never tired of reading it, but he'd only heard her say it a few times. He prepared her tea the way she liked it with a tiny squeeze of lemon and lots of sugar. Then he poured himself one and sat in the cushy chair at a forty-five degree angle from hers.

She read the first page, smile lines beginning to form. Resting an ankle on his knee, he took a sip of the weak brew, observing her over the cup, listening to the sound of pages being turned. Watching as her shoulders lifted and fell in a sigh. As her hand touched her throat, then her heart.

"Oh, Reeve. It's wonderful. I can't wait to read the whole thing, but I must put it aside and not use up our precious time. How are you, my dear? You look marvelous."

"As do you."

"Thank you." She gave him a quizzical look. "Interesting dedication in your book."

"So it is. How's your foot? Still bothering you?"

She accepted the change of subject and, as with every time he saw her, the hours flew by while they talked nonstop.

"It's not a home, Maman. Not like this." He swept his arm in front of him, indicating her room.

"It needs a woman's touch," she said.

He nodded. "Please, take the place in hand and do what you will."

"No, no, not me. I'm terrible at that kind of thing. Now, Flossie, being an artist and all, I imagine she'd be quite good. Perhaps you could hire her. She'd welcome the extra work, I'm sure."

He raised a brow. "I will not be hiring Miss Jayne. Shame on you for trying to maneuver me."

She pouted. "My Herschel was much easier to influence."

"Well, you know what they say about children. They're all so different."

She gave a soft laugh. "I see you brought an extra book."

"I did."

"And who might that be for?"

He gave her a pointed look. "You know good and well who it's for. Will you see that she gets it?"

"I most certainly will not. You want her to have it, you can go put it in her room same as I can."

He pressed back into the chair. "I can't go way up into her attic room. That would be unseemly, don't you think?"

"She's not in the attic anymore."

"She's not?"

"No, she's moved."

Uncrossing his legs, he pulled himself up off the back cushion. "Moved? Away?"

"No." She pointed a crooked finger toward her door. "Across the hall."

He blinked, then followed with his gaze the direction of her finger. "Across the hall? To, to *my* room?"

Picking up her knitting needles, she began to click them together in a staccato rhythm. "Mm-hm."

He gripped the armrests. "Is she in there right now?"

"No, she keeps the door closed so that her paints don't smell up the whole downstairs."

He eased his grip. "Why didn't you tell me she'd moved?"

"You didn't ask."

He narrowed his eyes. "I didn't ask about Mrs. Holliday, yet you told me when she went to and from Texas to visit her parents. I didn't ask about Oyster, yet you told me when he left. I didn't ask about Miss Love, yet you told me when she got a new roommate."

"You did, too, ask me about Mr. Oyster—and that's when Flossie moved to your room, by the way."

He stared at his, or *her*, door.

"Don't worry," Maman said. "You needn't go in if you don't want to. She should be home in fifteen minutes and you can give the book directly to her."

He glanced at a clock on the wall, then surged to his feet. "I'll be right back."

Swiping the book off the dresser, he crossed the hall, opened his old door, and froze. The potent odor of oil paints and turpentine hit him full force. The bed was in the same place as before, but it was covered with her white, fluffy linens. His desk held a palette, jars with brushes, tubes of oil paints, rags with an assortment of colored stains, and a jar of dirty turpentine.

His chair had been moved by the window, where she had an easel set up. Resting upon it was a canvas with a partially painted child wrapped in winter clothing and attempting to skate on the ice.

Completed paintings covered the walls. All of them with her signature in the corner. Of their own volition, his legs carried him inside her self-made gallery. A young girl with yellow sausage curls fed ducks at Central Park, a scruffy boy sold newspapers on a corner, a nanny pushed an elaborate baby carriage down a walkway.

But it was an oversized portrait of Cat that drew him like the gravitational pull of the earth. Cat was on her back and her paws swatted at a man's hand, a hand that was obviously playing with her, a hand that looked very familiar.

Swallowing, he turned away, then froze again. Wedged between the wall and the mirror was the phenakistascope he'd left behind. Removing it, he studied the photographs. The feelings he'd had for Flossie that day resurfaced in a surprising rush.

He held the phenakistascope in front of the mirror, spun it, then watched the two of them dance. He didn't think he'd ever forget the dress she'd been wearing or the way her hair had loosened or the scent of rosewater on her neck. He squeezed the handle. Die and be blamed, but he missed her. He returned it to its spot, wondering if she ever watched it anymore or if it was there merely to keep from hurting Mr. Holliday's feelings.

Tossing the book onto the bed, he exited the room, closed the door, crossed the hall, and pulled Maman to her feet. "I have to go."

"Running away, are we?"

"Absolutely." He gave her a fierce hug. "I love you. I'll try to see you within the next couple of weeks—before Christmas, in any event."

"Coward," she mumbled.

"Shrew," he quipped back. Then he gave her a kiss and all but flew out the door to the streetcar stop, until he realized Flossie would be disembarking there. Spinning around, he walked to a different one. He didn't want to force her into a meeting with him. Fifteen months might have passed since he'd last seen her, but that didn't mean time had healed her wounds. Of course, she'd sent him that Christmas card last year, but no matter how many times he read it, it was simply too cryptic. It left too much room for interpretation.

Even if it had been an olive branch, what if she didn't like the new him? With all the things that were different about him, he wouldn't even know where to start with her. What to say.

No, he'd done as she'd asked. He'd written her a book, and there was nothing cryptic about it. He'd laid himself completely bare. Either she'd accept the new him or she wouldn't.

By the time he arrived at the unfamiliar streetcar stop, he was cold, wet, and nervous. Yet his thoughts kept circling back to the notion that through the summer, the fall, and well into the winter she'd been working at his desk, sitting in his chair, and sleeping in his bed.

"Friendship is a sheltering tree." —Samuel Taylor Coleridge, 1797

CHAPTER

80

Opening her door, Flossie stepped into her room and closed her eyes, filling her lungs with the wonderful scent of paints. It was good to be home. She pulled off her gloves, then noticed a black book making an indention on her white downy bed.

Picking it up, she glanced at the spine, the title embossed in gold. *Beneath a Sheltering Tree.* Frowning, she opened it, then froze. *By I. D. Claire.*

Reeve had written a book? How had it gotten in her room?

She looked over her shoulder, then walked to her door and peered down the hall. It was empty. The *click-click-click* of Mrs. Dinwiddie's knitting needles drew her attention.

She crossed the hall. "Mrs. Dinwiddie?"

"Hello, my dear. Welcome home. How was work?"

"Fine, fine. Um, I found this on my bed." She lifted the book.

Mrs. Dinwiddie nodded. "Yes, it's Reeve's new novel. Isn't it marvelous?"

"I didn't know he'd written one."

"Oh, my, yes. He started working on it right after Christmas."

Flossie rubbed a thumb against the spine. She'd asked him to write a book in the Christmas card she'd sent him, but he'd not bothered to respond, hadn't so much as acknowledged the candy or fruitcake, nor the card she'd painted—though Mrs. Dinwiddie had assured her he'd received them.

She shook out her skirt. "Had he been working on the book before Christmas?"

"No, he had no plans whatsoever to write fiction again until suddenly, right after Christmas, he started a book out of the blue. Finished it in February, sold it in March. Now, here it is. He brought it over himself."

Flossie looked down at it again. Had her card been the impetus for it after all? "He was here? At 438?"

"He certainly was. You just missed him."

Crinkling her brows, she glanced again down the hallway. She would have loved to have seen him. He had to have known she'd be home any minute. If she'd just missed him, then it was because he'd wanted her to.

Mrs. Dinwiddie pulled at the yarn in her basket, then continued to knit. "I told him it was okay to leave the book in your room. I hope that's all right."

"Yes, of course. It was very generous of him to give one to me. Did he bring one for everyone?"

"Generosity had nothing to do with it. And no, he brought only you a copy. And me, of course."

"Of course." Generosity had nothing to do with it? What did that mean? But she couldn't quite get up the gumption to ask. Mrs. Dinwiddie was well ensconced in Reeve's camp. Flossie had seen the deluge of letters he'd written to the woman and feared that anything said might very well be reported back to him.

If only Mrs. Dinwiddie had shared his letters with her, but the woman had never offered and Flossie had never asked.

She bit her lip. "How is he?"

"Handsome and charming as ever."

"I see." In a bit of a daze, Flossie took a step back. "Well, thank you. I was—I was just wondering."

Mrs. Dinwiddie continued to knit, the *click-click-click* of her needles loud in the sudden silence.

Flossie returned to her room, then closed the door and leaned against it. He'd been in her room. Her gaze shot to the painting of Cat, then to the phenakistascope, then to the collection of scrapbooks by her bed. They appeared undisturbed, but that didn't mean he hadn't seen them.

Rushing to them, she picked up the one on top. It had all of the features he'd written this year. The scrapbook below it held his articles from last year. The scrapbook below that had each installment from *The Merry Maid of Mumford Street*. She'd saved them even before she'd known who I. D. Claire really was.

She'd almost burned them when she'd discovered the identity of Marylee Merrily, but something had kept her from it, and that same something had prodded her to glue them into a scrapbook.

She sank down onto the bed, her stomach bobbing like a buoy. What if he'd seen them? What would he think? And what had he thought when he'd discovered she was in his room? Had he thought she was pining for him? How desperate she must have looked. Just like the old maid in the board game.

She covered her face with her hands, then remembered he'd brought her a book. A book he'd started writing after he'd received her Christmas card.

She peeked up over her hands at the black volume she'd tossed on the bed. Grabbing a buttonhook on her side table, she undid her boots, pulled them off, then removed her watch pin from her shirtwaist. Six o'clock already.

She took off her skirt and shirtwaist, draped them over her chair, then crawled up into bed in her petticoats and held the book in her lap.

Who was the heroine? Was it Marylee? Or someone like her? Surely not. Still, her heart began to hammer.

She opened it.

BENEATH A SHELTERING TREE
by
I. D. Claire

She studied the frontispiece of a man standing beneath a leaf-less tree in the winter, alone and exposed. She tried to read the artist's signature, but couldn't make it out. She read the caption beneath it.

> *"Friendship is a sheltering tree."*
> —Samuel Taylor Coleridge, 1797

She turned the page.

DEDICATION
To my little magpie.
The songbird who changed my winter to spring.
You are never far from my thoughts, my mind, my heart.
I'm sorry.

She covered her mouth with her hand. Her pulse shot up. Her face turned hot. Her breathing became labored. She read the words over and over, trying to comprehend, wanting to believe. Believe that perhaps, just perhaps, he hadn't forgotten about her after all.

He was sorry? For what? Then she knew. For something she'd forgiven him for so long ago that she'd almost forgotten their last words. Her last words.

A pox on you, Reeve Wilder, you spineless, arrogant, lily-livered, son of a sea cook!

Oh, how she'd regretted those words, wished she could take them back. She'd read Marylee's story over and over. At first, she'd read it as a sort of self-flagellation, but the more she'd read it, the more she saw when Reeve's feelings for her had begun to change. When he'd begun to respect her as a person, then desire her as a woman. That's when she'd realized he was Mr. Bookish.

As the year progressed, her older and wiser self began to recognize the naiveté he'd seen in her and then portrayed in Marylee. At first, he'd portrayed it in a most uncomplimentary fashion. But as Marylee and Mr. Bookish began to walk down the path of The Old Maid Board Game, the things that Bookish had at first despised, he eventually came to cherish. When Marylee's foolishness endangered her, Bookish stepped in and protected her, saved her, even when, at times, he was saving her from herself.

The only thing Flossie never could reconcile was that Marylee hadn't been able to continue with the photography she'd loved. She'd been forced to choose between her passion and marriage. Shocking as it would have been, Flossie almost wished Marylee had chosen to marry and still maintain her photography business. It was fiction, after all. It would have done no harm.

But she'd never been able to ask Reeve about it, for she'd judged him and found him guilty when she was the one who owed the apology. Well, maybe not *the* apology, but certainly *an* apology, one that mirrored his. Only, he'd offered his the minute she'd thrown a book at his wall.

I can hear you and I'm sorry.

Shut up. Just shut up.

She'd offered an apology of sorts with the Christmas gifts and card. Hadn't he seen that he was the snowman? That she was the cat, wanting to get close but was too skittish to make the first move?

Yet her apology had been returned with nothing but silence.

Shut up. Just shut up.

She'd thought he was flinging her words back at her, but now he'd offered yet another apology. Only, this time he'd laid it out in print for her parents, her friends, her housemates, her workmates, and thousands of others to see.

Taking a handkerchief from inside the neckline of her chemise, she dabbed her nose, turned the page, and began chapter 1.

> I love winter. Its desolate snowscape. Its absence of bird song. Its leafless trees coated with ice. Ice so heavy that the limbs bend down to the point of breaking.

At nine o'clock her stomach growled. She'd made it a third of the way through, but she didn't want to stop and eat dinner. Opening a drawer, she fumbled around until she found a lemon candy stick, then continued to read.

> Her Ohio buckeye had already begun to leaf, the foolish tree. It was much too early and was in danger of the frost damaging those virgin leaves. Yet Miss Cheery Cherie came down her walk, her step light, her smile intoxicating. "Look, Mr. Glumb! Spring is coming."
>
> I stood in solidarity beside my Kentucky coffee tree, confident it had nothing to fear. It would be the last tree in the neighborhood to leaf out. Always had been, always would be. No frost damage for it.
>
> Miss Cherie opened her gate, a basket hooked on her elbow, her hat sporting the very songbirds she longed to hear. Only these had been snuffed out, never to whistle a merry tune again. I wondered if she saw the irony of it.
>
> "Nice hat," I said. "What kind of birds are those?"
>
> "Chickadees. They're my favorite." She tilted her head. "Do you have a favorite?"
>
> "The crow."
>
> Instead of believing me, she laughed, the sound so pure, the leaves on her buckeye produced more buds. She was half-

way to the corner when I realized I was no longer standing beneath my coffee tree, but had ventured several steps away so that I might keep her in my sights. She laughed, waved, and called out greetings to those she passed, upending the entire neighborhood the way spring and songbirds upended the forest. The way she was upending me.

At midnight, Flossie undid her corset, took off her undergarments, and put on her nightdress. Crawling back under the covers, she continued to read, pulling one hairpin out at a time. For the next few hours she laughed, she sighed, she cried. But most of all, she fell in love with Reeve all over again. The entire book was a love letter, and if the dedication were to be believed, it was a love letter to her. The songbird who'd changed his winter to spring.

> Her entire yard had come out in full glory. The cotton-woods, the spicebushes, the chokecherries, and her beloved Ohio buckeye, but it was the clove currants lining her house which produced a magnificent scent. Soon its fruit would ripen. I longed to taste it.
>
> My coffee tree lay in the height of dormancy, as I knew it would. At that moment I decided to plant a new tree—maybe even two—just as soon as the weather permitted. Something that would fill out the yard a bit and bloom a little earlier. Maybe some cottonwoods. Of course, I'd need to get one male and one female or they'd both wither.
>
> I stood at my gate staring at her yard, an unexpected longing filling me. I flicked the latch open and closed. Perhaps tomorrow I would venture forth and ask her for some cuttings.

At three in the morning, Flossie turned the final page.

Cheery and I sat on a swing suspended from our Kentucky coffee tree, its leaves full, its shade unsurpassed. Fifty years had come and gone since we'd said our vows from this very spot. Across the street, fast-growing trees had squeezed out and replaced the chokecherries and spicebushes of our youth, but the buckeye and cottonwoods still stood.

The cuttings we'd planted together in my yard gave us early blooms, late blooms, and fragrant blooms. But no matter what time of year we sat beneath our tree, be it dormant or thriving, we always found friendship and love within the shelter of each other's arms.

Swiping her tears, Flossie slid down beneath the covers and hugged the book to her. If she'd interpreted the metaphors correctly, he wasn't lonely. He'd learned to make friends. He'd made himself a home, and he'd extended her an invitation to be a part of it. All she needed to do was say yes.

But had he really changed so much? It was one thing to write all that into a piece of fiction. It was another thing altogether to put it into practice. Either way, it was as if she didn't even know him anymore. The man who'd written this book was a far cry from the one who'd lived in this room, the one who'd written *The Merry Maid of Mumford Street*.

She closed her eyes and considered everything she'd just read. It was then she realized the question wasn't how could she say yes, but how could she possibly say no?

She turned onto her side, confused, then hopeful, then confused again.

She fell into an exhausted sleep and dreamed of barren trees grabbing her, entangling her, and never letting her go, no matter how much she struggled and screamed.

CHAPTER
81

Reeve's hands shook as he opened the missive, the familiar handwriting telling him who it was from.

My dearest RW,

Thank you for the book. I stayed up half the night reading it and the other half thinking of you. It was beautiful, and the dedication moved me deeply.

Mr. Holliday is giving Mrs. Holliday a birthday party this Sunday after church. I know it would mean a lot to her if you came, too. Unfortunately, it is an ice-skating party, but I am not bringing my skates. I will be sitting on your bench drinking hot cocoa and, I hope, becoming reacquainted with you.

Very truly yours,
FRJ

Lowering the letter, he frowned. He'd spent months pouring himself out into that book, had agonized over the dedication, and the most she could say was that she wanted to get reacquainted?

Sighing, he took a piece of paper from his lap desk, dipped his pen into his inkwell, then gave his wrist a shake.

Dearest FRJ,

Bring your skates, for I am bringing mine. I will see you at our bench.

Yours,
RW

CHAPTER
82

Reeve stood half hidden behind a cluster of trees several yards away from their bench. She wasn't wearing the maroon gown she'd worn the last time they went skating. Was that a sign? Was she trying to tell him nothing would ever be the same again?

Or maybe she didn't wear it because she didn't want any more reminders of that skating debacle. Or perhaps her mother simply made her a new gown. All three were likely possibilities. He wished he knew which one it was. He'd have asked Maman, but she hadn't come to the party. Said the cold was simply too much for her these days.

Lifting his hat, he ran a hand through his hair. He wanted to go over there, but had no idea what to say. Couldn't decide where to start, which thing was the most important, which issue she wanted to hear about first.

Should he start by telling her that he hadn't used any of the money he'd earned from the Marylee piece? At least, he'd not used it for himself, only for others. The financial gain from it continued to mount. Every time he turned around, another paper was running it. The blasted story simply would not die.

No, maybe he shouldn't mention Marylee at all. But how could he not? That's why he'd left Klausmeyer's. That's why she'd never wanted to see him again. He'd pretended to be her friend while he'd used her to further his own purposes.

But that wasn't true, either. He hadn't pretended—at least not toward the end. He really had been her friend. He'd cared deeply for her then and cared deeply for her now. He blew out a breath, a puff of vapor forming. If he'd treated her like that when he cared for her, it wasn't much of a recommendation.

A breeze ruffled his scarf, the cold air stinging his ears. He couldn't stand there all day. It was time to pay the piper. He'd just say whatever happened to pop into his head. Taking a deep breath, he slung his skates over his shoulder and made his way toward the bench.

SHE SAW HIM COMING and he looked so magnificent, she almost rose to her feet the way men did when a lady entered a room. Instead, she forced herself to stay seated, gripped her gloved hands in her lap, and simply absorbed all the changes.

He wore his hair a bit longer. His shoulders had broadened. And his skin tone had darkened. With an index finger, he held a pair of skates over his shoulder. The fringe on his blue plaid scarf swirled in the breeze. His legs nudged the hem of his frock coat open with each step.

Then he was there, his eyes still green, yet changed. They were clearer, less opaque. Happier? Could eyes be happy?

"You look beautiful," she breathed, then slapped a hand over her mouth, her eyes widening.

Smile lines gathered on either side of his mouth. He tugged the brim of his hat.

Her face heated, despite the cold. *Please, earth, just swallow me up right now.*

"May I sit down?" he asked.

"Oh!" She scooted over. "Of course. Yes. I'm sorry. Sit. I mean . . ." She took a deep breath. "Won't you have a seat?"

Dropping the skates beside him, he sat and almost took up the whole bench with his long legs, the added breadth of his shoulders, and his very being. Whiffs of peppermint shaving soap came and went as he angled himself to better see her.

Perfectly relaxed, he crossed his legs and perused her without trying to camouflage his examination in the least. He started at the top of her peacock-feathered hat, then moved to her hair, which hadn't cooperated at all this morning. She'd been ready to chop it all off by the time she was done with it. It took every bit of control she had not to reach up and see if the Gibson girl coif had sagged like a goose down pillow that needed fluffing.

He continued his survey, studying her oversized sailor collar and the leg-o'-mutton sleeves it rested on. His gaze lingered on the big buttons running down the front of her shirtwaist, the revers that flipped out at her waist, then the braided trim running up the edge of a reverse pleat in her sky-blue skirt.

"What does the R stand for?" he asked.

His voice ran straight through her, producing a warmth as potent as a forbidden gulp of her father's whiskey. With a shiver, she looked down at her skirt, pressing her hands against her chest and waist to see what he was referring to. "What R?"

"The R in FRJ."

She lifted her gaze. "You mean Rebecca?"

He tilted his chin up slightly and gave a self-deprecating shake of his head as if he'd lost a bet with himself. "Rebecca. Flossie Rebecca Jayne."

"Florence Rebecca Jayne."

He smiled. Her insides turned to mush. She didn't remember this happening before. Had he always had this effect on her? If he had, she certainly couldn't recall it. Maybe it was that book. That book with all its metaphors about trees and fruit and flower buds, about songbirds turning winters into spring.

"Florence," he said. "Of course, I'd forgotten."

She stared at him. "Forgotten? When did I ever tell you my name was Florence?"

"You didn't, I heard it through the wall."

Her lips parted, then she narrowed her eyes. "What else did you hear through the wall?"

"Everything."

Her stomach bounced. She looked at the skaters gliding by, but didn't really see them. Instead, she tried to remember all that she and Annie Belle had said to each other. Had she ever talked about him? She was sure she had. What she wasn't sure of was what she'd said.

She crossed her arms. "It was in very bad form of you to eavesdrop."

"It was. I apologize."

She turned back to him. He still leaned lazily against the bench at a cockeyed angle.

"You don't look sorry."

His smile broadened. "That's probably because I'm sorry that I acted in bad form, but I'm not really sorry I heard all your conversations. That's when I first started to fall in love with you, listening to all that jabber. Completely fascinated me."

Her jaw slackened. How in all the world was she supposed to respond to that?

She began to tap her foot. "You know, I spent many hours as a young girl fantasizing about how the man of my dreams was going to tell me he loved me. Never, ever in all of my imaginings did I think he'd say it was my 'jabbering' that did the deed."

He propped an elbow on the back of the bench and rested a cheek on his fist. "Am I the man of your dreams, Flossie?"

She flattened her lips. "Nightmares, more like it."

He reached over and snagged a tendril that had come lose from her unruly coif and gave it a gentle yank. "Want to go skating?"

"No."

"Want to kiss me?"

She jumped to her feet. "No."

He stretched his arm against the back of the bench. "I'm afraid it's going to have to be one or the other because if I don't get my hands on you soon, I'm going to go stark raving mad."

Spinning around to face him, she planted her hands on her waist. "What in the world has gotten into you? You never used to act like this."

"I might not have acted it, but I thought it. I definitely thought it. Do you not like it? Because now that I've been unleashed, I'm afraid there's no going back."

Oh, she liked it. She definitely liked it, but they'd only been sitting there for fifteen minutes, yet they'd been apart for fifteen months.

"You are not kissing me anytime soon. I haven't seen you in forever and a day. So if you want that kiss, then you have some courting to do. And a lot of it."

He came to his feet. "Let's get our skates on, then, and I'll show you what I've learned."

She eyed him with suspicion, a breezed flipping back her collar. "What have you learned?"

He smoothed down her collar. "To dance, little magpie. I've learned to dance."

1/14/2021

ROSENBERG FLORENC

Item Number: 31901057793210

Contra Costa County Libraries are open for front door pick up of holds. Masks and social distancing are required. For faster service, book an appointment at: https://ccclib.org/front-door-service/ Book drops are available for returns. All Contra Costa County Libraries will be closed on December 24th and 25th, and January 1st and 18th; and will close by 5:00 pm on December 31st. Pinole Library and Ygnacio Valley Library remain temporarily closed. Items may be renewed online at http://ccclib.org, or by calling 1-800-984-4636, menu option 1.

Hold Shelf Slip

CHAPTER

83

Taking her right hand, he placed his other hand on her back, dug in with one skate, and pushed off. Surprised, she responded automatically and followed his lead.

"You've learned to skate," she said.

"To dance." The green eyes that had been so bright and clear before now darkened a shade.

"Watch where you're going," she said. "I don't want to bump into anybody."

He lifted a corner of his mouth. "No running over any fingers today. Now, close your eyes and give yourself over to me."

Close her eyes? Give herself over to him? Not likely.

He began to hum *The Blue Danube*. At first, she didn't trust him to navigate the ice, but then realized that though he wasn't the best skater on the pond, he was certainly competent. Average, even. And there was nothing wrong with being average.

Once she relaxed, it all came rushing back. The Fourth of July, their first dance. Her storming into his room, music box in hand, forcing him to connect with her. She allowed her eyes to close a moment and listen to him hum, memories flooding her.

The feel of his hand on her back, the rhythmic pattern of their steps, the scent of peppermint from his soap, and the rush of desire roaring through her veins. How many times had she tried to recapture those feelings in that very same room where she now slept? How many times had she opened her music box, closed her eyes, and done the one-two-three steps in an effort to evoke the feelings now coursing through her?

Many times. Too many times. All of them falling far short of this.

Reeve swerved around a wobbly skater. Breath catching, she jerked her eyes open and missed a step. He pulled her close, then spun them in a circle while she regained her balance. She looked into his eyes, eyes she'd tried to remember. Eyes she'd tried to forget.

He winked, then pushed off again, his humming starting anew.

The wind rushed at her back and she reveled in the feeling of being free, even while she was within the confines of his arms. But his arms weren't confining. They were . . . how had he put it?

No matter what time of year we sat beneath our tree, be it dormant or thriving, we always had friendship and love within the shelter of each other's arms.

His hand spanned the small of her back. He flexed his fingers, spreading them, lightly caressing her through her jacket. Her head fell back, her eyes slid shut. His humming began to slow, as did their skating. Slower and slower until they turned in a tiny circle. Finally, he stopped. She opened her eyes, her limbs heavy.

He brought the hand he held to his shoulder, then slid his hand down the whole of her arm and the entire length of her side until he rested both hands against her waist.

Sweet heaven above, but she wanted to kiss him. But they were in the middle of Central Park and she'd just told him no kisses until he'd courted her properly. Until she'd learned about this more mature, more confident, more open and alluring Reeve. Still, she was reluctant to step away from him just yet. He moved his hands to her back, his fingers brushing the curve at its base, his thumbs skimming her sides. Her fingers tightened on his shoulders.

"*Shhhhh.*" He smoothed a tiny piece of hair from her face, then brushed her eyebrow with his thumb.

She leaned her face into his hand, her eyes closing, her heart hammering.

"Watch out!" An out of control skater headed toward them.

Reeve shoved her behind him, then grabbed the youth's arm and steadied him, before sending him on his way. She smiled to herself. Imagine that. Reeve protecting her on the ice.

He turned around and she drank her fill. The wide cut of the frock coat across his shoulders tapering down to his trim waist. The windblown curls peeking out beneath his hat. The green of his eyes, so brilliant in the sun. The curve of his lips, more alluring than she remembered.

"You've become quite good on your skates," she said with a breathy sigh.

"Thank you."

She brushed a bit of snow from his shoulder, relishing the task. "You've gotten broader."

"So I've heard."

She grabbed a curl at his nape, then let it spring from her grasp. "You've grown your hair out."

"It needs a cut."

"You've . . ." She stopped herself.

"I've what?"

Become more handsome, she thought, but it wasn't just his looks. He'd always been attractive. It was something else, something deeper, something she couldn't quite put her finger on. She realized with a start that if her feelings for him had changed at all, they'd become stronger, not weaker.

"I've what?" he asked again.

She shook her head, refusing to put her thoughts into words.

The voices of the other skaters faded. The scraping of blades against the ice diminished. Her chest rose and fell, her breath fluttering her sailor collar.

"Will you watch the sunset on Klausmeyer's roof with me?" he asked.

Her heart squeezed. "I'm sorry."

Confusion filled his eyes. His lips turned down. "Why not?"

"Because if I go on that roof with you, I'll succumb to what my heart wants instead of what my head wants. And it's too soon, Reeve. It's too soon."

He didn't deny it, for they both were cognizant of the connection they'd once again felt in each other's arms. Something they'd gone without all these many months.

"Then dance with me one more time. After that, we'll go find the Hollidays and I'll pay my respects."

This time when he took her in his arms, she closed her eyes and gave herself completely over to him.

"Cinched in by an overly wide band of ivory satin at her waist, her skirt was draped with four strips of exquisite scalloped lace bordered with rose designs and tied by true-lovers' knots." [41]

CHAPTER

84

Winter passed and spring blossomed. The affection and love Reeve had for Flossie multiplied exponentially as he courted her with single-minded determination. Much to his surprise and pleasure, she responded to his wooing with equal amounts of warmth.

He stood in the Public Hall of the Y with her, humbled and heart full. Her mother and Maman had overseen the hall's transformation into a bower of pastel blooms and noble palms. An array of food along the east wall drew a crowd of men. A display of gifts along the west wall drew the women.

Two years ago he wouldn't have had a single friend to invite to his wedding. Today the room was filled with men who lived at the Twenty-Sixth Ward YMCA, teammates from his basketball and baseball teams, fellows from work, Holliday and Nettels, and even a handful of new neighbors.

The Tiffany Girls arrived in full force, Mrs. Driscoll included. Miss Love, Mrs. Klausmeyer, Flossie's art-school mates, and many friends of Flossie's parents all made appearances.

He'd been hugged, clapped on the back, and poked in the ribs. He'd been congratulated, badgered, and toasted. The melee was much more than he was comfortable with, but the party had only begun. It would be past noon before he could abscond with his wife.

IT WAS EVERYTHING FLOSSIE had dreamed of and more. Papa had spared no expense and Mother had outdone herself on the dress. Cinched in by an overly wide band of ivory satin at her waist, her skirt was draped with four strips of exquisite scalloped lace bordered with rose designs and tied by true-lovers' knots.

Mirroring her waist, a tall collar of lace encased her throat, a bouquet of orange blossoms pinned to its left side. Softly draped satin sleeves of great width gathered to her elbow, then hugged her arm, extending low on her short white gloves. She fingered a slender branch of her wedding day chatelaine made up of orange blossoms and falling artfully along the right side of her skirt. It was the only time in a woman's entire life when she could wear orange blossoms. Flossie couldn't believe her day had finally come.

Reeve rode a hand along the lower curve of her back, staking his claim and looking marvelously handsome in his black cutaway and double-breasted formal white vest. He smiled, he greeted, he thanked people for coming, but she could tell he'd have preferred a quick ceremony and an even quicker getaway with his bride.

She smiled at him, appreciating his sacrifice in letting her have her day.

He gave her a wink, then squeezed her waist. "For a magpie, you've been awfully quiet."

"For a newlywed groom, you've been awfully patient."

His eyes darkened. "Only because I've been thinking that once I get you to myself, I just might forgo all the fuss of a train ride and honeymoon and simply keep you locked in my house for the next thirty days."

Her eyes widened, goose bumps skittering over her body.

"Mrs. Wilder, you are the loveliest bride I have ever seen—second only to my own, of course." Her former boss approached them.

Flossie placed a hand against her throat. "Mr. Tiffany. My goodness, how do you do? Thank you so much for coming."

"My pleasure."

She'd done a lot of growing up at Tiffany Glass and Decorating Company. She'd learned what it was like to be a New Woman on her own. It wasn't exactly what she'd been expecting. Oh, she'd been free from the normal restrictions put on the fair sex, but with the lifting of those restrictions had come responsibilities.

The responsibility of taking care of herself on a streetcar full of resentful men. Of walking home alone in the dark during a snowstorm. Of paying her rent when hard times came. Of realizing that she couldn't take everyone at face value simply because she wanted to believe the world was full of good people.

She'd take away the lessons she'd learned at Tiffany's and enter into life as a wife and, hopefully someday, a mother, with joy instead of resentment.

One thing was certain, she would always be proud to have been a Tiffany Girl. She felt sure it would be something future Wilder generations would be proud of, too. And if that weren't enough, she still had her painting. She'd always have her painting.

Reeve extended his hand. "Reeve Wilder."

Mr. Tiffany pumped his hand. "It's an honor. I confess my daughters were quite envious of me and made me promise to ask for an autograph from Mr. Claire, if I could be so rude as to impose."

Reeve pasted a smile onto his face. "I'm certain that can be arranged."

Flossie bit her cheek. Somehow word had leaked out that Reeve was the one and only I. D. Claire. It was inevitable, since everyone at 438 had known his identity after the big argument she'd had with him that long ago day. Annie Belle had heard their quarrel through the wall and had wasted no time in informing the rest of the boarders.

More recently, with the huge success of *Beneath a Sheltering Tree*, the men he worked with at the newspaper had somehow found out. But it was the fellows here at the Y who gave him the hardest time—throwing in as many "I declares" as possible into their conversations.

Reeve tolerated it as best he could, but she knew he hated to call attention to himself, and even more, he hated the pseudonym. Still, it wasn't every day Mr. Tiffany asked for an autograph.

A bit after one o'clock, when only Mother, Papa, Mrs. Dinwiddie, and their very best friends were left, Reeve helped her up into a carriage complete with white horses.

He shook Papa's hand, kissed Mother's cheek, and pulled Mrs. Dinwiddie up into a bear hug. The woman whispered something into his ear that made him laugh. He put her down, kissed her flush on the lips, joined Flossie, and shook the reins.

Twisting around, she waved at her parents as the rice they threw pebbled the carriage.

CLAPBOARD HOUSE[42]

"Reeve pulled the horses to a stop in front of a clapboard house
with a white picket fence and a shaded front porch."

CHAPTER
85

Reeve pulled the horses to a stop in front of a clapboard house with a white picket fence and a shaded front porch.

"Oh, Reeve," she said, catching her breath. "It's beautiful."

Her parents had seen it, Mrs. Dinwiddie had seen it, his friends had seen it. Only she hadn't seen it. It was his wedding gift to her, and she'd not been allowed to have her first glimpse until she shared his last name.

The yard was more dirt than grass, but there were three bushes, a good-sized shade tree, and he'd built the place with his own two hands. A sense of well-being rushed through her. This would be the house she'd live in for the rest of her life. The house she'd birth their babies in. The house she'd welcome their grandchildren to. Of a sudden, she wanted it to be the house she consummated their marriage in.

"How much time do we have before our train leaves?" she asked.

Setting the brake, he hopped down. "Hours, I'm afraid. I didn't want you to be rushed at the reception, so we won't need to leave until almost dark."

Placing his hands on her waist, he lifted her from the carriage. She'd not changed into her traveling gown, but still wore her wedding dress. He'd told her in advance that he wanted to be the one to remove it. Mother had been quite scandalized, but it was the only request he'd made. He'd allowed Mother, Flossie, and Mrs. Dinwiddie to plan everything else. So she'd stood firm against Mother's objections.

At the door, he swooped her up into his arms and crossed the threshold. "Welcome to our home, Mrs. Wilder."

With her arms about his neck, she surveyed the living area. Two rockers sat before a red brick fireplace. One large and brown. One dainty and upholstered in a flowery brocade. Cat had curled up on the brown one, not deigning to even acknowledge their intrusion.

"She thinks it's her chair."

She bit her lower lip. "It's good to see her. I've missed her."

"Well, don't bother calling. She won't budge unless bodily moved."

On the mantle, right in the center, her Christmas card held center stage. Her heart warmed and she wondered how long it had been there. "You never replied to my Christmas card."

"That's because I was busy writing the novel that very card demanded."

"I didn't demand it, and you could have at least acknowledged the candy and fruitcake."

"I did. Don't you remember in chapter eight of the book? I ate them rather enthusiastically while I watched Miss Cherie flitting about her garden."

"Miss Cherie." She rolled her eyes. "That woman was always so cheerful. Everyone loved her, she never did anything wrong. I thought it an awfully high bar to live up to. Couldn't she have been average? You know, flawed?"

His kissed her forehead. "She was flawed, but the story was about him."

"I see." She adjusted his collar. "Speaking of Cheery Cherie and Marylee Merrily, I do declare but I'm stating here and now that I will choose the names of all our children."

He chuckled. "All? How many are you planning on having?"

"At least ten."

He shook his head. "We'll only need nine."

She leaned back to better see his face. "What's wrong with ten?"

"Nothing, but we only need nine players to field a baseball team."

She smiled. "What if we have some girls?"

"Then we'll put them on the team, too. After all, their mother was a New Woman. By the time our little ones are ready to play ball, women will probably be wearing trousers."

She snorted back a laugh.

Giving her a squeeze, he turned to the right and carried her to an empty bedroom. "This is your art studio."

Her easel stood next to a window in the barren room, but it was the portrait sitting on it that captured her attention. It was of a woman leaning against a railing, her red hair flowing in the breeze, the sea behind her blue and sparkling. *F. Jayne* was scrawled across the bottom corner.

Her hands loosened. "Let me down, please."

He placed her on her feet.

At first, she simply stood, absorbing the unexpected surprise. "Where, how did you find it?"

"I hired a detective. I'd hoped to find the Trostles and Bourgeois. Make them answer for their crimes."

She placed a hand against her neck. "And did you?"

"No, but the detective did find your painting at a shop on the East Side."

Her eyes watered. "I can't believe it. I . . . I thought it was lost forever."

"So did I."

She approached it, studying it. It really was one of her best pieces.

Reeve shifted his weight. "I used the money I'd earned from Marylee's story to hire the detective." He looked at the tips of his shoes. "I want you to know, I never used that money for myself. Only for others."

"Oh, Reeve. You didn't have to do that."

"I didn't use it for this house, Flossie. Not the house or the property or the furniture. All of that was purchased with money I earned on the *Sheltering* book and my articles."

"What things did you use it for, then?"

He studied her. "I used it to pay off your debts."

She took a shuddering breath. "You? You paid them?"

"Yes."

She looked to the side. "I had no idea. Why didn't you tell me?"

"I guess I was afraid it would make you feel beholden to me and that's not why I did it. Not at all. It was my pleasure to pay them off."

Tears stacked up against her throat. "Thank you. I don't know what to say. You didn't have to."

"There's lots of that money left and more coming in. I donated some of it to a settlement in Greenpoint. Some of it to buy Christmas gifts for the kids at the Sheltering Arms orphanage in Manhattan. I bought Maman a Tiffany hat pin with it—but that was back when she was just Mrs. Dinwiddie. Since she became my Maman, I've only used my money for the things I buy her."

"The money from the Marylee story is your money."

"It's dirty money."

"It's not. It's . . . wait a minute." She went into the parlor and pointed to her trunks amassed against the wall, waiting to be unpacked. "Can you open this one for me?"

He took down the trunk stacked on top of it, then unlatched the one she'd indicated and held open the lid.

She rummaged through it, then pulled out her scrapbooks. The first one she opened held the story of *The Merry Maid of Mumford Street*. "I saved all of the installments. I've read them over and over."

He took the scrapbook, turned the pages, then closed his eyes. "I'm so sorry."

She put the scrapbook back in the trunk. "Don't be. It's a story I will cherish for as long as I live. I will read it to our children, to our children's children, and even to their children, if I live long enough. So do not ever again let me hear you refer to it as dirty. Do you understand?"

Throat working, he nodded. "Don't move."

He crossed to a desk facing the window and opened the roll top, then removed a cigar box. Inside were stacks of tiny slips of papers. All had questions written on them. All had her artwork on their edges.

What is your favorite winter activity?

What is your earliest childhood memory?

What was your last thought before going to sleep?

She pressed a hand against her throat. "You saved them?"

"Every single one. Even the ones people left behind on the table."

"I never saw you take them."

"I asked Mrs. Klausmeyer to save them for me."

Closing the lid of the box, she hugged it to her. "Oh, Reeve. We've wasted so much time."

"I know." He shook his head. "I know."

He returned the box to his desk while she walked back to once again peek inside the studio, still trying to comprehend that she'd have the room all to herself for painting.

Stepping up beside her, he slipped a hand into his pocket. "If you want to sell your paintings, I want you to know, I'd never take your earnings away from you."

"Oh, Reeve, I'm not a good enough painter for that kind of thing."

"You're not hearing what I'm saying. I'm saying that if you ever earn any money, it'll be yours, not mine."

She studied him. "You know what I'd really like?"

"What?"

"I'd like it to be our money—not mine, not yours, but ours."

He looked out one of the curtainless windows lining the side wall. "I suppose we could do that, but if we did, then it seems like we should do that with what I earn, too."

She sucked in her breath. "You'd let your money be our money?"

"I would."

She stared at him, stunned. Never had she heard of a man doing such a thing. Gratitude filling her chest, she ran her hands beneath his lapels, grasped them, and brought his lips to hers.

He stilled for but a second, then pulled his hand from his pocket and wrapped her in his arms, deepening the kiss. "I've been wanting to do that all day."

"Me, too." She slid her fingers up the back of his neck and into his hair. "Thank you for my art room—for everything."

He kissed her again, his hands slipping lower, pulling her closer. Her knees weakened.

Breaking the kiss, he rested his forehead against hers, his breathing labored. "I haven't shown you the rest of the house."

"No, you haven't," she whispered.

He led her to the kitchen. An Acme Wonder cook stove sat against the wall. Along its back, the Tiffany tea screen she'd helped Mrs. Dinwiddie pick out shielded a coffeepot.

"I used to touch the tea screen," he said. "Just because I knew you'd touched it first."

She bit her lip, then turned around and noticed the table that Mrs. Dinwiddie had told her of. Even if she hadn't, Flossie would have immediately known he'd made it. Compared to everything else in the house, it was glaringly rustic.

Heart squeezing, she pulled out a chair and sat, her lace flounces spilling around her. "We're going to feed our family at this table someday."

He said nothing, his shoulder propped against the doorframe, his eyes hooded.

Holding his gaze, she removed her glove one finger at a time, then ran her hand along the table's scarred top. The gold band on her fourth finger caught the light and reflected it back. "Take me to the bedroom, Reeve."

CHAPTER

86

Pushing himself off the doorframe, Reeve swept his hand in front of him. The muscles in her lower abdomen clenched in a way that made her think of his kisses, his embraces, and the smoldering way he looked at her sometimes. The way he looked at her now. Swallowing, she made her legs carry her to the only room she had yet to see.

A massive iron bedstead dominated the room. Instead of having four posts at each corner, the top rail curved into one continuous piece. A washstand and tiny mirror stood in the corner. A side table held an oil lamp and the metal figurine from the fair. It would be the last thing he saw each night before he extinguished the light.

She fingered the orange blossoms hanging from her waist.

"I didn't want to buy a vanity without you," he said. "I wasn't sure what was required."

She walked to the bed. It looked nothing like the white fluffy one of her youth. It was draped with a crocheted cover she'd seen Mrs. Dinwiddie working on for months last year.

"I don't need a vanity."

"You do. And I'll get you one. Just as soon as we return from Niagara Falls."

Moistening her lips, she placed her hands on the mattress and pushed, testing the springs. "It's a lovely bed."

"It's not very frilly."

She picked at the cover. "I don't want frilly, just warm."

He approached her, then encircled her waist from behind and kissed her neck through the lace of her high collar. "It'll be warm. I can assure you of that."

The nerves along her neck tingled. She leaned her head back against his chest to give him more access. He moved his lips to her jaw, her ear. His hands spread. His fingers skimmed.

She grabbed his wrists, her breathing rapid. "Reeve?"

He stopped moving.

She threaded her fingers with his, feeling his wedding band, loving that she'd put it there. "How, how long does it take for a girl to become a woman? Does it, does it take all night?"

He rested his lips against her head, his hands gripping hers. "It doesn't take all night, but I wouldn't want to rush it."

She swallowed. "How long?"

"Not long."

Her pulse raced. Her legs trembled. "I-I know it's still light outside. And that it's the—the middle of the day, but . . ." She took a tremulous breath. "Would you think me terribly wicked if I . . . if we . . . if . . ."

Releasing her hands, he took her by the shoulders and turned her around, then cupped her face. His eyes were close, so close she could see streaks of blue shooting throughout the green of his irises.

"I would never think that," he said. "You will be my wife in daylight, in moonlight, in the dark of night, in every moment. There will never be anything wicked about it." Taking her by the arms, he brought her to him for a sweet, slow kiss. "Where's your buttonhook, my love?" he murmured against her lips.

She wondered if her skin was as flushed as his, her breathing as rapid as his, her eyes as dark as his. "In the carpet bag by the front door."

He nodded. "I'm going to get the bag. All right?"

"Yes." She stood by the bed, fingering the lace of her skirt, trying to remember why she'd been in such a hurry. For now that the time had come, she was very unsure.

A dog far away barked. Children playing a game of some sort shouted and laughed. She couldn't believe they were going to do this in the middle of the day. What had she been thinking? God would surely strike her dead for even suggesting it.

Reeve returned and placed the bag on the bed.

She rummaged through it, then clasped the buttonhook, her hand shaking. "Maybe this isn't such a good idea. Maybe we should wait. I-I wouldn't want to rush."

"We won't rush." His voice had dropped. He unfurled her fingers and took the buttonhook. "Hold out your arm, little magpie."

She held out her arm.

Beginning at her wrist, he released the tiny white buttons with deft movements. "There's a lot of buttons."

"There's even more running down my back. You should have let my mother help me change."

He stopped, the hook half in the buttonhole and half out. "I've been dreaming about doing this for months."

Her lips parted. "I've been dreaming about my wedding day for a lifetime." She lowered her voice to a whisper. "But not this part of it, of course. And certainly not in broad daylight."

He continued to work the buttons. "But this is the best part. If you weren't dreaming about this, what were you dreaming about?"

"Don't be silly. This isn't the best part. The best part is getting ready for you. Putting on all new garments. Bathing in water that smells like a vat of roses. Watching you when you first saw me in my gown. Listening to you pledge your life to mine. Putting the ring on your finger and making my vows. Hugging everyone. Riding off in the carriage. Being carried across the threshold. Those are the best parts."

The fitted section of her sleeve fell free. He moved to her other arm. "When we get ready to board the train tonight, I'll ask you again what the best part is and then we'll see what you say."

She blinked. "You think you're going to upstage a lifetime of dreams and fantasies?"

"I know I am."

She lifted her brows. "My, my, my. Aren't we sure of ourselves."

A corner of his mouth lifted. "How could you dream about this day when you didn't even know what I looked like? That's a pretty big component of the whole thing. At least, I hope it was."

"Oh, but I did know what you looked like. You were tall. Terribly handsome. Had a bit of a dimple right here." She ran a finger down his left cheek.

He fumbled the hook.

"You had broad shoulders, though I admit even I hadn't realized they'd be this broad." She ran a hand from his arm to his neck. "And you had beautiful curly hair."

He shook his head. "I hate my hair. It's like a girl's."

"There is not one single thing about you that is even remotely like a girl. And I love your hair. Especially when it gets long in the back." She tried to twist a lock of it around her finger, but it was too short.

He ignored her, concentrating on his task.

She removed the orange blossom chatelaine from the waist-band of her skirt. "For quite some time, I've been wondering how Papa managed to pay for such an extravagant wedding. Mother always prevaricated when I asked her about it." She lifted the blossoms to her nose. "You paid for our wedding, didn't you?"

He shrugged one shoulder. Her second sleeve fell free.

"Thank you," she whispered.

Straightening, he took the orange blossoms and draped them across the side table next to his figurine. "You're welcome. Now, turn around, my love."

She glanced at the bed.

"It's all right." He brought her hands to his lips, the sleeves of her gown hanging, then he lifted her arms and turned her slowly around as if they were dancing.

Once her back was to him, she lowered her chin, heart thumping. He undid her sash and tossed it on the bed. Next, the skirt. The minute he let go, it fell to the floor. He sucked in his breath, then held her elbow while she stepped out of it.

Bending over, she retrieved it, then draped it on the bed. "It's beautiful, isn't it?"

"Yes," he breathed.

"Did you see the true-lovers' knots along the edges?" Placing a hand beneath a lace flounce, she lifted it.

He wasn't looking at her skirt, though. He was looking at her petticoat peeking out from beneath her bodice.

She smoothed her hand over it, admiring the ribbons and beads her mother had sewn above the bottom ruffle. "It's pretty, too, isn't?"

"Yes." His Adam's apple bobbed.

"Wearing it, all of it, I felt like a princess."

"You look like a princess."

She gave him a warning look. "Now you're sounding like my mother."

"No, it's true."

"It's not. And I want our marriage to be based on nothing but truths. And the truth is, I'm average."

"You're not. Not in your smarts, not in your wit, not in your social graces, not in your heart, not in your looks, not in, um, not in, you know, not in your form." He ran his thumb up and down the buttonhook.

She placed a hand on her hip. "You haven't even seen my form yet."

His thumb stilled. His eyes darkened. "Then what do you say we correct that?"

Her knees wobbled. She touched the iron footboard, steadying herself.

Taking her by the shoulders, he turned her around again and worked the buttons from the top of her collar to the hem of her bodice. Cooling air rushed in where the gown gaped.

His movements stopped. The shoulders of her bodice became heavy and threatened to fall. He tossed the buttonhook onto the bed, then took the sleeves from behind and slid the bodice down her arms. He gathered it into one hand and with the other released the tie of her petticoat. It fell to the floor.

"Death and the deuce," he whispered. He relinquished the bodice, slipped his arms around her, and ran his hands along her white silk corset. Finally, he stepped back.

She faced him, self-conscious in her chemise, bloomers, corset, and stockings. But he looked at her with such obvious appreciation, she decided that if he wanted to think she looked like a princess, she may as well let him.

"Your hair," he whispered. "Please. Can I see your hair?"

She lifted her hands and began to remove the pins. He held out his palm. Soon, he needed both hands. Finally, she untwisted it, shook her head, and let her hair tumble. It very nearly touched the floor.

"Great Caesar's ghost." He dropped the pins onto the side table, several scattering to the floor. Without taking his eyes from her, he whipped off his jacket and slung it onto a chair. His cufflinks went the way of her pins, making sharp clanks when they hit the table. He yanked his cuffs out and threw them to the side.

With her chin up, she ran her fingers along her scalp, scratching and fluffing. When she looked at him again, his vest was gone, his suspenders hung down against his legs, his shirt was unbuttoned, and his undershirt peeked through the gap.

Reaching out, he burrowed his hands into her hair and draped it over her shoulders. "You are gorgeous."

So are you, she thought.

He gathered her hair into his hands, rubbing it between his fingers. "When I built this house, I thought I would finally discover what it was like to have a home where I belonged, but it didn't feel like I thought it would. So I began to fill it with furniture and a knick-knack or two. Nothing ever lived up to my expectations until now." He brushed her hair behind her shoulders. "It's not the furniture, or even the house that makes the home. It's you, Flossie. With you is where I belong."

Love for him surged through her, and with it a great calm. Pushing the opening of his shirt to the side, she slid her hands up his chest and onto his shoulders, then lifted onto her tiptoes. She brought her lips within an inch of his. "Welcome home, Reeve. Welcome home."

Crushing her to him, he kissed her, swooped her up into his arms, and gloried in the gift of home, sweet home.

"Bustle pinchers were a real problem, but it wasn't until
1909 before women were given their own car."

AUTHOR'S NOTE

Although *Tiffany Girl* was based on a real premise (the lead glass workers really did go on strike, and Louis Tiffany really did hire women art students to finish the chapel), I always have to do a bit of fudging. Sometimes it's because I couldn't find the actual facts—in which case I just make them up as best I can—and in other cases, I change things up in order to make my story work. (I know. Terrible, but there you have it.) This is where I confess all and tell you which of the historical facts I tweaked.

I add these notes in all my books because I'm afraid there are historical details you won't believe are true, even though they really are and I want you to know which is which. So, let's start with the Tiffany Girls. My main source of information for them was through a series of handwritten letters Clara Driscoll religiously sent to her family once a week. The discovery of these letters is brand-new—uncovered by scholars as recently as 2005. I read all of the letters she wrote during the 1890s. Unfortunately, none before 1896 survived. So right away, there's a big gap.

In most of these early letters, Mrs. Driscoll writes about her life in New York as a single widow in her thirties. Occasionally, however, she'd tell her family what was happening in Tiffany's studio. Her letters are the only known first-person account of what it was like to work there, and they revolutionized what we know about the design and manufacture of Tiffany goods. They also revealed, for the first time, the significant role women played. Up to the discovery of the letters, the women had basically gone unacknowledged (because no one knew what all they did).

Throughout the novel I referred to Clara as "Mrs. Driscoll" because that's how Flossie would have referred to her. But I've read hundreds of letters from Clara and have become quite fond of her. I would like, with your permission, to refer to her throughout this note the way I think of her—as "Clara."

Her claim to fame, and her most touted contribution to Tiffany's, was her lamp designs. The scene I wrote with Mr. Mitchell—Tiffany's VP and brother-in-law whose mutton chops I made up—was taken from an incident described in Clara's letters. The two of them did not get along in real life, and as much as Mitchell was against her extravagant lamps, they took Tiffany's company in a completely new direction. They won her (and Tiffany) many, many awards and were tremendously expensive to make. The lamps weren't produced in 1893, though. They came later, but I couldn't write this entire book without giving Clara's lamps a shout-out, particularly her iconic Dragonfly Lamp.

In a wonderful book called *A New Light on Tiffany*, the authors list all the Tiffany Girls by name in the back. Then they have another section called "Other Women Associated with Tiffany Studios." I never understood, however, what distinction the scholars made between "Tiffany Girls" and "Other Women." So, for the purposes of my novel, I picked some of the most interesting and made them all Tiffany Girls. (I know—typical fictional author behavior. Sorry!)

Tiffany (who really did have a lisp) had a small women's department as early as 1888, but they didn't do any "mannish" work. That didn't occur until the men went on strike in December 1892 and Louis hired six additional women from the School of Applied Design, the YWCA, and Coopers Union. He chose those locations because they didn't charge tuition, and he wanted to find women who were very likely to be breadwinners and would, therefore, profit by the employment. That, however, messed up my whole plot (about Flossie needing to work so she could pay tuition for art school). Without this piece, my story falls apart. So, I pretended that the School of Applied Design charged tuition. And since we already had the YMCA make an appearance, I didn't want to muddy the waters by throwing in the YWCA at Coopers Union. My apologies for the inaccuracies there.

I indicated in my Note to Readers at the beginning of this novel that all the Tiffany Girls—other than Flossie and Nan—are based on real ones. I used their real names, and if I could find out something about them, I used that, too. I don't know what any of them looked like, other than an occasional hint in Clara's letters: "*The two or three youngest ones have turned up their hair, but the old girls all look just the same.*" (The phrase "turned up their hair" means they quit wearing braids and pigtails and put their hair up to show they'd graduated from being a girl to a woman. This usually occurred around the age of sixteen.)

Someone that Clara did describe at length was Aggie. She really was a six-foot Swede who was sixteen and engaged to a forty-year-old butcher and, from what I could tell, Clara was particularly fond of her. She didn't start working for Tiffany until 1894, and she cut out the templates (not the foil). She was a larger-than-life character (no pun intended) and I couldn't help but include her—even though she wasn't there prior to the fair. She'd originally planned to put off marrying her butcher for two and a half years so she could get the hundred and fifty dollar commission for any girl who stayed at Tiffany's that length of time. She ended up staying for four entire years and, according to Clara, went from being all skin and bones to 180 pounds, *"a young giant of nineteen."* At twenty, she was *"a most noticeable and attractive woman"* who had a beautiful soprano voice and sang in the choir.

Four months after Aggie left Tiffany's to marry her butcher, Clara learned via the newspaper that Aggie committed suicide by drinking carbolic acid. In Aggie's pocket was a letter she'd written, stating that the butcher had revealed he'd never had any intention of marrying her. Ever. Clara left work immediately to seek out Aggie's family in the tenements and to offer what comfort she could. So, so sad. I should mention that they didn't call her Aggie. Her name was Agnes, but since the premiere designer's name was Agnes Northrup, I nicknamed our Swede "Aggie" to avoid confusion.

Here's an inside peek at some of the others who make cameos in my book:

ELLA EGBERT: In my novel, she was the selector who worked with Elizabeth, and that "team" was Flossie's and Nan's major competition. None of that is true. What is true, is that at twenty-eight years old, Ella was one of the oldest, one of the six originals, and she had a penchant for tea. She couldn't say enough against marriage compared to a life of work in the realms of art. At age thirty-five, she married a man sixty-seven years old and *"was nearly two years bringing her mind to it."* When he died three years later, she returned to Tiffany's.

LOUISE KING: She designed windows for Tiffany in the early 1890s and really did marry her instructor (though she did it in 1892). Together they painted the dome I described in the Manufacturer's Building—though her husband, Kenyon Cox, was the one who was noted in all the write-ups about the fair. According to the scholars, she wasn't classified as a Tiffany Girl, but as one of the "Other Women." Whatever that means. (Unless otherwise stated, all the girls listed are considered "Tiffany Girls.")

LOUISE STURTEVANT: Since there were two Louises,

I nicknamed this one "Lulu." I have no idea of her temperament. I
made all that up—about her being shy, and a fast cutter, all that. It
was simply a story device on my part to up Flossie's level of concern.
She did, however, study at the School of Museum of Fine Arts in
Boston. She is classified as one of the "Other Women."

AGNES NORTHRUP: One of the six originals who really
did hate being manager of the girls and was only too happy to
have Clara come back and take them over. She was one of Tiffany's
most talented and coveted designers. As such, she had her own
private studio—as indicated in my book, though her studio was
not adjacent to the girls' workshop. It was a small room located
down a labyrinth of halls, with flower studies and manila paper
tacked to her walls. She won several awards for Tiffany. (She was
part of the "Other Women" group.)

MARY MCDOWELL: Her cartoon pictured at the begin-
ning of Chapter 30 was the exact one exhibited at the Chicago
World's Fair. She briefly shared an apartment with Clara and left
Tiffany's in 1898 when she married. She was considered an official
"Tiffany Girl."

GRACE DE LUZE: Grace was one of the six originals. She
designed windows and had sketches displayed at the World's
Columbian Exposition in Chicago. She's considered an official
"Tiffany Girl."

LYDIA EMMET: She designed Tiffany windows for Mark
Twain's house and painted a mural in the Woman's Building. I
didn't have room for Flossie to go see two murals, so I chose Louise's
instead. Lydia was considered one of the "Other Women."

ELIZABETH COMYNS: In my book, she's the one who
got sick and couldn't go to the fair. None of that happened. Total
fabrication on my part. She had, however, illustrated books and
had three designs for china painting published. She designed
windows for Tiffany and was one of the "Other Women."

THERESA BAUR: She was a typewriter girl, but as far as I know she never painted nude figures in Paris and never had stiff fingers or hands. I made that part up. She landed her job as a "Tiffany Girl" because her brother was an office boy of Clara's new fiancé. (Clara didn't end up marrying the guy, though.)

As for the 1893 World's Columbian Exposition, the chapel was, in fact, late in being finished. How late? I don't know. I was never able to find out. So I had it there by the end of May—a total guess on my part. None of the Tiffany Girls went, though—not even Clara. The Tiffany Girls did, however, have a display in the Woman's Building and there was no way I was going to write this whole book and not go to the fair and see it! So, I made up the competition and the demonstration at the Woman's Building. In that vein, I have no idea if Louis Tiffany had intended to keep the newly hired Tiffany Girls permanently from the get-go or not. I have no idea if he laid anyone off or not. So, I took creative license there as well and pretended like they had a probationary status. Might've been true, might not have. I could never confirm it one way or the other. For my purposes, I needed Flossie to have her job in jeopardy, then I needed her to get laid off, so that's what I did.

My description of the chapel was accurate. I don't know if the whole thing was completed by the men, other than the windows, but I could never find any reference to the women working on anything for the chapel other than the windows, so I decided to keep things simple and focus on those. The chapel really did win fifty-four awards—more than any other exhibit in the entire World's Fair—and it launched Louis to stardom. He squeaked his exhibit in under the "Ecclesiastes" umbrella as described in my book, which gave him a tremendous advantage over his American stained-glass competitors, since none of them were allowed to exhibit. That said, his first love was portraying nature, not religious figures. So, he cherished it when he was able to get private commissions for nature-themed pieces.

Tiffany really did have the chapel sent back to New York and had it reassembled. After that it changed hands several times, spent some time in basements, all kinds of things. Down in Winter Park, Florida, though, the Morse Museum has taken what original parts of the chapel they could recover and have re-created it in full for us to walk right into and experience. Is that the coolest thing ever? You must, must put it on your bucket list.

I really struggled to describe the window-making process in a simple and engaging manner. If someone were to ever ask me what my weakness in the craft of writing is, that's what I'd list. It's so hard to weave in factual information without what the publishing industry calls "information dumps." So I work really, really hard to have no dumps. None. Sometimes I manage it. Sometimes I don't. (The reviewers are quick to let me know.) In any case, I have to gather a plethora of information so I can educate myself, and as hard as I looked, there was scarcely a peep on how Tiffany windows were made back in the day. There were tons of books about his glass, but none about his process. I ended up piecing it together through a lot of different sources—the majority of which were from the 1890s. I also spoke with museum curators and other art professionals.

When I was weaving it all into the novel, I so wanted to compare the carbon copies of the cartoons to paint-by-numbers, but they didn't have paint-by-numbers back then. Argh! And it took me forever to realize that an "easel" was a big old honker of a piece of glass that they leaned against the window and to which they stuck their glass fragments. You wouldn't believe how many times I had to rewrite those scenes as I'd uncover a new source (or picture) and realize I'd originally depicted it all wrong. I hope you were able to picture the process without too much confusion. And though I think I exhausted the sources, there's always the chance that I still have something wrong. So I'll state here and now that any and all mistakes are solely mine and I apologize profusely for them.

Before we shift gears, let me just mention that though Clara

506   Author's Note

described in her letters a couple of receptions Tiffany invited her to, none of the Tiffany Girls other than her and, perhaps, Agnes Northrup, were ever included. I made that part up because I needed Reeve to find out about the bustle pinchers, and—what can I say?—I'm a devoted fan of Cinderella and balls. So, there you go.

The other theme touched upon in the book—other than the New Woman theme which I cover in the Note to Readers at the beginning—is the boardinghouse. What a surprise that turned out to be. I'd merely set out to research a place for Flossie to live and instead ended up in a swirl of controversy about appropriate places for single, unmarried women to reside in. At the time, a home with wife, children, and a picket fence was nirvana. Boardinghouses, however, took that ideal and commercialized it—charged money for it. Horror!

As such, it became fodder for essays, political cartoons, sermons, novels, and serializations. Women who lived in them were suspect. Men who lived in them were of questionable character. You'd think that all-women boardinghouses would solve the problem, but they were cast under even more suspicion than coed ones, because brothels would disguise themselves as boardinghouses.

As a defense mechanism, boarders—particularly female boarders—tried to turn their boardinghouses into homes the way Flossie did. They, in essence, tried to pretend they were one big happy family. I ended up reading several books and not a few first person accounts of life in boardinghouses. I only had time to give you a glimpse of it here, but it was a very fascinating look at a country trying to adjust not only to an industrial revolution, but a women's revolution as well.

The Trostles' shenanigans were based on a real swindle done back in the day. Not the art gallery part—I made that up—but the part about them moving in, ingratiating themselves with everyone, the husband "going out of town," while the wife stayed behind with promises of payment as she stole from fellow boarders, then one day disappeared completely. All in all, the whole boardinghouse thing made for some very interesting research. I wish I could have included more of it, but it wasn't germane to the story, so I had to leave it out.

In conclusion, a few miscellaneous items: The Twenty-sixth Ward YMCA in Brooklyn didn't open until November 1893, yet I have Reeve moving in in August. Also, this particular Y didn't have rooms, but I needed Reeve to be close to the Gusmans, so I gave it rooms. Everything else about it, right down to the Women's Auxiliary decorating it for Christmas, was accurate. Basketball was a brand-new sport back then, and it was invented as described. I should point out, though, that the "International YMCA Training School" was actually part of Springfield College, not the YMCA— which creates a lot of confusion over basketball's birthplace. As for the boys at the Twenty-sixth Ward, they did, indeed, have to play around the support columns in their gym.

Bustle pinchers were a real problem, but it wasn't until 1909 before women were given their own car. They absolutely loved it, but the men kicked up a fuss and launched a newspaper campaign ridiculing it. Reporters referred to the cars as the "Jane Crowe Car," the "Hen Car," and the "Old Maid's Retreat." Some men stormed them, claiming discrimination. The railway company said it was no different than having a smoking car for the men, but that didn't go over very well and within three months the ridership dropped off and the program was abolished.

As an interesting footnote, in 2012 the *New York Times* reported that Czech Railways, as well as railways in Austria, Japan, Egypt, Iran, Brazil, and India, all have women-only compartments. These were established in response to women complaining of men groping, exhibiting lewd conduct, thieving, and even molestation. Men aren't banned from these cars, but women have priority seating.

Thanks for coming along with me on this ride. I've loved linking my three most recent books—*It Happened at the Fair, Fair Play,* and *Tiffany Girl*—to the 1893 Chicago World's Fair. It was a fun, exciting, and fascinating place to camp. Glad you joined me!

Speaking of which, I'd love to get to know you better, so come on over to my website (www.IWantHerBook.com) and drop me a note. While you're there, be sure to sign up for my newsletters, because my subscribers are privy to exclusive perks, inside peeks, contests, deleted scenes, and giveaways. You can also find me on Facebook at Facebook.com/DeesFriends.

See you there!

Deeanne Gist ♡

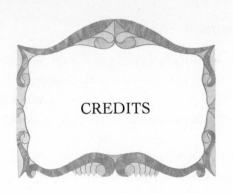

CREDITS

1. Henry Collins Brown, *Valentine's Manual of Old New York* (New York: Valentine's Manual, Inc., 1928), 39.

2. "Gown of Black Plissé Crépon with Velvet Sleeves," *Harper's Bazar*, November 9, 1895, vol. XXVIII, no 45, 913.

3. "Back View of Worth Cape on Front Page," *Harper's Bazar*, September 14, 1895, vol. XXVIII, no 37, 744.

4. Moses King, *King's Handbook of New York City* (Boston: Moses King, 1892), 285.

5. "Selecting the Plating," *The Cosmopolitan*, January, 1899, vol. XXVI, no 3, 244.

6. Monica Bruenjes, *A Woman Selling Flowers*, ©Pressing Matters Publishing Co., Inc., 2014. Original Bruenjes artwork specifically commissioned by Deeanne Gist for *Tiffany Girl*.

7. "Making a Cartoon at the Tiffany Studios," *The Art Interchange*, October, 1894, vol. XXXIII, no 4, 86.

8. Monica Bruenjes, *Place Card*, ©Pressing Matters Publishing Co., Inc., 2014. Original Bruenjes artwork specifically commissioned by Deeanne Gist for *Tiffany Girl*.

9. Gold Dust Washing Powder Advertisement, *Harper's Bazar*, May 27, 1893, vol. XXVI, no 21, 433.

10. Monica Bruenjes, *Game Card*, ©Pressing Matters Publishing Co., Inc., 2014. Original Bruenjes artwork specifically commissioned by Deeanne Gist for *Tiffany Girl*.

11. The Acme Giant, *The Sears, Roebuck Catalogue*, 1902, 825.

12. "The Making of Stained-Glass Windows," *The Cosmopolitan*, January 1899, vol. XXVI, no 3, 243, 246, 250.

13. Hubert Howe Bancroft, *The Book of the Fair* (Chicago: The Bancroft Co., 1893), 71.

14. Library of Congress, Prints & Photographs Division, L. Prang & Co. Collection, LC-DIG-pga-04050.

15. "How Miss Miggs Fitted Herself For Matrimony," *The Cosmopolitan*, March 1899, vol. XXVI, no 5, 511.

16. "View of the Glass Room with Women at Work," *The Art Interchange*, October, 1894, vol. XXXIII, no 4, 87.

17. "The Gathering of the Winterbournes," *The Ladies' Home Journal*, September 1894, vol. XI, no 10, 1.

18. King, 603.

19. Maud Howe Elliott, *Art and Handicraft in the Woman's Building of the World's Columbian Exposition* (Chicago: Rand, McNally & Company, 1894), 50.

20. Henry Collins Brown, *Delmonico's: A Story of Old New York* (New York: Valentine's Manual, Inc., 1928), 50.

21. Bancroft, 553.

22. Ibid., 392.

23. Monica Bruenjes, *Tiffany Chapel*, ©Pressing Matters Publishing Co., Inc., 2014. Original Bruenjes artwork specifically commissioned by Deeanne Gist for *Tiffany Girl*.

24. Elliott, 290.

25. King, 575.

26. *Shepp's World's Fair Photographed* (Chicago: Globe Bible Publishing Co., 1893), 513.

27. "The Board Game of Old Maid," Courtesy of The Strong®, National Museum of Play, Rochester, New York.

28. "Paris Dinner Toilettes," *Harper's Bazar*, April 30, 1892, vol. XXV, no 18, 349.

29. Brown, *Valentine's Manual*, 85.

30. "Garden Party Gown," *Harper's Bazar*, July 27, 1895, vol. XXVIII, no 30, 597.

31. Peter Fauerbach, *1910 Fauerbach Beer Wagon*, http://www .fauerbachbrewery.com (Madison, WI), May 24, 2013.

32. *Telegraphic Journal and Electrical Review*, January 24, 1885, vol. XVI, no 374, 3.

33a. "The Zoopraxiscope: A Couple Waltzing," Library of Congress, Prints & Photographs Division, Eadweard Muybridge Collection, LC-DIG-ppmsca-05949.

33b. Helen Campbell, *Darkness and Daylight: Lights and Shadows of New York Life* (Connecticut: Hartford Publishing Company, 1899), 691.

34. "Dragonfly Lamp by Clara Driscoll," Courtesy of Lillian Nassau LLC, New York.

35. *Fifty Photographic Views of Greater New York* (New York: Rand, McNally & Co., 1900), 41.

36. "26th Ward Branch of the YMCA," Courtesy of the Gomes Collection, http://www.tapeshare.com.

37. "Winter Costumes," *Harper's Bazar*, November 16, 1895, vol. XXVIII, no 46, 936.

38. Monica Bruenjes, *Christmas Card*, ©Pressing Matters Publishing Co., Inc., 2014. Original Bruenjes artwork specifically commissioned by Deeanne Gist for *Tiffany Girl*.

39. Monica Bruenjes, *A Little Girl in Central Park*, ©Pressing Matters Publishing Co., Inc., 2014. Original Bruenjes artwork specifically commissioned by Deeanne Gist for *Tiffany Girl*.

40. Monica Bruenjes, *Frontispiece*, ©Pressing Matters Publishing Co., Inc., 2014. Original Bruenjes artwork specifically commissioned by Deeanne Gist for *Tiffany Girl*.

41. "Miss Consuelo Vanderbilt's Wedding Gown," *Harper's Bazar*, November 9, 1895, vol. XXVIII, no 45, 908.

42. *Honor Bilt Modern Homes* (Chicago: Sears, Roebuck and Co., 1926), 118.

43. Library of Congress, Prints & Photographs Division, LC-USZ62-91532.

READING GROUP GUIDE

Tiffany Girl

Deeanne Gist

Introduction

The heir to Tiffany's jewelry empire is left without a staff when glassworkers go on strike just months before the opening of the much-anticipated 1893 Chicago World's Fair and the hyped mosaic Tiffany Chapel. Desperate and without another option, Tiffany turns to a group of female art students to finish the job. Flossie Jayne answers the call, moving into a New York City boardinghouse with high hopes of making a name for herself as an artist and defying those who say that the work can't be completed in time—least of all by a set of young, inexperienced women. As Flossie flouts polite society's restrictions on females, her ambitions become threatened from an unexpected quarter: her own heart. What or who will claim victory? Her dreams or the captivating boarder next door?

Topics & Questions for Discussion

1. What is the historic significance of Louis Comfort Tiffany's idea to hire women workers as replacements for the striking glass cutters? Do you think the move would have been as controversial had their employer and his project been of lesser notoriety? Would it have been as significant? Why or why not?

2. On page 6, Flossie compliments her mother: "every gown you make is nothing short of a work of art." Do you think Flossie's glass cutting or Aggie's foil wrapping are merely supportive to Tiffany's art or are they art forms in and of themselves? How would you define what is and is not art?

3. Why is Flossie's father so upset about her living in a boarding-house? Explore the concept of a lifestyle that is "appropriate" for a woman of her station. What types of behaviors, tasks, activities, and even purposes are clearly designated as belonging to the world of women in the novel? What about the world of men? Do you find these boundaries logical, or are they rooted in something else? If you can, use examples to support your opinion.

4. It's clear all along that Tiffany has created an enormous opportunity for both the Tiffany Girls and for the greater "New Woman" move-ment, but in doing so also creates enormous tension. After all, the women's opportunity comes at the expense of the "hundred-plus men who were striking for reasonable hours and better wages" (p. 38). How does this factor influence your feelings about the situation? Imagine yourself in Flossie's shoes—what would you do?

5. What is it about the New Woman that so threatens and offends men and women alike? How do you feel about the reasons characters give in opposition to the movement?

6. Flossie "merely wanted to be paid for her labor so she could go to art school. She had a hard time seeing how that was going to lead to the deterioration of the entire human race." (p. 84) Reeve's arguments against the women's liberation movement were drawn from actual articles written at the turn of the century. How do his opinions differ from Flossie's parents' or the striking protesters? If you had to take a position against Flossie, would you go with Reeve's, Papa's, or the strikers?

7. Identify some of the ways in which Flossie and other New Women suffered for their efforts to step outside of their prescribed roles. Discuss the dichotomy of the men in the novel who are against the women's movement because they want to respect and protect the "fairer sex," yet they mistreat the working women and even students. How did you expect Flossie to react to the men who harassed her? If you were a nineteenth-century woman, what would you have done in her place?

8. Reeve acts out of deep hurt caused by abandonment and isolation in his childhood. In what ways does he re-create these familiar environments and feelings as an adult? Why do you suppose present-day society is accepting of depression, yet loneliness is taboo?

9. Why do you think Reeve has such affection and feelings of obligation toward Mrs. Dinwiddie? What is it about Flossie that at first drives him mad and then later drives him mad with love? Discuss these two primary relationships in Reeve's life and consider their differences and similarities.

10. Despite Reeve's initial impression of the New Woman, he comes to understand that there are many reasons a woman may choose to take on a "man's responsibilites." For example, when he visits his childhood home he finds himself discussing finances

with Mrs. Gusman. How does this make him feel? How does he ultimately come to grips with the situation? Identify some of the circumstances in the novel that necessitates women taking on roles commonly ascribed to men.

11. When Nan goes home ill, Flossie takes it upon herself to make new choices for the glass panels she will cut to use in a nativity scene, and the results are not as she expected. What does this experience teach Flossie about her work and about herself?

12. Reeve thinks Flossie is spoiled. Do you agree? Why or why not? When Flossie berates herself for being selfish on page 320, do you think she's finally getting clarity or is she being too hard on herself? Do you think a modern woman would assess herself the same way? Would you?

13. Reeve seems to suffer from two main "walls": the emotional one that maintains his isolation, and the one that bars his understanding of what the New Woman truly wants and why. What begins to open his eyes to the realities that girls like Flossie face? What instigates the first trickle of empathy for their cause and how does he react to this revelation? Did his reaction surprise you? Why or why not?

14. Flossie decides before ever moving into the boardinghouse that all the other borders will become the large family she never had but always longed for. What series of events cause Flossie to realize that her "family at 438" is not what she thought? How does this realization change her? Do you think it's for the better, or for the worse? Why?

15. When Flossie discovers that Reeve is the infamous I. D. Claire and that he has based his protagonist on her, she is furious because she feels he's made a public fool of her. But Reeve protests that she

and his fictional character Marylee are not the same person. At what point does Reeve himself begin to understand this distinction? Later, how does Flossie identify with Marylee?

16. In many ways, this novel plays with the theme of perception, or how you see yourself versus how you are seen by others. What do you think the novel says about the weight you give to what others think of you? Do you believe there is value in questioning perspectives and ideas, either about others or about yourself? Why or why not? How might the story have unfolded differently if Flossie did not challenge her own perspectives, or Reeve's his?

17. In the end, Reeve has what he always wanted—a home where he belongs. What is it that Flossie wants most, and do you think she gets it? Why or why not?

Enhance Your Book Club

1. One of Deeanne's passions is learning about the period clothing worn by her characters. She even hired a historian seamstress to sew her an authentic Victorian gown so she could experience what it was like to wear all those layers. (See pictures and videos of her in an article that appeared on the front page of the Wall Street Journal at http://www.FrontPageWSJ.com.) Since taking "old time" photos—sepia or black-and-white—of yourself in period costume has become a worldwide amusement, you might be able to find a novelty photo studio near you where you, alone or with your book club, can take photos in Victorian dress. Check out your local listings or visit the Antique and Amusement Photographers International website at http://www.oldtimephotos.org/. Be sure to send your pictures to Deeanne or post them on her Facebook page. She'd love to see them!

2. In order to create bonds among her new family at the boarding-house, Flossie writes insightful and sometimes light-hearted questions for the boarders to ask one another over dinner. Host a dinner for your book club members. Have each person write one question on a slip of paper, then before everyone comes to the table, place them randomly underneath the plates. Enjoy listening to each other's answers and see if you don't know everyone a bit better by dessert!

3. On her website (http://www.iwantherbook.com/dees -inspiration-for-her-characters), the author reveals celebrity and modeling photos that inspired her to create her characters for each novel. Before visiting the link, cut out photos that reflect how you envision characters like Flossie, Mr. and Mrs. Trostle, Reeve, Mrs. Dinwiddie, and more. Paste them on a board or piece of paper and share your choices with your book club. Did your picks match Deeanne's? Were you surprised by the ones she chose?

4. If you enjoyed reading about the 1893 Chicago World's Fair, Deeanne's last two releases, *It Happened at the Fair* and *Fair Play*, are set in Chicago at the actual fair (as opposed to in New York the way *Tiffany Girl* is). Read and compare those stories to that of Flossie and Reeve in *Tiffany Girl*. How are they similar? How are they different?

5. Do you wish you could go back in time and visit the 1893 Chicago World's Fair? During your book club meeting, connect a laptop to the host's TV, then go to Deeanne's website and play her interactive animated four-minute game, "A Romp Through 1893," where the hero from *It Happened at the Fair* becomes sep-arated from the heroine and has to find her. At the end of each 60-second vignette, your club will have to make a choice about what the hero should do to resolve a dilemma he finds himself in.

The object of the game is to get through the adventure without making a wrong turn. You'll find the adventure at http://www.iwantherbook.com/video-adventure. Don't let your group spend too much time making a choice, though, because you only have a few seconds to click an option! For an extra bonus, have the host of the group go (in advance) to Deeanne's "Insider Information" link on her website and pull photos of Deeanne and her family members and print them out. Then show them to the group and have a contest to see who can spot Deeanne and her family members' cameo appearances during the video game. (http://www.iwantherbook.com/dees-family-makes-cameo-appearance)

A Conversation with Deeanne Gist

1. This is your third novel to feature aspects of the Chicago World's Fair. What is it about that event or moment in history that so attracts you?

The breadth and scope of this particular fair not only wowed the world back then, but it would wow today's most jaded visitor. It had something for everyone of every age and every nationality. It was not just an event, it was the event of the century—a watershed moment in our country's history. It's where the inspiration for today's American products, industries, corporations, and cultural movements began. And even though I camped there for three novels, I still only touched the tip of the iceberg.

2. When did you first learn the story of Louis Comfort Tiffany's chapel and the "Tiffany Girls?" What compelled you to write a novel about a fictional woman rather than one of the actual Tiffany Girls?

The discovery of the Tiffany Girls is brand-new. Everyone has always assumed Louis Tiffany was the exclusive designer of all his iconic objects. Then in 2005, scholars uncovered a trove of letters written by Clara Driscoll. Those letters made it abundantly clear that she and other Tiffany Girls were the principal designers of a vast majority of iconic lamps, windows, and other pieces produced by Tiffany Studios.

I found out about them in 2011 when my mom was watching a documentary on PBS. As soon as the show was over, she sent me the following email:

"Dee, Louis Comfort Tiffany was planning a crucially important display of his stained-glass windows for the Chicago World's Fair. Not of his lamps, but I think a fairly new direction for him at this time. Anyway, his glass artists (an all male profession) went on strike. He went to the art schools and recruited female artists and taught them the process. They became known as the 'Tiffany Girls.' About a dozen of them, I think. This is the first time women were given the opportunity to enter the commercial art profession according to the PBS program I was watching. This information was from a PBS History Detectives episode that was focusing on one of these girls who was originally from Duluth, Minnesota, and was somebody's grandmother. I didn't get the name of the collection of information on the 'Tiffany Girls,' which I think is in the archives in a church in NYC. They have a number of stained-glass windows by these women done through the years. Anyway, if you haven't picked your heroine's career, this is a unique point in women's career opportunities and, of course, Tiffany is a fantastic name and tradition. I was fascinated, even though this info was peripheral to the program. Love, Mom"

I knew as soon as I read her email that I'd one day write their story. I fictionalized my girl so that I would have more creative freedom with the storyline while still giving an inside glimpse of the real Tiffany Girls, their department head, Clara Driscoll, and their accomplishments.

3. As the bestselling author of ten historicals, have you developed a unique approach to blending truth and imagination? Tell us about your writing process and how you decide when to stick with the facts and when to let your imagination take over.
I spend months and months on research. I interview experts. I visit historical societies. I explore museums. I read newspapers of the time. I spend days in the city where my book is set. And I read a great many books and articles. I make notes in the margins of everything I read, then index those notes so the information will be at my fingertips during the writing process.

I do this because I very much want to get the historical facts correct. Sometimes, however, the facts don't fit in with the timeline of my story. For instance, in 1893 the Tiffany Girls had not started designing the iconic lamps they became so famous for. That didn't happen until several years later. Still, I could not bring myself to write an entire novel about the Tiffany Girls and not give the lamps a shout-out. So, I bent the timeline a little and had Clara Driscoll design one of her most famous—the dragonfly lamp. In the very first novel I ever wrote, I did this kind of thing with a handful of details and received emails from readers who were unhappy with me about it. So now, I always include an Author's Note where I confess to the details I've cheated on so the reader will know fact from fiction.

4. How has your background in education and journalism influenced your work as an author? Has it helped with the nonwriting activities as well, like speaking to groups or promoting your work online?
The background in journalism helped me learn how to meet word counts and deadlines. The education background helped me with organization. As for speaking to groups, I have a minor

in Theatre Arts. If I hadn't found true love and married the week after I graduated from Texas A&M, I'd planned to head to Hollywood and give it a whirl. I have no regrets, though. I got me a keeper. We celebrated thirty-two years of wedded bliss a few months ago.

5. You donned appropriate period garb for the making of your video adventure, "Romp Through 1893: The Invitation." Though the video was created to promote your previous novels, the clothing must have been pretty similar to what was worn in the period of *Tiffany Girl*, also set in 1893. Did you love wearing the clothes? Hate it? Was there anything about the experience that surprised you?
I will find ANY excuse to play dress up. I love costumes. I love pretty gowns. I love fancy hats. The reason I had a period gown made for the video adventure RompThrough1893.com is because I thought we were going to shoot it with live actors. For a lot of different reasons, we ended up animating it instead, but the historial clothing helped the artist Monica Bruenjes, who did the stop-animation. For *Tiffany Girl*, since Flossie is an artist, Bruenjes took on the heroine's role so that "Flossie's" illustrations could be sprinkled throughout the novel. It was a real treat for me to see sketches and paintings I made up in my head become a reality.

6. On your website you have a fun feature where you reveal the photos of real people—many of whom are celebrities—that you used as inspiration for your characters' appearances. Who did you have in mind when you created Flossie Jayne and Reeve Wilder? Do you find photos for your secondary characters as well?

For each novel I write, I put together a thick, thick binder where I keep copious notes on the characters, the plotting, the setting, and the research. In the "character" section, I have written notes about eye color, hair color, hobbies, talents, personality traits, family members, goals, regrets, internal conflicts, and all kinds of things. I also find a real person to use as visual inspiration for my characters. This helps me be consistent throughout the novel when I am picturing them in my mind (and then describing them in the book). For Flossie, I used Sandra Bullock as my inspiration. For Reeve, I envisioned a muscular and tall Jude Law minus the receding hairline. (When it comes to my male protagonists, they are predominantly tall and muscular with a head full of hair. So I usually just use a real man's facial features for inspiration.)

I found several group photos of the Tiffany Girls, but the images weren't very clear. So other than Clara, I used random tin-type photos for those girls. Jean Dujardin was the inspiration for Monsieur Bourgeois. For the boarders, my inspiration came from the following: Betty White for Mrs. Dinwiddie; Hugh Grant for Mr. Oyster; Richard Gere for Mr. Holliday; Melissa Sue Anderson (who played the older sister on *Little House on the Prairie*) for Mrs. Holliday; Jerry Stiller (with a goatee) for Mr. Trostle; Maggie Smith for Mrs. Trostle. I used old tintypes for Annie Belle, Mr. Nettels, and Mrs. Klausmeyer.

7. You begin the story with a Prologue that shows us Reeve as a small boy viewing the body of his dead mother. Why did you choose to open the novel—the main themes of which involve women and women characters—this way?

Basically because Reeve acts like a bit of a jerk at the beginning of the novel and I wanted the reader to know that deep down he was a good guy and it would be okay to root for him. Showing this scene was the quickest, cleanest, and most compelling way I could think of to do this.

8. You and your husband have four children. What was it like for you to get inside the minds of Victorian parents like Mr. and Mrs. Jayne, who love and want the best for their daughter, but whose ideas about what's best are very different from Flossie's? Do you find that much of your life ends up in your novels, or do you prefer to use fiction as a way to explore experiences that are different from your own?

For this facet of the novel, I read several resource books about the only-child and collected notes about what many of them have in common. An overwhelming majority of them have parents who devote a lot of time and attention to the child and who also, often inadvertently, put a lot of pressure on them. In addition to that, many sources explored what they call an epidemic in our country of kids who are told they didn't misspell a word on their test but simply spelled the word "creatively." Or kids who get trophies for simply showing up. As a parent, when I read these books, even though I have four children, I was guilty of doing many of the things depicted. I had the best of intentions, but the end result wasn't always the healthiest. In *Tiffany Girl*, I decided to explore some of these themes and therefore assigned to Flossie and her parents some of the characteristics I read about.

9. At first, Flossie is overjoyed to live among so many people in the boardinghouse—perhaps Reeve would say that she is simply enjoying her role as the sun around which they all orbit. But in the end, he seems to have been right when he chastises her about mistaking their fellow boarders for family, as they become less congenial to her as soon as her role shifts from boarder to housemaid. Did you intend a lesson for readers in all this?

I actually based this part on things I'd read in journals from the time period and other resources. Because boardinghouses were so suspect, reputable boarders attempted to "pretty them up" by trying to turn them into homes—albeit unsuccessfully. I found that fascinating and decided I'd have Flossie do that very thing. So her actions (and the results thereof) were based on historical data as opposed to a "lesson" of some kind.

10. Mr. Jayne seems committed to ignoring his role as the instigator for Flossie's venture into New Womanhood, not to mention the financial ruin his gambling problem causes for his family. Despite that, you've portrayed Mr. Jayne as a man who loves his family and who in general seems to be a decent person. Was it challenging for you to balance his flaws as a provider with his charms as a father? What were the biggest challenges of writing this book?

In the general scheme of things, I've found that be it villain or hero, no one person is all bad or all good. We humans are a complicated mixture of both. There are a lot of fathers (and mothers, as well) who love their children, but who make disastrous personal decisions that adversely affect the ones they love most. I'd certainly like to go back and change a few choices I made along the way. So that wasn't so much of a challenge. For me, the biggest challenge of writing this book was finishing it after the sudden loss of my own father. Sitting down day after day, pushing my grief to the side and finishing my pages was, my friend, one of the toughest things I've ever done in my life.

11. In your Author's Note, you explain that for many of Reeve's essays you used actual newspaper clippings and other writings from the 1890s so as to accurately reflect the opinions of the day. How did you feel sifting through these opinions? Did you find what you expected?

I knew the views were strong, but to see it in black and white like that was quite startling. Some of the things I read I intentionally left out of Reeve's writings because they would have made him so unheroic I was afraid the reader would find him unworthy of holding the male lead of the story. I really came to appreciate just how hard my female forbearers had to fight to overcome the prejudices of the time. I also saw that the motives of the men were not nefarious or self-serving. They truly thought they were protecting the women, society, and all of humankind. So at the end of the day, it was hard not to extend them a little grace.

12. In an interview with *RT Book Reviews*, you described your journey from being the "bad girl" of inspirational fiction to being a "good girl" now that you've crossed into the general market. Do you find that your writing is significantly different now that your audience has broadened? Why or why not?

My writing hasn't really changed all that much. When I wrote for the inspirational market, my editor simply pointed out the parts she thought might be troublesome, and together we figured our what parts to keep in and what parts to take out. And even though I have a very deep faith, I feel a book can be inspirational without proselytizing. My editor agreed and always allowed me to incorporate the inspirational aspect of the story in a way I felt comfortable with. For me, it was like weaving a fine gold thread into a colorful plaid—it wasn't anything that dominated or jumped out at you, but was instead something that added a bit of beauty in a very subtle way. With my general market books, both the hero and heroine still have Christian worldviews—which is very true to the times—but there isn't an underlying faith element.

13. Flossie seems happy that Marylee Merrily marries Mr. Bookish, but disturbed and unhappy that Marylee gives up her

photography career, secretly wishing that the heroine could have had both. Though Reeve agrees to Flossie's proposal that all their earnings be "our money," it isn't clear that she will continue working, especially since Tiffany has a policy against employing married women. Did you imagine that Flossie would work after marriage? Why or why not?

As much as I wanted Flossie to continue working after marriage, it would have been grossly inaccurate from a historical perspective, especially if she was a Tiffany employee. His stance on this issue was well documented and adhered to. Even Clara Driscoll had to leave his employ after marriage.

In the ending of *The Merry Maid of Mumford Street*, Mr. Bookish might have been willing to let his wife continue with photography, but he would not have allowed her to earn wages doing it. My concession for Flossie in *Tiffany Girl* was that even though Mr. Tiffany would not keep her on as an employee, Reeve was perfectly willing for her to earn—and keep—any wages produced through her painting. It might not have tied everything up in the pretty little bow we often long for, but it was as much as I was willing to compromise on the historically accurate scale.

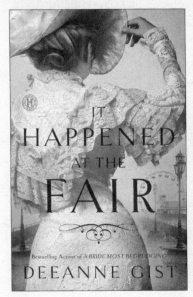